PRAISE FOR
T.L. HINES'S NOVELS

"... fans of breathless suspense that's a little off-center will enjoy this."

— *Publishers Weekly* review of
The Unseen

"... continues Hines' hot streak of quality thrillers with delightfully bizarre twists."

— review of *The Unseen* by Jake Chism,
thechristianmanifesto.com

"Hines excels at writing gripping supernatural thrillers with plenty of twists and turns; he'll pull you in from page one."

— *Library Journal* review of *The Dead Whisper On*

"A wonderful debut, by a prodigiously talented writer!"

— Michael Prescott, *New York Times* best-selling author of *Mortal Faults*, on *Waking Lazarus*

"Provocative from the first line, intriguing to the last. *Waking Lazarus* is a thriller of strategic pacing, colored in tones of mystery and wonder. Don't miss this exceptional debut."

— Brandilyn Collins, author of *Violet Dawn* and *Amber Morn*

"[Hines] plays some clever bait and switch games with the good and the bad guys, and creates an excellent genre-mix that's reminiscent of Dean Koontz, Peter Straub, and Stephen King."

— *Infuze Magazine* review of *The Dead Whisper On*

"*Waking Lazarus* is going to have people talking. It's a rare novel of perfectly executed suspense . . . T.L. Hines has himself a new fan; I'll be picking up all his books."

— Colleen Coble, author of *Anathema* and *Lonestar Sanctuary*

"The plot twists like the mine tunnels under Butte and made it difficult to stop reading. Nothing is as it first appears. [Hines] raises troubling questions that tie in with our current fears and apprehension. Who, or what, is really our enemy?"

— *TitleTrakk* review of *The Dead Whisper On*

"Sharp, finely drawn and compelling. *Waking Lazarus* is a supernatural suspense on steroids."

— Alton Gansky, author of *Angel* and *A Ship Possessed*

". . . *Waking Lazarus* is the smart, stylish, compassionate, life-affirming thriller I've been waiting for . . . a page-turner, and a remarkable debut."

— C.J. Box, author of *Blood Trail* and *Blue Heaven*

THE UNSEEN

OTHER BOOKS BY T.L. HINES

Waking Lazarus

The Dead Whisper On

Faces in the Fire

THE UNSEEN

T.L. HINES

THOMAS NELSON
Since 1798

NASHVILLE DALLAS MEXICO CITY RIO DE JANEIRO BEIJING

Published in Nashville, Tennessee, by Thomas Nelson. Thomas Nelson is a registered trademark of Thomas Nelson, Inc.

Published in association with the literary agency of Alive Communications, Inc., 7680 Goddard Street, Suite 200, Colorado Springs, CO 80920, www.alivecommunications.com.

Thomas Nelson, Inc., titles may be purchased in bulk for educational, business, fund-raising, or sales promotional use. For information, please e-mail SpecialMarkets@ThomasNelson.com.

Publisher's Note: This novel is a work of fiction. Names, characters, places, and incidents are either products of the author's imagination or used fictitiously. All characters are fictional, and any similarity to people living or dead is purely coincidental.

Page design: Walter Petrie

ISBN 978-1-59554-585-5 (trade paper)

Library of Congress Cataloging-in-Publication Data

Hines, T. L.
    The unseen / T. L. Hines.
      p. cm.
    ISBN 978-1-59554-452-0 (hardcover)
    1. Supernatural—Fiction. I. Title.
PS3608.I5726U67 2008
 813'.6—dc22

2008019839

Printed in the United States of America
09 10 11 12 13 RRD 5 4 3 2 1

For cancer survivors everywhere

ONE

PERCHED ON TOP OF THE ELEVATOR, LUCAS PEERED AT THE WOMAN BELOW and created an elaborate history in his mind.

Elevators and their shafts were easy places to hide. Easier than utility chases. Much easier than ductwork, popularly portrayed in movies as cavernous tunnels through which a man could crawl. Lucas knew better; most ductwork was tight and narrow, and not solid enough to hold 150 pounds.

But elevators. Well, the film depictions were pretty accurate with those. You could indeed crawl through the small access panel in the ceiling, sink a sizable hole with a hand drill, and then watch the unknowing people below as they stepped through the bay doors all day long. Provided you bypassed security, of course. And did your drilling outside of regular office hours.

Most of the time he preferred to work in DC proper, but with height restrictions on the buildings, he never got much of a chance to do elevator surfing; for that, he had to move farther away from the city, where skyscrapers were allowed.

He returned his attention to the dark-haired woman who was currently inside the car with four other less interesting people. In his history, she was a widow. True, she was probably in her early thirties, if that, but her stern look, her rigid posture, suggested overwhelming sorrow in her past.

Lucas recognized such sorrow.

So she was a widow. She had moved to Bethesda from her rural home in Kansas after losing her husband, an auto mechanic who had been crushed by a car in a tragic mishap.

Below Lucas, the dark-haired woman moved to the side for another person entering on the eighth floor. As she did so, the overhead light in the elevator car flickered a moment, then returned to full strength.

Puzzled, the dark-haired woman raised her eyes to the ceiling and looked at the light. It happened. For a moment, she stared directly at him, directly at the secret peephole he'd carefully drilled in the ceiling, directly at the constricting pupil of his own eye.

Then she dropped her gaze back to the other people in the elevator with her, offering a little shrug of the shoulders.

She had looked, but she hadn't seen. Like so many others.

When she had looked toward the ceiling, his heart had jumped. He had to admit this. Not because he was worried about being discovered, but because the *knowing* had started—the long, taut band of discovery that stretched between his eyes and the eyes of a dweller, then constricted in a sudden snap of understanding.

The Connection, he liked to call it.

Once he'd spent several weeks holed up in an office center on Farragut Square; during that time, his favorite target had been the reception area of an attorney's office. A one-man show named Walt Franklin, the kind of attorney who chased ambulances. And so, Walt Franklin was chased by people with grudges.

Lucas's observation deck in that office was one of his most brilliant ever: the lobby coat closet, a small cubicle not much bigger than an old telephone booth—something, unfortunately, he didn't see much of anymore. The closet had an empty space behind its two-by-four framing and gypsum board, leaving enough room for him to stand. An anomaly in the construction, one of many he'd seen over the years.

But what had been so wonderful about this space, this anomaly, was its perfect positioning between the reception desk and the lobby waiting area. By drilling holes on two opposite sides of the small space, he could simply turn and view the woman who usually sat at the front desk—a large, red-haired woman with a genuine smile—or the people in the reception area. No need to change positions; he could simply turn his head and watch whoever seemed the most interesting.

Over the several hours he'd spent cramped in that space, he'd seen dozens of intriguing dwellers—people with complex, magic-filled histories, he knew—sit in the lobby's molded plastic chairs and wait to speak with Walt Franklin. Their savior.

Once he'd experienced a Connection with the large, red-haired woman who sat at the desk. One minute she was working away, doing some filing. The next moment she simply stiffened, then looked nervously around the room.

"Whatsa matter?" he heard a man's voice ask from the lobby area. Lucas turned quietly and looked through the peephole at the man. White hair. Too much loose skin under his chin.

Back to the redheaded receptionist. "I . . . don't know," she stammered. "I just feel like . . . someone's watching."

The jowly man in the reception area half snorted, half laughed. "Wouldn't doubt it, the kind of stuff old Walt's involved in. Either the mob's watching him, or the CIA. Or both." He offered another snort-laugh.

The receptionist didn't share his humor, obviously, but she smiled at him. Except, Lucas could tell, this wasn't her usual smile. Her normal smile. Lucas was a student of the smile, and he knew this particular one was forced; it barely turned the corners of her mouth.

She hadn't seen Lucas. But she had sensed something of his presence, and his mind kept returning to that. Returning to all the people, maybe a dozen in all, who had made the Connection and intuited his presence in a closet. Under a floor. Above a ceiling. Hers was all the more special because she hadn't actually seen any evidence of him. She'd only felt it.

I just feel like someone's watching.

As Lucas left his daydream and returned his attention to the dark-haired woman in the elevator below, now staring at her feet, he wanted her to make that Connection too. He liked this woman; he wanted to feel something more than the typical subject and observer relationship. He wanted the Connection.

Instead, she lifted her face toward the doors, caught in midyawn, as they chimed and opened on the twenty-third floor. She slipped through and into the offices beyond.

So much for Connection.

Still, he would wait. It was early morning, and he'd have another half hour of steady traffic. If no other interesting dwellers stepped on the elevator before then, he'd choose the dark-haired woman. She was, after all, the only one who had inspired a secret history in his head all morning. That had to count for something.

Maybe, just maybe, this dark-haired woman with the full lips and the eyes like bright marbles and the overwhelming grief at the loss of her husband would pull him back to the twenty-third floor. Maybe she would make the Connection after all.

He could wait.

LATE THAT EVENING, WHEN THE DARK-HAIRED WOMAN HAD LEFT THE office and returned to her modest home in her Ford Taurus (this is what he imagined she drove), when the entire office building had emptied, Lucas let himself into the company offices where she worked and began to search.

This building didn't have much security. A few cams, but those were on the building's exterior. And the janitors here weren't all that attentive. They often left their industrial vacuums or their carts filled with cleaning supplies sitting alone in the hallways, rings of master keys jangling loosely from them. So really, it was easy to take master keys and make copies—he even knew of a key machine he could use after hours just a few blocks away from the building—then return the keys, safe and sound, to their carts or vacs.

So the dark-haired woman's office space was only a key turn away.

He slipped the key into the front door of the office and turned it.

He pushed open the door, listening for the telltale click or buzz of an armed alarm system. Nothing. Alarm systems weren't common in these kinds of office parks, because the tenants seemed to rely on the buildings' inept security guards. But he'd run into a few.

Closing the door behind him, he looked for light switches and began to examine the space. His mind took in all the architectural details as he explored, looking for his first target: the break room.

He found it on the far end of a row of cubicles, a smallish office behind a glass wall, with a table, some chairs, and a soda machine. Casually, he strolled the floor to the break room and entered. Just behind the door he found an under-the-counter refrigerator and opened it.

No funky smells. Good. Often, when you opened these refrigerators, you were greeted by the whiff of month-old Chinese food or curdled milk, long forgotten by the office workers who had stashed them there. Usually he ended up cleaning out rotten leftovers from these office refrigerators, performing a crude service in return for the edible food he took.

That was his real reason for seeking out office break rooms and refrigerators: they always held whole lunches packed and brought from home, leftover pizzas from office parties, takeout orders left untouched. Lucas couldn't remember the last time he'd had to buy food for himself. Occasionally he liked to go to a restaurant or get a special treat, but usually he found more than enough in the many offices of the greater DC area.

For that matter, Lucas didn't need to spend money on much of anything. He was happy with clothing from Goodwill, and his home constantly rotated from office building to office building. No rent, no food, no clothing—without those expenses, Lucas had been able to stash away several thousand dollars over the last few years, all while doing menial cash-under-the-table jobs.

In this particular refrigerator he found a full wrapped sandwich (turkey and tomato), a couple unopened cartons of milk, and some apples. Dinner. The cupboard held a few bags of chips; he took one of the bags and put it in his backpack for later.

As he sat at the small table and ate, listening to the low rumble of the HVAC system deep within the building, he stared at the small metal refrigerator. He knew all about these office refrigerators, yes. But what about refrigerators in homes? Those had to be different, didn't they? Surely no one just put food in the refrigerator and forgot it, did they? Home refrigerators, well, they were like small gathering spaces. Always near breakfast nooks or dining tables where families congregated over cookies and milk, talking about their days at the office or their projects at school or their meetings at Junior League. Yes, the home refrigerator had to be more like . . . home.

Not that Lucas knew. Or would ever know, for that matter. He'd grown up in an orphanage, never known his parents, never known anything about the traditional ideas of a home. A real home. It was all so foreign to him, so *other*. That's why he preferred the institutionalized feel of offices and commercial buildings. They felt more comfortable. His forays into the dark, hidden spaces were always in public buildings, never private residences. He wasn't a Peeping Tom, or a stalker, or anyone sick and demented like that.

He was an artist.

An artist who worked in concrete and glass and fiberboard, creating menageries out of the colorful existences lived by the dwellers inside his monitored offices. Yes, they had existences outside of those walls, but Lucas wouldn't cross that threshold; his imagined existences for dwellers were always more interesting anyway. He didn't, couldn't, understand their private lives in private homes. His own sense of ethics told him it would be wrong, and so he didn't question it.

After finishing his last bite of turkey and tomato, he cleaned the table and threw everything in the garbage, noticing that the janitorial staff hadn't emptied the office cans yet. That meant he'd have to be on guard as he worked.

He wiped his hands on the front of his jeans, adjusted the pack he wore on his back, and went outside the break room, scanning the middle cubicles and looking for the space where the dark-haired woman sat. Was she a receptionist? He didn't think so. She didn't have quite that disaffected air, and she'd been entering the building later; most receptionists were among the first to arrive.

He stood motionless, studying and considering as he scanned the offices. If they could be called offices. They were small cubicles, partitioned by cloth dividers, filling a large, open space. The place had a boiler room feel to it. Lucas hadn't bothered to check the name of the business at the front, but he was guessing this was a telemarketing facility of some kind. Maybe a phone support center.

He began to work his way through the cubicles, a Minotaur winding his way through a maze, looking at individual desks.

Eventually he found her. Even in places such as this, especially in places such as this, people tried to bring a bit of themselves to their workspaces. Photos were common. Knickknacks and trinkets. Comics and cartoons clipped from newspapers.

It was a photo that identified the dark-haired woman, and when he saw it, he knew he had been drawn to a very special dweller indeed.

The framed photo that sat next to her computer terminal proved it. In it, she had her arms wrapped around two preteen kids—one boy, one girl—and a look of pure joy on her face, matched, amazingly enough, by the joy in the children's faces.

As he stared at this photo, Lucas imagined the family camping on the Kansas prairie, enjoying a long weekend together. This would be when the father was still alive, he decided. Just before snapping the photo, the father had made a particularly funny comment, an inside family joke they all loved—*everybody say 'nubbins'!*—and then clicked the shutter.

He went to the desk, opened her top drawer. A time sheet for the next day lay neatly inside, the name Noel Harkins printed neatly at the top. Noel liked to be organized, he decided.

Of course, she would have to be organized, to bring her family through the tragedy of her husband's death. She would have to be strong, and steady, and an inspiration to her two beautiful children.

And that was why she kept this photo on her desk: it was a reminder of happier times, of together times. The photo was a totem for her, a bit of magic that could transport her to her Happy Place with one glance.

(*Humpty Dumpty had some great falls.*)

Lucas closed his eyes for a moment.

These words were his own personal totem, of sorts, but an incomplete one. They were brief whispers of a past he couldn't remember, memories he couldn't bring to the surface. Haunted whispers of the Great Before, which was pretty much anything before the orphanage, anything before his sixth year. These words were, in fact, the only thing he had from the Great Before, and they were mere shadows of whispers, maddeningly brief.

(Humpty Dumpty had some great falls.)

The orphanage. A cliché, really, the loner kid who never had close relationships with anyone because his parents had been killed when he was young and he'd been raised in an orphanage on the outskirts of DC.

Except he'd never known his parents. He knew they were dead—that's what the people at the orphanage had told him—but he'd never been told anything about his past, and so he remembered nothing of it.

Nothing about the Great Before except . . .

(Humpty Dumpty had some great falls.)

Yes, except that, a nonsense line that came back to him at the strangest times, meaning nothing, doing nothing, representing nothing. And yet it leaked from the cracks of his memories even now, more than two decades later.

His memories, what fragile shells of them existed, began at about age six. Before that, there was nothing. Just a solid expanse of white, stretching from horizon to horizon. He had existed in that time, he knew, and yet he had not existed.

It wasn't bad, as orphanages go, he supposed. Certainly not like the fanciful orphanages of literature, where young children were whipped into silence by angry and sadistic nuns wielding leather strops. No nuns at all in his orphanage; in fact, Lucas hadn't even seen a nun until he left the confines of the orphanage at age eighteen.

Still, even his most vivid memories of the orphanage were painted in broad strokes. He hadn't formed any close friendships with anyone there, couldn't even really say the names of any other kids, now that he thought about it. He saw their faces in his memories, of course, but that's all they were: faces. Even the teachers and staff were little more than that.

Instead, he remembered the roof. From his room, shared with so many other children, he had a clear view of the window. And through that window, when he ventured to it, he saw a far-off land of light and magic. He would find out later that those lights were the Metro DC area, but in his six-year-old mind, they were simply a promise. A promise of something he didn't fully understand but wanted to find.

He spent many hours in the dead of night admiring the far-off lights, imagining himself in that mystical place. Later, when he was older, he would open the window, crawl through its narrow space to the asphalt-shingled roof, and lie on his back staring at the lights, reaching out now and then and imagining himself grasping those lights in his hands.

That's what had started his creeping. Staying outside on the roof for a few hours invariably led to searches by the staff, and Lucas would catch glimpses of them inside the house, looking for him. After watching them for a while, he would pick a time to climb back through the window, wander down the hallway with the wood-slat flooring, and innocently ask, "Were you looking for me?"

Why the other kids never said anything, he did not know. Maybe it was the bond of a shared secret. But it continued for several years, without his increasingly longer sojourns being discovered.

This, he knew, is what had awakened the Dark Vibration inside.

And for the many years since, he had been feeding that Dark Vibration.

(Humpty Dumpty had some great falls.)

These words weren't a totem that transported him to his Happy Place. They were cruel reminders that he had no Happy Place.

He slammed a hand against Noel's desktop, jarring the framed photo out of its place a fraction of an inch. He bit his tongue, kept his eyes tightly closed, blocked the uninvited words from his mind.

(Humpty Dumpty had some)

(Humpty Dumpty had)

(Humpty Dumpty)

When he opened his eyes again, he was in control. The door to uninvited whispers of his past had been shut, and he was firmly in the present. Here in Noel's cubicle.

To watch Noel, to see her at work, he would have to build an observation deck. And in the open like this, there was really only one place to do it.

He looked above him at the acoustic tiles of the ceiling, calculating what he would need to do. Then he moved. Even though he'd spent several hours today lying motionless on top of the elevator car, when Lucas decided to move, it was smooth. Effortless. Liquid. He boosted himself up onto Noel's desk, reached overhead, and pushed one of the ceiling tiles out of the way. He smiled at what he saw. Just as he'd hoped, the poured concrete floor of the next story was hidden a few feet above the tile.

More than enough room.

He unshouldered the dusty blue nylon backpack—his constant companion—and unzipped the main compartment. Inside were all his tools of the trade: a flashlight, a utility knife, some climbing rope, a few sets of webbed rigging he'd built himself, and several other items. He selected a small hand drill and set down the pack for a moment. He tested the divider between Noel's space and the adjoining cubicle, then stepped on the thin edge and balanced himself there effortlessly. His head was now in the space left by the removed tile, and he held up the hand drill just in front of his face as he began drilling into the concrete. It wasn't easy, and he knew he'd burn through a couple of bits, but he didn't mind the work. He enjoyed it. He had the whole night if he needed it.

Later, when he'd completed drilling three holes, he tapped anchors into them and turned the screws inside; they expanded to fit the holes and wedged themselves in place. Then it was just a simple matter of affixing his small hammock, handmade from several sections of climbing rope, to the anchors.

Finished, he stepped down from the top of the divider and admired his work. With the hammock in place up above the tiles, he could hang comfortably, facedown, to peer into Noel's world below. Not so much different from the elevator, really. But more intimate. And therefore more exciting.

He put all the acoustic tiles he'd pushed aside back into the track, save for the one that was directly over Noel's head and computer terminal. In this one, he drilled a small hole—so small it looked like the simple pattern of the tile—and then put it in its place as well. Now he had an observation deck, complete with a peephole.

He jumped down from Noel's desk, noticing the thick layer of concrete dust he'd let filter down. Sloppy, yes. He usually wasn't so. But no matter. He brushed the dust off the desk and chair, sweeping it to the floor. He left, found the janitor's closet on that floor (unlocked, of course, but no janitor around), and returned with some towels, cleaner, and a small hand vac.

Five minutes later, all evidence of his being there was gone. And Noel's cubicle was probably cleaner than it ever had been with the regular janitorial staff working. He'd worked up a bit of a sweat and could use a good cleaning himself, so he'd probably have to shower soon. The Y and the homeless shelters were always options, but Lucas knew more than a few offices in the neighborhood that provided workout areas and locker rooms with showers for their employees. Mostly high-tech companies, pouring on benefits to keep workers healthy and happy. And in those places, the hot water never ran out in the middle of your shower.

Finished with the immediate work, Lucas readjusted his backpack and found himself staring at the photo of Noel and her kids again.

A beautiful photo, really.

He took it and added it to the items already in his pack.

TWO

THE NEXT DAY LUCAS MADE HIS WAY TO THE BLUE BELL CAFÉ FOR HIS early morning dishwashing shift.

The Blue Bell was an ancient cube of stucco, weathered gray by decades of grime. Just down the street, a new strip mall was rising, a nod at gentrification. But here, on the shady side of the street, the Blue Bell refused to give up its many ghosts.

He put a hand on the side of the Hobart. Room temperature; no way Briggs had run it in the last couple hours.

"Did it to you again, huh?"

Lucas recognized Sarea's voice and turned around. She was smiling, as usual, and her eyes shimmered. Lucas thought again of the photo he'd lifted from Noel's desk, and realized he was drawn to the photo because that look on Noel's face—that look of absolute joy—was much like the look Sarea always had on her face. He blushed a bit at this thought.

"Yeah, I guess," he offered.

"Should at least ask you to kiss him first, before he goes and does that."

Lucas smiled. "I could probably live without a kiss from Briggs."

"We all could." She turned and was gone.

Sarea was like that; one moment, she was in the room with you, carrying on a conversation. Then, without warning, she was gone. An hour later, she might be back, picking up where she'd left off. For Sarea, life was one long conversation with several pauses.

Lucas, smiling, turned on the hot water and started rinsing dishes.

HE DID A DOUBLE SHIFT, AND SAREA DOUBLED OVER WITH HIM. SHE EVEN spent an hour helping him load dishes after the late dinner rush.

When they punched the clock and left the café, twilight was spreading its fingers over the city; purple light burnished the bright windows of the strip mall down the street.

Outside the back door, Sarea took out her pack of cigarettes and pointed them at him. He didn't smoke, but he always took one when Sarea offered. It was a familiar ritual, and it kept her around for a few minutes, talking to him.

Sarea put a flame to both their cigarettes, then leaned her head back against the stucco wall of the café, blew a cloud of smoke from the side of her mouth while she eyed him.

Lucas looked down, uncomfortable with the attention.

"You ain't much of a talker, Lucas."

He shrugged, and she laughed at that. He wasn't sure why.

She took another drag on her smoke. "Where you from, anyway?"

He knew a shrug wasn't going to help him here. He also knew he couldn't answer the question, because he had no idea where he was from, unless you counted an orphanage. "Long story," he tried.

"Yeah," she said. "And you don't do long stories."

She put one of her sneakered feet up against the wall behind her, picked a fleck of tobacco off her tongue. "So where do you live, at least?"

"Staying in a place over by Howard University."

Another laugh.

"What?" he asked.

"Howard U-ni-ver-si-ty. How's a white boy like you end up in the District, working for cash under the counter at the Blue Bell, and staying at a place filled with black folks?"

He puffed on his own cigarette, looking down at the ground. "You mean I'm not black?" he asked.

That made her laugh again. It felt good to make her laugh.

She dropped her cigarette, crushed it with her foot. "Guess that's as much as I'm gonna get from you, huh?"

He shrugged again.

"It's okay," she said. "Mysterious is always more interesting."

She turned and walked up the alley, and Lucas watched her figure disappear into the haze of twilight.

TWENTY MINUTES LATER, HE WAS HOME. HE'D TOLD SAREA HE WAS STAYING in a place near Howard University. That was true enough, in a way, but it wasn't really near the university as such.

It was inside it.

Specifically, he was currently staying inside one of the underground tunnels attached to the steam plant. He'd been here a couple weeks now, and he was comfortable hanging around for at least another two weeks before moving on. He'd been scouting an abandoned floor in an old office building several blocks away, and it seemed like a logical next step.

For now, though, he had his own space down here, below the pipes that occasionally clinked, occasionally roared as heated air moved through them. The sounds were comforting to him, more comforting than the utter silence he'd experienced in some other spaces.

He moved his electric candle—a miniflashlight with a removable top that became a base—and sifted through his backpack. He found the photo of Noel, the dark-haired office worker. She had her tragic history, which meant Lucas had his magic hopes she would turn out to be a truly interesting dweller.

He fingered the frame of the photo, looking at the bright, familiar smiles of Noel and her children.

Genuine smiles.

At least he had this.

He crawled to a space near the head of his sleeping bag and placed the photo among all the others; he had arranged more than two dozen of them in a deliberate, almost geometric pattern. Noel's picture fit the overall mosaic well.

Of course, his minishrine didn't hold just photos. There were other mementos that had spoken to him as well. Jewelry, notes, children's artwork, a purple scarf. They were all here, these totems of Happy Places. And they were here to comfort him. To let him know Happy Places did, in fact, exist.

He turned off the electric candle and crawled into his sleeping bag, letting the sound of air hissing through the pipes above lull him to sleep.

DEEP IN THE MIDDLE OF THE NIGHT, A SCRAPING SOUND AWOKE HIM. A scuffling. He lay awake for a few minutes, remaining absolutely still, listening to the sound and establishing the pattern in his mind.

It wasn't one of the pipes; he'd memorized their various sounds over the past few weeks. Rats? No. Plenty of them down here, to be sure, but he could recognize their movement by the scuttle of their claws. Nor was it a mechanical sound. It was, he guessed, another person. Dragging something, maybe.

Seccies? No, it wouldn't be security guards at this time of night, certainly not underground like this. And if it were, he'd hear more sounds; seccies weren't exactly light on their feet, in his experience. This scraping was slow, deliberate.

Already he had an idea what it might be, but he thought he should investigate, make sure it didn't get too close to his home base.

No one knew where he was, and he wanted it to stay that way. He had, after all, an altar of wondrous mementos to protect; the thought of anyone else touching that perfect photo of Noel and her children, for instance, made him sick.

He felt with his fingers, finding where he'd left his electric candle, and detached the base to screw the head back in place. Now he had a flashlight, but he didn't turn it on. No need yet.

Lucas crept down the tunnel toward the steam plant, the apex of the underground system beneath the university. Like so many other college campuses, the university had been built on top of a network of these tunnels, which carried heat from the central plant to the various dorms and buildings through pipes belowground.

He took several steps, paused at the wall several yards from his home base, listened again for the sound. It was closer.

He felt the pipe above him, then put his foot against the adjacent wall and boosted himself up, scrambling so he was astride the giant pipe. Quickly he crawled along its length, sliding through the opening in the barrier wall while he stayed on top. There was very little room above the pipe at the wall, but Lucas fit through it easily; he was able to sneak into tight spaces few other people would dare try.

A few minutes later he stood inside the main plant itself, next to the boiler, which radiated pipes in all directions like a giant, mechanical octopus. Steam hissed in the heavy air, and the whole room smelled like rust. Rats scratched at the floor in dark corners. He began making his way around the boiler, pausing to put his hand on each pipe as he listened.

At the fourth pipe he felt a vibration, followed by the familiar scuffling.

He hoisted himself to the top of this pipe and began to follow it away from the boiler, past the barrier wall and beyond. Ahead, the steady scuffling continued with slight pauses in between. Still Lucas refused to use his light; he knew, soon enough, he'd see another light to guide him.

A few minutes later, he saw what he was expecting: the light of a miner's helmet, obviously attached to someone who was inching along the pipe. He couldn't quite make out the form in the darkness, but he was sure he knew what he was looking at now.

An infiltrator. A creeper. Someone who loved to explore the hidden spaces behind KEEP OUT and AUTHORIZED PERSONNEL ONLY signs.

He lay still for a few minutes, watching the other figure struggle. Move-pause-scuffle . . . repeat. Every thirty seconds or so, the figure stopped to sweep the light across the underground tunnel. A few times, Lucas saw the flash of a digital camera.

So what did this one like to call himself? Lucas had run into them inside buildings, drains, sewer systems. The more highbrowed bunch liked to call themselves infiltrators. Others preferred urban explorers or hackers. Some identified themselves by the kind of areas they preferred to explore: drainers, tunnelers, steamers. For slang, they all answered to the term *creepers*.

Usually they were teens or twentysomethings, chasing a few thrills to see if they could break into unauthorized areas or explore the unexplored. Some liked to "sign in"—infiltrate spaces and leave their own unique tags or markings as bits of communication with other creepers. Others, again usually the more highbrow among them, frowned on leaving any trace of themselves.

The question was, should he let this one know he was here? He felt a certain kinship, he supposed, with these creepers—he was, after all, something of a creeper himself—but he didn't like too much contact with unknowns. Not that the thought paralyzed him with fear or anything; in fact, he was rather comfortable communicating with others.

He just didn't enjoy it.

Washing dishes, sharing a smoke with Sarea, okay. Beyond that, though . . . just give him a dark hole he could crawl into.

Lucas sighed. He supposed he could just return to his space, lie awake for a few hours while he listened to this kid fumble about like a rhino on a tightrope. Or he could help the kid out, get him inside the central utilities building, let him take a few photos, and send him on his way.

So be it.

Lucas switched on his flashlight. "Need some help?" he asked as he shined the flashlight in the kid's eyes. He smiled. Cruel, yes, but he couldn't help himself. This kid had pulled him out of a pleasant night's sleep, after all.

He was surprised to see it wasn't really a kid. It was a guy in his thirties with a few extra pounds packed on his frame. Odd. The usual infiltration crowd tended to be thin, wiry, pasty-skinned.

The guy, to his credit, only had that doe-in-the-headlights look for a few seconds. It disappeared when he lost his balance and tumbled from the pipe, hitting the concrete floor four feet below.

"Oh . . . hey. You okay?" Lucas found him with his flashlight beam again, now sitting up on the floor's concrete surface. He turned the beam of his own light Lucas's way, and Lucas stayed immobile.

"Yeah, I'm okay," the guy answered. "Might need a new set of underwear, but I'm okay."

"Sorry."

"Didn't know anyone else was poppin' this space."

Lucas slid down from the pipe and landed on the floor lightly, then walked to the guy. "Where'd you find out about it?" he asked, helping the guy to his feet.

"Infiltration.org. Steam tunnels aren't really my thing—I'm more into buildings. But . . . you know. Live a little." The guy took off a glove and held out his hand. "I'm Donavan," he said.

Lucas took the hand and shook it. He didn't like to give out his real name. "Call me Humpty," he said.

"Humpty. Yeah, make fun of me falling, why don'tcha?" Donavan patted concrete dust from his clothes.

The name had nothing to do with Donavan's fall, but there was no harm in letting him think that.

Donavan looked back into the beam from Lucas's flashlight again. "You aren't gonna tell anyone about that fall, are you? Post it online or anything, I mean?"

"Nah. Everyone craters once in a while."

Lucas himself never fell. But he wanted Donavan to forget about it. He changed the subject.

"You got a barrier wall up here a couple hundred yards," he said, pointing his flashlight behind him. "Kind of a tight squeeze around the pipe to get into the CUB. But I can get you in through a back door." He threw in a few bits of infiltration lingo for Donavan; they always liked to run into kindred spirits who spoke their language.

"Huh? Nah, forget it. Like I said, I'm not much of a steamer. Don't know what I'm doin' here, anyway."

"You want some pictures of the CUB?"

Donavan squinted into Lucas's flashlight beam, his pupils glowing red. "You'd do that?"

"I'd do that." Mainly because Lucas knew if he got Donavan some pictures, it would be marked off the guy's list; he wouldn't talk himself into coming back later, and he'd move on to his next target. These infiltration types always had new targets.

"Okay, then. You got a deal." Donavan handed him his camera, then shoved his thumb back over his shoulder. "You don't mind if I get a head start, do you? I pretty much suck at this balancing-on-a-pipe thing."

"You don't really have to stay on the pipe. You could have walked this whole corridor until you got to the barrier wall."

"So I just wasted forty-five minutes."

"Call it a learning experience."

"Well then. Since this is a learning experience, maybe I should just follow you to the barrier wall, see how you get by?"

"Suit yourself." Lucas turned and walked the two hundred yards to the wall, with Donavan close behind. At the wall, he reached for the pipe overhead, then wedged his foot against the wall and scrambled up as he'd done before.

Donavan whistled. "Man, I never seen anyone chimney like that. Should get a picture of that."

Lucas smiled from the top of the pipe. "I don't do pictures."

"What, they're against your religion? Feel like they'll steal a part of your soul or something?"

"Something." Lucas scrambled across the pipe, sliding through the narrow opening, and dropped to the ground inside the central utilities building. He powered on the digital cam and snapped half a dozen photos before reversing course.

On the other side of the wall again, he pitched the camera down to Donavan.

"Thanks, man," Donavan said as he fumbled with the camera.

"So where do you post your photos?" Lucas asked, watching Donavan's reaction closely. He needed to make sure this guy was nothing more than an infiltration junkie out for a few late-night ya-yas.

"Lots of places. Start with infiltration.org. You been there, I'm sure."

Lucas gave a noncommittal nod. He wasn't into the whole online world of infiltration, but he was happy to let Donavan think that way. Just another guy, out for a late-night expedition.

"Actually, I publish the photos to Flickr," Donavan continued. "But the photostream shows up at infiltration.org, my blog, a few other places."

"Been infiltrating long?"

Donavan considered. "Buildings, yeah. Few years."

"Why?"

"Why not? Isn't that the creed? Go into the places, see the things no one wants us to see?"

Lucas smiled. "Yeah."

"What about you?" Donavan asked.

"What about me?"

"How long you been doing this? Obviously for a while. You stick mostly to the underground tunnels?"

"Do a little bit of everything," Lucas said.

"Maybe you could . . . you know . . . show me some tricks."

"Maybe."

Lucas began to lead the way out of the tunnel, and Donavan dutifully followed. Five minutes later they were in the basement of one of the university buildings.

"How'd you get in?" Lucas asked.

Donavan led him to the elevator shaft. "Told you tunnels aren't my thing. But I like buildings."

With that, Donavan moved up the iron rungs on the wall of the elevator shaft. Lucas had to admit he climbed well, especially for someone with added bulk.

Lucas followed him, then perched on the iron rungs, waiting for Donavan to force open the elevator bay doors with a crowbar. After a few tries, Donavan wedged the doors open a few feet and jammed the crowbar into the opening to hold it. He crawled through, then waited for Lucas to follow him before pulling out the tool and letting the bay doors close again with a metallic shriek.

Donavan mopped at his forehead. "Okay, I guess I owe you one." He looked at his watch. "You up for a little late-night breakfast?"

"Don't worry about it."

"No, really. I'd like to. There's an all-night cybercafé a few Metro stops over. The LiveWire. You know it?"

Lucas shook his head.

"I can post my photos, and you can tell me how you got those Jackie Chan moves."

Lucas stared at Donavan's face, his skin now a dark, sickly yellow in the overhead streetlights.

"Gotta work in the morning," Lucas said, which was true.

"Some other time, then? Maybe we can connect through the infiltration forum? How do I find you . . . um . . . Humpty?"

"Sitting on a wall," Lucas said, then spun around and walked away.

THREE

LUCAS WORKED HIS MORNING SHIFT WITH LESS THAN TWO HOURS OF sleep, but two things made it bearable. First, he didn't follow Briggs from the previous shift; it had been Ernie instead, who had left the dishes in good shape for him. Second, he didn't double over.

Make that three things: Sarea worked the shift with him.

At the end of the shift, they walked out the back door together, letting the cook and the other waitress coming off shift recede down the alley before their familiar ritual began. She took out the smokes, offered him one, lit them both.

The Pause button came off Sarea's previous conversation.

"I thought about enrolling at Howard University once," she said.

He nodded. "Why didn't you?"

She smiled, exhaled a plume of smoke. "Long story."

He smiled, took a polite puff of his own cigarette. "Good one."

He wanted to say something else, so he tried it. "You should go. To college, I mean. You're smart."

She grunted. "Yeah, I aced all my tests to get this waitressin' job."

He took another drag on the cigarette, coughed.

She turned her head to the side, keeping her eyes on him. "You don't have to take a smoke just 'cuz I offer, you know."

He shrugged. It was all he could come up with.

They smoked in silence for a few minutes, until Sarea came to the end of her cigarette and dropped it on the gooey tar surface of the alley.

"Oh, hey," she said, remembering something. "Your friend ever talk to you?"

He felt a mild shock course through his body, dropped his own cigarette. "Friend? What friend?"

"Guy was in here earlier today. Sat at the counter for a while, asked me if you were working."

"What did he look like?"

"I dunno. You white boys all look the same." She smiled and must have noticed something hard on Lucas's face, because the smile slid off her face instantly. "Sorry. He was bald, stocky, looked like he worked out. Didn't see him standing, but I don't think he was very tall. Kinda blocky, if that makes sense."

Someone looking for him? Bad news. He tried to hide his stress. "How long ago?"

Now it was her turn to shrug. "Don't know. He sat there nursing a cup of coffee for a while, then on one of the refills he says, 'Hey, Lucas washing today?' I said you were in back, did he want me to get you. He said he didn't want to interrupt you, he'd just wait until you went on break or something." Her eyes narrowed. "Doesn't seem like he stuck around too long after that, though, come to think of it."

Lucas was looking at the pavement. He felt her hand on his shoulder, flinched. She pulled her hand away, then let it settle there again. He looked up at her.

"You okay?" she asked. "You in some kind of trouble?"

"Fine," he said. "Probably just . . . um, Bobby checking up on me. Bobby's like that; I don't see him for a while, then he just pops in out of the blue."

She wasn't buying it. "Yeah," she said, tight-lipped. "Bobby." She held his gaze for a few seconds, then dug in her purse. She brought out a pen and a receipt, turned over the receipt and scribbled on it. She held it out to him.

"Here," she said. "My cell phone. You need anything, you just call me."

He took the receipt. "Okay," he said.

Now her hand was on his face. This time he didn't flinch.

"No, I mean it, Lucas. I don't know what you've got going, but you can tell me. I grew up around here, and I've seen stuff that would make your head spin. So there's not much chance of you surprising me."

He nodded slowly. "Okay."

She patted his cheek and then she was off, down the alley.

He waited a few moments, sprinted down the alley the opposite way, then turned and ran five blocks to the east. He came to a run-down hotel, then went inside and nodded at the clerk behind the front counter as he moved by at a fast walk. Seemed like there was always a new clerk every time he came through, and none of them took much interest in him beyond the obligatory nod; their mags or TV programs were more important. Next to the elevator, he came to a door marked AUTHORIZED PERSONNEL ONLY. Without hesitating, he pulled the door open; he'd broken the lock on it nearly two months ago, and he was sure no one but he had opened the door since.

Glad to leave the scent of stale urine behind him in the hotel lobby, he took stairs down to the subbasement of the building. Once again, another AUTHORIZED PERSONNEL ONLY door greeted him. He opened this one, pushing hard against its rusty hinges, and went out into a tunnel that connected to the city's sewer system.

Half a block away, a small cover, something like a horizontal man-hole, was bolted to the side of the sewer tunnel. He opened it and went through, putting himself in a Metro tunnel. No trains were coming, so he boosted himself through, staying on the catwalk until he came to a third door. Behind this door was the platform for the Eastern Market stop on the Orange and Blue lines; he could transfer over to the Green or Yellow at L'Enfant and be back to Howard University just four stops later.

Several other people were standing on the platform when he came out of the door, but no one seemed to notice him.

This he knew he could count on. People looked, but they never saw.

Twenty minutes later he stepped off the train at Howard University, slipped onto another catwalk, and found the entry into his own steam tunnel no more than a hundred yards away.

It was midday, but here, underground, it was always dark. Energized by his conversation with Sarea, he fired up his electric candle, then squatted on his sleeping bag and held the candle up to his shrine.

Immediately, he noticed something was wrong. Someone had moved the totems; his precise geometric pattern was broken. Whoever it was had tried to keep everything in the right place, he could tell; the correct order was there, but it was all wrong.

Someone had been in his space. Looking for something.

After a few moments of hesitation, he gathered the photos and totems, sweeping them into his backpack. Then he stuffed his sleeping bag into its sack and left.

It was time to find a new home.

THE NEW PLACE WAS THE FOURTH FLOOR OF A NOT-QUITE-ABANDONED office building near Tiber Island, built in 1910, according to the cornerstone on its front—long before the Tiber Island development just a few blocks away. The ground floor was retail—Dandy Don's Donuts and the Sole Provider shoe store; floors two and three were populated by small one-room and two-room office suites (many of which were empty), and floors four and five were entirely vacant.

Lucas chose the fourth floor because it seemed to be the most abandoned; floor five had signs of construction, though none that looked recent, while four was only populated by dusty steel desks, a few marred file cabinets, and a thick layer of dust.

He chose one of the back rooms near the fire escape (it was still intact; he'd checked), closing the front door and locking it. If anyone snooped around during the day, they would think the office was locked and abandoned. Meanwhile, Lucas was able to enter and exit his new space via a back window, directly onto the fire escape.

He settled in, began placing all his mementos in their comforting geometric pattern, and forced himself to relax. Yes, his home had been invaded. Yes, someone was looking for him at the Blue Bell. But Lucas was above that; nothing rattled him, because he had perfect control over all his actions, all his emotions.

He had discovered these amazing abilities while growing up in the orphanage: he could be ice-cold in any situation.

Still, he needed to think, and the best way to think was to crawl into an observation deck and watch someone. Let his subconscious mind do some of the work. If he sat here and tried to piece it all together, his brain wouldn't function; the Dark Vibration he always felt inside would shatter him into a thousand pieces. He could feel his hands starting to jitter even as he placed his mementos in the proper order.

Perhaps Noel, but that was a long way from here; he needed somewhere closer. He knew a regional library just a few blocks away. Greater Southeast Hospital would be easy to get to on the Metro, and it was always interesting, filled with people who had wonderful histories; he had built several still-functioning observation decks there. But it didn't appeal to him either.

Maybe relief was as close as one of the businesses downstairs. Dandy Don's Donuts seemed like a decent enough place. He'd noticed good traffic whenever he scouted the area before, along with a few tables inside so people could sit and get their instant sugar fix.

Usually he'd prefer to see the place after hours, do his work under the cover of darkness. But this wasn't usual.

He went inside Dandy Don's and bought a glazed doughnut, surveying the surroundings. The ceiling was out; it was one of those industrial chic monstrosities that exposed all the HVAC, ductwork, and wiring. No dropped acoustic tile.

He took a bite of the doughnut. Not bad, especially for this time of day. Obviously, Dan's whipped up fresh batches well into the afternoon.

The breezeway by the front entrance might hold some possibilities, but not in the middle of the day. He'd need some more time to explore what looked like fake walls on either side of the entryway.

He scanned the rest of the shop, his eyes settling on the public restrooms at the west side of the building. Those were a good possibility; they'd been built out into the middle of an essentially square space.

Lucas finished the last few bites of his glazed treat and moved toward the men's restroom, wiping his hands on his pants.

Once inside, he locked the door, turned, and scanned the room. Just as he'd hoped: a utility closet. He tried the closet's door. Locked, but he could get around that; it was just a knob lock. No deadbolt. Gripping the handle in both hands, he gave it a strong, steady twist. After a few seconds of resistance, the lock broke, and he felt it rattling loose inside the handle as he opened the door.

Knob locks on interior doors. Useless.

Inside the closet, he saw the usual array of toilet paper, cleaners, an extra trash can, a mop bucket. But there was more than enough room for him to stand, and the bare wall directly in front of him faced the main shop. He wouldn't be able to do anything too elaborate right now, but he could probably rig up something makeshift.

He twisted off his backpack, searched inside, and found his hand drill again, then changed out the bit to the thinnest he had. Not electric. He hated electric, and for good reason. No way he'd be able to fire up an electric drill and just bore through the wall of the shop without notice.

But with his hand drill and a slow, steady pace, he just might.

He placed the bit against the gypsum board wall and methodically started to turn the crank, one revolution every two seconds. The drill sank into the chalky surface and began coring a small hole. When he eyeballed a half-inch depth and felt the resistance lightening just a bit, he backed out the drill. If he kept drilling and went all the way through, he was likely to take off a chunk of the surface on the other side and attract attention.

He looked at the hole. Perfect.

Next, he found a small nail tacked into one of the shelves in the room; he took the nail, put it in the drill hole until it met resistance, then gave a quick tap. Now he had a small pinhole in the utility closet, offering him a view of three customer tables when he pressed his eye against the wall. Couldn't see the order counter, which is what he'd prefer, but this wasn't the time to be picky. After hours, he could punch holes and build observation decks all around the shop if he wanted to.

Now it was time to check his work from the other side, clear the bathroom for a few minutes. He backtracked, closing the closet door behind him, then unlocking and pushing open the small window on the opposite wall, and finally unlocking the men's bathroom door and walking back out into the shop.

"Thanks," he said to the pleasant woman behind the counter, and heard her say "Come again" as he walked out the breezeway and the front door.

Little did she know.

Without stopping, he immediately went around the corner of the building and circled around the block to the alley at the back. He'd already seen an exhaust vent jutting out of the brick wall there. Scanning the alley to make sure he was alone, he took the utility knife from his backpack and pried the exhaust fan away from its mooring on the brick wall. He set the fan on the ground and scrambled into the massive ductwork behind it, then turned around and pulled the fan back into place behind him.

Normally he never trusted ducting, but this was a commercial space with an industrial fan and HVAC system; he knew it could hold his frame for a short distance, and that's all he needed.

He scrambled down the duct, slid out one of the panels, and looked into the space beyond. Following his instincts, he stepped across a few rafters, then dropped down through the utility closet that still had ceiling tiles in it from a previous remodel. Perfect.

Now inside the closet, he put a wedge under the door from the bathroom and went back to the pinhole. No one at any of the three tables he could see, but that was okay. Someone would come. Someone with an interesting history to tell.

He placed his ear against the backside of the gypsum board, listening to the thrum of the HVAC system around him, punctuated by occasional conversation in the doughnut shop. He couldn't make out any words, but again, that was okay. Just knowing he was there, near the conversations, calmed the vibration in his own chest.

He went into his semi-catatonic trance, standing absolutely still and peering through the pinhole. Cold, he was ice-cold. Simply because he wanted to be.

Now. What had happened? He'd been discovered, yes. Someone had been able to trace him. How?

He thought immediately of Donavan. Was it any coincidence

that this happened the day after his first "chance" meeting with Donavan? He thought probably not.

A young man, maybe in his late teens, walked into view and sat at one of the tables. Good. He was long and lean, shaved head. Probably an athlete of some kind.

He was just out of school for the day, Lucas decided. He liked to drop by this doughnut shop on his way home from school three, maybe four, times a week. Had always been a latchkey kid; his mother worked swing shifts, so she wasn't ever home when he returned from school. Still, he'd stayed out of the drugs, embraced sports—played third base on his high school's baseball team. Never knew his dad, like so many kids these days.

The kid took a bite out of his doughnut—glazed, good choice—set it down on a napkin, and retrieved a notebook and pen from his backpack.

Yes, that was part of the kid's ritual. He wanted to be a writer. Couldn't afford a computer, but that was okay; his notebook and pencil worked just fine, especially for his free-verse poetry. He read a lot of Yeats, Whitman, all the classics. But he was most drawn to the unconventional stylings of William Carlos Williams. Lucas himself had discovered these poets and others on weekly trips to the library near the orphanage.

Lucas felt his heart beat once. Just once. When he slipped into his observation state, his body went dormant. Once he'd taken his pulse and found it was only 20: about one beat every three seconds.

Another thump.

Donavan. He needed to investigate Donavan. But was that all? Something else was bothering him, and he didn't want to admit it.

Sarea.

So where you live anyway?

She had asked that; he heard her question rattling inside his mind. She'd asked where he lived, and he had told her he was staying near Howard. Then Donavan, and the rearranged totems, and . . . this. Was she part of it?

Maybe. He didn't want her to be, but maybe.

He should investigate her as well.

The lean kid at the table turned a page in his notebook. He worked fast. That was good, Lucas decided. Part of the kid's style: he slammed out the verses as they came to his brain, then poured them out through his pencil to the waiting pool of the page. The kid was preparing, practicing, for an upcoming poetry slam. He kept it hidden from the other guys on the baseball team; no way you'd want to admit to writing poetry in a dugout filled with testosterone. But that made it a secret joy, and secret joys were the best ones of all.

Lucas knew that very well.

FOUR

THE LIVEWIRE, THE HANGOUT DONAVAN HAD SO ADMIRED, DIDN'T SEEM very live at all. Lucas guessed it had once been a pub or bar; no windows anywhere in the place. Dark concrete floors and ceiling, drab gray walls. Abstract artwork hung on the walls with museum lights focused on each canvas. Bad call, Lucas decided, after taking a close look at a couple of the pieces.

He ordered a cup of coffee and a Danish, then sat down at one of the free computer terminals along the wall.

He launched the Firefox browser and watched it load the home page, which, not surprisingly, was The LiveWire's home page. "COME GET WIRED!!!" the page said in overly enthusiastic all caps and exclamation points, floating over a giant cup of coffee.

Come get wired. Yeah, he got it.

He typed in infiltration.org and pressed the Enter key. After a few seconds the page loaded, offering several articles on the art of infiltration, along with a photo section and forums. He clicked on the forums.

The third thread from the top was titled "Anyone know Humpty?" He clicked it. As expected, it was a thread started by Donavan, just this morning at six thirty. The post breathlessly exulted about his foray into the steam tunnels at Howard and included a link to photos of the CUB.

No mention that he'd never actually been in the boiler room. Surprise, surprise.

The post finished by saying he'd met a fellow traveler who went by the street name Humpty. He hadn't been able to find any posts from a Humpty at any of the typical online outlets and wondered if anyone else knew who Humpty was.

Two replies to the post exulted over the photos and said they'd never heard of a Humpty. A third reply also loved the photos but ignored the Humpty question.

Lucas clicked on the profile for "DonavanRox" and read. It listed a few interests (Washington Redskins, Halle Berry, *The Matrix* but not *Reloaded* or *Revolutions*), and a link to his MySpace page.

The MySpace page blared a hip-hop song, and Lucas immediately turned down the volume. Amazingly enough, "DonavanRox" also gave his full name on his MySpace profile: Donavan Roxwell.

Lucas shook his head, wondering why people were so willing to give away information about themselves online.

He opened a new tab in the browser and went to Google to search for "Donavan Roxwell" and "District of Columbia." No hits. Then he started filtering through all the suburbs around the DC area, finally hitting on a phone listing and address for "Donavan

Roxwell" and "Silver Spring, MD." The address was 4403B, Rock Harbor Apartments.

He had an address and a phone number. He looked at his watch: 3:30 p.m. Decision time. For as long as Lucas could remember, he'd never broken into anyone's home; it was his own code. Public buildings only, because . . . because he didn't quite know why; he'd never questioned it before, in the same way he'd never questioned the light from the sun. It was just a fact of his existence. And now here he was, looking up addresses and thinking of breaking into someone's home for the first time.

He expected to feel self-disgust, something inside telling him this was a line never to be crossed. That voice was there, but it was overpowered by a new voice, one that demanded he find out who was on his trail—who had been at the Blue Bell, who had dared to invade his own space.

He sighed. Besides, it wasn't like he was going to make this a habit. Desperate times, desperate measures, and all that. He needed to find out what was going on, quell a potential danger, and that called for him to do things he wouldn't normally do. It would just be Donavan's apartment—someone, he was now sure, who hadn't met him by accident. Donavan had to be the key to it all, and Donavan had invaded his own privacy, hadn't he? This was a righteous cause, a case of self-defense. And there was no guilt in self-defense.

He swallowed, not wanting to admit how much his nerves tingled when the decision solidified in his mind. He could be there in forty-five minutes on the Metro. If Donavan worked regular office hours and commuted, Lucas could have a couple hours alone in apartment 4403B.

ABOUT FIFTEEN YEARS AGO, ROCK HARBOR APARTMENTS WOULD HAVE been a new development, and probably a place you'd want to live. Now, however, the whole place had the feel of a slowly sinking ship; the guard gate wasn't even staffed and, from the looks of it, hadn't been used for a few years.

Lucas found building 4403 and walked around the perimeter. He didn't like newer buildings very much; less wasted space, fewer opportunities to slide into various nooks and crannies. But he always liked a challenge.

First things first. He went to 4403B and rang the doorbell. Waited. Knocked a few times. No answer. Even better, no barking dog inside. Donavan had proven himself to be a bit lax on security issues, so Lucas guessed he'd find a hidden key somewhere.

He felt on the framework above the door. Nothing. Same under the welcome mat, generically marked WELCOME MAT. That Donavan was a real joker. He turned, spied a mostly dead plant of some kind in the corner by the railing. He tipped the planter and found the key hidden beneath.

Well, at least Donavan hadn't hidden it on the sill above the door.

The key slid into the deadbolt and turned easily. Lucas returned the key to its hiding place, went inside the apartment, and shut the door behind him, sliding the deadbolt back into place.

After a short, five-foot hallway, the apartment opened into a large room consisting of a living area, a small dining area, and a kitchen. Farther along, the hallway continued with a doorway at the end and a turn to the left he was sure led to a second bedroom.

He could smell old cheese, leftovers from last night's late snack, perhaps. But beneath that smell was another: mold, as if the apartment had been steeped in moisture at one time and never really dried.

Lucas went to the phone first. He pressed the caller ID and looked for numbers that appeared more than once. He wrote those numbers down, then pressed the answering machine button to play saved messages. Two messages were of the "Hey, give me a call" variety, but the third sounded interesting.

A woman's voice: "Hi, Donavan, just wanted to talk to you about Howard, wondering if you found anything interesting. Call me when you get a chance."

Was it Sarea's voice? He played the message again. No, it didn't quite sound like her, but he couldn't rule it out.

He took out the receipt Sarea had given him, looked at the number, scrolled through all the caller ID numbers again. No matches.

That made him feel a bit better.

Okay, enough of this. He needed to get ready for Donavan's return.

He went down the hallway and checked out both the bedrooms and the bathroom. One bedroom, which was obviously Donavan's, had a running computer on a Kmart Blue Light Special desk. He moved the mouse. No open documents or applications. He looked under recent documents, found a list of addresses. Those might be important, but he didn't have time to copy them right now. Instead, he let his eyes flick over the list, committing the names to memory.

He opened the Firefox browser to check recent pages loaded into the cache. Donavan's MySpace page, a couple other blogs, forums at infiltration.org . . . and something called the Creep Club.

He scrolled to the Creep Club page and let it load. A username and password came up. Unfortunately, Donavan didn't have the autofill feature turned on. Lucas could change that, turn on the autofill, and capture Donavan's username and password. But Donavan seemed like something of a computer geek and would likely notice. Lucas had other ways of finding that information.

After closing the active browser window, he explored the closet. Dropped acoustic tile ceiling in here as well—no surprise, as that was the cheapest ceiling to install.

Inside the closet, he pushed aside one of the tiles, clicked on his flashlight, and shined it above the ceiling.

Donavan lived on the top floor of the apartment building, so wooden ceiling joists and particleboard were hidden above the tiles. Good. Wood was faster to work with than concrete.

Lucas stood on a chair he retrieved from the dining room and slid aside the ceiling tile directly above Donavan's desk. He took out his tools and started working.

Half an hour later, with the chair safely returned to the dining room, Lucas was cocooned in another webbed hammock, hanging directly over Donavan's desk with a clear view of the screen through a pinhole in the tile.

He went still, silent, listening as his heart rate slowed.

Now all he had to do was wait.

But sometimes, waiting brought unwanted memories. Memories of who he once was, who he once wasn't. He thought of the orphanage, which had nursed his early inclination for infiltrating because of his bedroom near the window in the converted attic. He remembered the many long nights, after being sent to bed; opening the window, crawling onto the roof, and listening to the sounds of dogs barking and cars humming. Most of all, watching the lights of the city—just across the Potomac, yet also across the universe.

Even then, so many years ago, the demonic mnemonic, wherever it had come from, had haunted him: *Humpty Dumpty had some great falls.* Even on the nights when he lay out on the roof of the building, his arms splayed behind his head, his subconscious would eventually take over as he dozed, repeating the maddening, yet somehow comforting, phrase. He didn't know why. He only knew that he couldn't scrub it from his head, no matter what he tried.

Even his dreams were filled with the demonic mnemonic. Not images of the nursery rhyme character, but of the words themselves. They floated in the empty spaces of his REM sleep, filling in the voids, the letters of the words creating backdrops of scenery everywhere he looked inside his dreams.

Humpty Dumpty had some great falls.

A scratching sound brought him back. For a few moments he was disoriented as he quickly stuffed all the memories back into their locked box. Where was he?

Oh yes. Donavan's apartment. And that scratching sounded very much like a key sliding into a deadbolt lock.

He heard the front door open down the hallway. Then nothing for a few seconds. A glass clinking, maybe.

More silence.

He caught a flash of Donavan walking by—dressed in a suit, certainly not what Lucas had expected—then he moved out of sight into the closet.

After a few minutes, Donavan returned and sat at his desk directly below Lucas, now wearing cargo shorts and a T-shirt. More like it.

Lucas noticed Donavan was wearing earbuds, the end of them

disappearing somewhere in the pocket of his cargo shorts. An iPod listener.

Donavan hummed an unrecognizable tune as he keyed in a Web address. The username and password screen appeared, and Donavan fingered the keys.

Lucas studied, letting his mind record the scene as Donavan's fingers tapped the board.

A few seconds later, a simple white screen with black type appeared on the monitor, with CREEP CLUB in all caps at the top. Below it, a variety of forum threads spooled out.

Donavan scanned the threads, checked his watch, uttered a curse, and closed the browser.

Obviously, he was late for something.

Seconds later he was out of view, and Lucas listened until he heard the front door close and the deadbolt slide back into place.

He waited silently for five more minutes. Donavan struck him as the type who might forget something and need to come back—especially if he were running late.

When Lucas felt confident Donavan had left for a while, he slid the tile out of its track and swung himself out of the hammock and to the floor. After wrapping his webbing and replacing it in his backpack, he sat down at Donavan's computer and opened the browser once more. At creepclub.com, he watched the screen come up as before, asking for the username and password.

Lucas sighed, cleared his mind, and rewound the images of the last several minutes. When he came to Donavan's hands, poised over the keyboard, he let the image play in slow motion.

He put his hands over the keys and mimicked the strokes that played in his mind. Username: DonavanRox. Password: HalleBerry.

And with that, he was in.

The main screen and its forums loaded on the monitor, and a post at the top of the forum said: August 23 Meeting, 8:00 p.m.; Stranahan Building. He opened the thread and read four names and times: Donavan—15 minutes; Hondo—15 minutes; Clarice—10 minutes; Boomer—10 minutes.

August 23. Today's date. Lucas looked at his watch. 7:27 p.m. He smiled.

He had a very good idea where Donavan was going in such a hurry. And after another quick visit to his old friend Google, Lucas had an address for the Stranahan Building.

IT WAS IN THE NORTHEAST QUADRANT, IN THE MIDST OF A GROUP OF buildings likely built sometime in the 1950s and '60s. Lucas immediately knew this because the architecture featured speckled granite offset by large turquoise panels. Every building erected in the fifties and sixties, it seemed, was required to use those turquoise panels, be they schools, hospitals, or office towers.

This one wasn't exactly an office tower; it was only three stories high. But it was obviously an office building of some kind. Or had been.

Lucas started with a walk around the perimeter. He pulled a small spotting scope from his backpack of tricks and examined the front doors from a distance. It was starting to get dark, but he could clearly see the chains barring all the doors. A realty sign hung in the window of one.

Next he scanned the front of the building, then walked around the back and checked the rear.

Off the alley he saw three small basement windows, one of

which looked to be open a crack. He paused a few minutes to watch for activity, then quickly walked to the window. Just above the window, he saw a symbol he'd seen at the Creep Club Web site: a large M with rounded tops, looking much like a McDonald's logo.

He leaned down to push the window open, and now, as he was leaning into the window and looking at the M sideways, he realized it wasn't an M at all. It was two capital Cs, turned on their sides. CC. Creep Club. Evidently, the folks in the Creep Club believed in signing in—leaving marks for other infiltrators to see.

Hearing or seeing no activity on the other side of the window, Lucas pushed it open and slipped inside. He dropped to the basement floor without a sound.

He pushed the window closed behind him again, lit his flashlight, and began walking.

Everything in the building smelled like mothballs, although he doubted mothballs had ever been used here. That would mean someone cared about something in here, wanted to preserve it, and that obviously wasn't the case. Maybe he was just smelling mold and rot.

He fell into a regular pattern. Ten steps, stop and listen, ten steps, stop and listen. Soon his light swept over an elevator shaft and, to the left of it, crumbling stone steps.

Lucas went up the first two sets of stairs to the propped-open door of the main floor. No activity. He continued to the second floor and checked. Down a long corridor, light spilled out of a room. Voices, and occasional laughter, filtered toward him.

After memorizing the location of the room, he went up the next two sets of steps to the third floor. The floors were solid poured concrete, so he had no worries about creaking or groaning boards as he walked down the hallway until he came to the room directly above the one the Creep Club occupied on the second floor.

Some of the windows in this room were broken, and the weather had seeped in. Dark rust stains smeared the walls by the broken windows. Lucas checked the room. No utility chase attached. Not that he'd expected one. A water fountain out in the hallway; he could maybe work with that, hear some of what they were saying, if he had to. But he was hoping for something more promising. He didn't bother to lie on the floor and try to listen; a couple feet of concrete would insulate the sound too much.

Okay, he'd have to try an adjacent room on the second floor.

He retreated down the stairs again and walked quietly down the tiled hallway toward the room where light came spilling out. As he approached, the sounds of the voices grew louder.

They were meeting in room 227; the door on room 225, just to the south of them, gaped open. Good.

He crept into 225 and looked around. No broken windows or leakage in this room, but that was about the best you could say for it. A couple of rickety old wooden chairs, a steel desk, some papers littering the floor. Above him the familiar acoustic tile. Whoever invented that stuff must be retired in the Bahamas, living off billions of dollars of income.

He grabbed one of the chairs and set it by the wall adjacent to room 227. Because this was a poured concrete building, with several beams supporting the weight of each floor, he knew this wall wouldn't be load-bearing. That meant it probably didn't even go all the way to the ceiling; instead, it was most likely a partition built of two-by-four framing.

As Lucas pushed aside the tile, he saw exactly what he wanted: the wall stopped about eight inches from the subfloor of the next story. Some electrical wiring and cables snaked across the space.

He kept a roll of duct tape in his backpack, and he pulled off a length of it, looped it around his hand, then stretched across the top of the wall to an acoustic panel on the adjacent room. When the tape stuck, he lifted it ever so slightly, being careful not to shake loose any dust. No good. It was wedged tight.

So be it. He'd just have to listen.

Right now, he only heard one woman speaking, sotto voce, at odd intervals. As if she were whispering a secret conversation on a phone.

"Huh? Of course he's here," the voice said. "Why wouldn't he be?"

Pause.

"I don't think that's a good idea."

Another pause, then a stifled giggle.

"Okay, okay. Just this once. I'll tell him . . . I'll tell him I'm running to the store for milk."

Lucas heard a click and saw cracks of light coming up through pinholes and cracks in the acoustic tile. Someone had turned on the overhead fluorescents.

Now a man's voice spoke, much clearer and louder. "And that is the latest chapter in the Kiernan family saga."

Scattered chuckles, followed by applause.

Lucas realized that they had been watching a taped phone conversation. On a TV, maybe? Or a projector? That's why the lights had come on after the woman finished speaking.

"Yeah, Hoffman," the man's voice said below.

"What'd you shoot that with?"

"I knew you'd ask that." A few more chuckles. "I shot it with an

M10 Minicam, using night vision settings. It's tiny, and it shoots well in low light. Adds some grain, but I think that goes nicely with the story line, don't you?"

What was this? The Creep Club was screening foreign movies or something? They were an amateur video club? A group of *America's Funniest Home Videos* enthusiasts?

A new voice. "Okay, thanks, Hondo. Next is Clarice, who's working on an interesting project up in Georgetown."

Clarice began to speak, and Lucas realized, finally, what he was listening to. These weren't just your garden variety creepers who broke into public buildings and office spaces. They'd taken it a dangerous step further, creeping into private homes. And on top of that, they were recording the residents of those homes, then sharing the recordings with other members of the group.

Lucas shuddered. "Creep" Club suddenly seemed all too accurate.

And yet.

As repulsive as it was, it was somehow also fascinating. Even now, part of him wanted to be in the room below, vicariously creeping into the homes of others with the assembled group watching. The unquestioned line that had always been drawn in his own mind was now wavering like a mirage. What did that say about his code of ethics, that he suddenly had this thirst for something he'd always found unthinkable before? He was like a pacifist who had killed for the first time and found he liked the sight of blood.

Lucas shuddered.

Suddenly he needed very much to get away, far away from this place. He backed out of the ceiling, off the chair, and quietly slipped down the hallway and stairs into the fresh air outside.

He took a couple deep breaths, feeling as if he'd just barely escaped being swallowed by something gigantic and terrifying. And yet, he longed to be swallowed.

He needed more answers, but he couldn't be this close to the Creep Club right now; it was radioactive, at once exciting and dangerous, and he wasn't equipped to handle it.

Without consciously deciding, he began moving toward the Metro, planning a return trip to Donavan's apartment.

FIVE

THE YOUNG BOY FEELS THE STRAPS ON HIS WRISTS AND ANKLES AS HE awakes, but he makes no effort to free himself. It's useless, he knows, as he lies still with his eyes closed. More than once he's managed to work his way free, but always finds himself unable to escape the large room of steel. There is a seam on the wall where a door opens into his room, but no handle of any kind; the door has to be opened from the outside.

And the giant mirror on the adjacent wall is there too. Behind that mirror, he knows, are eyes that are always watching him. Studying him.

Knowing this, the boy lies quietly. Waiting. Listening. Trying to sift his mind for memories of his earlier childhood. It's something he always does, this attempt to remember. He never finds anything. Every fiber of his existence, it seems, is tied to this giant room; his only past recollections involve long sessions listening to odd sounds and sequences played on a brand-new record player while images from a slide projector play on the mirrored wall in front of him, grueling tests filled with odd questions and statements followed by shocks he can feel in his brain and his bones.

And, of course, the needles.

The needles have been a constant companion for so very long. He's been injected everywhere: his arms, stomach, thighs. He's been subjected to liquids of every color inside those large syringes.

He hears the steel door whisk open and a person enter the room.

"How did you sleep?" a voice asks him. It's the voice of the man who calls himself Raven, the only real, live person the boy has seen or heard for . . . he doesn't know how long. Certainly he must have seen other people, talked to other people, sometime before. A mother and father, at least. But he can only remember Raven. Raven has always been his entire universe.

The young boy refuses to answer. He doesn't feel like talking. Instead he listens as Raven returns to the door, knocks, then wheels in the metal cart holding the syringes. The young boy doesn't need to see this to know what's going on, because he's seen it so many times before.

After a few moments he feels a pinprick, this one in the bottom of his bare foot. Without meaning to, he speaks. "A bee," he says, not quite realizing he's said it out loud.

"What's that?" Raven asks him.

The young boy opens his eyes, stares at the man injecting a purple liquid into his foot. "The needle. It feels like a bee sting."

A smile creases Raven's face, the horrible smile the young boy has seen too often. "Funny you should say that," Raven says, returning his attention to the syringe.

"Why?"

Finished, Raven pulls the needle out of the boy's foot, sets down the syringe. "Because this medicine," Raven says, "is something like bee venom. More of a wasp venom, a synthetic version we've been able to produce in the lab."

Raven pauses, smiles again as he pats the top of the young boy's foot. "But of course, you don't need to know all that. You only need to know it's medicine that will make you feel better."

The boy watches in silence as Raven wheels the cart back to the door and knocks again. Raven always tells him the injections are medicine to make him feel better, but he knows this is a lie.

He knows, because he never gets better.

SIX

AN HOUR LATER, LUCAS WAS BACK AT DONAVAN'S APARTMENT. AFTER letting himself in the front door, he went into the kitchen, checked the phone messages (nothing new), and spent a few more minutes exploring the apartment. Surely there was more to be discovered here, and it would probably be another hour at least until Donavan was back; Lucas had left while they were in the middle of the meeting. As he searched the apartment he thought about the Creep Club, the pull he was feeling from two directions. Was the Creep Club dangerous, unsavory, deadly? Yes. Was it exciting, enticing, intoxicating? Yes.

As he pondered, he heard the deadbolt of Donavan's front door turning for the second time that day. He froze in the middle of the living room. Quickly, he looked around; no immediate hiding spots.

Donavan had returned from his meeting, and Lucas was about to be discovered. He listened as the door swung open, then shut again. The deadbolt slid back into place.

He could hear Donavan humming; obviously he had his iPod cranked once more. That meant he couldn't hear. Lucas could slip down the hall, get into the back bedroom—

But then Donavan strolled around the corner, a bag of chips in his hand. He looked up as he entered the living room and flipped on the lights—

And saw Lucas, prompting him to drop the chips.

Lucas smiled as Donavan popped out his earbuds. A few moments of silence, then Lucas nodded toward the bag on the floor. "Those things will kill you."

Donavan stood, staring and speechless. His eyes darted around the room for a few seconds before they held Lucas's gaze again. "I think you're what's gonna kill me. What, do you make it your mission to pop out of dark places and scare people?"

"One of my missions."

"What are you doing here?" Donavan bent down to pick up his bag of chips, then moved slowly to a chair opposite the sofa.

"Tell me about Creep Club."

Donavan took a handful of chips, stuffed them in his mouth. "Creep Club? Hmmm, doesn't ring any bells."

"Rings a few bells on your computer. You seem to visit the forums quite a bit. How was the meeting, by the way? Lovely space, that Stranahan Building."

Donavan slowly munched his chips, studying Lucas. After a few moments, his shoulders slumped and his body relaxed. Lucas could tell he was going to come clean. Or at least pretend to.

"Snake said some bad juju was gonna happen. You bad juju?"

"Nah. I'm Humpty, remember?"

Donavan started to dig around in his teeth with his tongue, trying to dislodge food stuck there. Lucas had to admit, the man made a quick recovery; he didn't seem too surprised or flustered to have a stranger sitting in his living room.

Donavan held out the bag of chips, offering some to Lucas. Lucas shook his head, but continued to stare. Waiting.

Donavan sucked air between his teeth a few times, dislodging more food, before speaking again. "How much do you know?"

"How much is there to know? Let's start with Snake. Who is he?"

"He's kind of the de facto head of the . . . um . . . organization, I guess. Pulled the original members together. Recruited me a few years ago. Well, didn't really recruit me, but let me in." He paused. "Guess it's like a family, because we understand each other. Most of us, we've been doing this for years. Since we were kids. I bet you did too."

Lucas ignored the remark. "What about Hondo, Clarice, Hoffman, Boomer?" he said, reciting all the names he'd picked up online and in the meeting.

Donavan did a better job of hiding his shock, but Lucas saw a flash of it. "Man, you got the membership roll memorized?"

Lucas thought of the contact list he'd found on Donavan's computer. A membership roll.

"They're all members, but Snake's the one you gotta talk to if you want in. The Creep Club was kinda his idea. A way for us to trade techniques, stories, ideas. A way for us to get inside places we never been inside of, you see? I can creep into a lot of places on my own, but I can creep into a lot more places with the others in the club. You know, live it through their eyes."

"So it's a support group. A twelve-step program for Peeping Toms."

Donavan made a sour face. "Please. You creeping into spaces so you can get a peek at women changing their bras? This is . . . this is a way of life, man."

"I don't infiltrate homes. Just public buildings."

"Yeah, and that's why you broke into my apartment, and you're quizzing me about the club. You're not interested at all, huh?"

Lucas stayed silent.

"Well," Donavan continued, "we do the public places. I mean— you saw me in the steam tunnel, didn't you? Trying to do a bit of old school, and look what it got me." Donavan shook his head, leaned back in his chair, getting more comfortable.

"Look, after a while, you need a bit more of a rush. There's some-thing . . . I don't know . . . magic about being in someone's house. On the opposite side of the wall, listening to a husband and wife argue about finances. Overhearing little Johnny at the dinner table, talking about the game he pitched. So much of this"—Donavan swept his arm around the room—"this stuff around us is fake. Fake ads, fake news, fake lives lived in the public. I'm fake, and you're fake when we know we're around other people. But in their homes. That's when people are real."

Lucas understood what Donavan was saying. Understood it a little too much to be comfortable.

"You get hungry for reality. And then, once you taste it, you get addicted to it."

Despite his effort at aloofness and coolness, things that usually came to him so naturally, Lucas felt himself being drawn in by the pep talk. He'd felt these things inside his own mind, inside his own body, but never allowed himself to acknowledge them. The public buildings . . . the thrill wasn't exactly wearing off, but he'd been hungering for something different. Something more. He just didn't know what. Until now.

And now that he knew, he wished he didn't.

Donavan grinned. "Yeah. You know just what I'm talking about. I can see it in your eyes. You gotta join us."

"I'm not part of any club. I work alone."

Donavan picked up his bag of chips again, rummaged round in them, stuffed a few into his mouth. "No, seriously. I saw that stuff you did in the steam tunnel—the parkour moves. You're, like, ten times better than anyone else in the club. You'd kill, man. Everyone would be asking you to show them how to do your stuff."

Lucas pondered. Parkour. A cousin of free running, both of them dedicated to moving through urban environments as quickly as possible. He wasn't into parkour or free running any more than he was officially a creeper, but he identified with the people who were. In an odd way, Donavan's offer sounded . . . enticing. It would be nice to be appreciated by someone for this thing he'd never been able to share with anyone else. When he noticed Donavan staring at him expectantly, he shook his head and leaned back in his seat.

"I'm gonna get a beer," Donavan said. "You want one?"

Lucas nodded and Donavan left, leaving him alone with his own questions for a few moments. Question #1: Did Donavan know something more? Was he the one who uncovered his hiding spot in the steam tunnel? Had he led someone else to that hiding spot? Was this whole Creep Club involved in some way?

Okay, that was four questions.

And he hated to add the fifth: Was Sarea also part of it?

Donavan returned and handed him an uncapped microbrew. Lucas smelled the sharp tang of the hops wafting out of the bottle, masking the apartment's odor of leftover food just a bit.

Donavan tipped his bottle, keeping his gaze on Lucas as he drank. "Like I said, we need to talk to Snake. But I can get you in. Be your sponsor, since you seem to like the support group concept."

Lucas stared at the floor, took a drink of his own beer.

Donavan leaned forward again, dropped his voice as if revealing a secret. "Tell you what. Before you make up your mind, let me show you something."

"Show me what?"

"The drug."

LUCAS AND DONAVAN STOOD IN A GARAGE, NEAR THE INTERIOR WALL with exposed two-by-four studs. Only a thin layer of gypsum board was between them and the home on the other side.

Lucas could feel the Dark Vibration cycling deep inside his body, reaching an entirely new harmonic. Something inside him, something dark, loved what he was about to do. It scared him.

Donavan pointed to a small nail in the backside of the gypsum board, then expertly grabbed the nail and pulled it. It came free easily. Next he retrieved a small, flexible tube from his hip pack and snaked it into the tiny hole, motioning Lucas to come over and see what the pack held.

A small monitor revealed a fish-eye view of the home's interior, obviously from a kitchen wall since Lucas could see the sink curving into the bottom of the frame.

Inside the house, a man and a woman were eating something—nachos, maybe—at a built-in counter on the far side of the kitchen. The man's lips were moving, but Lucas heard nothing.

Donavan's hand reached out toward him, and Lucas stepped back in surprise until he saw what was in it: one of the earbuds Donavan was so fond of wearing. Lucas took the earbud and put it in his own ear, immediately surprised at the clarity of the sound.

The man was in midsentence.

"—know we have to do it. And we have to do it at Split Jacks."

The woman stayed silent, looked down at the plate in front of her.

"Come on," the man continued. "We've talked about this . . . I don't know how many times."

Lucas noticed Donavan nodding his head in agreement, a smile on his face and a manic energy twinkling in his eyes. As if he were on a drug high.

"Are you listening?" the man asked.

The woman finally spoke. "It's no good. I mean, he has people everywhere. You know that. And if we screw up something like this . . ."

"His car."

"His car?"

"Yeah. He has a few drinks at Split Jacks, gets in his car . . . you fill in the blanks."

The woman stood up and carried her plate toward the camera. Lucas and Donavan stood absolutely still, watching as she came to the sink. Her face was now filling the fish-eye lens as she rinsed her plate.

Lucas saw she was under duress, debating, making a decision she wanted and didn't want at the same time. She closed her eyes, breathed deeply, kept her eyes closed.

"You sure about this?" she asked weakly.

His voice came from behind her. "I already told you: it's perfect."

She opened her eyes, and Lucas saw a change come over her face. She was going to say yes, he could tell, even before she spoke.

"Okay. I'm in."

She turned around, the back of her head now filling the frame of the camera.

"Yeah, you're all in, baby."

The woman receded from the camera, walking across the room and disappearing around a corner. She said something from down the hall, something Lucas couldn't hear because she was too far away, prompting a laugh from the man, still sitting at the counter.

"Oh, you can count on it," he said, then stood and left the frame.

Quickly Donavan pulled the tube out of the small hole and replaced the nail. He stuffed the tube camera back into his bag, paused, and looked Lucas in the eyes. Lucas could see that manic energy still there, dancing.

The only problem was, he could also feel that same manic energy burning behind his own eyes.

SEVEN

BACK IN HIS ABODE, LUCAS UNSCREWED THE BOTTOM OF HIS ELECTRIC candle, slid out the batteries and replaced them with fresh ones, then turned it off and put it in his backpack. Outside the window on the back wall, streaks of pink and purple were painting the eastern sky.

A new day in the District.

One advantage to the steam tunnels and underground spaces: it stayed dark there all the time, which he found comforting. Rats weren't the cleanest of neighbors, but in many ways they were better than humans.

Lucas hadn't slept since returning from the sojourn with Donavan six hours earlier. Instead, he had knelt before his makeshift shrine, picking up each of the assorted totems, holding them in his hands and caressing them before returning them to their proper places.

It still pained him to think someone else had touched these things, found his inner sanctum and violated something so pure. An action that told him, *I know where you are. I can invade your space.*

It was a notice, he was sure of it.

The question was, a notice of what?

Even so, he'd barely been able to control the Dark Vibration inside, now more ravenous than ever. A vibration that wanted more of what Donavan had shown him the night before.

So what were his options? He wanted, desperately, to find out more about this Creep Club; it filled a gnawing hole deep inside that nothing else had.

But he knew this wasn't the time to start making new contacts with the outside world. Someone had tracked him, and what he really needed to do was go deep underground. Make no contact with any- one for a few months, let his trail go cold. He'd stashed away a few thousand dollars from his odd jobs over the past years; after all, he rarely needed money to do what he wanted. His rent was free, and most of his meals he took from the lunchroom refrigerators of the office spaces he frequented. And his entertainment budget . . . well, watching people was always free.

The plan meant, unfortunately, no contact with Sarea. Especially because she could be part of it.

Logically, it also meant no part of Creep Club. His mind knew this. But inside, already, he could tell that wasn't going to happen. He was going to find out more about Creep Club, taste more of what he'd so long forbidden himself. Because he had to.

He might as well accept it now.

And if he knew that's what was going to happen, he'd best make some contingency plans.

A drug, Donavan had said.

Yes, that was true. And already, his body was jonesing for more.

LATER THAT DAY, INEXPLICABLY, LUCAS FOUND HIMSELF AT THE SAME house Donavan had shown him the night before. The place where the couple had been debating . . . well, he had to admit it: murder. They were planning to murder someone; that much was obvious. Now he had to figure out who.

The house was in the large swath known as Silver Spring, a few miles from Donavan's apartment. A nice suburban home—but not too nice. Instead of the exhaust and concrete you smelled in the city, you could detect tree blossoms. The smells of the city were still there, of course, not far below the surface. But nature at least competed.

As he always did when checking out a new place, Lucas started by walking the perimeter. First by taking in the street in front of the house, paying attention to the hedges and chain-metal fence that framed the yard. Then by walking the alley, pausing to dig through the garbage cans lined up there, in case anyone was watching. He could pass for a homeless person, he knew, and digging through garbage cans would complete that illusion.

He'd played the part of a vagrant many times before, even panhandled on the street. He was amazed at the amount of money he made panhandling—far more than he could make washing dishes or doing short-term construction cleanup—but he didn't keep it up very long. Panhandling was preying on others in a way that made him uncomfortable. Sneaking into their offices and watching everything they did all day—well, yes, that was okay. Panhandling was out. He knew it was a twisted sense of ethics, but there it was.

Of course, planning to break into someone's home was even worse, but he forced himself not to think of that right now.

The wire fence and hedge continued along either side of the house, but only the fence lined the back of the property. This was the way Donavan had brought him in last night: they opened the back gate, then moved quickly across the lawn to the patio, where a back door led to the garage. Amazingly, the door was unlocked.

Lucas wondered how many people left the back doors to their garages open.

He spent an hour watching the house from vantage points around the neighborhood and saw no activity. That was good. No dog at the house, or at the house on its east side. The house on the west side had a dog in the backyard, but he hadn't heard a peep out of it the whole time. When he walked by in the alley, the dog had simply lain on the grass, watching him from the yard and occasionally wagging its tail.

He considered his options. He didn't have the names of the couple who lived here, so he couldn't do a phone call. He could probably do a reverse-lookup on the Internet, using the address to get a phone number. But he'd have to find a nearby Internet café or public library to do that, and he didn't want to get sidetracked just now.

Maybe he could just walk to the front door and ring the doorbell. Maybe. But he was looking pretty ragged right now—he'd already wandered the neighborhood as a homeless vagrant, and it was unlikely anyone would open the door for him. He really needed to head to a Salvation Army for a couple new sets of clothing.

In the end, he decided just to do the back door of the garage again, see if any cars were inside. If the garage were empty, he felt there was a good chance the home would be empty.

Without pausing, he walked across the street, opened the front gate, went directly to the hedge at the fence line, and followed it to the backyard. He paused, listening for a few moments, then went across the backyard to the patio and the back garage door. A small water fountain trickled on the patio. Nice. One more bit of nature out here in the 'burbs.

Once again, the garage door was unlocked. The garage was empty; last night one car had been there, even though there were two stalls. And even though he hadn't seen the front of the home last night, he'd noticed no cars parked directly in front of the house this morning.

Inside the garage, he crept to the door that led into the house. Would they keep this door locked?

The knob twisted easily in his hand. No.

With the door open a crack, he listened for sounds inside the house. No TV, no footsteps. Just the steady thrum of the refrigerator's compressor nearby.

He slipped through the door and shut it softly behind him. Now he was standing in a small mudroom, with a coat closet to his right and a few pairs of shoes on a mat directly in front of him. No children's shoes, he noted.

Lucas walked out of the mudroom into the kitchen area, just past a short, five-foot wall. He remembered the kitchen layout with perfect clarity from the night before: the sink would be back to his right from this doorway, adjoining the garage. The refrigerator and some cupboards were on the other side of the short wall he'd just walked past. Opposite, the oven, stove, and under-counter cabinets, as well as some hanging cabinets. To the left, at the far end of the kitchen from the garage, the counter ended in an L-shape, forming the area where the couple had been eating the night before. Beyond that lay the rest of the house.

He stepped into the kitchen. No lights on. Good sign. He relaxed, knowing no one was home, and ventured through the kitchen to the living area just beyond.

A small black cat came out of one of the bedrooms and rubbed against his legs, purring. He reached down to pet it a few times, then went down the hallway where it had come from.

Several framed photos hung on the painted wall here. A wedding photo, several old black-and-white photos of ancestors and relatives, and a photo he was particularly drawn to: a couple, the woman smiling at the camera—almost laughing—and the man staring at the same spot with a hard intensity. The woman in the photo was the woman he had seen last night. He knew her face well, because she had stood so close to Donavan's surveillance camera.

But the man in this photo, wearing a suit and standing behind the woman, was not the man he'd seen. This man was black-haired, lantern-jawed, tall.

The man in the home last night had blondish hair, seemed stockier, shorter.

His eyes moved to the wedding photo. It was definitely the woman and the dark-haired man, not the guy from last night.

So the two people in the house the night before weren't a couple. At least, they weren't a married couple.

Interesting.

Lucas felt the Dark Vibration starting in his gut. But it wasn't over-whelming at all, or painful, or consuming. It was warm, comfortable. Pleasant.

The cat wandered past him, pawed open a door down the hall-way, and slipped through. Lucas followed and saw the cat curled up under a desk. It was a home office. A computer and telephone sat on the desk against the wall. Next to the desk, a black file cabinet and a bookcase. More file cases on the opposite wall.

Above the computer, framed on the wall, was a news article from the business section of the local paper. PARTNERS FORM NEW ATM VENTURE. The accompanying photo showed three people: the mar-ried couple and the blond-haired man Lucas had seen last night. The caption below the photo said: "L to R: Viktor Abkin, Anita Abkin, and Ted Hagen want to see more ATMs in restaurants, convenience stores, and other businesses."

Lucas scanned the story; their company, ATM2GO, licensed ATM machines to other businesses, giving them a split of the usage fees. According to the date on the paper, the article was just over three years old.

Lucas memorized the article, then began replaying bits and pieces of the previous night's overheard conversation.

Now he had to make a decision. Someone had invaded his space, and the most likely suspects were the Creep Club; Donavan could have been a diversion while other members of the club found his space. The easy way to solve that was to keep moving, drop everything, leave everything behind; he'd done it so many times before.

The only complication was, he knew someone was planning a murder, and that, in no small part, was also tied to the Creep Club. He couldn't just walk away and leave this guy to be murdered by his wife and partner. He had to help. And by helping, he could infiltrate the club, get more information, find out how they operated, so he could stay better hidden in the future.

The cat came from its hiding spot beneath the desk and began entwining itself around his feet again.

"Kitty," Lucas said, still looking at the article, "you've been very helpful."

HE WAS WAITING ON THE COUCH WHEN DONAVAN RETURNED HOME FROM work that evening.

Donavan only paused for a moment this time before taking out the earbuds and heading for the refrigerator.

"I'd offer to make you a key," Donavan said, "but I guess you don't need one."

Lucas grinned. "Nah, I'd just lose it."

Donavan rummaged around in the refrigerator, pulled out some cold cuts, stuffed one in his face. "Want a beer while I'm here?"

"Sure."

Donavan took his place in the chair, pitched a bottle to Lucas, crammed another piece of ham into his mouth. He chewed a few times. "So, am I gonna find you on my couch every night from now on? Roommate from hell?"

Lucas ignored the question. "When's the next Creep Club meeting?" He already knew the answer—he'd logged in to the site from

Donavan's computer—but there was no need for Donavan to know this.

"Day after tomorrow."

"Day after tomorrow? That might be too late."

"Well, a member can call a special meeting any time. I could do one for tomorrow, post it on the Web site. Probably can't get to the blackboard, though."

Lucas had no idea what the blackboard was, but filed it away for future research. "Yeah," he said. "Call a special meeting."

They had to, after all; there was no telling when Ted and Anita were going to kill Viktor. They had to get to Viktor and warn him before something happened.

A knowing light spread across Donavan's face. "You interested? Like I said, I think I can get you in."

"Yeah," Lucas said. "I'm interested."

"Cool, too cool."

"I wanna help."

Donavan considered. "Well, I guess I owe you for the steam tunnel. And, I don't know, it could be like . . . a collaboration or something."

"It's not really about owing anything . . . it's the right thing to do."

Donavan shrugged his shoulders.

How could he be so noncommittal?

"Aren't you worried something could happen? Sooner than you expect?"

Donavan shook his head. "Look, I know you're worried we're going to miss something. I got it covered. Really."

Lucas didn't like the way that sounded: *I know you're worried we're going to miss something.* But he let it slide. "How?" he asked instead.

"I got a few tricks up my sleeve."

"Like?"

"Hang on." Donavan left the room, and Lucas heard him digging through some things in his closet. A few moments later he returned and held up . . . nothing.

Lucas squinted his eyes and realized Donavan was holding what looked to be a thin, translucent button.

"Geopatch," Donavan said proudly.

"Geopatch?"

"Nifty little gadget. Has a microchip inside that emits a signal for geopositioning at all times."

"Like GPS, then."

"Not like it. Exactly it." Donavan held out his arm and stuck the small wafer on his jacket; instantly it became nearly invisible. "Stick it on someone, and you can log in to track their movements."

"Really?" Lucas immediately knew this was something that could be potentially useful to him.

Donavan shrugged. "At least until they shake it—it's good adhesive, but it doesn't stay on forever or anything." Donavan cocked a finger at him. "Come have a look." Lucas followed him into the bedroom and waited while Donavan opened his browser and logged into a numeric IP address.

"You have to use a numeric IP?" Lucas asked.

Donavan shrugged as they watched a hybrid satellite photomap load on the screen. "Well, to activate them, you have to bind them to a specific Web address, but it doesn't have to be numeric. This is just what I like to use for extra security."

Lucas nodded, staring at the screen and committing the numeric address to his photographic memory.

Donavan continued, pointing at three blips on the screen; two were very close to each other, while the other was at least a few miles away. "These two here are our friends from last night, Ted and Anita, at the office. They work together. Actually, all three of them work together officially, although I can't say I've ever seen Viktor at the office." He pointed to another spot on the screen.

"Instead, Viktor seems to spend a lot of time at this bar, kind of a low-rent place. And as you might have guessed from listening last night, Anita and Ted are . . . um, more than business partners. Even though Anita is married to Viktor." Donavan smiled. "So you see, none of them does anything without me knowing about it. I check in on 'em several times a day—lots of times, leave this running while I'm working at the office."

"And you just stuck the geopatch on—"

"Viktor's is hidden inside his briefcase; goes with him pretty much everywhere. Anita and Ted, they do love their cell phones. So I have geopatches on them. Inside their phones' battery compartments, actually."

"Their cell phones?" Lucas asked. "How'd you get their cell phones?"

"What do you think this is? Amateur hour?" Another big, beefy grin. "They have company-provided phones, same model. Suppose the manufacturer recalls the original batteries in their phones; suppose the manufacturer sends both of them new batteries to replace the old ones."

Lucas nodded. "Okay, you did your homework."

"Always. Which is how I know Viktor spends most of his days at Split Jacks. Heck, I'd say he spends about half his evenings there too. Man must know how to drink. But I can guarantee you, if Viktor's away from his house more than an hour, Ted's over there." Donavan smiled through a fresh mouthful of ham. "Anyway, relax, man. I got it covered."

Lucas tried to relax. But he noticed he was bouncing his leg, feeling jittery. He wasn't sure exactly what Donavan had covered.

EIGHT

THE NEXT DAY, AFTER CHECKING THE GEOPATCHES TO MAKE SURE ALL three people were still moving, Lucas attended his first Creep Club meeting. When he arrived with Donavan, the others were already there: seven of them in all. Three were sitting in chairs in front of a television, which in turn was attached to a Mac PowerBook. The others were in the back of the room, talking among themselves. One, a guy with long shaggy hair who looked like a throwback to the sixties flower generation, was drinking a latte.

All of them stopped their conversations and stared when Lucas and Donavan entered room 227.

"Hey, everybody," Donavan said. He pointed at Lucas. "This here's . . . uh, Humpty. Met him in the steam tunnel at Howard. I think some of you saw my photos." Donavan glanced at Lucas before he continued.

"You should see him work; he's good. Not just at creeping, but maybe free running and parkour too." Donavan paused, as if hoping Lucas would confirm this.

Lucas stayed quiet.

Donavan, a bit flustered, continued. "Anyway, he's . . . uh, gonna help me with my current project."

Lucas felt himself shudder a bit; Donavan spoke about it in such clinical terms, as if saving Viktor was simply something he was doing for the science fair.

Hippie Boy walked over, extended the hand that wasn't clutching the latte. "Snake," he said, introducing himself.

Lucas took his hand and shook it.

"You want us to call you Humpty, I take it?"

Lucas shrugged. "Humpty works."

"Sure it works. None of us here use our real names anyway." Snake smiled and turned around, started pointing out others. "Over there by the TV we have Hondo, Clarice, and Stocklin." He turned the other way, indicating the three he'd been speaking with at the back of the room. "And this is Kennedy, Mya, and Dilbert."

A few awkward moments of silence as everyone stared.

"Nice to meet you all," Lucas finally said.

Snake pulled a chair over to him, and the others who were standing at the back of the room slid chairs in front of the TV as well.

"Have a seat," Snake said. "I think you'll see some interesting work tonight."

Lucas took the indicated seat. Snake walked to the front of the room, waited for everyone to settle in, and turned on the television. The computer's desktop illuminated the TV monitor.

"Okay," Snake said. "I think Dilbert has something for us tonight."

Dilbert stood and approached the computer. He slipped a disc into the slot on the front of the laptop, opened a movie file.

It was easy to see how he got his name; he had close-shaved hair and round glasses, like the hapless cubicle-dweller from the daily comic strip.

"Okay," Dilbert began. "I've spliced this together from about four weeks of footage, and I have to say, this is probably my most interesting project since that Iranian diplomat in Georgetown."

"Yeah, that was a good one," chimed Mya. She was thin and pretty with dark eyes. Lucas thought she looked faintly Asian.

"Thanks. Anyway, I like to call this 'Symphony of Violence.'"

"Oooh," someone said. Lucas didn't catch who it was.

Dilbert pressed the Play button on the movie file, and a title screen appeared: SYMPHONY IN VIOLENCE | *Music by Johann Strauss | Subjects: Kleiderman and Leila Delgado, 4815 Suncrest, Alexandria, VA.*

The opening strains of "The Blue Danube" started on the screen, mellow violins. On the screen, a quiet suburban home, which dissolved to a couple sharing a kiss, then cooking together in the kitchen, and then the same couple hosting another couple at dinner, all of them laughing.

Suddenly the music dropped and a horrible scene filled the screen: the husband yelling at the wife and then backhanding her.

The music cued again, and the scenes of tranquility were back. The two of them heading out the door for an evening jog, the woman curled up on the couch with a book.

Another pause in the music, and more scenes of destruction: the man throwing a bottle of something at his wife, tipping over the dining table in an uncontrollable rage.

Lucas shifted uncomfortably in his seat and looked around.

Everyone was rapt, their attention focused on the screen. Donavan had that goofy grin on his face.

After a few more seconds, Lucas couldn't watch anymore. He let his gaze drop to the floor, waiting for the video to end. Mercifully, after three minutes, it did.

When he finally looked up again, as applause rang around the room, he saw Snake staring at him over his shoulder.

Snake stood. "Wonderful, wonderful work, Dilbert. Very artistic, as usual."

Kennedy had his hand in the air. He was thin, very thin, and pasty-faced. He wore a flannel shirt, jeans, and boots. A cowboy wannabe in DC.

Dilbert acknowledged Kennedy's hand. "Yeah, Kennedy."

"I loved your edit points. I mean, you can feel the tension between those two worlds. You did all that in Final Cut?"

Dilbert grinned sheepishly. "Yeah."

Kennedy whistled. "Lot of work."

Now Clarice wanted to speak. She was also very thin, with white, wispy hair and very angular, almost masculine features. "You done with this couple now?" she asked.

"I don't know. I mean, seems like on the surface there's really only one story to tell there. But I feel like there's something else waiting to happen. So I'm still shooting some footage. We'll see."

Dilbert sat down, and the applause started again. Lucas felt a sick ball of revulsion in his stomach, and he couldn't control himself. He stood.

Snake leveled a gaze at him, and the others turned to stare as well. "Something to say so soon . . . Humpty?" Snake asked.

"Yeah. I . . . is she okay?" he asked Dilbert.

Dilbert shifted in his seat. "What do you mean?" he asked.

"The woman—in the video. Who was getting beaten. I mean . . . how did you get her out of there?"

Dilbert seemed puzzled. "I . . . didn't."

Lucas was dumbfounded. "He's gonna kill her. You can't just let that happen. You can't just . . . watch that and do nothing."

Snake spoke. "Dilbert didn't just do 'nothing,' as you put it. I bet he has a hundred hours of editing alone in that piece."

"The video? So you just do it all for your own kicks?"

Silence.

"No," Snake said coolly. "He did it for us."

"I don't understand—" Lucas stammered.

"Obviously not."

"You mean, this is just about . . . watching? You don't try to help these people?" Lucas, horrified, thought of the ATM company; he spun and looked at Donavan. "The ATM people—are you just going to let them kill the husband? That's what they're going to do, you know."

Donavan's eyes twinkled. "Of course I know," he said.

"You've obviously misunderstood Creep Club," Snake said, with a sideways glance at Donavan. "It's not just about infiltrating the homes. You'll find lots of punks out there who get their kicks from doing that kind of thing. We're more than that." Another glance at Donavan.

"It's about . . . art. Art focused on depravity, yes, I suppose. But that helps us understand more about ourselves, doesn't it?"

A few nods and murmurs of agreement in the room.

Lucas scanned their faces, their smiling upturned faces. And suddenly, he found himself turning to leave the room, running down the long hallway toward the granite stairs. He wanted to get out of the Stranahan Building as fast as he could.

LUCAS DIDN'T STOP RUNNING UNTIL HE'D WORKED HIS WAY THROUGH A sewer tunnel and onto the platform for the nearest Metro station.

When the doors whisked open, he rushed into the car and sat. The car was only about half-full, which is why he was surprised when a bald man in a black suit sat right next to him.

The man turned and nodded, pulled out a pack of cigarettes, offered one to Lucas.

"You can't smoke on here," Lucas said, pointing to a sign at the front of the car.

The man smiled, pulled out a cigarette with his lips, and lit it. He stared straight ahead. "I often find," he said, "that I most want to do the things I'm told I shouldn't."

He blew a haze of smoke out the side of his mouth. A woman sitting with her son gave him a glare, then stood, grabbed her son's hand, and moved to the back of the car.

The man in the dark suit took no notice and tried another deep drag. After a few moments he spoke again. "Now you know why they call themselves the Creep Club."

Lucas felt his breath leave his lungs, almost as if it were leaking directly out of his skin.

"What?" he asked weakly.

"I have a proposition for you," Dark Suit said, still staring straight ahead as the train rolled to a stop at the next station. He stood and left the train without saying anything; after a few seconds of shock, Lucas scrambled out behind him.

The man walked to a garbage can several feet away, stopped, and turned. Now he did look at Lucas. "Are you interested?" he asked.

"Interested in what?"

"My proposition."

"I haven't heard it yet. I've only heard you say something about the Creep Club." Lucas was getting his feet under him a bit now. "That got my attention."

"I want you to help me bring it down."

A pause stretched out between them. Dark Suit spoke again. "You're not one of them. You know it."

"No, I'm not." Lucas said it a little more forcefully than he'd intended.

"You see, then? And really, how could they? Just stand there, just record all that and do nothing?"

Lucas waited. He'd noticed that the man had a tendency to look anywhere but his face while he was talking; he only looked at Lucas's eyes when he was listening. Even then, he blinked too often, as if he was constantly trying to clear his vision.

Dark Suit threw his cigarette into the garbage can without crushing it first, right beneath the sign that had a cigarette with a large red slash through it.

"First off, how'd you even find me?" Lucas asked.

The man smiled. "I followed you."

"From the meeting? Through the tunnels and everything?"

Another smile. "For starters."

"And now you want me to help you."

"Not just me," Dark Suit continued. "You could help those people. Use the Creep Club's work against itself." He was staring at the wall as he said this.

"How?"

"By saying yes."

"But I have to sell my soul to make it happen. Something like that, huh?"

Dark Suit laughed. "Tell me, do you really think you're dealing with the devil here? Or did you see something of the devil back there?"

Lucas shivered, even though it was hot and muggy. Late August in DC.

"But what would I need to do? Testify or something?"

"Eventually. But what I'm asking you to do now is: creep the creeps."

Lucas stared. "What's that mean?"

"That means you document everyone there. You follow them, find out their real names, bring them to me."

"You mean you don't know their names?"

"Some of them. But not all."

"But you obviously knew what was happening in the meeting tonight."

"Oh, the meetings and such. Yes, I know all about those. I know all the people involved—more than just the ones who were there tonight, by the way."

"You obviously have people, resources, whatever. Why don't you call up a couple of your James Bonds, have them track the Creep Club?"

Dark Suit turned his neck to the side, and it made a ripple of cracks. He twisted it the other way. More cracks. "Not really tracking that's the problem. At this point, we need some inside information. Someone who's one of them."

"But I'm not one of them."

Dark Suit blinked rapidly a few times. "I did say that, didn't I?"

"Besides, I just blew out of there; I doubt they'd welcome me back."

"Do they need to?"

Lucas thought about it. He knew where they met, although he was pretty sure that would change after his stunt tonight. Still, he knew how to track Donavan; he could follow him to a new meeting spot once they established it.

A sudden thought flashed in his mind. The conversation with Sarea. "Hey," he said. "You were the one at the Blue Bell. Waiting for me."

"When you had your encounter with Donavan, you showed up on our radar. Once it became obvious you were perhaps going to attend a club meeting yourself . . . it seemed a good idea to let things develop naturally. Which brings us to tonight." Dark Suit took a deep breath, exhaled, waited. Blinked some more.

Lucas pondered. Something inside him did want to bring down the Creep Club, punish them for . . . doing nothing. And doing so would feed the Dark Vibration deep inside him, wouldn't it? Two birds with one stone, as the old cliché went. "I don't know who you are, who you work for. How do I know you're not setting me up for something?"

"You don't," Dark Suit said.

"And how do you know I'm not going to set you up, double-cross you somehow?"

"I don't," Dark Suit admitted again.

The Dark Vibration inside began to cycle up, creating a steady

hum in Lucas's ears. "Okay," he said. "As long as we're clear on that."
He held out his hand.

Dark Suit took his hand. "Crystal."

They shook hands to seal the pact.

"I'll meet you tomorrow. Give you a few things to help," Dark Suit
said. He was staring at a spot somewhere over Lucas's head as he said
this; Lucas fought the urge to turn around and see what it was.

"Okay. When?"

"Three in the afternoon."

"Where?"

"You seem to know your way around these stations," Dark Suit
said. "Pick one."

Lucas thought. "Shaw-Howard, on the Green Line." Right next
to his old quarters. Dark Suit had already admitted he'd sent people
there, so he wasn't giving up anything.

"Done."

Dark Suit turned, walked up the stairs to street level, and was
gone.

Lucas checked his watch. Just a bit after nine. If he was lucky,
Donavan would still be at the Creep Club meeting—providing Lucas's
little outburst hadn't ended it all early.

He wanted to get to Donavan's tonight; something told him all
the locks would be changed by morning.

NINE

LUCAS SHUDDERED AWAKE THE NEXT MORNING, ROUSED BY DREAMS FILLED with giant letters in the background.

(Humpty Dumpty had some great falls.)

After a few seconds, he realized he was in his web hammock, perched above the computer in Donavan's ceiling. He listened for a moment before he allowed his body to come awake and move.

His watch said 8:23 a.m. Had Donavan been home, and he was just too exhausted to notice? No. Not a chance.

Lucas unfolded his body, pushed aside the tile, dropped to the floor, and retrieved his hammock webbing. Yes, the apartment was exactly the same as it had been last night. Just no Donavan.

Maybe he'd left with one of the other Creeps; Lucas himself had interrupted the regular flow of the meeting just a bit.

Even though he'd been in his deep state, sleeping even, he didn't feel refreshed. He felt . . . violated. First, someone had found his home, touched his things, moved them around. Then, this guy from last night—the guy in the Dark Suit—had easily tracked him from the Creep Club meeting. Had *known* things about him. Was he slipping? Maybe it would be best just to get out, maybe even leave the DC area. There was nothing tying him to this place.

But if he did that, Viktor Abkin would be murdered. Worse, Donavan or one of the other Creeps would record it. And he couldn't let that happen.

So. He'd just retrieve a few things from Donavan's closet, use his computer, and be on his way. He had a few hours before his meeting with Dark Suit, and there were some things he needed to take care of first.

In Donavan's closet, he found a stash of equipment. He took two of the flexible tube cameras, some wireless microphones, and four of the geopatches.

Next, he found Donavan's bag and looked through it. Good, the minidisc recorder was still in there. He flipped the button to Video and replayed the last few minutes of captured video. Anita and Ted, talking about Split Jacks and Viktor. That was what he needed.

Lucas fired up Donavan's computer, hooked the minidisc recorder into a USB port. He let the computer start converting the video into a Web movie, then wandered into the kitchen. Might as well see what was in the fridge.

Nothing. Unless you considered a couple bottles of beer, an opened pack of deli meat, and a bottle of ketchup.

He returned to Donavan's bedroom and decided to go online while he was waiting for the video to finish converting. At the Creep

Club home page, he used Donavan's name and password to sign on. No new posts since the meeting last night. Evidently he'd shocked them into silence.

The computer beeped, letting him know the video was done converting. Lucas slid a DVD from Donavan's desk into the slot; while burning the DVD, he easily found the ATM2GO home page and clicked the "Contact Us" link. He'd briefly thought of sending an e-mail directly to Viktor, but he had no real way of knowing where that e-mail would route to, did he? The wife or business partner might see it, and he wasn't a hundred percent certain what might happen in that case. After a few moments of staring at the screen, he noted the phone number and dialed it on his TracFone.

A pleasant voice answered. "Good afternoon, ATM2GO."

"Hi. Is Viktor available?"

"Viktor's out of the office at the moment. Can I put you through to his voice mail?"

Okay. Lucas thought for a second. Then: "Maybe I'll just call him on his cell phone, but I'm on the road right now, and I don't have his card with me. Do you have that number?"

"Certainly."

After she gave him the number, he thanked her and dialed it. Viktor's voice answered, a bit raspy, with a hint of an accent. Russian, maybe?

"This is Viktor."

"Viktor. You don't know me, but . . . I have some information I think you'll be interested in."

A few moments of silence. "What kind of information?"

"About your business. About your . . . um . . . partners."

"What partners, exactly?"

"What do you mean, 'what partners'? Your wife and Ted."

"Oh."

Lucas expected the man to ask or say something else, but he didn't. Lucas shook his head and continued. "Look, it's probably easiest if I just show you. Some video. I think it will all make sense then."

"Is everything okay?" Viktor asked.

"Everything's fine. It's just—I'm trying to do you a favor."

Another pause. "So what do you want?"

"Look, I think you just need to see what I have."

"Okay. You can bring it to me."

"Um, actually, I was thinking more along the lines of sending it to you. E-mail or mail, or something."

"No, I think . . . you say this is something very important. I believe you, and something important like this you don't trust to mail or computers. You do it in person."

He had a point, but this conversation wasn't going the direction he'd intended. He closed his eyes. He didn't like the idea of meeting the guy, but he at least deserved to know his wife and partner were planning to kill him. "Okay, okay. How about I meet you at Split Jacks? It has something to do with this."

"Okay."

"When?"

"What about now?"

Lucas shook his head, even though he knew Viktor couldn't see it. "I can't right now. Later—this evening."

He felt the pause from Viktor.

"You call and tell me you have something very important for me to see, and then you tell me to wait for several hours."

"I know, I know. And I'm sorry."

Viktor sighed. "Okay. I'll be at Split Jacks all evening."

"Okay," Lucas said, but he was already talking to dead air; Viktor had hung up.

Right now he was too frazzled to meet Viktor or anyone else. He needed some downtime, some alone time before his meeting with Dark Suit.

He caught the Metro, riding it back to his new digs above Dandy Don's Donuts. There he decided it was time to freshen up, prepare himself.

The bathrooms on the fourth and fifth floor of his building had been ripped out, but the third floor did have a restroom with a lockable door. He washed, then shaved and changed into fresh clothing. Last clean set; he needed to head to the Laundromat or the Salvation Army soon.

That done, he returned to his small space. All the totems were there, placed in the soothing pattern he'd created. He picked up a few of the photos and looked at them. Once again, it occurred to him how very long it had been since he'd felt the Connection with anyone. So long since any dweller had been aware of his presence, sending that electric wave of excitement radiating through him. Now, more than ever, he needed a Connection like that, a link to something real, because he felt lost and alone.

He had always been lost and alone, ever since his days in the orphanage. But participating in the lives of others, the lives of people represented by all these totems spread out before him, had erased the fears and longings he'd felt when he was a young and scared boy. His hobby, his lifestyle, had filled a purpose inside—especially in those moments when he felt a Connection.

He put down the photo, picked up his most recent one taken from Noel's office. Looking at it calmed him, made him feel secure. Before the Creep Club meeting, he was sure he had found a permanent Connection, of sorts, in the one group that would understand him. And he was excited to find that creeping into private homes could actually help him do something good. Something meaningful. Like what he was trying to do for poor Viktor, who obviously spent every day drinking his liver into oblivion while his wife and partner plotted his death.

But then he'd seen the video from Dilbert, and every image stayed stuck in his mind. The curse of a vivid memory. And since then he'd felt untethered, lost. So quickly, he had found something profound, something beyond the Connection he'd felt with other individuals; just as quickly, it had been yanked away from him.

Now he needed something else sure and solid. Something to make him feel better.

Her face popped into his mind immediately. Sarea. He needed to talk to her, let her know he was going to disappear. Dark Suit had already admitted he'd been snooping around at the Blue Bell, so it was best if Lucas just cut off contact with everyone there. Keep them out of it.

He dug through the pocket of his old pants and found the receipt Sarea had given him. He powered on the phone and dialed her number. It was morning, and she most often worked mornings, so she probably didn't even have her cell phone on.

The connection went through, and Sarea's phone started to ring. This was Friday, but he couldn't remember if she was on the schedule for—

"Hello?"

He paused, long enough for her to repeat the hello.

"Uh . . . hi, Sarea. It's—"

"Lucas."

"Yeah."

"You missed a few shifts."

"Well, yeah. I, uh . . ."

"You in trouble?"

"No, no. I'm actually good. I just . . . I'm not gonna be around. I won't be back to the Blue Bell."

Silence from her end. Then: "Oh."

"And I just wanted to say . . . to you, I mean . . . I didn't want to just disappear, because you were always so nice to me."

He could hear a clicking noise on the line. Was she tapping her fingers?

"Musta been the free cigarettes."

He grinned. "Yeah. Musta."

"Listen, Lucas. Are you sure you're okay?"

He closed his eyes. "No, I'm not sure. But I gotta . . . take care of some stuff."

"All right. You take care of yourself. I suppose this just means Briggs is actually gonna have to wash some dishes."

A smile. "Yeah, I suppose it does."

"Good-bye, Lucas."

"Bye."

He hung up the phone. All these years, he had concentrated so much on the Connection with other people. Now he felt that Connection, stronger with Sarea—someone he'd never spied on— than with anyone else, and he was saying good-bye to her.

But maybe it had worked out much better this way.

No one could be close to him. A freak. A man who watched other people because . . . because why?

Because the Dark Vibration inside demanded it.

Lucas thumbed off the phone and turned his attention to his collection of totems, reminding him of smiling faces in happy places.

Once again his eyes returned to the most recent photo: Noel, camping with her kids. Their eyes sparkling with joy.

(Humpty Dumpty had some great falls.)

Yes, indeed. You never really heard anything about Humpty when he was whole; only that he was broken, irreparable.

Just one more thing Lucas understood well.

He looked at his watch. It was time to go see Dark Suit.

LUCAS WATCHED THE SHAW-HOWARD STATION CAREFULLY FOR HALF AN hour before showing himself. First he scouted the underground platform, searching for people who seemed to be hanging around but not waiting for a train. After three trains had pulled into the station and left again, he noticed a woman who had been standing on the platform the whole time. She looked to be of Asian descent, professionally dressed in a skirt and blazer. Not exactly the place he'd expect her to be hanging out if she were waiting to meet someone.

After the fourth train disgorged its passengers, however, she left and walked up the concrete stairs with a very tall, very lean man.

Two more trains came and went, then Dark Suit was standing on the platform, appearing as if by magic: one moment he wasn't there, the next he was standing tall, an unmoving boulder in a river of people exiting and entering the train.

Lucas expected Dark Suit to retreat to the far end of the platform, to hide in the shadows. That was, after all, how it was done in
all the spy movies. But Dark Suit made no move to blend in with his
surroundings; he seemed content to stand on the island platform, his
jacket fluttering in the tunnel's slight breeze as he waited.

Lucas paused a few more minutes, studying Dark Suit, watching
his lips to see if he spoke into a hidden microphone, watching his
eyes to see if he furtively glanced at a surveillance camera, watching
his hands to see if he clutched at a hidden weapon of some kind.

Dark Suit, however, simply stood mute and motionless.

Lucas heard the approaching whoosh of the next train, pushing
the heavy organic smells of the world aboveground toward him. It
was time.

He waited for the train to pull into the station, then stepped
through the security door in the midst of the disembarking crowd.
Quickly, he mixed in with the others as he approached Dark Suit
from behind.

"You're a bit late," Dark Suit said without moving, staring at the
concrete floor.

"A bit. Missed a connection before this train."

Dark Suit turned to him, smiling. "Not much of an excuse for
you, since you weren't on it."

Lucas chose to say nothing. He didn't like the man's penetrating
smile. They stood, facing each other, on a thick slab of dark bricks
between the two sets of tracks—just them, the map kiosks, and a
few concrete benches. Even at busy times of the day, people never
hung around here; it was simply a stop on the way to other places,
and the platform always emptied within a few minutes of each

train departure. Part of the reason why Lucas had chosen it as a meeting spot.

Overhead, the station's arched ceiling seemed to glow. Lucas always thought most of the Metro stations, with their recessed white squares, looked like giant frameworks for spaceships under construction.

"So I assume you're ready to go to work. To do some . . . creeping." *Blink, blink.*

"I'm ready to listen."

"Fair enough." Dark Suit finally motioned toward a nearby bench, and they walked to it and sat. From the other side of the platform, Lucas could hear the sounds of an acoustic guitar drifting down the steps. At least, it sounded acoustic; had to be amplified for him to hear it down here. A musician at street level, playing a few notes for notes.

Lucas leaned back on the bench, putting his back against its hard concrete surface, trying not to concentrate on the geopatch he was cupping in his hand. In his ever-present backpack, he imagined the minidisc recorder spinning—no video signal, but capturing every word of their conversation.

"How's this gonna work? From now on, I mean?"

Dark Suit nodded thoughtfully a few times. He looked at the top of Lucas's head. "We'll meet twice a week, and you can give me updates."

"Here?"

"It's a big city. I think we can find more interesting spots."

Lucas listened to the guitarist upstairs stretching a note, then breaking back into a tune he didn't recognize. "And what if I just say no after all, walk away from it?"

Dark Suit retrieved his pack of cigarettes, shook one out, tilted it toward Lucas. The motion reminded him of Sarea with a stab of regret; if it had been her, he would have taken the smoke. Now, however, he shook his head. Dark Suit shrugged, flipped the cigarette into his own mouth, and lit it. He let a long stream of smoke slide from his mouth as he fixed his gaze on Lucas.

He repeated Lucas's question, but from his mouth, it was a statement. "What if you just say no." A pause as his eyes searched Lucas's face.

Lucas wanted to drop his gaze, but somehow felt that would be a mistake.

"I guess that would call for Plan B," Dark Suit said.

"And what is Plan B?"

"Ah, well, let's not give up on Plan A quite yet."

"I'm just saying, you don't have anything on me. You've admitted you have trouble tracking the Creep Club—"

"But as we've both said: you're not one of them."

"No. No, I'm not. But . . . I could just disappear and be gone forever."

Dark Suit smiled. "That's pretty much what Plan B is." *Blink, blink, blink.*

Lucas felt his face getting cold, but plunged on. "You'd have to find me first," he said weakly.

"Would I?" Dark Suit offered the smile a vampire might show his next meal.

Lucas took a deep breath, tried to lean back on the bench casually and hide the sickening vortex of fear gnawing inside his stomach. He felt sweat beading on his hands and absently hoped it wouldn't ruin the geopatch he was still trying to conceal. These were all strange sensations for a man who had worked so hard to make his whole existence robotic and emotionless.

"Okay," he offered, hearing his voice crack a bit despite his best efforts. "Let's not give up on Plan A quite yet."

Dark Suit tossed his cigarette stub on the concrete floor without crushing it. "Ah, so we do speak the same language after all." He reached down beside him, and for the first time, Lucas saw a briefcase by Dark Suit's feet. Was he carrying that briefcase earlier? Had to be. Dark Suit pushed the case toward him. "Merry Christmas."

Lucas eyed the case. "What is it?"

"Your signing bonus. Some files—paper and digital. A few other surprises."

Lucas made no move to retrieve the case; he would take it when he left. "Okay."

"Now then," Dark Suit said. "I believe the next meeting of the Creep Club happens . . ."

"Tomorrow, actually."

"What say we meet after? Coffee? My treat."

Lucas nodded. His brain felt as if it were swelling. Okay, he needed to make a move now, if he had a chance of planting the geopatch.

He bent, opened the briefcase, pulled out a file of papers. He let a few sheets of paper fall from the file as he lifted it, then grabbed at the papers as they fell to the floor next to Dark Suit's unmoving feet. As he retrieved the papers, he turned his right hand to the side and rubbed the geopatch against Dark Suit's shoe in a smooth, fluid motion. It stuck easily, and a quick glance confirmed it was mostly invisible.

"Sorry," he said, playing up the gee-I'm-clumsy routine. "Guess I didn't expect quite so much paperwork."

"Well, you are working for the government now." *Grin. Blink.*

"Am I?" He sat up again. "What branch of the government would that be?"

"That would be my branch," Dark Suit said.

Lucas turned his attention back to the contents of the case. More files with photos and documents, some small packages wrapped in plain brown paper. He nodded, as if this was what he expected to see inside the case, then closed it.

Dark Suit rose, turned toward him. Lucas followed the motion and clasped his hand.

"Um, what should I call you?" Lucas asked hesitantly.

"Ah. Well, I guess you could call me Saul."

"Saul. Why?"

"Because that's my name." He began to walk away, toward the steps that led to street level. Up above, the guitar abruptly stopped pumping out its lonesome wail. "We'll see you on Tuesday . . . Humpty."

Lucas stared across the station for a few minutes after Saul's departure, thinking as a few more trains pulled in and emptied their passengers.

Finally, he opened the briefcase again. He considered the folders and wrapped brown packages inside for a few moments before unslinging his backpack and transferring them to it.

Up above, the guitar began in earnest again, yet another blues-tinged riff that sounded faintly familiar to Lucas; the tune, in an odd way, felt hypnotic. He listened to a few bars, closing his eyes as the chords seemed to fill the air around him. After a few seconds, he opened his eyes and looked around him, trying to see if anyone else was listening to the music. Another train stopped, emptying fresh passengers onto the platform, but the sounds of the crowd didn't seem to overpower the music from above at all.

Curious, Lucas stood and went toward the concrete stairs, his pack strapped to his back and the now-empty briefcase clutched in his hand.

At the bottom of the steps, he paused. A few people coursed around him. The music beckoned, and now he could hear a faint growl of someone singing, accompanying the tune. No distinct words that he could make out, just a dark growl that punctuated the chords strummed on the guitar.

He kept his gaze above as he climbed the stairs to the street level, pulled along by the siren sound of the music. At the top of the stairs he paused again, seeing the guitarist sitting on a crate near a bench. Lucas was aware of traffic noises, shuffling feet, honking horns, but somehow they all faded into the distance. The guitar and the low, guttural voice of the musician forced it all to the background.

The musician threw back his head and let out a wail, then launched into an intricate solo, making the guitar wail along with him. His eyes were closed, as if he were in pain, but Lucas could see a glint of white teeth shining in the light. A porkpie hat perched on the man's head and seemed in danger of falling off, but it refused to move in spite of the musician's gyrations. Through it all, the man kept his left leg bent, perched against the crate, as his right leg stretched in front of him and tapped out a beat.

Lucas stared around him again, noting the people moving up

and down the stairs without taking notice of the wondrous sound in their midst.

He smiled, felt his feet taking him toward the figure on the crate.

He stopped in front of the musician, and as he did, the guitarist straightened his head again and opened his eyes. Another smile, another flash of white teeth. He nodded his head to Lucas, continuing to play but lowering the intensity of the music.

Lucas felt a smile come across his own face, found himself fumbling in his pocket and pulling out a few bucks. He dropped them into the man's guitar case, feeling like a robot; his own movements seemed stiff, awkward in the presence of . . . of this amazing sound.

Another nod from the guitarist as his fingers moved on the frets, shifting to a new tune but somehow flowing from the last one. The musician spoke.

"You wanna hear somethin?" he asked, continuing to play.

Lucas opened his mouth, but it was dry. He swallowed, feeling a click in his throat. "Just . . . this," was all he could stammer.

The musician nodded. "You look like a man who could go for one of the old-time spirituals," he said. His eyebrows arched, and he held Lucas's gaze as his fingers etched out a new tune. The man threw back his head and began to sing in that low, feel-it-in-your-bones tone.

Sometimes I'm up, sometimes I'm down
Oh, yes Lord
Sometimes I'm almost to the ground
Oh, yes Lord
Although you see me goin' along so
Oh, yes Lord

I have my troubles here below
Oh, yes Lord
Nobody knows the trouble I see . . .

Lucas smiled. Could be his theme. The man opened an eye and peeked at Lucas, who nodded back encouragement. For a few minutes he stood, transported to another world filled only with shifting chords and plaintive singing; the man performed the song, and Lucas simultaneously felt like crying and laughing. The music gripped him deep inside, matching the Dark Vibration that was always there. But while the music played, the Dark Vibration didn't demand to come to the forefront. It stayed in the background, comforted by the sounds.

Finally the musician finished, going back to some filler. His eyes opened again, the smile spreading from his mouth across his whole face.

"That's . . . amazing," Lucas said.

"Ain't it, though?" the man said. "You feel it. Not many folks do. Not many folks do at all. They hear, but they don't feel."

The familiarity of the phrase struck Lucas; it sounded so much like *They look, but they don't see.* He understood this man very well, he thought.

The musician's eyes took on a faraway look for a few moments, as if lost in some memory. "Hard to feel it if you don't understand," he said.

"Understand what?"

Another gleaming smile. "Ah, that's the question, ain't it?"

Lucas listened to the musician play for a few more minutes, then turned sadly back toward the steps that would lead him underground again. As he turned, the man spoke behind him once more.

"You just keep listening, son," he said.

Lucas spun around, thought a moment. "You just keep playing, and I will."

"Got yerself a deal there."

Lucas listened to the sounds of the guitar fading away as he retraced his route to the underground. Back in the station, he scouted the platform and backtracked through the security door to bypass the gates, then out to the back tunnels of the Metro system. A few hundred feet down the catwalk adjacent to the rails, he paused and threw the now-empty briefcase out onto the tracks; it tumbled to a stop, resting askew on one of the rails. In a few minutes, the next train would rumble through, pushing the case back toward the station, mangling it in the process. He smiled, thinking about potential bugs or tracking devices hidden in the soft cloth lining of the case; let Saul's spooks kick around the dark stones on the floor of the Metro station, looking for broken pieces.

He turned down an access tunnel and toward the basement of a nearby office building he'd called home some months ago.

Of course, there was also the matter of the files and the wrapped packages Saul had given him; they were just as likely to carry tracking devices, so he couldn't very well take them with him. He'd hide them in the basement up ahead and come back to them at a later time for closer inspection.

Then it would be time to pay a visit to his good friend Donavan.

Even down here, in the bowels of the Metro system, he swore he could still hear the music from above.

But that was impossible.

TEN

DONAVAN WASN'T HOME; LUCAS COULD TELL THAT AFTER A FEW MINUTES of watching his apartment. Amazingly enough, though, the key was still hidden under the planter. When Lucas let himself into the apartment, it was immediately obvious Donavan hadn't been back since his last visit; the nearly empty bag of chips Donavan had left in the hall was still there, undisturbed.

Lucas made his way through the apartment, cataloging images and comparing them to the ones he had in his mind. The bed, still unmade, with one pillow on the floor and the other plumped into a small hump. The dirty dishes next to the sink, unrinsed. The mail, haphazardly opened, sitting on the small end table in the living area.

Donavan hadn't come home after the meeting last night; that was obvious. The question was: Where had he gone? Stayed with Snake or one of the other Creep Clubbers? Or was Donavan avoiding his home, in hopes it would help him avoid Lucas? Possible. Maybe even probable after his walkout the night before.

Wait. Viktor Abkin's house—that's where he had to be. Probably getting more shots for his big "project." At least it kept him out of the way for the time being; once Lucas talked to Viktor, Donavan's precious project would be done.

Lucas went to the bedroom and woke Donavan's computer, then opened the Web browser.

First he typed in the numeric IP address to make sure the geopatch he'd attached to Saul's shoe was active. It was. Lucas would come back to that later.

He started to leave the site, then thought better of it and checked the locations of the geopatches attached to Viktor, Ted, and Anita again. As expected, Ted and Anita were at the Abkin house, while unsuspecting Viktor whiled away his time at the bar.

Next he pointed the browser at the Creep Club home page. He entered Donavan's username and password, and was relieved to discover it still let him in.

Still no new posts on the page, though. There was no telling when Donavan would sign on and change his log-in information, so Lucas's online link to the Creep Club was already iffy.

He needed a real link to them. Maybe he'd be working with Saul, maybe he'd be working alone. In either case, he was sure he wanted to pay another visit to Creep Club. Eyes wide open this time.

He checked his watch. He'd left his meeting with Saul about an hour and a half ago. Now it was time to log in to Donavan's geopatch site.

He considered, for a moment, whether or not to barricade the front door of Donavan's apartment. Donavan could return at any time, especially since he hadn't been here at all in the last twenty hours or so. But he doubted Donavan would be surprised to see him there; in an odd way, Donavan had seemed to welcome his presence in the apartment.

He was fairly certain the apartment was under some kind of surveillance. Maybe Donavan even had a few tricks hidden inside the walls or ceilings. And again, this did nothing to change his plans. He was only here to use the computer and then would be on his way. He could always return later, when Donavan was back.

The front door was locked; that was good enough for now.

Lucas recalled Donavan's numeric IP address in his mind's eye, then keyed it into the browser window; instantly, a satellite/map hybrid of the greater DC area began to load on the screen. In a pane off the main window, he clicked on a drop-down text box and selected the number of the geopatch he'd affixed to Saul's shoe. A few moments later, a red dot began glowing on the screen as the image zoomed; it stayed stationary as he watched it for a few minutes.

Nodding, Lucas clicked on the history link and traced the geopatch's movements since its activation ninety minutes ago. Looked like Saul had made two brief stops, then a third at his current location, where he had been for the last fifteen minutes.

Lucas made a mental note of the three addresses, filing them away in his memory banks. He had some exploring to do.

AS LUCAS FOLLOWED SAUL'S RECENT TRACKS, HE THOUGHT THE MAN'S first stop was innocuous enough: a local coffee shop, carved out of the lobby of a blue glass building just south of the Washington Monument. Lucas went inside the shop to look around, ordered a latte to give himself a caffeine kick. Brushed nickel tables and chairs circled the L-shaped bar, with bright drop-down lights overhead. Everything in the coffee shop was sharp and angular—no soft curves or lines.

Something like Saul himself.

Lucas sipped at the latte—hotter than molten lava—as he pulled up the image of the computer map in his head. The next location he'd known immediately when he'd seen its address: the Lincoln Memorial.

It wasn't exactly a short walk from where he was—almost a mile—but he felt like hoofing it. Walking would give him some time to clear his mind, keep him off the Metro for a while.

Half an hour later, he stood in front of Honest Abe, looking up at the giant marble face. The mammoth statue of Lincoln, he thought, looked sad, as if seeing something that disappointed him.

Lucas took another sip of the latte, now only slightly cooler, and walked to the top of the steps, standing by one of the giant columns to take in the general area. Trees and lawn stretching away from him, leading to the Walking Mall's shimmering sheet of water. Washington Monument and Capitol Hill, wavering in the hazy distance.

His eye stopped on a long, low concrete bench adjacent to the base of the steps. It felt right: it was open, offering a long view in any direction. This felt, to him, like a place Saul would . . . would what?

He wasn't sure of that. Yet.

He walked down the steps to the bench, sat on it. Yes, Saul had been here. After another sip of the latte, he decided to give up on it and stood to walk it over to the nearest trash can.

He looked across the long stretch of the Walking Mall, toward Capitol Hill on the other end. His next destination was near the Hill, and he'd already done a bit of research on the address. A government office building, but no online records to indicate exactly what kinds of offices the building housed. A quick Google search revealed no private businesses or official government divisions using the address.

He moved north toward the Foggy Bottom Metro stop, where he could catch the Orange or Blue Line to Capitol Hill; he had less than an hour to work with if he was going to make his meeting with Viktor at Split Jacks.

He listened to his feet shuffling on the pavement as he walked, replaying the events of the past few days in his mind. Immediately, the world around him began to squeeze in. For a moment he wished he were in a dark, smooth place—a cool place—with his menagerie of totems surrounding him. The photos, the wonderful photos, the smiling faces and the scarf and the trinkets.

Lucas made himself take a few deep breaths as he continued walking. Had to keep it together right now. The itch was there, to be certain, but he could live with the itch for now. He'd be back home tonight.

A few blocks from the Metro stop, he went into a giant brick office building whose entrance was guarded by a spraying water fountain, feeling tiny drops of the water pricking at his face like grains of sand as he walked by. Inside the building, he moved confidently to the stairs and down them to the basement.

He'd spent a lot of time in this section of town, to be sure. He was, after all, something of a permanent tourist. He'd come here from . . . well, from the orphanage, drawn by the bright lights. But like anyone else, he wanted to see all the machinations of government, the memorials and statues and gardens and cemeteries. So he'd infiltrated many office buildings in this area, and the images of the buildings—their floor layouts, their utility grids—were carefully filed away inside his mind.

In the basement he pushed open a glass door, obviously not the original door to the basement, and went into the darkness beyond. After a few steps, just as he'd remembered, a motion detector flicked the light switch and illuminated the way for him. He took a right just past some built-in storage areas framed by wire and came to a door marked DANGER: ELECTRICAL HAZARD in big, bright letters.

Most people shied away from danger signs. Lucas knew there was little danger from electrical hazards behind the door; instead, there was a short passageway that led to an underground tunnel and, eventually, a door to the Metro system.

A few minutes later he stood in a Metro car, crowded on all sides by commuters, their faces mute masks of indifference, headed to Metro Center or L'Enfant Plaza to catch different lines to their homes in Maryland or Virginia.

He let his gaze drift around the car, focusing on the distinct faces, trying to picture what their homes must be like. This one, a stocky man with a perfectly coiffed head, he imagined in a small condo. A divorced father of two, he sat forlornly in his seat tonight because this wasn't a weekend with the kids. The condo would be immaculate, because this man—Lucas decided his name was Dexter—was fastidious, ordered. The living room would be more of a great room, with a large picture window out the front and—

Lucas shook his head, consciously clearing his thoughts. Something was wrong inside his own mind; usually, when he invented these elaborate stories for the people he watched, he focused on their lives and loves. Now, he found himself fixating on their homes, wondering what they looked like inside, how the people he stared at would interact with their surroundings.

It frightened him, this new feeling. Frightened him the way a new junkie might be afraid of the next score: you want it, oh yes, but you're trembling because you want it.

He dropped his gaze to the floor, closed his eyes, tried to appear as if he were getting a bit of shut-eye on his own commute.

But behind his closed eyelids the cinema of imagined possibilities continued to play, and by the time he arrived at the Capitol South stop his mouth was dry and metallic.

The way a junkie's mouth would feel in the midst of a deep craving for another hit.

SAUL'S BUILDING—OR WHAT LUCAS ASSUMED TO BE SAUL'S BUILDING—was an old one several blocks from the Hill. That meant it would have room in the utility chases, as well as unused spaces and other creases where he could fold his body into the building itself.

It was past typical office hours now, but he didn't really believe this was a typical office, did he? Officially, at least in terms of Google and phone listings, no business or government agency used this building. Even its location seemed to isolate it; in a largely residential area, it was surrounded by row houses rather than other commercial buildings. And yet here it was, heavily fortified with scanners and guards just inside the front entry and signs posted on the building's exterior warning "unauthorized personnel" to stay away. He loved those kinds of signs; they always led to easy entries.

He took out his spotting scope for a closer look. Inside, on three of the building's five floors, he saw fluorescent lights illuminating office spaces. Still plenty of light right now, at least an hour or two from sunset, but people seemed to turn on overhead fluorescents from force of habit. That meant there was probably still a fair amount of activity inside. Even at this hour. Even on a Friday night. Interesting.

He checked his TracFone; he didn't have long before his meeting time with Viktor. Lucas was regretting even agreeing to see the guy. Why get involved in something potentially complicated and messy? This was exactly why he avoided most interactions with others. Invariably, it led to something more complicated.

And yet, maybe that was part of the reason, wasn't it? Because he'd had no personal contact with much of anyone for years. A chance to make up for his past transgressions.

Whatever those might be.

He sighed, knowing he would have to leave this building for later exploration. Maybe it would be a quick meeting with Viktor, and he could get back here for some initial recon. Maybe he could find a computer at an Internet café and log on to Donavan's geopatch site to track Saul's most recent movements. Provided Donavan hadn't discovered a few of his geopatches moving and deleted the entire site.

Split Jacks it was, then.

ELEVEN

IT WASN'T THE KIND OF PLACE LUCAS WOULD BE DRAWN TO NORMALLY. Or even drawn to abnormally, for that matter. The sign above the door was a stark, black-and-white thing: the words SPLIT JACKS stacked on top of each other in big block letters, with a large notch of white cut out of the middle in a jagged slit. A split in the words, then; someone was trying to be clever.

Behind the garishly lit neon of the front door, a decidedly mundane bar, of sorts, waited. It wasn't one of those classic old establishments, family run for generations, with a giant, thick-wood main bar and the feel of history in the air. Neither was it a sparkling new club, awash in shining metal and glass.

It was stuck somewhere in the middle, trying to be a bit of both and succeeding on neither count. Old diner-style stools topped with red leather were mounted to a sticky floor in front of a fake-wood bar mirrored with panels of chrome here and there.

At the far end of the long, rectangular space was a hallway, probably leading toward the restrooms and a few illegal card tables and a phone room with sports books. A name such as Split Jacks, after all, would be no accident.

He scanned the room, breathing through his mouth to keep the cloying mix of sweat and stale cigarettes out of his nostrils. Plenty of people in the bar, but he could tell the festivities hadn't hit full stride yet.

He began walking down the long, metal-plated bar, scanning faces. About halfway back he saw the angular face he was looking for, seated in a booth just across from the bar. Viktor was on his cell phone, a glass of caramel-colored liquid with a wedge of lime—more of a dull yellow than the proper green—jammed haphazardly on the rim. A few file folders sat on the booth seat next to him, papers spread out on the table.

Lucas approached the table, and Viktor looked up. He jutted his chin at the seat on the opposite side of the booth, and Lucas sat.

Viktor listened to several more seconds of someone on the phone, then spoke. "You will call me later on this. I have something else now." He closed the phone without saying good-bye, put the phone on the seat next to him, stared at Lucas a few moments, and said nothing.

Lucas decided to break the ice. "Eight o'clock, and here we are."

Viktor let a brief smile crease his face. He held out a hand across the booth. "Viktor Abkin," he said.

Lucas took his hand and shook it; Viktor was obviously one of those guys who believed you should have a firmer grip than anyone you meet.

"What shall I call you?" Viktor finally asked, releasing Lucas's hand from his death grip. Viktor's accent gave a slightly odd cadence, somewhat robotlike, to his speech patterns.

"You shouldn't."

"A comedian."

The barmaid approached and gave Lucas an uninterested glance. "What can I get you?" she asked, glancing over at Viktor nervously before turning to Lucas.

Lucas wondered why she looked so uncomfortable. "Water's good," he said.

"Not here, it isn't," Viktor answered.

The waitress, obviously unsure how she should react, tried a pained smile before retreating to the relative safety of the bar.

They sat in silence a few moments, Lucas watching Viktor drum his fingers on the tabletop as they waited for the barmaid's return. Finally, she slid a highball glass filled with ice and water in Lucas's direction, along with a small basket of pretzels.

Over in the corner, someone had slipped money into the CD jukebox, and an old song Lucas dimly recognized—Lynyrd Skynyrd, some kind of southern rock like that—was punching out of the semi-fried speakers.

Viktor took a sip of his dark liquid, grimaced, set it back down. Looked into it as if he'd lost something valuable in there. "So," he said, a little too low.

Lucas leaned in to hear him.

"What do you have for me?"

Lucas took a sip of his water, listened to the ice shift inside the glass. The water tasted faintly of sawdust. Not that he was surprised.

"I think I should just show you," he said. He dug in the backpack, retrieved the minidisc recorder and DVD, and pushed the recorder across the table toward Viktor. "Take a look," he said. "I burned a DVD too," he said, holding it up.

Viktor looked at the recorder for a few seconds as if it were a venomous animal, then glanced at the DVD Lucas held.

"I didn't actually record it myself," Lucas said, feeling a sudden urge to explain. "A friend did." He paused. "Not really a friend, I guess. A guy I know."

"A guy you know." Viktor smiled. "And he just decided to show it to you, and you happened to know who I am, how to find me."

Lucas squirmed in his seat a bit.

"Yes," he said slowly, deciding not to go any further down this conversational path. "Something like that."

Viktor flicked the sickly lime off the side of the glass, pushing it into the liquid. He picked up the minidisc recorder and thumbed the Play button. After a few seconds, he held the recorder close to his face, listening intently while trying to block the sounds of a long guitar solo coming from the rattling jukebox.

Several seconds later, he turned off the minidisc recorder and set it back on the table. "So," he said, and waited.

"So," Lucas repeated.

"So now would be the time when you tell me what you want."

Lucas shook his head. "I don't want anything. I . . . I thought you should just see this."

"A Good Samaritan."

"I guess so." Lucas was feeling more uncomfortable by the second; there was a sense of menace hanging in the air all around Viktor. No wonder his wife was looking elsewhere for . . . whatever she was looking for.

"So," Viktor continued, "since you're just a Good Samaritan, you probably know nothing about the company I own with these two." He waved a hand, indicating the minidisc recorder still sitting on the table between them.

"Well, yeah, I do know about that. ATM2GO."

Viktor smiled, but it was a smile that did nothing to comfort Lucas. "You seem to know much more than the average Good Samaritan."

Lucas took a sudden interest in his own glass, took another drink of the sawdust-infused water.

"Let's talk a moment about the life insurance policies—policies, I'm sure, you know nothing about. Impossible for you to know such things, being a simple Good Samaritan."

Lucas said nothing. It seemed his best strategy at the moment.

"The company pays the premiums," Viktor said. "Any one of us dies, the policy buys out that partner's shares. The shares revert to the company, and the surviving family gets half the money." He brought his gaze up to meet Lucas's once more.

"What about the other half?"

Viktor smiled once more. "Ah, well. The company will have a hard time replacing me—let us just say it is me who has died—and so the company must be compensated for the loss of my services."

Lucas nodded, waited.

Viktor leaned back, let his fingers start tapping in time with the tune on the jukebox. The throaty voice was singing about the smell of death. Yeah, it had to be Skynyrd; Lucas had heard it before. Maybe even on a beer commercial once.

"What are they giving you?" Viktor finally said. "It can't be enough, if you are coming to me with this." A derisive snort.

Lucas stared back. "They're not giving me anything. I've never met them."

"I will give you twenty-five thousand dollars."

Lucas let out a small sigh. "To do . . . what exactly?"

Viktor motioned to the barmaid, held up his glass to ask for another drink. "So twenty-five thousand will do it."

Lucas said nothing, so Viktor continued. "Our business arrangement—the life insurance—is a succession plan. To keep the business operating if any of us dies, or decides to leave. A fund has been set up specifically to buy the shares of any partner who wants out."

"So you're going to sell out and leave?"

Viktor laughed, just as the barmaid returned with another drink for him. The lime on this one looked marginally better. Viktor waved her away, and she left without a word.

Viktor took the thin straw out of the glass, tossed it aside, and had a long draw on the drink. Over in the corner, the jukebox changed songs.

"The answer to your question," Viktor finally replied after setting his glass down again, "is no. I'm not going to sell out. They are."

Lucas sat back, tried not to show a reaction.

Viktor arched an eyebrow. "Perfect, eh? That is why I need you. You see?" Viktor was using his hands to gesture now.

Lucas wasn't sure if it was a result of his excitement or of who-knew-how-many drinks.

"I show them the tape—all the tapes. There are more, I assume?"

Lucas nodded his head. "I think so."

"Perfect. I show them the tapes, tell them it is time for them to retire. If not . . . perhaps authorities will be interested in hearing about their plans."

Lucas suddenly felt thirstier than ever; he drained the rest of the water before speaking again. "So you just pay them out? Give them the money and let them go?"

Viktor licked his lips. He pursed his lips. "No, they do not get the money."

Lucas saw the light now. "You want it."

Viktor closed an eye in a slow wink, pointed at Lucas with the glass still clutched in his hand. "The money comes out of the company. They are allowed to go free."

"But . . . what about taxes and stuff? I mean, isn't that going to show up as income for them—how do they account for it?"

Viktor shrugged. "That is their problem. They are smart people; I am sure they will figure out how to pay taxes on money they never received." Viktor smiled, obviously enjoying this.

Amazing. Here Lucas sat across from a man whose marriage had obviously crumbled long ago, whose business must have taken a turn for the worse—at least among the partners—and he was smiling because he'd inflict damage and get money out of the deal.

He studied Viktor's features, tried to dream up a history for him on the fly. An athlete while growing up in Russia; played hockey, of course. Following the crumbling of the Iron Curtain, he saw opportunity in the United States, and so came with a dream. Met his soon-to-be wife soon after, a nice Midwestern girl with a bright smile and—

"I said, are we agreed?"

Lucas brought himself out of his reverie, finally registering that
Viktor had spoken to him. He leaned forward in the booth and spoke
slowly. "I already told you, I don't have a dog in this fight. I gave you
the tape; I gave you fair warning. Do what you want with it."

Viktor's eyebrows furrowed, and his face registered confusion.
Obviously trying to figure out how someone could turn down an
easy 25K. Once again, he pushed his lime into his drink, then let his
fingers drum on the table. A sigh. Then: "I need more tape. More
evidence. For this, I might be willing to double my offer."

Lucas stood. This conversation was over, as far as he was concerned.

Immediately, a hard look crossed Viktor's face, and he stared up
at Lucas through slitted eyes. "What are you doing?"

"Leaving."

Viktor relaxed his face a bit, shook his head. He offered his hand
for a parting shake.

Lucas stood at the end of the booth, considered. Well, fine, at
least he could end on a positive note. He took Viktor's hand and
shook it, but Viktor immediately sealed Lucas's hand in that vise
grip and pulled him down to his level, leaning forward and speaking
through clenched teeth.

"You consider what you are doing here, my Good Samaritan," he
said. "You know who I am, so you know I do not like to be turned
down. Some might even say I am quite unreasonable on this." He
finally released his grip. "I would hate for your selfless deed to go
unrewarded, after all."

Lucas stood and looked down at Viktor, still seated at the booth.
Over in the corner, the jukebox had gone silent again.

He turned and walked from Split Jacks, eager to breathe the air outside.

LATE THAT NIGHT, IN HIS SLEEPING BAG ON THE FOURTH FLOOR ABOVE Dandy Don's Donuts, Lucas dreamed. It began with his earliest memories of the orphanage, dreams of his bed in the converted attic. In his childhood bed, he lay awake, staring at the ceiling and wondering what was above. What secrets the sky held. Then he was creeping to the window, carefully, slowly, making his escape to the world outside.

But when he reached the window, it didn't lead to the roof outside; instead, it put him in a stark room, painted a dull, eggshell color. A single lightbulb hung from the ceiling above him, and he stared intently at the bulb, repeating the words he knew so well, the words that would transport him away from this room that smelled of slick sweat and oil.

(Humpty Dumpty had some great falls. Humpty Dumpty had some great falls. Humpty Dumpty—)

The window behind him opened again, this time on its own, and now it was pulling him, like a vacuum it was pulling him toward it—

He was sucked into the window and spit out in the tunnels beneath DC. He recognized the area immediately; he was in the northeast quadrant, not far from Union Station. Straight ahead, he knew, was a small hatchway that led to the underground sewer system, and he had to reach that hatchway soon, because a deep, guttural growl stalked him in the tunnels.

He sprinted to the hatch and opened it, splashing his way through a couple inches of standing water, then continued running because it seemed like the right thing to do. And soon he came to the iron-rung ladder that led to the street above. Just a manhole cover between him and freedom as he scrambled up the rungs, the guttural growling directly below him.

He pushed at the manhole cover, and it opened easily, so easily, sliding away and revealing another impenetrable hold of darkness.

But it was safe, of course it was safe, it was a manhole cover leading to the world aboveground so it had to be safe. So he boosted himself through the opening and into the space beyond.

Something was wrong. Something was very wrong. He hadn't climbed into the light above at all; he'd climbed into . . . a monster. The monster that had been chasing him. He looked behind him, and now saw the gaping maw of a mouth closing, lips sealing over the jagged teeth. Soon all contact with the outside world was gone, and he was surrounded on all sides by wet, sticky darkness, and he felt the monster diving, diving deeper, and—

Lucas awoke in a drenching sweat, his lungs huffing in gasp after gasp of oxygen. A dream, yes. He fumbled around in the dark for his electric candle, found it, then thumbed the button. He picked up the candle, turned toward his arrangement of photos and mementos, and scanned the smiling faces he saw there.

(*Humpty Dumpty had some great falls. Humpty Dumpty had some great falls.*)

He repeated it to himself again and again, and lay staring at the photos of smiling families until the sun rose in the eastern sky.

TWELVE

THE TEENAGED BOY LISTENS TO THE INCESSANT HUM IN HIS EARS, SMILING
to himself as he waits for his secret visitor.

At first the hum—the all-encompassing, inescapable hum—drove him
nearly crazy. So much so that Raven, and a team of others, started new
medications to combat the side effects. After several weeks of experiment-
ing, they found the combination that worked. The chemical cocktail he now
took twice a week didn't deaden the sound of the hum swirling about him
at all; it stayed the same volume, the same exact pitch, all the time. But
somehow, the hum stopped being maddening and started to be comforting.

And so, when he awakes, especially on the days after his most recent shot
of the new chemical cocktail, he enjoys lying still for several minutes, letting
the noise envelop him, transport him to some place none of these people can
understand.

He is the only traveler on these journeys.

Beneath the buzz he hears the steel door slide open, and his smile widens. His secret visitor is here.

"And how are you feeling today?" the secret visitor asks.

The teenaged boy licks his lips, smiles, looks at the secret visitor. "Better than ever."

"Good, good. And you haven't told Raven about—"

"I wouldn't tell Raven anything," the teenaged boy says. And he means it. Raven is the enemy.

The secret visitor nods, puts a hand on the bed beside the boy. By this time the boy has figured out how to release the restraints in mere seconds; he can get free anytime he wants to. He can slip past Raven, if he chooses, make his escape, explore the world outside this room of steel.

Someday, he knows, he will do just that. Someday, his secret visitor will make it possible.

"Do you think you're ready to start taking on some other . . . duties?" the secret visitor asks. The voice is almost a whisper.

"I was born ready," the teenaged boy says. For all he knows, this is absolutely true. He has no idea where he was born, who he is, how he got here. There is only this room, Raven, and an endless parade of nameless faces poking and studying him.

At least, that was true until his secret visitor appeared, someone who has promised to unlock the world beyond.

When he's ready.

"I'm glad to hear it, because . . . well, I'm not sure the wasp pheromone experiments you've been participating in have been entirely successful. Surely you must feel this."

"Yes."

"Not that we feel the pheromone road is a dead end at all; we think there are others who might do . . . more with the resources. Maybe you."

"Yes."

The secret visitor smiles. "So eager to participate, to do what is asked. In that respect, at least, the wasp pheromones haven't been a total wash." The secret visitor takes a deep breath, holds the teenaged boy's gaze steadily. "You realize what the next steps are. More than that, what the eventual steps are."

"Yes."

"There will be more . . . medicines. To help you learn. To help you digest what Raven and his crew have been doing. To help you create new ideas— ideas Raven will, ultimately, be unable to explore. You'll have intense daily sessions, absorbing all there is to know. Perhaps a brilliant mind such as yours will help us win the Cold War, defeat the Soviets."

"How can war be cold?" the teenaged boy asks.

The secret visitor pauses, brushes a hand against the boy's cheek, and smiles. It's that radiant smile the teenaged boy loves to see, and in that moment, the boy knows he would do anything—anything—to keep the visitor smiling.

He would kill, if he had to.

THIRTEEN

IN THE MORNING, LUCAS HAD AN URGE TO GRAB A COFFEE AND A DONUT at Dandy Don's, but figured he'd wait until he got to The LiveWire Internet café; there, he ordered a coffee and a scone before sitting down at the ancient PC and punching in the numeric IP address to track Saul's geopatch. It showed the patch had been at the same location since 10:07 the previous evening, about twenty miles away in Bowie, Maryland.

Good to know; most likely Saul's home. He'd visit it soon. That would mean a ride to the end of the Green Line, and then a bus from there, but it would be doable.

Lucas backed up through the history logs to see where else Saul had been since their meeting the previous day. Other than the stops Lucas had already investigated, it didn't look like he'd been anywhere interesting—he'd stayed in his office until eight thirty the previous evening, actually.

"All work and no play," muttered Lucas as he sipped at his coffee. The scone was too dry for his taste, but he wasn't about to complain. It filled his stomach.

Next he pulled up the Creep Club home page and typed in Donavan's username and password. It still worked, so that was good. There were several new posts, including one posted within the last half hour from "Hiss"—had to be the guy who called himself Snake—promising a new meeting announcement within the next twenty-four hours.

So far, so good. If Donavan had tried to log in with his old information, Lucas was sure he would have contacted the admin for a reset. That hadn't happened.

The question was: what was Donavan up to?

Maybe Lucas should drop by Donavan's for another look later on. Right now, though, he had a few other stops to make.

LUCAS TOOK HIS TIME WALKING AROUND THE PERIMETER OF SAUL'S OFFICE building; eventually he found a nice hiding spot in the hedge and planting area that separated the building from a string of row houses right next to it. There, he took out his spotting glass and scanned the windows on the nearest floors.

No immediately obvious activity; it was a Saturday, so he hadn't expected much to be happening. Part of the reason he was there now.

He'd already checked the front entry and other doors on the main floor. The front doors had a security station and a metal detector, or at least a setup that looked like a metal detector, while the other doors all required a swipe of an ID card.

He scanned the perimeter of the building and found two cameras pointed at the sidewalks. Also expected. He was sure, with a bit of looking, he would find surveillance cameras on the other sides of the building.

The building was only four stories tall. Part of the reason, certainly, had something to do with the District's height requirements—no buildings higher than 288 feet—but just as much, he knew a building like this wouldn't want to draw any attention to itself.

At The LiveWire he'd searched for information, but no publicly available records existed. He'd even logged on to Google Earth to check the location, but the satellite photos of the area that should have appeared told him "no image available." It was a building that didn't officially exist.

He could try to break in today, but it would take a few hours to put together a workable plan. He needed an entrance plan, an exit plan, a bit of time to construct an observation deck in the right spot—and he didn't even know exactly where Saul's office was hidden inside the building. On top of that, he only had a rudimentary understanding of the building's security system at this point. Best to wait for now; he didn't really need to get inside yet.

He closed his spotting scope and returned everything to his backpack. Saul's office would have to wait; right now, it was time to visit the man at home.

SAUL'S HOME, AND HOMETOWN, WERE A BIT OF A SURPRISE: AN OLDER, country-style cottage in the villagelike atmosphere of Bowie. Lucas had half expected a large condo filled with chrome appliances after meeting Saul. But this home looked like something straight out of the pages of Mother Goose.

He wasn't sure if Saul was in right now—most likely, he was—but Lucas wasn't terribly worried about being spotted. Most people paid no attention to what was happening around them, too wrapped up in their own thoughts. What was it the musician had said at the Metro stop? *They hear, but they don't feel.* Even though Saul was a government spook, it was doubtful he would be any different. Saul wouldn't see him in his neighborhood simply because he wouldn't expect to. So much of the typical person's perception of the world centered on what he expected to see. Lucas had used those expectations, those perceptions, to his benefit many times before.

Still, he was careful as he strolled around the perimeter of the house. He stayed on the opposite side of the street. He wore a hat and sunglasses. He carried a large, handled department store bag (into which he'd put his backpack), playing the part of an unassuming man who had just made a big purchase and was now walking home down the pleasant streets of Bowie, Maryland.

Saul's home was a pale yellow, with white trim and accents outlining both the house and the attached one-car garage. A stone walkway in front of the house meandered across a small, well-kept lawn.

An alley had once run down the back of the property, he was sure, but a new development was butted up against the rear of Saul's neighborhood now, half-finished homes and cement pads adorned by Realtors' signs. So much for Saul's village setting. Right behind him, the Whispering Pines subdivision was rising, offering "Relaxing Old-World Living."

Bad for Saul and his neighbors, perhaps, but good for him. Lucas walked quickly into the subdivision and found a half-finished home just north of Saul's cottage. The exterior walls were in place, protected by wrap and tar paper while waiting for the permanent siding, but there weren't any interior stud walls yet. Holes had been framed in the exterior walls for windows, but they were just that right now: holes.

Lucas climbed some makeshift wooden steps to the unfinished home's second story and set down his shopping bag. He retrieved his backpack, unzipped it, and found his spotting scope.

The back of Saul's home had a small patio with a couple of chairs and a small table. A metal fence across the back property line was almost entirely covered by a lush, green hanging vine.

Behind the patio, he studied a door that led to the garage for a few moments before sliding the scope's lens over the roofline of the house. At the end of the garage, a fan spun slowly, providing exhaust from the ceiling rafters.

Lucas slipped the scope into his pack again, listened to the birds chirping. He took a deep breath, inhaling the aroma of fresh-cut grass. A plan had formed in his mind, and it was time to put it into action.

Shouldering his pack, he quickly moved out of the half-finished house he was occupying and went across the tracks rutted in the mud to Saul's vine-covered fence. Without hesitating, he vaulted the low fence and went to the patio. The door from the patio to the garage was unlocked, just as it had been at Viktor Abkin's house. Inside the garage, he carefully closed the door behind him as he scanned. A car was there, which most likely meant Saul was home. The interior of the garage was dark, but light spilled onto the roof of the blue sedan from a window on the garage's exterior wall—just enough light for Lucas to make out the general interior.

Several tools hung on the wall. Overhead, a few extension cords snaked across the ceiling. One connected to the exhaust fan high under the roof apex, he guessed. The other went to a small refrigerator over in the corner, right next to the door that led into the house.

He wasn't interested in that door right now. Instead, he continued to study the ceiling of the garage, scanning the bare gypsum board. Then he found what he was looking for: a small trapdoor providing access to the garage's ceiling rafters, just above Saul's vehicle.

Quietly he moved to the car, then stepped up onto the front bumper and crept along the front fender. He was careful to stay on the edge of the fender's seam, where the metal was strongest—further in on the fender, or on the hood, he knew, the metal would bend or buckle as he stood on it.

He pushed at the small piece of gypsum board, sliding it to the side and setting it on the adjacent rafters. Warm air bled from the space above the ceiling, in spite of the exhaust fan.

Effortlessly, Lucas put his hands on either side of the space, grabbed the tops of the two-by-six framing with his fingers, and boosted himself up through the hole like a gymnast. His head and chest inside the hole now, he moved his hands to adjacent rafters to get a better purchase, then scrambled onto the ceiling. He pushed the chunk of cut board back into place and crouched on top of the rafters for a few minutes, catching his breath and listening for movement below.

None came.

It was even darker up here—just some angled slats of light from the grille of the exhaust fan at the end of the garage—so he slipped off his backpack and found his flashlight, then flicked it on and let the beam explore the space where he now stood.

The garage ceiling wasn't insulated—only the framing covered by the gypsum boards. In spite of this, he saw mice droppings dotting the rafters and heard a mouse scurrying several feet away. Saul had a bit of a rodent problem.

The thought made Lucas smile, for some reason.

Over in the corner, he noticed that the exhaust fan was spinning slowly from a slight breeze; it wasn't even turned on, which was why the top of the garage was holding in so much heat. It felt like a steam tunnel in here, which was oddly comforting to him. He'd always liked steam tunnels.

To his right, the garage was attached to the house. It had obviously been built sometime after the house, as he could see some of the home's exterior trim above the ceiling line. But, just as he'd hoped, the rafters and joists of the garage were attached to the framework of the house. From here, above the ceiling, he could simply walk across the garage and into Saul's home.

He went onto the joists of the home, being careful to step only on the two-by-six framing; if he made a mistake and stepped down into the spaces between the boards, he'd probably fall through the ceiling of Saul's home—a major surprise for both of them.

Above the home, the ceiling was padded with spun fiberglass insulation, which made it easier for him to find what he was looking for: another trapdoor leading to the home's interior.

He was making his way to the trapdoor when he felt and heard a door open and then shut somewhere below; the compression caused by the door's movement created a suction effect up in the rafters, moving air past his face.

He paused, listening. Another door opening, this one a car. Finally, a loud rumble started, and he immediately recognized it as the electric garage door.

He smiled. Good timing on Saul's part. Or bad timing, depending on your view.

The car started and backed out, then the garage door rumbled back into place again. Lucas remained still, listening, waiting. He had no way of knowing if other people were inside the home. Saul didn't exactly seem like the wife-and-2.3-kids type, but then, he didn't seem like the historic-cottage type either.

He could probably go back through the garage ceiling now, enter the home through the door between the garage and the main house. But it still felt better to be up here; he'd check to make sure no one else was in the home before dropping through the ceiling.

Satisfied it was safe to proceed, Lucas went to the small square of gypsum board that accessed the home underneath. He felt the edge of the board with his fingers, lifting it out of its place and putting it to the side. Below was a hallway with honey-colored wood floors.

Lucas stuck his head through the opening, surveying the hall, listening for other sounds. Nothing, save for the heavy tick of an old-fashioned pendulum clock somewhere out of sight. He couldn't see it, but he recognized the sound immediately; an image of a tall clock with glass doors, weights you pulled down each day to keep the clock running—

Where had that come from? Had he ever actually seen such a clock? Not that he could remember. So why was he getting that mental picture?

No matter. Satisfied that the interior of the house was empty, he pulled out his nylon rope and knotted one end of it over a ceiling joist. He wrapped the rope around his forearm, then dropped down through the hole and into the home.

The home smelled warm, inviting. Saul had obviously cooked himself some breakfast recently, and the smell of it still clung in the air. Sausage or bacon, maybe.

Lucas went down the hallway, looking at some photos that had been mounted on the wall—old black-and-white photos, including one of a balding man, grin stretching across his whole face, with an arm draped around the shoulders of a woman who wore her hair pulled back into a severe bun. The woman was smiling as well, but seemed somehow embarrassed, as if someone had just told an inappropriate joke, and she was staring down at the ground in front of her.

A happy moment, a totem that drew him immediately. Yes, this would make a nice totem.

The end of the hall opened into a sitting room, and the old-fashioned clock he had heard was against the wall in the corner. Its face was engraved with scrollwork and Roman numerals, and the clock's cabinet was made of dark stained wood, buffed to a sheen in places by its many years of service.

It wasn't exactly the clock he'd pictured, but it was close—close enough to make him stand there, staring at the brass pendulum swinging back and forth for a few moments, comforted by its reassuring arc.

Yes, this clock—well, not *this* clock, but one very much like it—brought back . . . something. He wasn't quite sure what it was, but it bobbed at the surface of his consciousness, begging to be remembered.

Tearing himself away from the clock in the sitting room, Lucas made his way to the kitchen and looked around. An old teapot, bright red, sat on the stove. Knickknacks and antiques adorned the shelves on the walls. Nothing interesting there.

He had turned to go back to the sitting room when he heard something that stopped him dead: a key going into the front door, just ten feet away from him past a small coat closet. There was a curtain across the glass pane on the front door, but Lucas could see a man's head outlined behind the curtain, struggling with the key.

He'd have no time to get back to his nylon rope and his escape route through the ceiling. Time to improvise. As he heard the bolt turning inside the lock, he stepped toward the door and into the space behind it; a fraction of a second later, the door opened and swung inward and toward him, creating a small pocket where he now hid. The figure made no effort to close the door behind him, instead hurrying toward the interior of the home. Footsteps made their way across the hardwood floors, and Lucas immediately recognized the gait of Saul himself. He could tell the man was muttering, saying something to himself as he moved through the home.

Saul disappeared for a few moments, then reappeared. He had his head down and was going back toward the front door when he stopped. He changed directions, and Lucas peeked, watching as Saul went to the ancient pendulum clock on the wall; he opened the glass doors on the front and pulled the weights on the chains, which would allow the pendulum to keep moving and the clock to keep running. Saul took a last look at the clock, nodded, and turned toward the door again.

Lucas pressed himself against the wall, feeling the door get pulled away as it closed. Saul twisted the key to relock the door and moved away from the house. Moving his head and peeking out of the curtain on the door, Lucas saw the man go back to his blue sedan, which sat haphazardly in the driveway with the driver's door still hanging open. Once inside, he backed the car out of the driveway and then pointed it west, chirping the tires a bit as he wheeled onto the street.

Lucas relaxed, realizing he'd been holding his breath for the last several seconds. Close call.

Okay, so Saul had obviously forgotten something at the house and came back to retrieve it before going to . . . wherever he was going. In the process, Lucas had nearly been caught.

This was one reason why he didn't ever creep into people's homes: too many variables. You never knew when someone was going to change plans or show up unannounced.

And yet, the thrill of it was coursing through his veins now. He had to admit, this was much more interesting than scanning the desks of secretarial pools. Much more dangerous.

After a few moments, Lucas tried to retrace Saul's steps. He hadn't seen where the man went, so he had no way of knowing for sure. However, Saul hadn't seen the nylon rope or open hole in the ceiling of the hallway, so he was pretty sure the man hadn't gone down his hallway. Good thing. Really, that only left the sitting area.

He'd been able to see Saul at the pendulum clock, but not in the rest of the sitting area. What had he returned to retrieve? Could be something as simple as a wallet, he supposed.

First things first. What if Saul came back a second time? After all, if you forget one thing, it's just as likely you'll forget something else.

Lucas went to the front door, found a vase holding some reeds sitting by the door. He pulled them in front of the door, so the door opening would hit the vase and topple it. If Saul came back, he'd knock over the vase, curse as he uprighted it and cleaned the mess, wondering how the vase had got behind the door. But he would dismiss it, thinking he had knocked over the vase when he left or something similar. Lucas knew this; it was the way people naturally thought. Part of looking but not seeing. Part of hearing but not feeling.

In the meantime, that would give Lucas enough time to make his way up the nylon rope and back into the ceiling. If Saul used the garage instead, he knew the electric door opening would give him plenty of time to escape.

He turned away from the front door, went back through the sitting room and down the hallway. In the hall there were three doors, all of them closed. The first was a bathroom, the second a bedroom, the third a guest room/home office. He smiled as he stared at the desk and file cabinet in the office. This was where he would start.

First he went to the file cabinet and opened the top drawer. Four or five years of income tax returns, some owner's manuals for various equipment, a file for warranties, and another filled with bank statements. He checked the front page of the first tax return, filled out for a Saul Slater. Lucas paused; so Saul really *was* his name. Go figure. Saul's occupation was listed as a federal agent for the United States government. That wasn't much help.

Lucas pulled out the tax file and checked the declared income, then compared it to what he found in the banking folder. Nothing looked suspicious, until he got to the back of the banking. In the past couple of months, Saul Slater had opened a Swiss account and made deposits totaling something more than $200,000. Lucas doubted those figures would show up on this year's tax return.

The second drawer held nothing of interest. Health club memberships, some medical records, various insurance policies. The desk held nothing he wanted, either, so he backed out of the room and went to Saul's bedroom. Something in his gut told him he was looking for something well hidden, something Saul wouldn't just leave out in the open. What it was, he didn't know. But he felt there was something in here. Still, after searching Saul's closet, dressers, and bed, checking for false bottoms and other hiding spots, he came up empty.

The banking files were there, suggesting Saul wasn't just your friendly patriotic secret agent, but that's all he had.

Disappointed, Lucas went back to the sitting room, sank into the easy chair with a deep sigh. He knew he should be cleaning up, moving things back where they were, getting out of the house—Saul could be back again any time—but he needed to think. He didn't want to leave the house without . . . something tangible. If he hadn't seen the bank records, he wouldn't be suspicious. Well, wouldn't be *as* suspicious, anyway. But something smelled fishy, and he needed to find the fish before he left.

A sudden whirring sound startled him, and he leapt to his feet, only to realize it was the giant wall clock across the room from him. It was the top of the hour, and a small mechanical bird came out of its perch behind a small door, tilting its head and chirping. After ten chirps, it retreated, and the small door shut behind it.

Lucas smiled. A cuckoo clock. That's what it was called. Had he seen a cuckoo clock? Once again, his gut told him yes, he had been around one of these things before. But he couldn't say when. It was something that existed in the Dark Years—the years before the orphanage, when he knew nothing about himself.

Still standing, he walked slowly across the floor and approached the clock, much like a bomb technician approaching a suspicious package. This was a powerful totem, he knew, a very powerful personal totem, and he didn't even know why.

Standing in front of the clock, he watched the large pendulum swing back and forth a few times, creating giant arcs in the air. The heavy *tick-tick-tick* of the clock was louder than ever, and he could hear gears and movements spinning inside the cabinet.

He touched the face of the clock, running his fingers over the surface. Then he moved to the glass over the giant pendulum, and finally to the closed wooden cabinet making up the base of the clock. He half expected the cabinet to be locked, but its dark walnut door opened easily for him. Nothing inside to see, but he felt around with his hands, knocking on the surfaces, and in a few moments he found a small lever at the very back of the space. When he pressed the lever, the side of the cabinet folded out, holding a sheath of papers.

His trembling fingers touched the papers, then grasped them and brought them out. He pulled open a seal on the sheath and examined the papers inside.

Lucas knew immediately that he was looking at dark secrets, secrets that could get him killed. The first several sheets were printed with vertical characters he faintly recognized: Japanese writing, or Chinese maybe.

Below these thin onionskin papers, he found a printout of an Excel file: names and addresses of several people—at least a couple dozen in all. Next, a stack of half a dozen photos. Surveillance photos, obviously, of several people he didn't recognize.

And a few he did recognize, from his Creep Club meeting. One in particular: Snake, the founder.

Okay, that shouldn't be too surprising. Saul had said, after all, that he was tracking the Creep Club, trying to break into their midst.

Next were a couple of compact discs in cases, and finally, several sheets of correspondence. He glanced at the notes and printouts of e-mails back and forth between someone identified as Native Son and another identified as Beast from the East. A quick glance at the correspondence told him it was setting up a series of meetings, drop-offs, exchanges.

Lucas thought of the bench near the Lincoln Memorial. Had Saul met this contact there the day before? He thought it was a good bet.

Lucas kept scanning the documents, his mind taking in the information and storing it. One word in particular caught his attention and begged for further consideration: *Guoanbu.*

Lucas put down the files, then swung around his backpack and dug around in it for a few moments. He came out with a small digital camera and began snapping images of the papers and photos. He didn't need the images for himself; his photographic memory was filing away information as he looked through the folder. But he thought he might need to show the images to someone else.

The more Lucas studied the documents he held, the more he became convinced Saul was, indeed, working for a secret government agency.

But he was also convinced it wasn't a government agency of the United States.

Lucas put everything back in the sheath, refastened the seal, and set it all back in the secret compartment. Part of him wanted to take the compact discs, but that would certainly alert Saul that someone had been in his secret stash.

That done, Lucas replaced the vase beside the front door, then combed through the house again, making sure everything was exactly as it had been when he entered. Finally, he climbed his nylon rope through the ceiling, one word flashing in his mind again and again.

Guoanbu.

FOURTEEN

BACK AT THE LIVEWIRE, HE PUNCHED INTO THE CREEP CLUB HOME PAGE again. Donavan's username and password were deleted from the system, which meant Lucas was now locked out.

It also meant he had no way of tracking the movements of the club; he had no idea where or when its next meeting would be, unless he made it back over to Donavan's house and trailed him. Something he'd have to try, just as soon as he did a bit of research.

He picked up the latte he'd ordered, took a sip, and typed *Guoanbu* into the Google search engine. Immediately several hits confirmed what he'd been thinking: Guoanbu was the intelligence agency for the Chinese government.

He sighed, setting down his cup. Saul was a double agent for the Chinese government. Lucas wasn't a hundred percent certain what that meant, but he knew it was big. He also knew that meant he couldn't work with Saul.

Or could he? Maybe his best bet was to be a double agent himself; work with Saul and pretend to be infiltrating Creep Club, but instead feed information to . . . to whom, exactly?

He didn't know.

Lucas felt his nerves getting jittery, and he knew it had nothing to do with the caffeine. For so many years now he'd cultivated his anonymity, made himself invisible, lived between the seams of society. He'd lived happily, comfortably, with his manufactured histories for the people he watched, his mementos snatched from offices.

He'd been alone, just him with his own thoughts, his own creations. Comfortably cocooned inside his shell.

But now, all of the events of the last few days had pulled him into the blinding light. He felt like exposed prey, waiting for death to come swooping down and clutch him in its razor-sharp talons.

He was no longer in control of his world.

Even worse, he wasn't sure who was.

Okay, it was time to make a plan. He closed the browser window on The LiveWire's computer, flushed the cache, and reset the app to erase its history. No sense leaving more tracks.

He picked up his cup and went to the door, making eye contact with no one else in the café.

He'd swing by Donavan's apartment before returning to his current hideout. That was the next step, the only step he could take right now. He wanted to leave it all behind—just head out on the highway, catch a ride headed west, and set up again in a new city, because he really didn't know what he was doing here in the District anyway. That was the logical thing, the sensible thing, the Lucaslike thing he had always done.

But maybe the Lucaslike thing wasn't what he *should* do. So long ago, as a young boy in the orphanage, he had stared at the lights of DC, dreaming that those lights held something for him, that they would one day draw him to something important. That they would make him part of something bigger than himself.

And now, despite the odds, they had. This was a chance to belong to something bigger, something he knew was far removed from spying on people at their desks. He was part of . . . something. He knew about a double agent, someone who was most likely selling state secrets to the Chinese government. He couldn't just walk away from that.

He had to walk into it.

He arrived back at Donavan's apartment in the late afternoon, taking half an hour to watch for movement or activity before approaching the door. He knocked and, when no answer came, looked for the key in its usual hiding spot. He was surprised to find it still there. He wasn't sure that was a good sign.

Inside, Donavan's apartment was the same as it had been the last few days. Same laundry, same dirty dishes, and now a slightly putrid smell—maybe something going bad in the refrigerator—hung in the air.

This made Lucas's stomach do a slow revolution, because it meant his last hope of a link to the Creep Club had gone into deep hiding. He shouldn't be surprised, really; after all, he himself had recently done the same thing. When your home turf is compromised, you move, leave everything behind. That's exactly what Donavan had done. Maybe even before Lucas had entered the picture. In retrospect, Donavan was just a pawn to get him into this game, wasn't he?

Maybe Donavan's "apartment" wasn't even really his apartment, but just part of the game.

Still, as he rode the Metro back to his fourth-floor apartment in the late afternoon, Lucas knew he was getting pushed out of this giant chess match before he'd even had a chance to plot a few moves. With Donavan missing, Lucas's connections were gone. With his connections gone, he had no way to string along Saul.

He needed to think, so he retreated to the hidden closet inside the bathroom at Dandy Don's Donuts. This late in the day, few customers were there. So he sat, staring at empty tables through his peephole, considering his options, trying to work his angles.

If he could somehow find the next meeting of the Creep Club, maybe . . . maybe he could present his evidence against Saul. But without Donavan, he was unmoored.

Maybe Saul had ears to the ground, people who could tell him when and where the next meeting was going to take place. Use Saul to get information, then turn it back around. Possible, but he didn't like it as his first option.

Besides, what would he do if he showed up at the next Creep Club meeting, anyway? His last one hadn't exactly been a rousing success, and he was fairly sure he wouldn't be welcomed back with open arms.

No, it would be better if he were at the meeting, but not part of it. If he could find the meeting and creep into it, he could get a better idea what they were discussing, and get a handle on Donavan again. Follow his movements.

If only he had a way to hook back into —

He smiled as his mind made a connection. There *was* a way back into the Creep Club.

He accessed his memory banks, replaying the video Dilbert had presented at the last meeting. The title cards for the video rolled by. First: SYMPHONY IN VIOLENCE. Then: *Music by Johann Strauss*. And finally: *Subjects: Kleiderman and Leila Delgado, 4815 Suncrest, Alexandria, VA.*

Dilbert had said he was still collecting video, adding to his work-in-progress.

Lucas had an address; if he visited Kleiderman and Leila Delgado's home, he was sure he'd find Dilbert.

And once he found Dilbert, he'd find his way back into the Creep Club.

THE DELGADO HOME WAS A LARGE, CAPE COD-STYLE HOUSE OF TAN AND cream tones in a well-to-do neighborhood. A mere facade for the things that happened inside the home, Lucas knew; images of Dilbert's hideous film floated back to him again.

Stereotypically, when you thought of domestic abuse, you thought of poor people in trailer homes, drunk men who lashed out at their families in impotent rage.

But this was more like Green Acres.

Lucas wasn't interested in the couple right now; in fact, he stayed away from the house entirely. Instead, he set up inside a garden shed in the backyard, squeezing in between the lawnmower and some other gardening implements that obviously never saw any use. In a neighborhood such as this one, you didn't mow the yard. You had a lawn service.

Inside the storage shed, Lucas curled into a ball and waited for night to fall. While he waited, he retrieved his spotting scope and cased the exterior of the home, looking for signs of Dilbert's presence.

He gasped a bit when he saw it: the familiar CC symbol—two uppercase letters, turned on their sides to resemble mountains—scratched under a water spigot near a basement window. Evidently the Creep Club members loved to leave their calling cards at every building or home they visited.

After seeing it at the Stranahan Building, Lucas realized he'd seen the symbol on several buildings around the DC area; he'd always written it off as just one more bit of graffiti left by a casual infiltrator, but now he realized the symbol was so much more than that. It was a sign to others within the Creep Club, a way of marking territory.

Lucas shivered, put the spotting scope away, sat down, and tried to relax while he waited for night to fall. Something inside told him Dilbert wouldn't show up until it was dark outside.

He pulled his jacket tighter around him and put his backpack over the front of him like a makeshift blanket, surprised at how chilly it was; the last several days it had been warmer than usual, but now the whole DC area was in the midst of a cold snap. In August. Go figure.

The astringent smell of gasoline from the mower, mixed with the earthy smell of grass clippings, made him light-headed. All in all, probably not the best place to spend a few hours waiting. But it was the safest.

He pulled his knees up toward his chest and rested his chin on his knees. Within a few minutes his mind was retreating to the past, to times he hadn't visited in so long.

The orphanage. The far-off lights of the city.

After several minutes, darkness fell, and Lucas saw lights inside the home flicker on. He moved, still peering through the tiny crack between the shed doors, but saw no activity in the basement beside the—

Wait. He saw shadows shifting, very subtly. He smiled, knowing instantly that it was Dilbert. He had no reason to know this, and yet he knew it anyway.

His smile was interrupted by something shattering inside the home, followed by a long scream.

Lucas felt his throat dry instantly. This was precisely why he had holed up in the garden shed; he knew things would happen inside that house he wanted to avoid. He remembered the images from Dilbert's presentation, and he had no desire to see them acted out live and in person.

So he had chosen this garden shed, where he could wait for a sign from Dilbert, then follow him unobtrusively, tail him until the next Creep Club meeting.

But the scream changed everything. How could he sit here and do nothing, knowing what was probably happening inside right now? For that matter, how could he tell himself the main reason he was here was to find Dilbert? He had sought out this shed, away from the house, in an attempt to smother what he knew he must do.

But the scream made it all crystal clear again. He was here first to help the woman inside that house. And second, if he got lucky, to figure out some way to tail Dilbert.

It might mean throwing away his chance at reconnecting with the Creep Club, but Lucas had to act. His body knew it before his mind did, because he was already opening the shed doors and moving quickly across the manicured lawn before he finished the argument raging inside him.

He moved quickly, quietly, hoping to escape detection as he approached the house.

Avoid detection. The words stuck in his mind for a few moments, and he suddenly had a plan.

A security system.

A house like this had to have one. True, it wouldn't be armed right now with people inside the house, but he could change that. He knew his way around security systems, and he knew one of the quickest ways to trip one was to bust off the access panel hiding the electrical system—usually on the exterior of the house.

He crept around the house, careful to stay away from the basement window where he'd seen the shadow of Dilbert. Nothing on the north side.

The scream had ended at least thirty seconds ago, and since then, he'd heard nothing. Nothing but an odd, unnatural silence settling over him. Which was more terrifying than the scream. Lucas tried to shrug off a shiver as he moved to the west side of the house. And there he found what he was looking for: a black panel, recessed in the siding of the west side, a giant SooperSentry sticker on its surface.

Lucas ran to the panel and pulled on its cover, breaking its hinges. Immediately a high, piercing alarm sounded throughout the house.

Still no other sounds, though. No screams. No sobbing, No anything. Lucas crouched down beside the home, closing his eyes for a few seconds as the alarm pumped its shriek into the still air. What about the neighbors? These were larger lots than average, but surely the neighbors had to hear what happened here. The screams, the . . . whatever. Didn't anyone ever try to help?

They look but don't see. They hear but don't feel.

Lucas was still crouched down in the darkness of the home's shadows; no security lighting on this side of the home, oddly enough. He glanced at the home across the street, saw the pulled drape in the front room moving slightly, then falling back into place.

He shook his head. Even out here, even among the so-called normal people, the rules were still the same. How stupid of him to think people were different anywhere. The folks in this neighborhood looked, occasionally. Opened their drapes, whispered to each other over the fences. But they never saw. They didn't want to. Because seeing would mean . . . they'd have to do something.

The alarm abruptly stopped. That would mean the alarm company had called to ask the residents if everything was okay before alerting the police. He had no doubt that the person who answered the phone had told them everything was fine, even given them the right code word; after all, he was Kleiderman Delgado, the home's owner. But to answer the phone, to give that code word, he'd been forced to stop . . . whatever he'd been doing.

And that was a good place to start.

The unsettling silence continued. No screaming, no dishes being thrown, no chaos of any kind. Lucas thought back to the video Dilbert had presented; silence was something definitely out of place at this home.

Almost as if on cue, he heard a muffled moan, and then something falling. Or someone. A door slammed.

Decision time. If he was going to do anything else now, he'd need to reveal himself to Dilbert, and probably blow his chance at finding the next Creep Club meeting. Once he showed his face, he knew Dilbert would leave immediately, probably abandon this whole home as a project. That was, after all, what he himself would do in the same situation.

But that was fine. It was horrible enough to know this kind of thing went on inside DC homes; it was an entirely lower level to watch it and document it.

And perhaps it was worst of all to realize that a secret part of him—the Dark Vibration—wanted to do that recording. Wanted to join Dilbert in the basement.

In the end, it was an easy decision. He needed to help the woman. Leila.

But before he moved again, an idea occurred to him. He spun around his backpack, shuffled through the items until he came up with what he wanted: another GPS patch from Donavan's. Maybe he didn't have to give up Dilbert to save the woman. Maybe he could find Dilbert, somehow attach the geopatch before he fled, and help the woman.

Maybe.

Shouldering his pack in place again, Lucas crawled around the exterior of the home, moving quickly and quietly toward the basement window with the CC marking. When he got there, he tried to peer inside, but by now it was too dark. Dilbert might see him coming in through the window, but he didn't know of a good way to avoid that right now. He'd deal with that, if it came to it.

He hoped, however, that Dilbert would be too intent on capturing the scene that produced the blood-curdling scream, too caught up in his work, to watch his entrance point.

Lucas wasted no time, pulling the casement window toward him, pulling it off it hinges, then boosting himself down into the darkness of the basement. He turned, thinking he would replace the window immediately, and stopped himself.

He might need a quick escape. He'd replace the window when he left. If Dilbert noticed in the meantime, so be it.

Lucas moved carefully, making no noise as he moved across the bare concrete floor of the basement, the smell of dust and earth in his nostrils.

Still no sound. Just that eerie silence. He continued moving, going toward the small shaft of light that spilled down unfinished wooden steps from the main floor above.

His eyes were having a hard time adjusting, especially now that he'd looked into the light from above, and he faintly wished he had some night vision goggles.

His foot hit something, and he nearly tripped over it before righting himself. Something soft and yielding, not bricks or stone.

He crouched, and his hand touched what he'd feared: someone's body. Alive or dead, he couldn't be sure.

He put the geopatch back in his pocket and stood again. This was wrong, all wrong, and he needed to get out.

Then the lights came on.

FIFTEEN

"THOUGHT HE MIGHT HAVE A BUDDY WITH HIM," A VOICE SAID BEHIND Lucas.

Lucas turned around and recognized the man instantly: the face of rage he'd seen displayed on Dilbert's films. What's-his-name, the homeowner. So much for his perfect photographic memory at the moment.

A quick glance at the body on the floor confirmed it was Dilbert, which, in an odd way, brought Lucas some relief. Stumbling over it in the dark, he'd been afraid it was the woman. Leila. Obviously, Dilbert hadn't been too careful, and he'd been caught.

The man wiped at his mouth, held up a baseball bat. "You guys aren't exactly the smartest burglars in the world, setting off the alarm."

Lucas said nothing, realizing what had happened. When the alarm went off, of course the homeowner—*Kleiderman Delgado, his name*

155

was Kleiderman Delgado—decided to explore the home and check for problems. He'd gone into the basement and caught Dilbert by surprise. It made perfect sense; it was what anyone would do. How could Lucas have been so stupid? He hadn't worked in private homes much, and it was showing.

The man wiped at his mouth again, then scratched at his cheek. His eyes were bloodshot, and a deep stench—like something chemical—emanated from his pores. The stench of fear, Lucas decided. Or rage. Or both.

"I . . . just . . . let's just talk," Lucas stammered, unsure what to say. He'd been caught as a cat burglar, and there was no way out of it.

The man sniffed, scratched at his cheek again. "No time for talking now," he said. "Only time for doing." He raised his bat and moved across the floor toward Lucas.

Lucas heard a mechanical click, then saw the man look up the stairs, faltering a little. His bat came down, and he stopped.

Lucas turned to look up the stairs. There stood the woman, pointing a cocked revolver at her husband.

"Stay right there, Kleiderman," she said through clenched teeth.

The bat stayed lowered, but Kleiderman Delgado smiled at his wife now. It wasn't a pleasant smile; it was a smile that promised pain. Lucas flinched, and the smile wasn't even directed at him.

"You go get yourself cleaned up," Kleiderman said to his wife. "I've got this handled."

The woman uttered a painful laugh, holding the gun steady. "Yeah," she said. "You've got it handled, all right. You've always got it handled."

"That's right," he said, starting toward Lucas again.

"I'll blow a hole in your gut," the woman hissed, and Kleiderman stopped. For the moment.

"Right now," she said, "I've got it handled for a change." She motioned toward Lucas with the gun. "Get your friend," she said. "Drag him this way. Can you get him up the stairs?"

Lucas nodded weakly, then cleared his throat and spoke. "Yes."

Kleiderman was regaining his confidence. "Oh, you're going to shoot me now?" he said to the woman, mocking her. "I don't know where you got the gun, but you really expect me to believe it's loaded? I know you better than that."

Kleiderman started to move toward Lucas again, and the report of the revolver echoed off the concrete walls of the unfinished basement. Kleiderman's leg collapsed beneath him, useless, and he uttered a high-pitched keen, even more despairing than the one Lucas had heard earlier.

The woman cocked the pistol again, kept it aimed. "You don't know me at all, Kleiderman," she said quietly.

She looked silently to Lucas again; he nodded, then stooped and grabbed Dilbert underneath the arms. Dilbert was thin, wiry, like himself, so he wasn't very difficult to maneuver.

Lucas began dragging Dilbert up the steps, noticing a large lump forming on the unconscious man's temple. Lucas cringed; taking a hit in the temple with a baseball bat. No wonder it was lights out for him. He'd be lucky if he didn't have any brain damage.

Kleiderman, still folded on the floor in the basement, was softly crying now. "Leila," he said, pleading with her. "Why did you . . ." He let the sentence trail off as he choked down another sob. Then he spoke again, leaving a single "Why?" hanging in the air.

The stench of Kleiderman was still there, permeating the air, but as Lucas worked his way up the steps, his fear subsided. He readjusted his grip on Dilbert and thumped him up the last few stairs until he stood even with the woman on the first-floor landing. She inclined her head toward the living room behind her, then returned her attention to Kleiderman, still in the basement.

"Why did I do it?" she said, repeating the question to her husband.

Kleiderman only answered with a small whimper as he tried to move his useless leg.

"Same reason you always give me," she said, and Lucas saw tears trickling from her eyes. "Because you made me." She slammed the basement door shut and twisted the deadbolt.

She turned to the living room. Lucas was down on his knees, checking on Dilbert. He was breathing. A bit shallow, perhaps, but breathing.

"He gonna be all right?" she asked.

Lucas looked at her, stood slowly. "I . . . don't know," he said. "I hope so."

She nodded, let the gun drop to her side, her finger off the trigger now. "So," she said, her eyes taking on a glazed glint as she stared across the room at nothing. "I suppose you should call for backup."

Lucas stood very still for a few moments before speaking. Backup? What did she mean by backup? Best to give a noncommittal answer. "Let's just take a minute to catch our breath," he suggested.

She nodded, the gun still hanging loosely at her side. From the door behind her, an indecipherable scream of rage floated up the stairs. She closed her eyes, a few more tears leaking out.

"Catch our breath," she said, almost in a whisper to herself. "Good idea." She took a few deep gulps of air, forced back the tears.

"So did you get . . . what you need?" she asked.

Lucas knew he needed to step carefully here. "What we need?" he said, parroting back her question.

"Footage. Surveillance tape, I guess. That's what you call it, isn't it?"

Lucas tasted something dark and bitter at the back of his throat. "You knew he was . . . recording you?" He looked down at Dilbert's body. Still no movement.

"Sure. I saw things, here and there."

"Like what?"

"Like . . . I don't know. This guy, different areas around town, in the span of a few days. A few strange noises in the house. Found a lens cap, actually, in the basement a few weeks ago. Guess he got sloppy."

Lucas wasn't sure what to say, so he nodded.

"So," she said, continuing, "that's when I figured it out: I knew the police were watching the house. Recording. Keeping it under surveillance. A stakeout."

The dark, bitter taste in Lucas's throat coiled like a snake. Here was someone who saw—who didn't just look, but who *saw*—what was happening around her. And yet she still needed to delude herself on some level. It was much more comforting to think of the police doing all this, because . . . because it was a way out.

Lucas started to speak, but his voice wouldn't work for a few moments. He swallowed hard and tried again. "So . . . you let him continue to beat you because—"

"I didn't *let* him do anything," she said, mad now. She crossed the room and sat on the couch, set the gun on the coffee table. "You don't really *let* anything in life happen to you. It doesn't ask your permission, it just happens. And so . . . yeah, I thought, the police are getting this on video, and so they'll build a case, and they'll do something." She stopped and looked straight at him for the first time. "That's right, isn't it? I mean, you're here to stop him?"

Lucas tried a smile, but he knew it was only coming off as a grimace. "Yes."

She nodded, staring down at the floor again. "So tonight, when you tripped the alarm, I knew it was time. I knew you guys had the place surrounded, and you'd come rushing in to help when that alarm went off. But then . . ." She trailed off, looking at the floor for a few seconds before lifting her gaze to him again.

"No one else is coming, are they?" she asked softly.

"No."

"And . . . you're not a cop."

He paused. "No."

She nodded at Dilbert. "Him neither."

He shook his head.

"So what are you?"

Now it was Lucas's turn to stare at the floor. "Still trying to figure that one out, I guess."

She was quiet for a few moments before speaking again. "He's been here. But you—this is your first time," she said.

"What makes you say that?"

"You're the one who set off the alarm."

He nodded.

"Why?"

Lucas shrugged. "Because . . . because I knew you were in here, and I knew . . . he was in here. I heard you scream."

She bit her lip, sat back on the couch. "Well," she said softly again. "At least there's that. At least there's that."

Lucas crouched back down again, hovering over Dilbert's motionless body. He dug around in Dilbert's trench coat pockets, finally finding what he was looking for: a few small digital tapes. He pulled them out of Dilbert's pocket, stood, and walked across the room, then set the tapes on the table in front of Leila.

"And there are these too," he said.

She looked at him, tears leaking from the corners of her eyes. "Do I want to watch these?"

"I don't think so," he said. "But I'm guessing the police, when they get here, might want to."

She nodded. "So I guess that's your way of saying I should call them now."

A low moan escaped from Dilbert's lips, and Lucas went to him, helped him sit up. Dilbert's eyes opened, but they were still wide, dilated. His hand went absently to the large knot on his head, his stare vacant.

"You feeling okay?" Lucas asked him, but he said nothing. Instead, he put his head back down on the floor and closed his eyes again, going immobile.

Lucas looked back to Leila, who was studying both of them. "You should get him to a hospital," she said.

Lucas nodded.

"But I'm somehow sure you don't want me to call an ambulance or the police until you're gone," she continued.

He set his jaw for a moment. "You need to call both, for your husband. But I don't want to be here when they show up."

From behind the locked door to the basement, they had initially heard Kleiderman's screams of rage. Now those screams had become occasional whimpers and crying. Each time a fresh bout began, Lucas saw Leila flinch.

"Maybe someone already called," Lucas said. "Maybe they're on their way. Neighbors."

She smiled grimly. "I've been in this home more than a year. Lots of times I've been scared to death the neighbors would call the police because of . . ." She let the sentence trail off, dropped her gaze to the floor. "No one's ever called," she whispered.

"Maybe they couldn't hear," Lucas offered. "Lots of plants around this house, it's on a big lot."

She studied him for a moment. "Maybe."

But neither of them believed it.

"Anyway," she continued, "most of tonight happened in the basement. The gunshot, I mean. And I think this house is pretty soundproof."

Lucas thought of the bloodcurdling scream—her scream—that had brought him running from the garden shed. The house was far from soundproof, but he said nothing. If that was what she needed to tell herself, he wasn't going to stop her.

She took a deep breath. "Anyway," she said, standing and walking toward the kitchen, "we need to get you two out of here."

He stood, leaving his spot beside Dilbert. "How?"

She disappeared into the kitchen for a few moments, then returned with keys and threw them to him. "Take my car," she said.

He looked at the keys, then back to her.

"It's the white Volvo in the garage," she said. "There's a hospital about ten minutes away. There's a GPS system in the dash, which should help you get there."

He looked again at the keys, as if they were some kind of foreign object that had just dropped from the sky. "But—"

"But nothing. Just do it." She brushed a lock of hair back from her face.

"But . . . the police will probably question the neighbors," he said. "Ask if they saw anything. Surely someone's going to say they saw a white car leaving the house."

She shrugged. "Maybe. But we both already know how attentive the neighbors are."

"At the very least, the police will ask where your car is."

"I'll tell them I left it there the last time I was at the hospital. That a friend picked me up."

"But they'll have access to the security cameras at the hospital, and—"

He saw a bit of anger bubble to the surface. "You think maybe, I show them this, they won't wonder why my car is at the hospital?" She lifted her shirt, revealing a network of purple and yellow bruises. "You think I don't know how to come up with lies to cover what's really happening?"

He nodded. "Okay. I'm sorry."

"I know you're wondering how it happened," she said. "How? Why? Because I loved him, once upon a time. Because I didn't want to admit I'd made a mistake. Because I tried, talked to people at the hospital, even had a few visits from the police. When your husband

is a diplomat, these things can be covered. But see, you don't understand my life. Who I am, where I come from."

She gestured to the basement door; behind it, her husband was
quiet now. "Him, for instance. Tell me you haven't looked at his
name and thought, what kind of name is Kleiderman? He's Hispanic,
he should be Jorge or Roberto or something. But you'd know, you'd
understand, if you were Venezuelan. Strange names, they're a badge
of honor. And so, for us, Kleiderman isn't strange at all; it's normal.
Down in Venezuela, you'll find many men named Kleiderman."

She looked at him hard, pausing to catch her breath. "Like you.
Someone who breaks into homes and videotapes people. To me, it's
strange. It's scary. But to you, it's probably normal."

He looked at her a moment, smiled. "No," he said. "There's nothing normal about it."

He crouched down beside Dilbert once more. When he touched
the man, his eyes opened again. The pupils looked a little better,
Lucas thought, but they still didn't register any recognition.

He coaxed Dilbert to a standing position, keeping the man's arm
draped around his shoulders as he worked his way over to the door
of the garage. After getting the door open, he glanced back at Leila
again. She was on the phone, speaking softly.

After getting Dilbert folded into the front seat of the car, he
returned. She met him at the door.

"Better get going," she said. "Police will probably be here in a few
minutes."

He nodded. "What are you going to tell them?"

She pulled a digital tape from her pocket. "I'll start by showing
them this," she said. "Tell them I set up some cameras around the

house. Then, tonight, he found the cameras and went psycho. Started ranting about some intruders in the house, grabbed a baseball bat and came after me. I knew he had snapped, and I knew he was going to kill me, so Annie Oakley got her gun and shot him down."

"Then locked him in the basement."

"He was already in the basement," she said. "That's how he discovered the cameras. If you had some psycho with a baseball bat in your basement, wouldn't you lock the door?"

Lucas nodded. "Okay."

She reached for a button on the wall of the garage and pushed it. The door behind the Volvo began to rise into the ceiling.

He held out his hand, offering a handshake. "Thanks," he said.

She stared at him a few moments, then, surprisingly, stepped forward and wrapped her arms around him, hugging him in a tight embrace. He stiffened, but then relaxed as he felt her sobbing.

"Thank you," she said in a hoarse whisper. "For doing what no one else would. Even me."

She broke the embrace, then held his head in her hands and stared straight into his eyes as tears continued to pour from hers. "Thank you for seeing," she said.

SIXTEEN

ON THE DRIVE TO THE HOSPITAL, SOMETHING LEILA HAD SAID KEPT replaying in his mind: *When your husband is a diplomat . . .* it seemed important somehow, but he couldn't quite figure out why. Yet.

He turned to look at Dilbert as they turned into the hospital parking lot. Dilbert was conscious and alert, but had said nothing. He'd only stared at the road in front of them, with an occasional glance at Lucas.

"Want me to drop you off at the emergency entrance?" Lucas asked. As he said this, a light mist of rain began to fall on the car, creating a steady white noise to fill the silence following his question.

Finally Dilbert spoke. "You followed me."

Lucas paused. "Yes."

"Why?" Dilbert was staring at the hospital lights, a liquid smear through the windshield of the Volvo.

Lucas sighed. "I want you to take me to the next Creep Club meeting. I know the location's changed, but I don't know where." There. He'd said it. No harm in being truthful.

Dilbert shook his head slowly. "You set off an alarm on my turf, almost get me killed, cost me a ton of equipment, and now you want me to take you to the next meeting."

Lucas ran his hand through his hair, sighed. "Yeah," he said. "That's pretty much it." He'd already committed to the straight-ahead approach with all this; might as well stick with it for the time being.

Dilbert chuckled softly until it turned into a cough. He cleared his throat. "No way I'm bringing you back to the Creep Club." He turned to face Lucas. "I never woulda brought you in the first place."

Lucas waited a few moments. "I could just stay here, follow you when you leave," he said.

"You could try," Dilbert said. "Think I haven't thought of that already? Think I won't have some way of getting out of here unseen?"

Lucas doubted Dilbert could really shake him, but no harm in letting Dilbert have a little overbearing pride in his abilities. It could work to his advantage. "That's why I asked you to take me."

"And now you have my answer." Dilbert opened his car door and stepped out into the rain. He was starting to swing the door shut when Lucas spoke again.

"You didn't lose all your equipment."

Dilbert stopped the car door, looked back inside. "What?"

Lucas held out his hand, and Dilbert looked at the object in it for a moment. "My mini camcorder," he said.

"I knew you'd want it," Lucas said.

Dilbert looked at him for a few moments, then reached in and snatched the camcorder from his hand before closing the car door and walking to the emergency room entrance.

Lucas watched as the car's interior lights dimmed and winked out. He put the keys to the car in the glove box, opened the door, and stepped into the rain himself. Its staccato pattern on the pavement comforted him as he began to walk.

Yes, he knew Dilbert would be very interested in taking his camcorder.

Which was why he'd attached a geopatch inside the camcorder's battery compartment.

LATE THAT NIGHT, IN HIS FOURTH-FLOOR COCOON, LUCAS SLEPT. AND dreamed.

He walked beside a running stream. No, not a stream, but a river: a large, deep ribbon of blue that gurgled over rocks and boulders to his left.

He was on a trail, a dusty path winding among tall pines, the scent of their needles bright and heavy in his nostrils.

At first, it was just him. But then, on the path ahead of him, he saw a couple. A man and a woman, their backs turned to him as they walked along hand in hand. He called out to them, but they didn't hear, even though the only sound in the air was the wind whispering through the pine boughs overhead.

He started to run, understanding in some way that it was very important to reach these people, to get their attention.

Ahead of him, they approached a concrete bridge that spanned a stream joining the large river. They walked onto the concrete path, barely pausing, oblivious to his shouts.

Seconds later, he was on the concrete pathway behind them, but they seemed no closer. They were only a few feet away, yes, but they refused to turn and acknowledge his cries. He stopped, winded by his running, and studied the small stream. Just before it reached the main river, it spread out into a large pool. Inside the pool, large bubbles rose to the surface.

Springs, his mind told him. These were springs, and they were beautiful. He stared deep into the bubbling water, imagining himself captured inside one of those bubbles, carried through the atmosphere of this earth to a place beyond. A place where he could breathe and laugh and live.

He turned again to look at the people walking on the path ahead of him. They hadn't stopped the entire time he stared into the gurgling springs, yet they were no farther away.

That's what these people were. His chance to escape this world. He began to run again, screaming at them to stop, feeling tears beginning to curl down his cheeks.

And this time, he did move closer. He ran, and he stretched out his right arm, impossibly long, reaching for the woman, now so close he could smell her perfume *(wildflowers and oranges, wildflowers and oranges)*, and his finger brushed the back of her shirt.

At the instant his finger made contact, he felt something snap deep inside, like a cord stretched too taut, and he fell to his knees along the path. Water to his left, water to his right, and he on this small, concrete wall in between.

Like Humpty Dumpty. On a wall.

He tried to scream at the couple again, but they were farther away than ever, still deaf to his cries.

And now, even the sound of his own voice was overpowered by the sound of something new: cracking. Stones, he thought, stones crumbling and breaking apart as if pounded by an earthquake. On his hands and knees in the middle of the path, he looked at his fingers splayed out before him and saw crumbling dust. The pathway was breaking up beneath him, turning to dust—

No, he realized with sudden horror. It wasn't the pathway breaking at all. It was his body. He held up his left hand, saw a jagged crack of darkness move from his wrist to his forefinger, followed by a spiderweb of smaller fractures.

Pieces of his hand fell away, crumbling into tiny fragments, scattered into the nearby river by the soft breeze.

His mouth opened to form a scream, to demand an end to this impossibility, but there was no mouth to scream, only his mind falling, falling toward the water and—

Lucas awoke, his face bathed in sweat. After a few moments of dizziness and disorientation, he realized he was in his fourth-floor home above Dandy Don's Donuts. But for a few moments, for a few brief moments after waking, he was a shattered chunk of concrete, sinking into the swirling water.

He sat up, the images of the dream continuing to blaze in his mind. He hadn't had that dream for so long. Years. The dream that always ended with one mournful thought as he sank into the river's depths:

(Humpty Dumpty had some great falls.)

THE NEXT MORNING, LUCAS KNEW HE NEEDED TO REGAIN HIS FOOTING. He'd been knocked off his game, his familiarity, by the previous night at the Delgado house. And today he had two main threads to follow up: track Dilbert and make contact with Saul.

Not necessarily in that order.

But first, he needed to clear his mind of the thoughts pushing their way in. Even the dream that had once haunted him had returned. He shuddered just thinking about it and made himself look at his left hand.

No cracks or fractures.

Nestled inside his perch from the utility closet, he stared out into the sitting area at Dandy Don's Donuts. This was a Sunday morning, and he knew it would be packed. Lots of people getting boxes of a dozen donuts to take home for a lazy morning, others settling in at the tables for a quick old-fashioned doughnut and a look at the Sunday morning paper.

Lucas closed his eyes for a second, consciously cleared his mind, took a deep breath. He was here now to . . . to leave all that other stuff behind. Or at least put it away for a while.

Over in the corner of the seating area, he watched two young children, a boy and a girl both under age five or so, using the chairs as makeshift monkey bars while their mother immersed herself in a story from the newspaper.

The family had just come from church, he decided, based on their clothing. The young boy wore a shirt and a messily knotted tie that clutched at his neck; the young girl was in a yellow dress and tights.

The mother was named Teresa. Mother Teresa. He smiled at the thought.

Teresa worked at a lobbying firm in DC. A firm that lobbied on behalf of oil companies. She was married, and her husband was on the staff of a congressional representative for a western state.

He thought for a moment.

Wyoming, it would be Wyoming.

The husband, whose name was Brandon, was a typical small-town Wyoming boy. Had surprised everyone in his hometown by taking an interest in politics while going to college at the University of Wyoming. Had surprised them even more by getting on staff for a representative, then meeting Teresa and falling in love while working in DC.

And yet, whenever they went back to Wyoming, whenever they visited, they were treated like stars. Everyone loved to see them in small-town Wyoming, and Mother Teresa was something of a celebrity when they were in town.

Teresa took a sip of coffee, turning a page of the newspaper.

On the other hand, Teresa was torn. In college, she had been active in progressive politics, taken part in a couple of marches on the Mall, her first taste of DC. An internship with the NAACP, followed by some lobbying. Her life, her path, had been set.

Until she met Brandon. The boy from Wyoming with blond hair and blue eyes. She loved him, yes, she loved him, but inside she always felt she was betraying who she was. Hadn't she fought for justice and change? And now, she had sold her soul to ply the legislation Big Oil wanted.

Lucas watched her eyebrows furrow as she read, and in the secret history he was inventing for her, this meant she was pondering the Great Questions of who she was, wondering where she'd gone wrong.

Mother Teresa picked up the section of the paper she was reading, held it in front of her and unfolded it, giving Lucas a clear view of the front page.

It was the Metro section of the paper, and a large photo occupied about a quarter of it.

A photo of his own face.

He caught part of the headline—MAN SOUGHT FOR—but that's all he could read before Mother Teresa refolded the paper and started another story.

Lucas sank to the floor of the utility closet, abandoning his peephole, abandoning his invented history for Mother Teresa.

His face.

In the newspaper.

How? Why? Officially, he didn't exist to the government. To anyone. He had no identification, no driver's license, no social security number. He moved from odd job to odd job, always getting paid under the table in cash or panhandling.

But that hadn't stopped Donavan or Saul from discovering him, had it? And now, his photo was on the front page of the Metro section.

Wait. Saul. Had to be Saul. After all, Saul had managed to discover him, track him, enlist him. And now, after a trip to Saul's home, he had a good idea the man was selling secrets to someone. Saul had to be behind this, trying to flush him into the open for . . . he wasn't sure what.

Without bothering to check the bathroom, Lucas clumsily stumbled out of the utility closet, surprising a young man in a hooded sweatshirt at the sink. The young man eyed him for a few seconds, his eyebrows arched in a question.

Numbly, Lucas looked around him. Back inside the utility closet, he saw a WET FLOOR sign and an empty mop bucket. Quickly, he grabbed the sign and slid it out onto the bathroom floor, then wheeled the bucket out after it. "Hard to keep this floor clean," he mumbled.

The young man at the sink finished washing and nodded, but said nothing. He dried his hands with a paper towel and threw it into the trash before disappearing out the bathroom's front door.

Lucas stood silently for a few moments, feeling the sweat trickle down his forehead as he collected his thoughts.

Lucas stepped up to the sink, splashed some water on his face and dried it. He studied his reflection in the mirror, looking for an answer that didn't appear. Okay, if he was going to step out into the donut shop—let alone the rest of DC—and if his face was plastered on the front page of the paper, it was probably best to change his appearance in some way.

That meant he'd have to go upstairs again. He swung off his ever-present backpack and unzipped the outer pocket, where he kept some gloves and a Washington Nationals baseball cap. He pulled the cap down over his head. Not exactly a wig or a change of hair color, but it was something.

He returned his attention to the backpack and pulled out a pair of wraparound sunglasses from a side pocket. Hiding the eyes, he knew, was the key to a disguise; without the eyes, people couldn't distinguish faces as easily.

With the cap and sunglasses in place, he replaced the pack on his back and went out into Dandy Don's. No one appeared to notice him leaving the bathroom, which was good.

At the counter, he greeted the young woman with short-cropped, kinky hair and heavy black-framed glasses. She offered a thousand-watt smile and asked what she could get for him.

He ordered an old-fashioned and a cup of coffee, and picked up a copy of the paper from the display near the counter. The young lady looked at the front of the paper, then at him, and announced his total. He thanked her and paid, retreating to a corner by the door.

Across the room, Mother Teresa was gathering up the kids, getting ready to leave.

Lucas bit into his donut, sipped his coffee, and folded open the paper, finding the Metro section.

There was his face again. Blown up, a bit out of focus and pixelated, but recognizably him. Obviously a still from a security cam somewhere. But where? MAN SOUGHT FOR QUESTIONING IN DISAPPEARANCE, the headline read. Below it, he read the story:

Metro police are searching for a man described as a person of interest in a kidnapping case involving two principals of ATM2GO, a DC-headquartered company.

The kidnapping victims, identified as Anita Abkin and Ted Hagen, were reported missing Saturday morning after Viktor Abkin, also a principal at ATM2GO and husband of Anita, found a ransom note in his home and agreed to a secret meeting with the alleged kidnapper at a local club.

The meeting between Viktor and the alleged kidnapper was caught on security cameras at Split Jacks and turned over to authorities, on Saturday morning.

Abkin said he received a threatening phone call from the alleged kidnapper shortly after finding the ransom note on Friday, and agreed to meet at Split Jacks. After the meeting, he went directly to police to report the crime, turning over the note and opening his home to investigators.

Police have since gathered security camera footage from the lounge where the two met, enhancing the images released to the public on Saturday. Police also hinted at other gathered evidence, but refused to disclose its nature, citing the case as an "ongoing and developing investigation."

Viktor Abkin commended the police department's fast work in a statement released late Saturday. "I intend to fully cooperate with investigators, and all of us at ATM2GO want nothing more than to see Anita and Ted safely returned."

The subject in question is described as . . .

Lucas stopped reading, turned to look at people around him. No one was staring. Mother Teresa, her two kids in tow, was walking out the front door of the shop.

He closed the paper and tried another bite of the donut. Between the first bite and the second bite, it had somehow lost its flavor. Lucas chewed slowly a few times before washing it down with a sip of coffee. But even the coffee now tasted bitter.

Viktor. He never would have imagined it . . . and yet, he should have. It was obvious, from their meeting, that he was a man looking only for the best angles for himself. Now he'd been able to finger Lucas for kidnapping his wife and business partner. Probably had his life insurance claims already filed as well.

And Lucas had done quite a bit to help him. He'd been in Viktor's house twice, leaving physical evidence—most likely a fingerprint or two, since Lucas hadn't exactly been careful while inside the home. He'd called Viktor's cell phone number, which would be verifiable with records. He'd have to ditch the TracFone now; he'd never be able to use it again unless he wanted to advertise his location to the police. He'd met with Viktor at Split Jacks, helpfully allowing his image to be recorded on security cameras.

Lucas propped his elbows on the table and rubbed his face. Time to plan his next move. Even with something as simple as a baseball cap and sunglasses, he wasn't horribly concerned about being recognized; as always, everyone looked, but few people saw. But physical evidence might lead a trail back to him at some point. He'd never been fingerprinted or booked into a police station. He didn't exist to the federal government. And that was just what he wanted. Still . . . perhaps something in the records from the orphanage? He didn't recall any specific tests or samples, but most of those memories were fuzzy.

This simply meant he would have to be more careful and plan his next moves. Viktor had added a huge wrinkle to all of this by putting Lucas in the middle of a police investigation, and that meant Viktor would need another visit.

But then, that's exactly what Viktor and the police would expect him to do. Which meant, if he did nothing for now, he'd confuse the issue. Keep quiet long enough, and he'd possibly convince the police it was time to take a closer look at Viktor's story.

There was a catch with that, of course: Lucas didn't know if the other two were, in fact, missing. Strike that. He was pretty sure they were missing but unsure if they were still alive.

If they were, waiting might not be the best option. True, they had been plotting to kill Viktor, but that didn't mean they necessarily deserved to die. In any case, he didn't feel any particular need to stick his neck back into a three-ring circus of people who were plotting to kill each other.

He stood and walked to the door, hearing the young lady at the counter call out a "Thanks!" over the tinkling of the attached bells.

Viktor would have to wait, he thought as he headed toward the Metro. The unwelcome publicity complicated matters, certainly, but it really had no immediate effect on him. He would let Viktor slide; right now, Saul was the priority. Then, the next Creep Club meeting.

Talk about the wrong priorities.

LUCAS DEPOSITED THE OLD TRACFONE IN AN ALLEY DUMPSTER, FOUND A kiosk, and bought a new one.

From there, he made his way back to his secret stash near the Washington Monument. After his first meeting with Saul, he had jettisoned the briefcase onto the tracks. But he had kept the files, discs, and wrapped packages, all packed away in the basement of an abandoned building. Now it was time to check on those; there might be clues that would tell him what his next steps should be. How to prepare for his next Creep Club meeting. How to prepare for his next Saul meeting.

For a man who loved to be alone, he was finding himself in a lot of meetings.

After a ride on the Metro, Lucas exited the underground tunnel and made his way to the old brick building. Instead of entering the building, however, he casually walked on the sidewalk in front of it, baseball cap low over his face and sunglasses hiding his eyes. He had to check out the vicinity, make sure the area wasn't being watched.

A quick sweep of the perimeter didn't show any obvious signs of surveillance crews or stakeouts. It had been a few days, and he thought it unlikely the stash would be watched for more than forty-eight hours with no sign of him anywhere.

Of course, that was before his face had been plastered all over the front of today's paper.

He cut down the alley, pushed aside a garbage can, and boosted himself through the basement window of the building. In a few minutes, he had uncovered the stash and now took a closer look at the contents.

He knew these items would be marked, tracked. After all, if people such as Donavan had easy access to things like geopatches, there was no telling what kind of technology was available to spooks who worked for the federal government.

He leafed through the dossier of papers. Background information and files on people known to be members of Creep Club. About half the files were complete; the others were sketched in with photos and some rudimentary information. A few had absolutely nothing on them except a name on the file tab.

He paged through the files, searching, and was surprised to find no folder—empty or otherwise—prepared for Donavan.

He put aside all the files, unwrapped a small rectangular package, and revealed a cell phone. He smiled. As if he were going to use a phone given to him by a government agent. Or a government spy, as the case might be.

The next package was a box with a few DVDs, tube-cams, a mini-GPS system, and a couple other pieces of electronic equipment he didn't immediately recognize.

He set all this aside and turned to the last package. He unwrapped it and stared at it for several seconds.

He had no idea what it was.

It was a cube, roughly the size of one of those old Rubik's cube puzzles, but solid. It felt like it was made of granite or marble or something similarly cold and hard. Its surface was the darkest black he'd ever seen—so black it seemed to actually suck light from the immediate vicinity.

The appearance made him expect the cube to be heavy and solid. And yet, it was light. He held the cube up to his face, shook it lightly. He thought something inside shifted, but he couldn't be sure.

A quick examination of the cube's exterior surfaces revealed no buttons, no clasps, no hinges. It was smooth and solid everywhere. Something told him this cube was a container holding something important, but he had no idea what. Or how to get to it.

With a tinge of regret, he wrapped the cube in its paper again, shoving it and all the other items back into his secret hiding spot behind the bricks.

Nothing immediately useful to him in Saul's packages, but he hadn't expected there to be. More than anything, he felt he had needed to take a look at the items before contacting Saul again; for now, he had to play along with the whole charade. Until he had more information on Saul and what he was involved in, Lucas had to look like he was working with him.

After hiding the packages and replacing the bricks, Lucas went back to the nearby Metro tunnel and took the train to L'Enfant Plaza station, where he walked across the giant tile floors and found a quiet bench near the corner. He pulled out his new TracFone and dialed Saul's number from memory.

After one ring, the line connected, but no one spoke. Lucas waited a few seconds before speaking himself. "I'm calling for Saul."

Lucas heard a creaking sound on the line, a chair maybe, then Saul's unmistakable voice. "Got something for me?"

Lucas watched people hurrying toward the gates that would carry them elsewhere. "Maybe." He paused. "How about we meet?"

"When?"

"Now."

"Now works. Where you at?"

Lucas smiled. "As if I'd tell you."

Saul chuckled. "Just because I'm a government agent doesn't mean you can't trust me."

Which government? Lucas asked himself quickly before pushing the thought away. He looked out the window and saw the giant white spire that was visible from almost anywhere in the DC area. "Let's make it easy," Lucas said. "Meet me at the Washington Monument in half an hour."

"I think I can find that."

Lucas let Saul's obvious sarcasm slip by without comment as he closed the TracFone and powered it down.

That's when he heard a sound he recognized: low notes on a guitar, floating through the air toward him, carried through the building from somewhere outside.

He stood and walked out the doors, pausing to get his bearings at the top of the steps. Across the street, next to a giant statue and spraying fountain, he saw a hunched figure on a box.

He crossed the street and stood in front of the man again, waiting for a pause. The guitar player tilted his head back, holding a long note, then opened his clenched eyes.

"Well now," he said as he segued into a new tune, his hand sliding up and down the guitar neck. "Seems to me you spend way too much of your time in train stations."

Lucas smiled. "You too."

"I got somethin' special for you," the guitar player said, and he slid into the tune without waiting, strumming the opening bars as his eyes closed again. After the first twelve-bar progression, he began to sing.

Got those crumblin' down blues, baby
Got me some crumblin' down blues
Got those crumblin' down blues so bad
Feel 'em clear down in my shoes
Did me some dancin' with the devil
Said he'd have to take his dues
Now I'm digging with that shovel
Cuz I got them crumblin' down blues

The guitarist did a quick flourish and finished the song, then opened his twinkling eyes and stared at Lucas again.

Lucas threw some money in the guitar case. "Keep playing that guitar," he said and turned around. As he walked away, he heard the answer:

"Keep digging with that shovel."

SEVENTEEN

TWENTY MINUTES LATER, HE SAT ON A BENCH ABOUT TWENTY YARDS FROM the base of the Washington Monument. Out here, with no nearby tree cover, the wind whipped across the ground, making the flags surrounding the base of the giant pillar flutter. Lucas tilted his head back, leaning against the bench and enjoying the sun beating down from a blue sky above. He closed his eyes, listened to the breeze, the nearby traffic, the chatter of tourists mingling softly.

"This seat taken?" It was Saul's voice, right next to him.

Lucas smiled, keeping his head tilted back and his eyes closed. Best to play this cool. "Knock yourself out," he said. "Free country, last time I checked."

He felt Saul settling onto the bench next to him.

"Don't know where you've been checking," Saul's voice answered. "All the stuff I've been reading, people seem to think we're living in a fascist state. Country's taking away all our rights, telling us it's hunting for terrorists."

Lucas smiled. "Are we?"

"Are we what? Taking away rights, or hunting for terrorists?"

Lucas cocked open an eye. "Both, I suppose."

"Funny, that's what I was just gonna say." Saul crossed his legs, letting his trench coat fall open, and stared up at the towering monument above them. He put a hand on his bald head and rubbed it for a moment, as if massaging away a headache.

"It's kinda warm out," Lucas commented. "You really need a trench coat like that?"

Saul had one eye closed as he squinted into the glare of the sky above. "Government spook dress code. No way around it. So what you got for me?"

"I'll have the date and place for the next Creep Club meeting later today."

"Really? You don't think they'll just go back to the Stranahan?"

"I didn't exactly make a great first impression," Lucas said. "They'll want to avoid me. Especially after they find out about . . . last night."

"What about last night?"

"One of the Creeps—goes by the name of Dilbert—got himself in a bit of trouble."

Saul smiled, picked a bit of lint off his slacks. "And you just happened to be there to save the day," he said.

"Something like that."

Saul nodded. "But not before he got himself knocked out with a baseball bat."

"So you know about it. Guess I shoulda figured that."

Saul shrugged. "Yeah, I'm a big baseball fan."

"He okay?"

Another shrug. "He'll live."

"What about . . ."

"The woman?"

"Yeah."

"She's in custody right now. Have to answer a few questions. I'm sure they'll book her on Attempted, but she's got money. She'll make bail."

"Will she beat the charge?"

"Like I told you, she's got money." Saul looked at him. "And a tape. She's probably looking good for self-defense, if she plays her cards right."

"Good."

"'Course, that's not the only videotape I got on my mind right now."

Lucas nodded. "Guess you're a newspaper subscriber."

"For the sports section, mostly. Baseball scores."

Lucas tilted the sunglasses up on his forehead. "You got any information on that?"

"You first."

Lucas nodded. "Tried to save the guy. I gave him some footage of his wife and partner planning to kill him."

"So you played Good Samaritan to a bad egg."

"You know the old saying. No good deed goes unpunished."

"Yeah, I've heard that one."

Lucas smiled. "I think he's trying to smoke me out with this story in the paper. Hope I make contact again, trap myself. Except—"

"Except you don't know Abkin; he's not . . . normal. Be careful."

Saul sucked air between his cheeks, pulled out a pack of cigarettes and offered one to him.

Lucas shook his head, waiting for Saul to put a flame to his smoke.

"So," Saul began, "we're gonna do a little tit for tat. You give me something useful, I give you something useful."

Lucas nodded, expecting as much. "I thought we were already doing that."

"Keep thinking that way, then."

"I'll have something from the next Creep Club meeting."

"I hope so, with that nice little prize package I put together for you."

Lucas nodded, not saying anything.

Saul stared at him a few moments, then smiled. "You're not gonna use anything in that package, are you?"

Lucas watched a couple stroll by on the sidewalk, hand in hand. "Would you, if you were me?" he asked finally.

"No, I don't suppose I would."

Lucas looked down at the bench they were sitting on, pretended to read something on the slats. "Made in China. Bench sitting here at the Washington Monument, and it's made in China. Seems like everything comes from China these days." He swung to look at Saul, searching his face for some kind of reaction.

Saul nodded, taking another drag off his cigarette before holding it up. "Yeah, well, smokes are still made in the good old You-Ess-of-A," he said. "We still got a corner on the cancer market."

He was good, Lucas had to admit. He didn't rise to the China bait at all.

"So that's it, Humpty? You called this little soirée to tell me you don't really have much now, but you're gonna get me something later?"

Lucas nodded. "Hey, I told you I got a good track on the next meeting. Also because I missed your witty conversation."

Saul flicked the rest of his cigarette to the concrete without crushing it. The butt rolled away, pushed by the wind. Saul stood, stretching his back as he did. He twisted his neck to the left, and then the right, resulting in a ripple of pops and snaps. "I'll leave you here on your Chinese bench, then," he said.

AT THE LIVEWIRE CAFÉ, LUCAS DECIDED IT WAS TIME FOR A FULL MEAL. He looked at his stash; still plenty of money left, but he hated to be draining it like this. He'd need to hit some of his other hidden stashes around the city before long. Better to have a job of some kind, keep adding to his savings.

Except he had a job now. One that didn't pay. One that just might kill him.

Not exactly the benefit package most people crave.

When his sandwich was ready, he took it to an open computer terminal and sat. Immediately, he went to Donavan's geopatch page. First he tried the patch he'd left on Saul's shoe. It hadn't moved in the last twenty-four hours, still at Saul's home address. Either Saul hadn't worn those shoes, or the geopatch had somehow rubbed off inside his home. Or maybe he'd found it.

Next he entered Dilbert's geopatch number. He scanned back over the last several hours of movement. From the hospital, Dilbert had obviously caught a cab or bus to his home—or at least a place where he'd stayed the next ten hours. This morning, however, he'd been busy, spending a few hours at a location down near Fort Stanton Park. Lucas felt certain this was the location of the next Creep Club meeting, and Dilbert was doing some setup. Lucas would find out soon enough.

He smiled, memorizing the two addresses as he took another bite of the sandwich. Soon he would attend his second Creep Club meeting.

EIGHTEEN

THE YOUNG MAN STARES AT THE SECRET VISITOR AND NODS. THE SECRET visitor seems happy, happier than the young man has ever seen. "Congratulations," the secret visitor says, holding out a hand. "Usually, we don't make such changes with someone so . . . young. You're a first. A prodigy."

The young man takes his secret visitor's hand, shakes it. He's been let out of the metal room many times now, seen the world outside this steel trap. And yet, oddly enough, he's always felt most comfortable here inside a place other people would call a prison cell. It's the only thing that's comfortable and familiar for him, and he needs to hold on to something comfortable and familiar.

Especially on the missions he's been performing for his secret visitor these last few years. Raven still has no idea. He thinks the young man is his experiment, his property. He thinks the daily tests, the prodding questions, the learning sessions, are the young man's only contacts with the outside world.

But the young man knows better.

The young man has been outside the steel room. He's learned all about Raven's pheromone research, and he thinks he knows why Raven has failed. He's shared these ideas with his secret visitor, as well as some new ideas in genetic research spurred by the new materials, new lessons.

And now, he's agreed to become part of another . . . experiment. To carry on with Raven's research, as well as to partner with some other researchers on new opportunities. He's ready, because his secret visitor has given him the ultimate training these last few years. Combat, strategy, physics, theoretics, and more, all of it implanted with the help of new cocktails brought to him only by the secret visitor.

And now, the secret visitor has offered him a promotion.

He stands, hearing the chair he was sitting in scrape against the bare floor. "I'm just wondering . . ." he says.

"Yes," the visitor prompts. "A good quality, to wonder. Something Raven hasn't been able to kill, despite his best efforts."

The young man returns the smile, only now becoming aware of the constant buzz in his ears. For several years now, the wasps have been his constant companions, fluttering about his head—drawn, he knows, by the experiments Raven has performed with wasp pheromones. Raven wanted to create a Drone Soldier, someone who would follow orders unquestioningly, much as the drone wasps sacrificed themselves to protect their hives.

He is a failed experiment, he knows. Raven hasn't given up yet, of course, but it's too late to go much further down that path alone. With the help of newer technologies such as gene splicing, coupled with the pheromones, there are possibilities—possibilities the young man has expressed to his secret visitor—but Raven is the proverbial dinosaur. He has no interest in using these new techniques.

"Your question," the secret visitor asks, drawing him from his reverie.

The young man looks the secret visitor in the face. "Where did I come from? My family—my mother, my father?"

The secret visitor takes his hand, pats it comfortingly. "I am your family. Your father, your mother."

"But . . . who am I?"

"Does it matter?" The secret visitor holds out a semi-automatic pistol; the young man recognizes it instantly as a Taurus 24/7 .45 caliber. He takes the gun, slides the action to make sure there's a round in the chamber.

"When?" he asks the secret visitor.

"Raven will be here in about ten minutes. You know that as well as I do. It's time for his project to end. Think what he's done to you, how he's failed you. And yet, here you are, the youngest agent we've ever promoted—more than that, the first one actually in our program. We have several teams of researchers ready to help you; you just need to lead the field team. And the first thing you need to do is take command. From Raven."

The young man sits in the chair again, the pistol relaxed and comfortable in his grip. He's shot several thousand rounds on firing ranges outside these walls.

The secret visitor moves to the steel door, knocks on it. It opens, and the secret visitor begins to leave.

"I'll need a name," the young man says.

The secret visitor stops, turns back toward him again. "What?"

"I've never had a name," he says. "I've always been . . ." he searches, realizing no one has ever called him anything. "I've always been here." He motions at the room with the pistol in his hand.

The secret visitor smiles. "Yes, I suppose you're right. And what would you like your name to be?"

The young man concentrates, listening to the buzz of the wasps floating around his face. Yes, they will give him his name.

He smiles at the secret visitor. "Call me Swarm."

NINETEEN

THE NEXT DAY, LUCAS CHECKED DILBERT'S MOVEMENTS AGAIN. SEVERAL trips back and forth between the two addresses he'd memorized, along with a few side trips along the way. More than ever, Lucas was sure he had the location of the next Creep Club meeting.

Convinced, he moved toward the Metro and started making his way south. An hour later, he stepped off the train and began walking toward Fort Stanton Park. He passed the famous Our Lady of Perpetual Help church adjacent to the park and kept going south, pulling the image of the map into his memory as he moved. At the next intersection, he turned east and walked for two more blocks, then south for another block.

Here was a neighborhood of buildings that stood largely empty; in contrast to the gleaming buildings of downtown DC, these structures held only ghosts and memories. Shattered panes of glass in the windows resembled the jagged teeth of animals, as if they were giant, beached sea monsters, fossilized by years of disuse.

Lucas found himself slowing as he walked, pulling his shoulders in, keeping his head down, warding off the eerie feeling these buildings gave him. Even though it was the middle of the afternoon, a sense of gloom infused the air.

He found the address he was looking for, an old cinder-block building that looked like it had once been a hotel. Or maybe an apartment building. He circled around to the back of the building, careful to avoid stepping on the trash that littered the old lot: cans, molded paper boxes, a rotting mattress, a partially disassembled bicycle.

He scanned the first-floor windows and found what he'd expected: the sideways CC symbol, scrawled on a concrete sill.

Lucas continued walking, moving to the abandoned building next door. A large sheet of plywood had been affixed over the building's back door, but the wood had been pried off and hung lazily by a few nails now, letting Lucas into the building easily.

He stopped once he'd stepped into the anonymity and darkness of the building, listening. Vagrants were obviously using this building—okay, every building on this street—for crash pads, and he didn't want to surprise anyone. People had an image of homeless people as pathetic figures looming in the shadows of the streets, wrapped in dirty blankets and old clothing, but quiet and docile.

There were those people, of course. Mostly the drinkers: people who poured themselves into bottles of fortified wine or, as they became steadily more desperate, cold medications and rubbing alcohol. By and large, when these people weren't drinking, they were in a stupor.

But Lucas had spent enough time on the streets to know that the drinkers were only a small portion of the homeless. More often, you met people who were mentally unstable, kicked out of group homes because they had no insurance and no families. Or people who went from high to high searching for more crack or crystal meth. Often, the people in the throes of their highs became violent and aggressive.

Inside office buildings, Lucas didn't have to deal with the people who inhabited the lost shadow city every night. But he met them, often enough, when he was returning from one of his various odd jobs, or when he was out on the streets doing a bit of panhandling himself. Or when he was at the Salvation Army picking up new clothes.

After a few moments, when he'd heard no screaming or thrashing inside the building, Lucas stepped farther into the darkness. He found the wall closest to the Creep Club building and lay down next to a cracked window smeared with pigeon guano. As if on cue, he heard the flutter of pigeons up above him somewhere.

He lay quietly for several minutes, studying the Creep Club building with his spotting scope and watching for any activity. Watching, especially, for signs of Dilbert. The guy had been here several times during the last few days.

Lucas thumbed on his TracFone and checked the time. He was guessing the Creep Club meeting would start at the same time as the previous one: 7:00 p.m. If that were the case, he had only about forty-five minutes before showtime.

Lucas moved back through the bowels of the derelict building he now occupied, then to the Creep Club building next door. Near the CC insignia scrawled on the basement window, he found an old wooden door with a padlock and a warning sign reading PREMISES

CONDEMNED. The only problem was, the door's padlock was broken, hanging uselessly on its hasp.

Without hesitating, he grabbed the door handle and pulled. It opened a few inches before sticking on the chipped concrete surface below him; obviously the door had sagged in its frame and was no longer able to open fully.

It opened more than enough, though, for Lucas to sneak inside. He squeezed through the opening, scanning the still hallway ahead of him. Somewhere deep inside the building, he heard a soft rumble. Something like an engine running.

He paused, adjusted the pack on his back, and moved forward. Down the first-floor hallway, he found the elevator, its doors closed and waiting. He didn't even bother, knowing the building had no electricity. He could possibly pry open the elevator doors, use the shaft to make his way throughout the building. But he only had forty-five minutes—less than that now, he reminded himself—and he couldn't chance being caught by a member of the Creep Club.

He had to be quick and light. His guess was they would again meet on the second floor. Perhaps higher, but the second floor was most likely. People were creatures of habit, and even in the Creep Club, they would unconsciously try to recreate their meeting space in the familiar Stranahan Building.

Near the elevator, Lucas found the stairs and began to climb. Most of the building's interior was covered with a thick layer of dust, but he noted that the dust on the stairs had been kicked away by recent activity. Many people had been on the stairs.

Or, more likely, one person had been up and down these stairs many times.

He made his way up one flight of the concrete steps, stopping on the landing before doubling back on the second flight. The noise was a bit closer, a bit clearer now, and he was sure he knew what it was. Lucas put his foot on the next step and easily moved up the second flight; the door to the second floor was propped open by a crumbling cinder block.

Staying on his toes to keep his steps light, Lucas moved down the hallway to the only spot on the second floor where he saw light. As he moved, he listened for movement, voices, any sound that might indicate other people on the floor with him. But all he could detect was the low rumble, closer and closer.

Finally he arrived at the doorway, noticing how the light spilling from it illuminated several footsteps in the dust of the abandoned floor. The light, weak though it was, exposed flecks of dust still airborne.

Lucas stepped into the light and looked at the room, knowing he was alone on the floor. For now.

Inside the room, he saw a red diesel generator on the floor, humming away. A length of flexible tubing led away from the generator's exhaust and to a circular hole cut in the glass of the room's window. The rest of the window was covered in dark plastic—garbage bags, he guessed—to cover the lights.

Next to the generator were a television on a small stand, hooked to a computer and cam, and a stand-alone lamp. In front of the TV, several chairs spread out in a haphazard pattern. The chairs looked like they were from somewhere else. Rentals, even.

Lucas breathed in the dust and continued to scan the room. It was on the small side, but not tiny. Maybe it had been a meeting room or break room in better days. A few pieces of furniture and junk were pushed against the back wall, thrust into the shadows. One of those pieces, Lucas saw, was an old Steelcase desk. The desk's back opening was against the far wall, with the modesty panel—complete with a small hole for cords—pointed toward the rest of the room. The hole was roughly the size of a coffee cup, more than large enough to give him a clear view of the entire room, provided he kept his face hidden in the shadows underneath the desk.

Perfect.

Lucas walked to the desk and pushed it away from the wall. Immediately, downstairs, he heard a woman's voice: "Hello?"

Okay, he'd have to move fast now. He squeezed behind the desk, then into the small space between the desk drawer and sides, finally lifting the desk slightly before pushing it back into place against the wall.

It was a tight fit, to be sure, but Lucas had been in much tighter spaces. He turned toward the modesty panel, making sure he could peer out of the small hole as he folded his legs beneath him. Now he sat, hunched in an extreme yoga position, and waited. He willed his body to go still, to turn off its self-awareness, and felt his breath and heartbeat slowing. Within seconds, he was able to switch into his monitoring mode, his body in a deep trance while his mind—his senses—crackled with heightened awareness.

Several seconds later, he heard footsteps in the hallway outside. A woman's step, he could tell. Eventually she entered the room, carefully clutching a handgun ahead of her. This one was new, Lucas noted; he hadn't seen her at the previous meeting.

"What are you doing?"

The voice came from out in the hall, and the woman spun the gun toward the voice. In a moment, she lowered the gun as Dilbert walked into the room.

"Oh. Hey, Dilbert," she said. "Thought I heard something."

"Probably me," he said, entering the room. "I've been getting this place ready all day." His hand absently went to the lump on his temple, scratched at the red surface. He winced a bit, decided to stop scratching.

The woman had put away her gun now. "What happened to you?"

Dilbert moved to the TV, made a great show of checking connections from the camera and computer. "Yeah. Well," he said, "guess we'll talk a little bit about that tonight."

"About what?" A third person stood in the doorway, this one a man Lucas recognized from the previous meeting. He couldn't immediately recall the man's name until he called up images of the meeting and replayed them in his mind. In a few moments, he had it: Hondo.

Within minutes, the room was filled with nineteen people; Lucas had counted each and every one as they entered. Almost all the people from his previous meeting, plus another five he hadn't met.

Obviously, attendance at this meeting had been highly encouraged.

The only person missing, as far as Lucas could tell, was Donavan. This gave Lucas an immediate queasy feeling in the pit of his stomach. He pushed away the queasiness, focusing on the meeting happening in front of him as Snake brought it to order.

"Okay," Snake said. "Looks like we have a good turnout tonight. Thanks for coming." He paused for a few moments, nodded at a few murmurs, and continued. "Obviously, we have some . . . issues to deal with. We're only missing a couple of people, and one of those people is Donavan." Another pause. "Anyone heard from Donavan?"

"Not since the last meeting," someone offered.

"Yeah, me neither," Snake said. "Now, those of you who were here last time know Donavan brought a . . . visitor. Someone he wanted to recruit into Creep Club. But that didn't pan out so well. His friend, who called himself Humpty, didn't have the stomach for what we're doing here. Fair enough. No hard feelings. Except."

Snake held up a copy of the Metro section of Sunday's paper, with Lucas's face on it. "Except this. Anyone recognize this face?"

More murmurs among some of the assembled Creep Clubbers.

"Yeah," Snake said, answering his own question. "That looks, to me, like our friend Humpty. And as you'll notice when you read the article, Humpty's got himself involved with one of Donavan's projects."

"The ATM people," someone said. Lucas couldn't see who it was.

"Bingo. So what does it mean? Don't know. Not for sure. But let's just say I'm not surprised to find Donavan missing. And I think we should all hear what Dilbert has to say."

Dilbert stood and walked to the front of the room. He nodded at Snake, clicked the trackpad on the computer. Immediately, footage of the Delgado couple flooded the screen—Dilbert's previous video, edited to the music.

"I think most of you remember my Delgado project," he said. "I've been working on it for quite a while. I showed a rough cut at the last meeting, for those of you who weren't here. But I needed just a few more shots—something special to complete it."

Dilbert paused, licked his lips, and Lucas shivered. Even from this distance, even in this cramped space, he could see the feral hunger, the madness, in Dilbert's eyes.

Dilbert paused his video. "Saturday night I was back there, doing some work in the basement. Getting some footage. But someone tripped the alarm while I was there, and . . . and that's all I really know about that. Someone hit me, that much I know." He rubbed at the huge red spot on his head again, making sure everyone saw. "But when I woke up, I was in a car with . . . Humpty. The guy Donavan brought."

"This was last night?" asked Hondo.

"Night before. Saturday night. Pretty late. But here's the thing: no one's seen Donavan since the last meeting."

"So?" said Hondo.

"So," said Snake, joining the conversation again. "We think we have a Benedict Arnold. Think about it: Donavan shows up with this Humpty guy out of the blue, who immediately tries to start a fight with us—comes in and insults who we are, what we do. Then they both disappear, and suddenly, Donavan's project shows up in the paper—with Humpty's face on it. Then, Saturday night, they show up at Dilbert's project—"

"Wait—you saw Donavan there?" said another. "I thought you said no one's seen him since last meeting."

Dilbert shook his head. "No, I didn't see him. But—"

Hondo stood up, cutting him off. "Think about it: it makes sense. Donavan waited until his buddy tripped the alarm, then knocked Dilbert out. They're working together. I can feel it."

Hondo, gaining confidence in what he said, stood and looked

from face to face. "Let's just say that's what's happening here. Maybe we can't say for sure yet, but let's just say." He paused, and a few heads nodded.

A man Lucas didn't recognize spoke. "So they're working together to . . . I don't know, sabotage our projects? Why? Doesn't get them anything."

"Blackmail," Dilbert said forcefully. "I had tapes—several recent scenes—in my pocket. Now they're gone. Now, I don't know that it means anything by itself, but when you put it together with the article in the paper—"

Dilbert waited for Snake to hold up the article before continuing. "You see a pattern. I think Donavan, and this Humpty guy, are going to try to blackmail each of our projects. Talk to our projects, show them footage, tell them they need to pay or they'll end up in the news."

"How do you know they won't try to blackmail *us*?" asked another unfamiliar voice.

"We don't," Snake said.

"So what do we do about Donavan and . . . Humpty?" asked Dilbert.

"That's easy," Snake said, looking around the room carefully before answering. "We kill them."

TWENTY

LUCAS STAYED UNDER THE DESK, IMMOBILE, FOR HALF AN HOUR AFTER the last person left the meeting. Only then did he allow his body to come out of its deep state; he felt tiny needles poking his hands and feet as blood flow returned to them. He guessed it was after eight o'clock, based on the twilight descending outside the windows. It would be dark in another hour or so.

Most of the meeting had been spent discussing Donavan's hangouts, his movements, his proclivities. Obviously, they felt finding Donavan was going to be the key to finding him.

His hole was getting deeper all the time. First the wrinkle from Viktor Abkin, putting his photo in the paper. And now the Creep Club, convinced he and Donavan were trying to sabotage them. So he had at least two dozen people who would like to see him dead. Probably more.

Lucas wasn't necessarily opposed to the idea of sabotaging the Creep Club, but he was insulted that they thought he'd do it by blackmailing their victims. The victims were precisely the reason why he wanted to bring down the club.

He pushed against the desk, moving it away from the wall and unfolding himself from the small space beneath. He stood, listening to his joints crack and groan.

The room was quiet, the generator silent and the television dark. He was alone in the building.

And evidently, he was back to being alone in the world. A stupid mistake, befriending Donavan. That had pulled him into this whole Creep Club mess, which led to the ATM2GO fiasco, and Donavan's disappearance, and who knew what else? He would have been much better off if he'd never revealed himself to Donavan.

He still wasn't sure, exactly, why he'd responded to Donavan in the first place. But now, look what it had done to him; one way or another, Donavan was in trouble.

Lucas adjusted his backpack and headed toward the door, wondering what his next move should be.

Maybe it wasn't too late to take his own advice: stay uninvolved. It had served him so well for so many years, and he was good at it. It had left an empty hole inside him, yes, but he could fill that hole just by watching people, inventing their secret histories . . .

He shook his head as he walked down the hallway. No good. He was into the mire too deep now. He was at least partly responsible for what had happened to the missing ATM2GO partners, as well as Donavan.

He thought again of the bright twinkling lights of DC, seemingly just out of the grasp of his ten-year-old hand as he lay on top of the orphanage.

This was his chance to grab those lights finally, be something more than a dishwasher or a panhandler. Or an orphan.

And what about Leila? He had helped her, hadn't he? If he hadn't been part of this whole scheme, she'd still be facing beatings, waiting while she thought the police were videotaping her and building a case. So he had done *something*.

He moved down the stairs carefully, checking his surroundings. No one else was left in the space. He made his way to the broken door and out into the humid evening air. In the distance, he heard a siren wailing; above him, streetlights flickered on and wavered in the gathering darkness.

Yeah, he was in it too deep now. Either he needed to sink, or he needed to keep his head from going under.

He moved down the street, turned back toward the Metro stop, pulled the TracFone from his pocket, thought better of it. He needed to get away from here before he called Saul.

He jumped on the Metro, suddenly feeling exhausted. So he closed his eyes and slept, Snake's words ringing in his ears.

That's easy. We kill them.

TWENTY MINUTES LATER, HE CAME AWAKE WITH A SUDDEN START, LOOKING around him. He was pretty far north now—just past Fort Totten, and only a few stops from the end of the Green Line. He'd have to ride the Metro back toward downtown. That was fine; he'd call Saul, and if Saul were able to track his location somehow, he'd assume Lucas had been somewhere up northeast.

He looked around, trying to see if anyone took an unhealthy interest in him—especially now that it was dark, and he was still wearing sunglasses—but no one seemed to notice.

That's easy. We kill them.

Lucas pulled the TracFone from his pocket and dialed Saul's number.

"Well, if it isn't Humpty Dumpty."

"I just came from a Creep Club meeting."

"Oh?" Lucas heard a bit of pleasure in Saul's voice, but no surprise.

"Got time for a cup of coffee?" Lucas asked.

"I've always got time for a cup of coffee. There's a shop over near the Washington Monument—"

"Java the Hut? It's on the ground floor of a blue glass building?"

"Yeah," Saul said. "You been there?"

"I know where it is," Lucas said, not telling Saul he'd discovered the place by following his movements with a geopatch. "I'm not far away."

"SO WHAT DO YOU HAVE, HUMPTY?" SAUL LIFTED A LATTE TO HIS half-smiling lips.

Lucas took a sip of his own decaf, set it down on the table. He locked Saul into a stare. "Donavan's your boy, isn't he?"

Saul set his latte down, thumbed off the lid, and blew on the liquid inside. "Way too hot," he said.

"I noticed," Lucas said.

"Part of the charm for me." He stared at Lucas, but his gaze flicked to the wall when he spoke again. "Like to see how hot I can stand it."

Lucas waited a few moments while Saul fiddled with the drink, then lost his patience. "Well?"

Saul, unhurried, set the lid to his drink aside, then pulled out his pack of cigarettes and offered one to Lucas.

"Not supposed to smoke in here," Lucas said.

Saul smiled, enjoying the game. "I know," he said as he lit one. He took a deep drag and blew it at the ceiling. "Now. Tell me why you think I've got Donavan in my pocket."

"One, you don't have any files on him—you gave me a bunch of files, but nothing on him. Two, he's gone now, and—"

"Is he?" Saul arched his eyebrows, and Lucas had to admit, he was a pretty good actor. "Where's he gone to?"

"I don't know. Hasn't been to his apartment. And no one in the Creep Club has heard from him either."

Saul nodded, flicking ashes to the floor. "Interesting."

"In fact, it seems everyone in the Creep Club is convinced Donavan and I are a team—out to blackmail all the victims. Oh, wait, *projects*, as they like to call them."

Saul was nodding more rapidly now. "Because of the article in the paper. The ATM folks you met through Donavan."

"Exactly."

He nodded and blinked several times. Sometime Lucas would have to count just how many times Saul blinked in an average minute.

"Makes sense," Saul said. "It's wrong, but it makes sense."

"I know it's wrong."

"No, I mean your little theory about Donavan being part of my plan," Saul said. He flicked more ashes to the floor.

Lucas was amazed no one ever seemed to challenge him on the smoking.

"So you're saying he isn't?"

"That's what I'm saying."

"And you just expect me to believe that."

"I do. But do a little more thinking here: if Donavan's my guy, why do I need you?"

Lucas grimaced, took another drink of his decaf.

Saul continued. "You don't see any paperwork on Donavan because I don't need anything on Donavan. I have all I need on him. It's the others I'm looking at—the ones you do have files on."

"So if you know everything about Donavan, why not just use him? He's already part of the Creep Club; he was a better contact than I'll ever be."

"Because he's a junkie."

Lucas stopped, his cup halfway to his mouth. "What?"

"A junkie. I talked to him a few times after he got in, but he was already hooked. He loved creeping, so there was no way he was going to cut off his high."

Lucas went cold, remembering the crazy look in Donavan's eyes as he talked about the Creep Club. The coldness turned to a shudder as he once again recognized the need inside his own skin, even now.

"So," Saul said. "No Donavan. But you—" Saul pointed at him, his cigarette clenched between two fingers. "You, I knew, would be different."

"How'd you know that?"

Saul shrugged. "I don't think you like yourself very much, Humpty. And I mean that in a good way, for what we're talking about here. You're not gonna be a junkie." He tossed his cigarette on the floor, picked up his drink, and tried another sip. "Ah, much better." He replaced the lid, leaned back in his chair, crossed his legs. "But now we have a problem, don't we?"

"What's that?"

"You."

"What about me?"

"You're becoming . . . a little too visible. Somehow I doubt I've seen the last of you in the paper."

"Fine. We're done. I didn't want to be part of your little game anyway."

Saul sipped at his latte, pursed his lips, sat the cup down on the table, tapped his fingers a couple of times. "Yes. Well. It's not quite that easy, is it . . . Lucas?" He smiled, watching Lucas's reaction.

Lucas went perfectly still. "You know my real name."

"I do."

Lucas felt his throat click as he swallowed. He tried another drink, but his throat stayed dry. He tried to look Saul in the eye. His hand was trembling, so he put his cup down, put his hands palms down on the table.

Saul kept that idiotic smile on his face the whole time.

"So what happens now?" Lucas finally asked.

Saul shrugged, an aw-shucks gesture that was somehow filled with menace. He saw Lucas's reaction and chuckled. "Ah, you think I'm going to pull out a pistol and shoot you here in the middle of

Java the Hut? Not my style. I don't kill informants." He picked up his coffee again.

Lucas waited a few moments. "But you have people who do."

Saul sat down the cup, dabbed at his mouth with a paper napkin, saying nothing. "You really have some trust issues. All I want is what I want," he said. "A bit of information—especially on the one who calls himself Snake."

"The guy who started the Creep Club."

"That would be him."

"So then you just kill me after that. Or have your thugs do it."

A pained look crossed Saul's face. "Please, please, Humpty. You think I'm a monster or something?"

Lucas thought it best not to answer.

LATE THAT NIGHT, HIS FLASHLIGHT CONVERTED INTO A CANDLE, LUCAS huddled in his small space on the fourth floor, cataloging his totems.

He picked up each item, lingering over it, before replacing it in its assigned spot. This was a pattern, a ritual, that calmed him whenever he felt uneasy.

But tonight it wasn't working. Images of Saul, of Leila in her home, of the Creep Club, kept intruding.

He had no family, no future, no past. And now he was a fugitive from the police, from the Creep Club, and from at least one government intelligence agency. He wasn't safe anywhere.

Humpty Dumpty had some great falls.

He caressed a photo, enjoying the smiling faces of the people in it. But now the smiles seemed sinister, as if the people knew what he held in his Dark Heart.

Nothing.

He was hollow, meaningless.

And the people in these photos—his mementos—knew it. He could see it in their faces now; why hadn't he before?

With a roar of rage, he swept his arm across his carefully constructed shrine, scattering photos and frames across the floor.

Not far away, he heard something move in reaction. A scrape.

He grabbed his candle, unscrewed the base, and extinguished the light. He moved quickly to the nearest wall, pressing against it, and waited in the darkness.

Was someone in the room with him, sent to take care of the problem for Saul? The man knew his real name, so it wasn't much of a stretch to figure he knew his location as well.

Then the noise came again. And this time, with his attention focused, he was able to make out what it was. A scraping sound, yes. But there was a deeper, more organic element to the sound as well—something like the slither of a snake. It was at the office's locked front door; someone, he realized, trying to pick the lock. He heard a soft click, and then the door swinging open in the darkness.

Lucas forced his body to relax, even as he felt his heart rate spinning wildly out of control. An unusual, almost unheard of sensation for him. He never sweated, but he felt a fine sheen of it oozing through his pores.

There was something . . . other . . . entering his room, and his whole body was telling him to get out.

He took a deep breath, surprised at the panic that was coursing through his body, and forced himself to relax. After a few beats, he held up his flashlight and thumbed it on.

A tall, thin figure, its face bathed in light, stared back at him. Lucas recognized the face immediately and wished he hadn't turned on the flashlight; he had to get away, as far away as possible. *Now.*

Flashlight and backpack clutched in his hands, Lucas turned and scrambled to the rear part of the office, then slid out the window onto the fire escape, stumbling to his knees as he landed on the steel steps.

But the . . . thing following him would expect him to run down the stairs, wouldn't it? Perhaps he could take advantage of those expectations.

Instead he raced up the iron stairs to the fifth floor, and then up a final flight to the roof of the building, dropping over the edge and pressing himself into the dark crease of the wall around the building.

A few seconds later, the main door to the fourth-floor fire escape slammed open below. The thing hadn't followed him out the window but had chosen to go out the emergency exit in the hallway. Odd. He paused for a few seconds, heard the labored breathing. A few exchanged words he couldn't make out (so the thing wasn't alone), and then the iron rungs of the fire escape began clanking: his pursuers were making their way down to the street.

Several seconds later the stairs stopped shaking, and Lucas dared a peek over the top of the building. In the glow of a single weak streetlamp down the alley, he saw two figures moving away at a brisk pace, guns drawn and held ahead of them. At this distance, they were blobs, so he couldn't see their features. But they had to be his pursuers. They hadn't shot him in his room, even though they'd had the chance. And now they were running down the alley as if they were still following him. Something didn't add up.

Lucas let out a small sigh, letting himself sink back to the surface of the roof. He waited, making his body go into its deep trancelike state. After half an hour without moving, and without hearing any other sounds, he removed himself from the dark corner, slipped over the edge of the building, and made his way carefully down the fire escape. The iron framework tried to quake with each of his steps, but he moved lightly, making sure it swayed only a bit. As he made his way to the alley level, he kept a careful watch on his surroundings, looking for danger.

Finally, on the relative stability of the paved alley, Lucas felt the fear amplifying in the back of his throat again. This was the Dark Vibration at work, yes, but in this guise, the vibration wasn't a hunger, a need.

It was innate, naked fear.

Because Lucas had looked at the first figure who had broken into his secret hiding place, and he had seen something that terrified him more than anything he could imagine.

His own face.

TWENTY-ONE

SWARM STOOD IN THE RETREATING SHADOWS AND WATCHED THE CITY around him awaken. Cars and buses belching exhaust on the street. People on foot, holding their arms close in the morning chill as they hurried to their destinations. Chain-link fences rolling away from storefronts with a dull chatter.

Even the cloud of wasps, his constant companion, showed more activity. He felt their incessant buzz in his own bones as their numbers grew from a few dozen to a few hundred in a matter of minutes. That number would stay constant until nightfall; some wasps would die, torn apart by others, while others would fall away listlessly. Even so, those left behind would be replaced by others as new wasps joined the cloud, pulled by some elemental magnetism.

Swarm felt one of the wasps alight on his forehead and begin to crawl across his skin. He smiled.

The End Game was beginning, and the person who would set that End Game in motion had left the building in front of him no more than an hour ago—just after he'd sent in his Dark Fear recruits.

He hadn't really wanted to send them into the building, but it had been necessary; this young man—this Lucas—had to be prepared. Watchful. And so Swarm needed to make sure he kept his edge.

He looked at the dark windows of the fourth floor, put his hand against the iron fire escape Lucas had used not so very long before.

Iron. Like steel. Like the room he could still feel, still smell and taste, all these years later.

Lucas had locked himself inside rooms as well, hadn't he? Kept himself isolated. And now it was time to throw open the doors, expose Lucas to the Great Wide World beyond.

He had big plans, very big plans, for this Lucas.

Swarm felt the wasp working its way down his face, across his cheek. He opened his mouth, stood unmoving as he felt the thin legs of the wasp make their way onto his lips and across his teeth.

When he felt the wasp on his tongue, he closed his mouth over it, feeling its panic as it desperately injected its stinger into the soft pink flesh of his tongue again and again.

He savored the wet taste of its fear before beginning to chew, crushing it between his molars.

And as he chewed, overhead, he already felt another wasp join the endless cloud that followed him.

TWENTY-TWO

UNDER THE HAZY TWILIGHT OF EARLY MORNING, LUCAS WALKED INTO A homeless shelter on the north side of DC.

He needed new clothes. But more than that, he needed new everything. Someone had found him *(it was me, I found myself)*, and he was sure he knew both who and how.

The who was Saul. The how was something he currently carried. Maybe his clothes, maybe something in his backpack, maybe the backpack itself. Surely a bug had been planted somewhere on him during his meeting with Saul. It made perfect sense. Which meant it was time to be reborn. Time to change every article he was wearing, donate every item he was carrying, and replace it all.

The clothing was easy; he was happy to pick out donated items from the shelter, and he regularly carried an extra set of clothes with him in his backpack.

The backpack and its contents would be more difficult. He had several stashes of cash all across the city, so money wouldn't be a problem.

At least, not an immediate problem; sometime soon, he'd have to start working again. Or panhandling.

He would have to make several stops, though: a sporting goods store for rope, utility knife, and flashlight; a hardware store for duct tape, drill, and other tools . . .

He sighed. No choice.

At least he could donate all his current items, make sure they went to someone else.

Before turning in the backpack, Lucas went through it and retrieved a few items he had to take with him. First, tapes of everything he'd recorded from Donavan's files, as well as Dilbert's footage. He'd buy new DVDs and make copies at The LiveWire café, then ditch the tapes in an alley trash can somewhere. Second, the remaining two geopatches he'd lifted from Donavan's; they might come in handy again.

He put the tapes and geopatches aside, and thought of what he'd been forced to leave behind. The mementos—the photos, scraps of clothing, and knickknacks that kept the Dark Vibration inside under control—were gone now. Certainly for the foreseeable future. Maybe forever. He'd have to leave them where they were, forever entombed above Dandy Don's Donuts.

He shook the last few items out of his backpack and noticed a small piece of paper flutter to the table where he stood. He picked it up, recognizing it as Sarea's phone number.

He hadn't talked to her for—well, it had only been a matter of days, but already it felt like several lifetimes. He felt an overwhelming urge to hear her voice. Something warm and comforting and familiar. Especially now that he had given up his totems.

He clenched the slip of paper in his hand and went to get a couple fresh changes of clothing. It would take a couple of hours to replace everything, and then he would call Sarea.

"HELLO?"

Her voice sounded warm, comfortable, familiar, and just the sound of her saying one word made tears well in his eyes.

What kind of reaction was this? Certainly nothing he'd expected. He sucked in a breath, switched the new TracFone to his other ear. "Hey, Sarea."

"Lucas." She spoke his name as if she'd been expecting his call.

"What are you doing?" he asked.

"I'm on shift," she said. "Pretty light right now, though. I'm gonna walk into the back so I can talk."

"Okay." He waited a few seconds, listening to her breathe as she walked, kitchen sounds filtering by. Then, abruptly, he spoke again without thinking. "It's good to hear your voice," he said. "Really good."

She laughed. "You act like it's been years since we talked," she said. "It's been—what?—three days maybe."

"Let's just say it's been a long three days," he answered.

"Okay," she said. "I'm back here by the old Hobart now. We both know it'll be quiet—Briggs is on."

"Piling 'em up for the next shift, huh?"

"Yeah. And the new kid can barely make it to the bathroom by himself."

"Sorry."

"Don't be. It's like you got . . . I don't know. A get-out-of-jail-free card or something. Some of us, we been here for years. So when someone goes on to a better place, that's good."

"What makes you think I'm in a better place?"

"Just an expression. You in trouble? You need help?"

"I don't know what I'm in," he said. "But I already feel better talking to you."

He heard a quick breath from her on the other end of the line. "Good to hear your voice too. I'm glad you didn't decide to just disappear on me."

"Yeah, well, it wasn't you I was trying to disappear from."

"You sure you're okay?"

"I am now."

"Listen," she said, her voice dropping to a whisper. "There's been guys coming in here. Looking for you. Not just that first guy."

Probably not a surprise. "What do they look like?"

"I don't know," she said. "Different guys. Three or four of 'em."

"Anyone . . . look like me?"

"What? No. No, not at all."

Lucas breathed a sigh of relief. He half expected to hear that the . . . thing . . . chasing him, the thing wearing his face, was out there. Wandering the streets. Living his life.

After all, he hadn't done a very good job of living it, had he?

"What can you remember about them?"

"Well, I've seen four of them, now that I think about it. Two were white, and they came in alone. But two came together, and they were Asian, I guess."

He held his breath. "Asian? Like maybe Chinese?"

"Chinese? Yeah, sure, I suppose."

Lucas nodded to himself. Guoanbu. Sending agents after him. Evidently Saul was pulling in reinforcements.

"How many people do you have after you, Lucas?" she asked.

"I'm losing count."

"So let me help."

"That would be a bad idea. A very bad idea."

"Why?"

"All these people after me, for one. And you haven't even met the most charming ones."

"Well, Lucas, there's a problem with guys who try to solve everything alone."

"What's that?"

"They die alone."

LUCAS NEEDED TO STAY HIDDEN, AWAY FROM THE PUBLIC EYE AS MUCH as possible. So late that afternoon he went back to a server room he'd found several months before. In older buildings, especially, Internet companies rented large rooms, filled with servers hooked to the Web via high-speed backbones. Techs would regularly come to the server rooms to do some maintenance, but 90 percent of the time, the servers were alone.

Which meant Lucas could be alone with them.

He popped open the door marked AUTHORIZED FASTECH EMPLOYEES

ONLY using the master key he'd swiped from the management office on the first floor long ago. Inside, the mechanical hum of a hundred computer hard disks flowed over him. He smiled, feeling at home here; in many ways, the hum of these servers mirrored the Dark Vibration he always felt inside.

A built-in desk on the west wall held an older computer the techs used as a workstation when they were here; he'd watched them, carefully logged their actions in this room, on two or three occasions. He knew he could use the workstation to do some searching; his actions might be logged on FasTech's network somewhere, but the thought didn't bother him. He'd be long gone before anyone came around to investigate.

He did a news search for the name Kleiderman Delgado and came up with a couple hits in local newspapers. Kleiderman, a diplomat on staff at the Venezuelan embassy, had been released from the hospital with a leg injury following an apparent robbery attempt in his suburban DC home. His wife, Leila Delgado, had been unharmed during the break-in.

Kleiderman Delgado was a diplomat. Did that mean diplomatic immunity? Was that why the whole story was apparently being swept under the rug? And what had happened to Leila?

Again, the whole diplomat connection seemed a bit uncomfortable to Lucas; it was part of a bigger picture, he knew, that hadn't yet fully focused for him.

Troubled, he backed out of the search and went to Donavan's geopatch site. It was still operational, but the two patches he'd planted—on Saul and Dilbert—had been inactive during the last twenty-four hours. That meant the patches had probably been discovered and destroyed, or perhaps simply fallen off; they were, after all, only meant to be temporary tracking devices.

On a whim, he went to the Creep Club home page. Instead of the familiar log-in screen, he saw a new one: "All messages are now being routed through the Blackboard."

The Blackboard? Lucas scanned his inventory of conversations with Donavan; there had been one previous mention, but no details. He did a quick Google search and found a piece of communication software called Blackboard. Was that it? If so, he had no way of finding it right now.

Lucas backed out of the Web browser and checked the workstation's clock.

The next Creep Club meeting was in less than an hour. The regularly scheduled evening meeting.

He was sure the Chinese version of the CIA was now after him, and he had Saul to thank for it. If he could back up, maybe start over with the club, he could explain the situation with Saul, convince them to help him bring it all down. But that was all out the window now; he couldn't very well show his face to them again, especially in light of his recent publicity.

Still, he had nothing else; going to the Creep Club meeting was the only thing he could think of to do, and he needed to do *something*. Quitting, leaving, dropping out of sight, and doing nothing wasn't an option. He felt a . . . well, *Connection* was the right word, wasn't it? That indefinable, extrasensory something that tied him to certain people over the years. He felt the Connection now, stronger than ever, more imperative than ever, and even though it wasn't tied to a specific person, he knew he couldn't cut it.

He sighed as he stood. Time to creep the creeps, as Saul liked to say. He needed to build a makeshift observation deck at the new building, hide away and find out what he could.

Maybe he'd be lucky.

TWENTY-THREE

LUCAS WATCHED AS THE CREEP CLUB MEMBERS SLIPPED INTO THE building—some through the broken door, some through old windows, some, he was sure, through entry points he couldn't easily see—and he felt a longing in his heart.

Here were people who should welcome him, who should understand him, who should accept him as one of their own. Or, maybe more appropriately, here were people he should welcome, he should understand, he should accept as his own.

And yet, as much as he understood one side of them—the side that hid an insatiable hunger to seek out other people, an uncontrollable need to feed the Dark Vibration—he was repulsed by their unseen side.

The side that simply watched while other people suffered.

He wasn't one of them. Couldn't be one of them. The Dark

Vibration that thrummed in his bone marrow didn't demand the suffering of others.

Did it?

He pushed the thoughts from his mind and hefted his new pack onto his back. Like it or not, he needed to find out more. Maybe he could use something he found out as a lure for Saul, a bargaining chip.

It had been several minutes since he'd seen anyone enter the building, and his TracFone told him it was now about a quarter past the hour; after looking at the time, he powered down the phone and slipped it into his pocket.

A quarter after. For him, it was showtime.

He would have preferred to arrive early, set up ahead of time, carefully conceal himself. Time hadn't allowed that, so he'd have to wing it, hope for the best.

No matter; he couldn't stop now. The front door, hanging loosely, had more than enough space for him to enter. He noticed, as he slid through, yet another CC scrawled into the surface of the door. Evidently the Creep Club folks were starting to feel at home.

He climbed the stairs, going to the next floor. He paused at the end of the hallway, noting the light spilling from room 227 about halfway down. He stayed silent, pressed against the wall as he listened. Murmurs from the room where they were meeting, but nothing else. He'd go to the adjacent room this time, as he'd done in the other building, try to overhear what they were talking about.

He stepped out of the shadows and began to move down the hallway, being careful not to make a sound. But after a few steps, he stopped again, shocked by who he saw step out of room 225. His

Bad Twin. The Bad Twin looked at him with his eyes, smiled with his mouth, held a finger to his lips for a quick *Shhh* . . . and stepped back into room 225, slamming the door shut behind him. The sound reverberated down the hallway, and Lucas heard scrambling inside room 227; without hesitating, he started to turn and run, but just as he did, he felt something solid hit him on the back of the head. He crumpled to his knees, dazed, caught a glimpse of the figure who had hit him running down the stairs.

Also his Bad Twin.

Two of them? He'd been set up, tricked, by two people who looked exactly like him. Impossible, yes. Unless he was becoming a split personality. Delusional. That wasn't so hard to believe.

He started to rise, but he knew it was already too late, even before he heard the mechanical click of a revolver's hammer being pulled back just behind him.

"I think you can stay on your knees right there," a woman's voice said.

He did as he was instructed.

"Put your hands behind your back," the voice said.

Once again he did as he was asked and felt a plastic tie-down slip around his hands and tighten.

"Stand up and turn around."

He turned, and the whole Creep Club was in the hallway with him. The woman closest to him kept her revolver pointed at his head. Snake, just behind, stood smiling. Down the hall, he saw a couple of people picking the lock on room 225's door.

"Well," Snake said. "You know how to make an entrance." Then to everyone else: "Okay, let's go back and talk about this."

The people began filtering back into room 227, and the woman motioned with the barrel of the gun, telling him to follow.

Inside the room, all was quiet as every set of eyes stared at Lucas. He shifted on his feet uncomfortably; he wasn't used to being the subject. Only the viewer.

"Odd," said Snake. "Here we were talking about how to track you down, and you save us considerable trouble by walking into the meeting for us."

Another man, whom Lucas recognized from the previous meeting as Hondo, spoke. "So where's Donavan? Was he one of the others with you?"

Lucas stayed in the doorway, returned the man's gaze. "I'm here alone," he said.

"Funny," Hondo said. "We saw one guy hightail it down the steps, another climb down the side of the building and run away."

"Did you get a good look at them?" Lucas asked.

"Why? Who are they?" Hondo returned.

"That's what I was going to ask you."

Hondo looked like he had something sour in his mouth. He pursed his lips, and Lucas thought for a moment he was going to spit. But he stayed quiet.

Lucas let his gaze slide back to Snake. "Seems like you're our favorite topic, Humpty. Had a special meeting all about you last night, and now this one tonight. Everyone still wants to talk about you. I don't suppose you have a project to show?"

Lucas held the gaze a moment. "I do, as a matter of fact."

"Really?"

"In my backpack. Some tapes I think you'll want to see. A man who's a double agent, trying to infiltrate the Creep Club."

Snake glanced at the red-haired woman who stood behind Lucas, keeping the gun pointed at him. "What do you think, Clarice?" he asked. "Should we let his hands free?"

Snake looked back at Lucas. "Sorry," he said. "Clarice says we can't untie you."

Hondo spoke again. "Yeah, I bet there's an agent trying to make it into the club," he said. "And he's standing right in front of us."

"Now, now, Hondo," said Snake. "We don't know that at all."

Hondo stood. "That's just it. We don't know *anything*. We never even had such a thing as open membership until we let Donavan in a few years ago. And now, just by coincidence, he comes dragging this guy in." Hondo gave him a dismissive wave. "Who's now here to tell us he can save us from some big federal investigation. Timing seems a little convenient."

Snake seemed to actually be enjoying the exchange. "Hmmm. Interesting point. So what do you think we should do, Hondo?"

Hondo didn't hesitate for a second. "Shoot him."

Lucas swallowed, tried not to show any emotion. This wasn't what he'd expected—these folks loved secrets, after all, so why wouldn't they be slobbering all over themselves to see what he had on Saul? But surely someone else would speak up.

"Shoot him," Snake repeated. "A good possibility. Anyone else have an idea?"

Lucas looked around the room, expecting an argument of some kind to start. But all he saw in their eyes was that Dark Vibration, wanting violence.

Hondo, sensing he was on the verge of something big, continued. "This isn't the Elks Club. You don't get voted in. You were either there in the beginning, or you weren't. Never should have taken in

Donavan, and good riddance to him anyway." Hondo sat back down, a satisfied look on his face.

Snake walked back and forth in front of the room. "So the proposal is, we have Clarice take him out and shoot him now," he said. "Anyone opposed?"

Lucas watched as they all stared, saying nothing. Looking, but not seeing, he thought. Just watching. After several seconds, another woman raised her hand.

Finally, Lucas thought. Someone's going to talk, start making sense.

Snake looked at the woman, nodded. "Yeah, go ahead, Mya."

Mya spoke. "When Clarice shoots him, someone's gonna tape it, aren't they?"

Nods and murmurs. Another man chimed in: "Yeah, I think I could use something like that in the project I'm finishing up."

Lucas stared in disbelief. He'd convinced himself, deep inside, that these people were like him—family, in a way. They did all this because they were driven by a compulsion, but they were human, and decent, underneath it all. He had been sure he could appeal to that human part of them, get them to realize that they were under attack, show them the evidence he'd collected against Saul, enroll them in a fight—a revolution—to save themselves.

But he'd been wrong. These people weren't human, and he didn't share anything in common with them. He was, after all was said and done, a true orphan.

"Sure, I think we could arrange that. Kennedy, you want to do the honors?" A man sitting in one of the chairs rose and walked toward the door, nodded at Lucas. As if they'd just been picked for the same dodgeball team or something.

"Don't you want to see the tapes, the files? Hear what I have to say?"

Snake smiled. "I'm a bit curious, speaking personally. But this is a democracy." He swept his arm, indicating the others in the room. "Majority rule."

Lucas turned to make a move, trying to drop his shoulder and bowl Clarice out of the way. But even before could do that, he felt his legs come out from under him and her body move away. Somehow she'd avoided his lunge while doing a foot sweep on him.

Unable to protect his fall by putting his arms down in front of him, he came down hard on his stomach, the cold tile floor knocking his breath away and immobilizing him.

She was on him now, the gun pressed tightly into the back of his head and her breath hot and sticky at his ear. "Don't make me shoot you right here," she hissed. "We don't even have a camera set up yet."

Someone else, Kennedy maybe, slipped a dark hood over his head. He tried to struggle again, tried to fight for his life, but then he felt an arm around his throat, constricting his air, stealing his breath until stars danced in front of his eyes (*lights from the city, they look like lights from the city*) and the world faded to black.

LUCAS AWOKE, HIS BODY A TANGLE OF ACHES AND PAINS. HE KEPT HIS eyes closed, tried not to move, until he got his bearings. He was in a moving car, obviously. Front seat? Back? Hard to say, and even harder to figure out, because the bag was still over his head, and his feet were now bound as well.

He concentrated, putting his body into a deep state, and heightened his senses, listening as carefully as he could.

Two people in the car; he could hear two distinct breathing patterns, even though neither one spoke. And both of them were in front of him, which meant he was in the back.

The car was moving slowly, and the lack of a high whine from the tires meant they were probably on a street rather than a highway—judging by the lack of other traffic sounds, he was guessing a suburban street.

He felt his body shift to the left as the car made a right turn and slowed to a stop. Ahead of him, both doors opened, activating a *ding ding ding* for a few seconds before both closed again. The door next to him opened, but he waited.

"You're awake. I can tell by the way you're sitting."

Clarice's voice. At the thought of her name, images of the Creep Club meeting came flooding back to him.

Yes, this was Clarice. She had brought him here to shoot him and dump him. End of story.

He felt a hand on his shoulder. A few seconds later, he felt a tugging at the binding on his legs, and then his legs were free. Hands pulled away the bag on his head, revealing Kennedy standing at the door, knife in hand. Just behind him, Clarice watched, gun pointed at him. It was dark now, but the parking lot where they had stopped was well lit by sodium lights. Everything looked flat and dusty in their harsh orange glow.

Kennedy clicked the knife closed and put it back in his pocket. "Follow us," he said, and turned to walk away from the car.

Clarice kept the gun trained on him until Kennedy was in the clear, then slipped it into the back of her pants and waited for him to get out of the car.

He refused to move. "You're gonna have to shoot me here," he said.

She looked at him, rolled her eyes. "I'm not gonna shoot you anywhere," she said.

"You wanna take me in that building over there, set up a camera, and pump a couple slugs into me. And you're gonna tape it all so you can get your jollies." He stared hard at her. "But you're gonna have to shoot me here," he repeated.

She leaned down. "And I already told you, I'm not going to shoot you anywhere. You don't have any idea what's going on here, so maybe you should just shut up and pay attention before you try to go all martyr." She produced her own knife, clicked it open, and cut away the binding on his hands, leaving him completely free. That done, she turned and began following Kennedy.

After a few steps, she turned around. "Come on," she said. "I think you'll want to see this."

He looked around. They were in an older neighborhood, in the gray zone between commercial and residential: a few crumbling buildings stood down the street, next to a Quonset hut and two small homes, but all of them were dark. They were parked in a small lot adjoining an ancient brick church of some kind; Lucas saw a large backlit cross above the front doors. He caught a glimpse of someone entering the church through these doors, just ahead of Kennedy. So they were meeting someone.

Lucas sat in the backseat of the car a few more moments, then turned his body and put his feet on the ground. At least his backpack was still with him, he noted. Small wonder, since he'd just replaced it. He didn't trust Clarice for a second, but he now knew he needed to see what she wanted to show him. Whatever it might be. Besides, he could run away right now and get killed by Guoanbu agents; if he had to die, he supposed, he might as well do it sooner rather than later.

He walked across the concrete lot toward Clarice, who stood at the church holding the door open for him. She nodded as he walked by her, then followed him inside.

The church itself had long ago been abandoned, obviously; the only current residents were pigeons and rats, judging by the scattered waste on the hardwood floors.

Clarice stepped in front of him again and led him to a dark wall at the front of the church. Some of the orange light of the streetlights spilled through broken windows high above, but the front of the church remained shrouded in darkness.

Ahead, in that blackness, a soft click startled Lucas, causing him to stumble. Clarice caught his arm as the front of the church was illuminated in a soft glow.

Snake stood in front of them, that impish smile on his face. "Dilbert does some pretty amazing things with generators, don't you think?" he said. "Come on up. Have a seat." He indicated a couple of chairs in front of him.

Lucas stepped up the two stairs to the raised dais and took one of the chairs, and Clarice sat next to him. Kennedy stood off to the side of Snake. But already, Lucas had lost interest in all of them, his gaze transfixed by the front wall of the church.

It was covered with hundreds of pushpins and nails holding photographs, notes, scraps of clothing, and other items.

Totems.

Lucas stared in wide-eyed wonder; compared to his clumsy attempts at a shrine of sorts, this was a masterpiece. And the pattern, the pieces, fit together exquisitely. He wanted to approach the wall and touch the items nailed there, pick them up in his hands and admire them.

Snake turned to look at the wall with him for a moment. "Our Blackboard," he said. "Been part of Creep Club since the beginning."

Lucas, unable to take his eyes off the wall, spoke softly. "When?"

Snake shrugged. "Don't know, exactly."

"But I thought Creep Club was your idea."

Snake nodded. "Donavan told you that?"

"Yeah."

"Well, it was just easier for Donavan to think that."

Lucas stared at the Blackboard a few more moments, then finally managed to overcome its magnetic pull by turning his head to look at Snake. Obviously, this was the Blackboard that had been referenced on the Creep Club site. "What is it?" he asked.

"It's . . . well, it's like our switchboard, isn't it?" Snake looked at Clarice, who gave him a nod. He looked back to Lucas again.

"Yeah, a switchboard. Where we post information and updates about projects, keep track of everyone in the Creep Club. Had to do it this way, you know—Creep Club started long before the Internet was around. Even before a lot of the recording technology we have today. And really, isn't this a better way to do it anyway? Old school."

Snake moved to the board, removed a hat nailed into the wall. He brought it to his face and breathed in, smelling. "You get to touch the projects, feel them this way. Can't do that online. Also, no need to worry about hackers." He turned to face Lucas again. "You know: unauthorized users who get into Web sites they're not supposed to."

Lucas remained silent.

Snake turned to face the wall once more, admiring items that hung on it as he replaced the hat. "Even the inactive ones. They all get boxed, archived. Every Creep Club project is in this building."

"So why'd you bring me here?"

Snake swiveled to look at him. "What, you'd rather have Clarice and Kennedy shoot you?" He laughed.

Lucas felt his eye twitch.

"See, I brought you to my safe place. The place that's more sacred to me than anywhere else. As a gesture of trust. I don't like you, but I've helped you. I could have killed you, but I didn't. I expect the same in return."

"But why did you pretend . . ." Lucas began, but cut himself off in midsentence. He stared at Snake. "You think there's a traitor in the Creep Club."

"Ah, I knew you were smart. You're partly right. Let's just say I don't think everyone in the Creep Club is a hundred percent trustworthy."

"Then why did you bring them into the club?"

"I didn't."

"But I thought—"

"Donavan again?" Snake said.

Lucas bit his lip. "Yeah."

"The only new person to join the club, since I've been in it, is Donavan. We let him in as an . . . I don't know. Call it an experiment."

"Evidently Hondo wasn't much in favor of the experiment."

"Not much. And he's not the only one. Just the loudest." Snake sighed. "Truth be told, all's not well in Creep Club land; bit of a power struggle going on. I'm kind of the old school guy, the one who started it all. But Hondo is all *viva la revolución*, stirring up the pot. He's harder, more brutal, more interested in the . . . unsavory side of this. He doesn't see it as art; he sees it as something to spike the adrenaline, and he needs more and more to keep that adrenaline flowing. He's getting dangerous."

Lucas looked at the wall of totems for a few more moments. "So I'm guessing you want to hear what I have to say. What I recorded."

"Like I said, I don't have a good handle on everyone in the club. Not anymore. Maybe once, but after a while, this changes you." He looked at Lucas grimly, his eyes suddenly looking tired.

Lucas thought of Mya, raising her hand at the meeting and asking if someone was going to record his death. He thought of Saul, talking about Donavan: *He's a junkie.* "I know what you mean."

"Anyway, this place—we just call it the Blackboard because that's always been what we primarily use it for. It's always been . . . holy ground for us. You know what I mean? Always off-limits for anything, really. You ever see *A Clockwork Orange?*"

"I read it."

"Oh, we got a literary boy here, Clarice. Anyway, you know how they program the main character to get physically sick at the thought of violence?"

"Yeah."

"That's how I feel when I think of anything happening to this place. That's how all of us feel. Hard to explain, but to even think about stealing something from here, or defacing something . . ." Snake's face took on a pained expression, proving his point.

Lucas spoke. "But someone has."

Snake wiped at his forehead, looked at him. "Yes. Someone has.

Over the past several months, I've found a few things missing. Nothing major—a few files and such—and nothing that seems to be connected. But still. Someone's crossed the line." Snake stared hard at him. "And I think you might have something that tells me who that is."

Lucas nodded. "I just might." He shrugged off his pack, pulled out the tapes, and held them up. "Let me tell you about a guy named Saul."

TWENTY-FOUR

TWENTY MINUTES LATER, AFTER THEY HAD TRANSFERRED THE TAPES TO a laptop computer and watched them on a screen, after Lucas had told them about his clandestine meetings with Saul, Snake sat silently for a few moments.

"So what you're saying is, you think this guy—this Saul—is working for the Chinese government."

"For Guoanbu, the Chinese version of the CIA."

"Okay. And you think he's trying to infiltrate Creep Club."

"I think so. I think he's a double agent; he works for U.S. intelligence in some capacity, but I found these folders in his house. I think he's turning over information on Creep Club to Guoanbu. And I think he knows I've figured it out—he sent someone after me last night."

Lucas thought it best to leave out the small detail about the someone in question looking just like him.

"And so who were the two people with you tonight? Neither one was Donavan?"

"Neither was Donavan. Neither was with me. In fact, I think they were there specifically to call me out—to let you know I was in the building."

Snake considered for a few moments, nodded. "I see," he said. "I think I'm putting some things together here."

"What things would those be?"

"Later. Let's get back to the Guoanbu thing. What do you think they're after?"

"Who knows? Maybe you have some information on a Chinese official they want. You said it yourself: every project is archived in this place."

Snake stared at the floor, thinking. "We've never done much for security here. Mostly because anyone in the Creep Club would get physically sick just thinking about stealing or destroying anything."

"What about people outside of Creep Club?"

"Well, it wouldn't make much sense to anyone outside Creep Club. All the digital files are encrypted, and the filing—everything's in code."

Lucas stood, went over to the wall. "Like a puzzle, then. You have to break the code to figure out what's archived in this building."

"Yes . . ."

Lucas looked at Clarice, then back at Snake. "That's it, then. Saul—and Guoanbu—want to decode what's in all your files. They need someone to help them crack the code. Saul was most interested in you, after all. Looking for leverage, I'll bet."

Snake was quiet.

Lucas paused a few moments before speaking again. "You don't agree?"

Snake let out a sigh. "I'm not sure. In some ways, it feels right. In others, not so much. For starters, none of us know the code, the encryptions."

"What do you mean?"

"I mean, none of us does the coding or encrypting. None of us could go through the physical files, or the digital ones, and unlock it. That's the point. It's all random, so it never gets unlocked. Which doesn't matter so much to any of us. It's a big puzzle, yes, but we don't need to see the big puzzle to go back. To remember."

He went to the wall, pulled off what looked like a severed hand. "We just need these puzzle pieces. This one, for instance, instantly makes me think of the Halden family. Joseph Halden was a little late with some payments to a . . . certain lending institution. This was his interest." He put the hand back on the board.

"So you cut off his hand?"

"Not at all. I just . . . borrowed it when all was said and done." He studied Lucas's face for a few moments. "I'm not a monster."

Lucas decided it best not to comment.

"So you keep all this stuff, you encode it, but no one knows how to decode it?"

Snake looked at him. "I didn't say no one knows how to decode it. I only said no one in the Creep Club knows how."

"So you're actually collecting all this data, all this information, for what reason? It seems too random."

"Things aren't always what they seem."

Clarice, evidently bored with the detour the conversation had taken, steered them back to the subject of Saul. "We're gonna have to creep this guy."

Snake looked at her. "That's what I've been thinking."

Lucas spoke. "I'm going too."

Snake looked at Clarice, who shrugged. Snake began to pace. "You say you have an address for the building where he works?"

"I do."

"Where is it?"

Lucas gave him an address, recalling it from memory, and Snake nodded immediately.

"Never been in that building specifically, but I know the neighborhood. I have some contacts who could help us get in, I think. Find more information."

Lucas considered. "Your contacts . . ." he said, making the connections in his mind. "Are they in the CIA?"

Snake stared at him. "Something like that. So you need to stay out of sight and let them do their work. Hondo thinks you're dead—everyone thinks you're dead. If you show up again, things could get ugly."

"Ugly for me, or ugly for you?"

"Ugly for everyone," Snake said. "But especially for you. I'd have to make sure of that."

"Point taken."

"Okay," Snake said. "Clarice and I will put together a plan, see what we can find out with this guy. Give us a phone number. And some time."

"Then what?"

"Then we meet again." Snake handed him a card with a phone number on it.

Nothing else: no name, address, or e-mail.

Snake spoke to Clarice. "When you get back to the car, put the hood on him again."

"I thought you said you brought me here to show a bit of trust."

"I did. But letting you figure out exactly where this place is wouldn't be just trust. It would be stupid."

Clarice pulled out a couple zip ties and moved toward Lucas.

He stepped back. "Can't we skip the restraints this time?"

Snake smiled grimly as Clarice pulled out the gun again. "That would be even more stupid."

"Okay, okay," he said, thinking quickly. He needed to know where this church was. "Just let me hold on to this for later," he said, holding up the card Snake had given him.

He put the card in his pocket and, at the same time, pulled out one of the two remaining geopatches, cupping it in his hand.

He turned and let Clarice bind his hands. Then, hands tied, he worked his way toward the door in front of her. At the doorway, he stumbled, acting as if he'd tripped over the mat placed there; he fell against the doorjamb and pressed the geopatch against it, then righted himself and went out the door. Outside, against the wall, was a chair. About ten feet away from the chair stood a camera on a tripod; beside the camera, two round lights spilled their beams on the chair, illuminating a small spot in the darkness of the night.

Lucas looked at Clarice, who motioned toward the chair with the gun. So now, after all this, they were going to shoot him anyway.

"Sit down," Clarice said.

"Just wait a . . ." he started to stammer.

Her answer was a crack on the head with the butt of the gun, which staggered him and sent fresh jolts of pain through his brain. Two hits to the head in the span of an hour. He wasn't having a good evening.

Clarice, surprisingly strong, half dragged him to the chair and put him in it. She picked up some cord that was coiled by the chair and wrapped it around him, tying him in tight. She checked her knots and stood back.

He looked up at her. "Aren't you gonna put the hood on me?" he asked. "For the execution."

She pointed at the camera. "Don't think the audience would like that. They'll want to see your face, you know." She took a few steps back, raised the revolver.

"Wait," he said. "You don't have to do this. We can—"

"Sorry, Charlie," she answered. "But we do have to do this." She pulled the trigger, fired six rounds, emptying all the chambers in the revolver.

Lucas, in a mad panic, felt his chair tipping over; he hit the ground hard and gasped for breath.

A few moments later, Clarice was crouched on the ground beside him, untying him. He looked at his chest, expecting to see a mass of hamburger, but saw nothing. He looked back at her in wonder.

She held up the revolver, tripped the hammer again. "Blanks," she said. "But they make a nice sound, don't they?"

"But—"

"Hondo and the others wanted to see you shot on camera." She nodded at the tripod. "We just gave them what they wanted." Next, she held up the hood. "Now you can have your executioner's hood."

THEY DROPPED HIM OFF AT UNION STATION, AND LUCAS WALKED AROUND the station for a few minutes to clear his mind, decided to stop for a coffee.

It was late now, near midnight, so he had to settle for a cup of off-color coffee from the vending machine. He waited for the cup to fill, pulled it out of the slot, sniffed at it, and tasted it.

It was cold, but it didn't taste as bad as he'd thought it would. Still, he added a couple packets of sugar to make it go down easier.

Sleep was what he really needed, but this would do for now. He sat near one of the legionnaire statues, sipping his coffee, trying to wrap his mind around the last several hours. The last several days.

The Creep Club had obviously been a large miscalculation. And he had to admit, now that he'd had a chance to chew on it for several hours, he knew exactly why he'd made that miscalculation.

Pride.

He'd seen himself above all the members of the Creep Club. They loved to creep into private homes; he sniffed at such things (even though the Dark Vibration inside yearned for it, oh yes), as they were beneath him. He had self-control; they had none. He had standards; they had nothing but their insatiable hunger. He was able to control his impulses; they were not.

Therefore he was smarter, faster, better than they were.

Hondo had crushed that pride easily. He wouldn't make the same mistake again. Now he understood that although he wasn't truly one of them, he was a kindred spirit. The same desires that burned inside them also illuminated his path, like it or not.

And he didn't like it.

The thought sickened him, saddened him, more than ever. Here were people who were so much like him, people who should understand him more than anyone else on earth.

And maybe, scarily enough, they did understand him. Maybe the problem, unfortunately, was that he had failed to understand them.

Which meant, in some ways, he'd failed to understand himself.

He shuddered, gulped down the rest of the coffee, and decided to make his way down to the loading platform. He had no pass, of course, nothing to be tracked, but he knew a back way about half a block over.

He pushed his way out the doors to the station and felt something hard poking him in the back of the head.

A voice spoke, dark and harsh, the breath scented with garlic. "How about we take a quick detour?" it said.

Lucas closed his eyes. This stuff was getting old. "A detour to where?"

"Little place called Split Jacks. You've heard of it."

Lucas opened his eyes. Split Jacks. The bar where he'd met Viktor Abkin, the owner of ATM2GO. He had a sinking feeling he was about to meet Viktor again.

And he knew it wasn't going to be a pleasant meeting.

THIS TIME LUCAS DIDN'T ENTER SPLIT JACKS THROUGH THE FRONT DOOR; Garlic Breath escorted him through a back door, led him through a dark, echo-filled room where he tripped over something unseen, and pushed him into a small corner with a folding card table and a dim lamp.

At first Lucas thought they were the only people in the room. But then he heard a scraping sound, and Viktor's face moved into the weak light of the lamp. Viktor moved the folding chair, adjusting it on the bare concrete floor, and motioned to an empty chair across the table from him.

Garlic Breath let go of Lucas's arm, so he moved to the table and sat. Viktor stared for a few moments, then his face tipped back and out of the direct light again.

Lucas briefly thought the man was tipping over, until he realized Viktor was filled with nervous energy; he kept rocking back on his folding chair's two back legs, dropping the chair to the floor with a scrape, then rocking back again.

Viktor's face came forward again, an illuminated leer in the incandescent glow. "Well now, my good Samaritan," he said. He put his front teeth over his lip and sucked in, as if he were about to say something he found very difficult. "It would seem you've been avoiding me. And here I thought we'd hit it off so well."

Lucas said nothing, deciding it would be best to go with the silent treatment. But that didn't last long. "How'd you find me?" he said.

Viktor's voice floated across the table toward him. "Ah, well, one of the benefits of owning an ATM company. They all have cameras inside them, you see. And we have several hundred ATMs across the DC Metro area. One near a place called Dandy Don's Donuts—where some of my associates wished to speak to you, until you slipped out the back—and one at Union Station. Where you just had a cup of coffee. It also helps that we have some rather wonderful facial recognition technology to go with our cameras—you can shave your head, you can hide your eyes, but you can't change your face."

Viktor tipped back in the chair again, forcing Lucas to listen to his disembodied voice. "You've been a real thorn in my side, I must say. I've not been able to figure out what to do with you."

Now Lucas spoke. "Why do you say that?"

Bam. The chair's legs came to the floor again, perhaps a bit more forcefully. Viktor seemed to be leaning forward. "Why? Well, I'd say because you don't seem to be afraid of me. Someone who isn't afraid is . . . well, a thorn in my side."

Lucas said nothing, but Viktor Abkin was wrong. He was afraid. Very afraid.

Viktor put his elbows on the table and propped his head on his hands. The careful, attentive listener. "Now then, what do you suggest I do?"

"I suppose 'go our separate ways' isn't one of the options?"

"Afraid not."

"But think about it. Those tapes I showed you aren't good for anything now. I saw the story in the paper: both Anita and Ted are missing."

"Don't believe everything you read in the papers," Viktor said. "They've been found. An unfortunate car accident, you see. They were hit by a drunk driver—guy came all the way across two lanes of traffic and—*bam!*" Viktor slammed his hand on the table, shaking it and startling Lucas.

Now Viktor decided to lean back in his chair again. "Near as we can figure, they were holed up in some little country cottage down in Virginia. Coming back after a few days off. I, not hearing anything from them for a few days, went to the authorities. But then, this. The two of them, carrying on, having an affair. How positively tragic for me, to lose my wife and my business partner . . . and to discover they were also lovers."

His face was back in the light now, smiling.

"You don't seem too upset."

"Well, there is the little matter of the insurance money. A few ends to wrap up, of course, but the money should be on its way soon. Help to salve my wounds." He paused. "Not the way Ted and I had planned it, of course. Lots of time wasted, with him wining and dining my lovely wife."

Lucas looked at him, stunned. "You were going to kill your wife."

Viktor's smile burned brighter than ever. "Ted was going to do the dirty work, but yes. Until you decided to be a hero. Not that I'm complaining. Double the money."

Lucas sighed. "So you're coming out ahead. You don't need me for anything."

"Oh yes, I'm coming out ahead." Now he put his top teeth on his bottom lip again, made that same sucking sound.

It reminded Lucas of a snake flicking out its tongue to taste the air around him. A fitting image.

"But you're wrong on the second part. I do need you for something."

A door opened behind Viktor, letting in a shaft of light. For a moment, a dark figure stood in the doorway, holding something; the figure turned to close the door, and Lucas felt the new person approaching.

At his ear, he heard Garlic Breath once again raise the pistol; its barrel settled against the back of his head, a little more forcefully than necessary.

The new guy was a small, dark man who refused to meet Lucas's stare. He stopped at the table and bowed; immediately, Lucas felt him strapping something around his leg. Great, they were tying him up again; hadn't been that long since he went through all this.

But a few seconds later, after a tugging sensation, Lucas heard a few quick beeps and saw lights begin to glow in the darkness.

"You might be wondering what's on your ankle right now," Viktor said.

He was half in/half out of the lamplight, frozen in midtilt; Lucas could see his mouth and jaw, but his eyes stayed in darkness. Viktor waited for Lucas to respond, but continued when Lucas didn't.

"It's a bomb." He waited for the information to sink in before continuing. "Thank you, Terry."

The small man rose to his feet again and retreated from the room while Lucas sat and stared.

"So you blow me up," he finally said. "It doesn't get you anything."

Viktor clapped his hands, let his chair legs drop to the floor again. "It doesn't! It doesn't! That's exactly right. Which is why I don't want to blow you up. Not at all. You see, I'd rather we work out a partnership. You run some errands for me, and I agree not to blow off your leg."

He made a swirling motion with his hands, smiled. "Not much of a bomb, I'll admit," he said. "Very little explosive charge, really. Just enough to blow off your leg. But you have some very large arteries in your legs. Did you know that? Blow off a leg, you could bleed to death in just a few minutes."

Lucas felt panic rising in his throat, but he forced it down. "Sounds like you're getting the better part of the deal."

"I think I've made it very clear, I don't want to blow off your leg. It is my wish that we continue to work together, that you perhaps do some collections for me. As a way of repaying my favor. Each time you complete a job for me, I reset the timer on your ankle." He paused. "The upside is, you get to live. You, of course, can choose to do none of this, decide to go throw yourself under a train. But I do not think you will do this. You are a hero, after all, the man who thought he was going to save me. So we will keep working together, and you will keep convincing yourself you'll figure out a way to beat this arrangement."

"And I'm guessing you have a first errand in mind."

"I do. I do, indeed. Your first assignment is: you will set up a meeting."

"A meeting with . . ."

"With whomever you're working with. Or for. You really expect me to think you're doing all this by yourself? You've got someone behind you. Someone interested in making a move on my operations, I'm guessing."

"Your guess is way off the mark."

"Well, there's one way for you to prove that."

"I could set you up."

"You could. But I'll have others following you. Your bomb has a built-in tracking chip. Plus, you're a hero. You'll do as I ask, try to figure out how to get yourself out of this mess. And I'll make it easy on you: I'm clearing my schedule for the next two days. You might say this is my top priority, so feel free to call me on my cell phone."

Lucas pictured the cell phone number, instantly pulling it from his mind. He nodded. "You said two days."

"Well, more like a day and a half—the timer's set at thirty-six hours before . . . well, let's not talk too much about what happens when the timer runs down. I don't want you to be discouraged, first day on the job and all."

Viktor stood, leaned over the table, put his face close to Lucas, and whispered, "So what do you think, my friend? Are you afraid of me now?"

Viktor straightened back up and disappeared in the darkness. Lucas listened to his footsteps on the cold concrete until the door at the back of the room opened again, spilling a shaft of light.

Just before Viktor disappeared through the door and into the light, Lucas shouted to him. "I'll beat this!" he said.

Viktor turned back to face him, standing in the open doorway. Lucas couldn't see Viktor's face, but he knew the man was smiling. "See? I told you—you will convince yourself you can find a way out of this. That will keep you going. But if you'll pardon your own American expression, you don't have a leg to stand on."

TWENTY-FIVE

After Garlic Breath and his gun had kicked Lucas out of the car at Union Station, he knew he needed to get back to the church. He looked at his watch; he'd been going all night, and it was just past four thirty. He was stuck in those dead hours between late night and early morning. The Metro wouldn't start running at Union Station for another hour, so he decided to splurge. He found a cab queue at one of the hotels, crawled into the taxi, and gave the driver the address for The LiveWire.

He'd told Snake he would stay out of sight. And he would—just as soon as he found the address he needed. He didn't even bother to buy a cup of coffee this time; he went into the café, fairly deserted at this early time of morning, and opened the browser on a vacant computer. Five minutes later, after typing in the IP address and checking the geopatch, he had the church's address. The Green Line or Yellow Line would get him there. He checked the time on his TracFone. Still another half hour or so before the trains started running, but he might as well head to the station and wait there. He checked his dwindling money supply, down to a couple hundred bucks. Time was more important than money at this point; he hailed another cab.

He knew, even as he slid into the back of the cab, why he needed to find the church. It was filled with mementos, totems. Some, detailing the currently active projects, were nailed to the Blackboard wall at the front of the church. And some were hidden elsewhere. But now that his own totems were gone, it was the only place he could go for comfort.

For home.

He closed his eyes as the streets flew by. He had a bomb attached to his leg. The thought should terrify him, but he was too exhausted to feel anything right now. In a strange way, the bomb had already given him clarity; he knew exactly what he needed to do, and he had no qualms about doing it. The bomb, after all, was at the least a way out of all this.

Of course, before he exploded, he needed to stop the Chinese secret service, stop the more brutal members of Creep Club from spilling more blood, and, oh yeah, figure out why the two guys who looked just like him had outed him at the Creep Club meeting.

Exhausted, he pulled himself into a tight ball and fell asleep.

He was jolted awake when the bomb on his ankle began to utter a high-pitched alarm. Quickly, he looked at the cab driver, who didn't seem concerned at all. He pulled up his pant leg and looked at it. The ring of lights continued to beat out their steady pace. He realized, his brain still fuzzy, that he'd been dreaming about the ankle bomb.

The cab slowed and pulled to a curb; as light began creeping across the eastern horizon, Lucas saw the dark outline of the church hovering.

He paid the cabbie and entered the church. He moved slowly to the front wall, found the switch that illuminated the Blackboard, and flicked it, listening to the steady hum as the lights drew a current from the battery cells. Clever, that Dilbert; he used the generator to power the batteries, then ran power from the batteries.

He stared at the Blackboard, following the trails of Creep Club members, the strings that connected their individual photos to mementos from their current projects. There was something big in here, he knew. Something very big. He just needed to figure out what it was.

Hondo's face was here, hanging on a nail. The nail had some string wrapped around it that led to another nail a few feet away. The string was wrapped a few times around this second nail (which held a family photo of a mom, dad, two children, and a golden retriever), then went to a third nail, which held a small tennis shoe, tied there by one of its laces.

Photos of other Creep Club members dotted the huge wall, each connected by nails and pieces of string to other mementos all across the board. Photos of all kinds. Newspaper clippings. A child's doll. A swatch of fabric. Several keys and key rings. Even the dismembered, mummified-looking hand Snake had lingered over before.

Lucas found Dilbert's photo on the wall, then followed the string that connected it to Kleiderman and Leila Delgado. He looked at

Leila's smiling face as she posed beside Kleiderman, the man who had beaten her for so long. Was that a fake smile she was wearing in the photo? No matter; it was a smile, and a familiar face of some kind. A friendly face. He took the photo off the wall and slowly sank to the floor, holding the photo carefully.

Once sitting, he put the photo on the floor and turned his attention to the contraption that now encircled his ankle. It wasn't big or heavy; his pant leg easily hid it. It was a dull lead color, except for the red LED lights that dotted its circumference every inch or so. The lights blinked on and then off in a steady pattern all the way around it, making it seem like a small flying saucer straight out of a science fiction movie.

A flying saucer that was attached to his leg.

A flying saucer that was attached to his leg and would blow it off in several hours. Unless he introduced Viktor to "backers" who didn't exist.

He put his hand on the—what was it, anyway? A manacle? Good a word as any. He put his hand on the manacle, feeling its solid metal surface, and turned it. It moved easily around his ankle. On close inspection, he could see the hinge at the back and the locking plate on the front with a small keyhole.

He didn't know much about bombs. But he did know they could easily blow if you tried to diffuse them and didn't know what you were doing.

But if he could get out of the manacle with the whole thing intact, maybe.

He took off his sock and shoe, flexed his foot down as far as he could. His joints were much more pliable than most people's, and if he could just . . .

Nothing. He could get close, tantalizingly close, to slipping the manacle over the heel and ball of his foot. But it wouldn't quite go. He was stuck with it. For now.

He put his sock and shoe back on, looked at the photo of Kleiderman and Leila again, then picked it up and cradled it in his hands.

(Humpty Dumpty had some great falls.)

He stared at the photo, at the fake smile. There was so much he needed to do. Get in touch with Snake and his crew. Find out more about Saul. Investigate the Guoanbu. Stay hidden from the rest of the Creep Club (and this was not the place to do that). And, yes, find a way to keep his leg from exploding.

But the veil of exhaustion smothered all those thoughts, and even as he struggled to stay alert, he was fighting a losing battle.

Soon, his body slept.

23:27:45 REMAINING

A toe in the shoulder wakened him. He came to immediately, jumping to his feet.

"Why am I not surprised to see you back here?"

Snake, along with Clarice and Kennedy.

"Guess I halfway figured you'd find your way back, but I had to try. 'Course, sleeping in the middle of the floor doesn't exactly count as staying out of sight. Makes it a little hard for Hondo to believe that staged video. Nice touch, making the chair fall backward when Clarice shot you. I smell Oscar."

Snake held out his hand, and after a few moments, Lucas realized what he wanted. He handed the photo of Kleiderman and Leila to Snake, who put it back on the nail on the Blackboard.

"You remember Clarice and Kennedy," Snake said as he finished hanging the photo.

Snake turned around to face them again. "After our little meeting last night, I made a few calls. Found out a bit more about Saul."

Lucas nodded.

Snake set down a briefcase, opened it, and started rifling through several papers inside. "Interesting character, this guy," he said. "Almost too interesting. Been in the intelligence community for the last seventeen years, first in the military, and for the last five as a civvie. Awards, plaques, the whole nine yards."

Snake stood, handed Lucas some of the papers. Lucas paged through them as Snake continued to speak.

"A Purple Heart in the first Gulf War, plenty of commendations, several rounds of classified training . . . I mean, this is the poster boy for our intelligence community."

Lucas looked from the papers to Snake. "Meaning?"

Snake shrugged. "Meaning I don't know. I told you, I don't think I can trust everyone inside the Creep Club. I'm not surprised to find some other branches of government intelligence trying to bust into our ranks, keep an eye on us, but not this guy."

Something Snake said jolted Lucas, but he couldn't quite figure out what it was right now; his mind was still waking. He looked down at a photo of a younger Saul, dressed in his fatigues.

"A little too obvious, is that what you're saying?"

Snake shrugged. "Yeah, I guess so. A little too visible; you send a guy to go snooping inside"—Snake stumbled just a bit, as though he'd started to say something he shouldn't—"inside something like the Creep Club, you send someone who doesn't have such a long trail. Someone who's an unknown."

"Someone who's expendable."

Snake looked at him. "Right."

Lucas thought about the manacle clamped to his ankle. "That's where I come in, I guess."

"Maybe."

"So what are you gonna do now?" Lucas asked.

"Well, we've been getting some things set up at Saul's office. Doing a little digging. Figure maybe tonight we'll have a look around, see what we can find."

Lucas nodded. "Sounds like a plan, but that building is a ghost building. Doesn't officially exist on any maps or sat images. No businesses listed there. Can't imagine it isn't loaded with security."

Snake smiled. "You leave that to me. My contacts helped me put this all together."

"You already have it done?"

Snake looked at his watch. "Past three in the afternoon right now. Didn't want to wake you; you looked like you needed some sleep. And we got it handled."

Lucas felt as if the manacle on his ankle were tightening. For roughly the first ten hours he'd had this bomb attached to him, he'd slept. Now he was down to twentysome hours.

"You okay?" Snake said. "I'm letting you into this, because frankly I need the extra boots on the ground, and there's no one I'd absolutely trust outside of Clarice and Kennedy here. But if you're not up to it . . ."

Lucas shook his head. "No, no. I'm good to go. I just—" He stared at Snake. "Kind of a rough night."

Snake nodded, then dropped to his knees and retrieved one more item from the suitcase. A newspaper page, folded to a specific story.

"Your rough night have anything to do with this?" he asked as he gave the paper to Lucas.

Lucas took the paper and scanned the story. "Body Found in River," the headline said. Lucas read quickly, noting the specifics: a man named Brian Ford had drowned in the Potomac, and his body had been recovered late the previous afternoon. Authorities withholding details due to an ongoing investigation, the standard fare.

Lucas, puzzled, looked at Snake. "I don't get it," he said.

Snake smiled. "So I guess you're trying to tell me you don't know Donavan's real name. Here I thought you two were close."

"His name is Brian Ford? I thought . . . well, I guess I thought it was Donavan Roxwell."

"It was his name, for everything he did with us. For everything he's done the last few years." Snake smiled. "For the trail he's been laying." Snake stared for a few seconds, waiting for Lucas to make the connection.

"You think . . . he's connected to Guoanbu too? Maybe he's been meeting with Saul?"

Lucas thought of Saul's geopatch movements. Was Donavan, née Brian, the person he kept meeting at the Lincoln Memorial? After all Saul's blather about not wanting to work with Donavan—the "junkie"—was he working with him after all?

"Doesn't sound like a bad theory to me," Snake said.

"What about Hondo?" Lucas asked. "He didn't seem like a big fan of Donavan's."

Snake stayed silent for a few more moments, glanced at both Clarice and Kennedy, then back at Lucas. "No, I don't think Hondo will be heartbroken."

Lucas held out his hand, and Snake grasped it. "Thank you," he said to Snake, meaning it. He half thought of showing Snake the manacle on his ankle, asking if he had some way out of the predicament. But that would be showing a weakness. He didn't want to show any kind of weakness to a snake.

"See you tonight. Nine o'clock," Snake said. "And do me a favor until then. I doubt anyone will be dropping by—whole club's in a bit of a frenzy—but maybe you could hide yourself just a bit better." Then the three of them were gone, leaving Lucas alone with the Blackboard.

And his thoughts.

And his bomb.

His eyes strayed back to the photo of Leila and Kleiderman. He scanned the other faces of Creep Club projects on the giant board, letting his mind soak it all in. In addition to photos of the people, he saw depictions of architectural plans, satellite images, coordinates. He saw actual microchips and circuit boards hanging on nails, along with passports, vials filled with liquids, plastic baggies containing hair samples.

A sudden thought bloomed in his mind, and he went back to Leila and Kleiderman one more time. He glanced at their faces, then checked off the faces representing all the current projects for the Creep Club, Viktor Abkin's face included.

This wasn't just a memento board—a blackboard, as the Creep Club liked to call it. Viewed as a whole entity, it became clear to him now. He was looking at an evidence board.

And he didn't like what the evidence was showing him.

TWENTY-SIX

Leila opened the door of her home, then stood in front of him silently.

"Well," she said. "You back to set off my alarm again?"

"Um, is your husband here?" Lucas asked.

"Hospital," she said. "Tore up his leg pretty bad when I shot him. Had to have surgery."

"Is he gonna be okay?"

She shrugged.

Lucas shifted his weight from one foot to the other. "Look, can I come in?"

She stared for a moment. "Why do I get the feeling I'm going to regret this?" she asked.

"I just figured something out," he said. "I think you should hear it."

She stared for a few more seconds before stepping aside. He walked into the house and waited for her to close the door, then followed her back to the living room and sat down when she did. He tried to put thoughts of his last visit to this house, just a few nights ago, out of his mind.

"So," she said, "you back for some more video, are you? Need a couple extra shots?"

He ignored her question, but offered one of his own. "So, your story—how'd it hold up?"

"You mean about my husband going paranoid, and seeing people in our basement, and beating me because he's sick?" She ran a hand through her long, dark hair. "So far, so good. I think they even bought it when I told them a friend picked me up at the hospital last time, let me stay at her house, and brought me home the next day."

"Which explained your car at the hospital."

She nodded. "Story's mostly true, anyway." She looked at him with her dark eyes. "All the important parts, anyway." She leaned back against her couch. "Now, you want to tell me why you're back?"

"I . . . uh . . . can you tell me what, exactly, your husband does? His work?"

"Diplomat for the Venezuelan embassy here."

Lucas nodded. "And what about you, if you don't mind me asking?"

"Don't mind you asking what?"

"What you do, your line of work."

She smiled. "So you don't buy the stay-at-home trophy-wife story, huh?"

He returned the smile. "Trophy wives, for the most part, don't know how to use a gun."

She nodded. "Okay, no harm, I suppose. I was a weapons designer once upon a time," she said. "Got my degrees here in the States, did some work for the U.S. government, designing . . ."

"Weapons."

She smiled. "Yes. Weapons. If I didn't know any better, I'd say you were a police officer suddenly."

He shook his head. "Just trying to put some things together."

"Like?"

"Like why your house was targeted."

"Targeted for . . ."

"For surveillance. A group that calls itself the Creep Club. Couple dozen people across the whole DC area, and they . . . well, they essentially spy on people in their homes."

She stared for a moment. "You're serious," she said. She shook her head, looked at the ceiling. "A bunch of high-tech Peeping Toms."

"I think Peeping Tom is maybe the wrong way to describe them. I think, maybe more like spies."

"Spies," she repeated.

He switched gears. "You and Kleiderman, you're both from Venezuela originally?"

She stared for a few moments. "Yes."

He bit his lip, unsure how to continue. "Venezuela's been through some . . . well, political turmoil is a good way of putting it, these past several years."

"*Some* is a mild way of putting it. Just spit out what you're thinking," she said.

"I was looking at the Blackboard today—"

"The Blackboard?"

"It's a large wall. Kind of a giant bulletin board, where people in the Creep Club keep photos, tidbits, souvenirs of the projects they're working on."

"Stolen pieces from the homes."

"Yes."

"What's there from my home?"

He squirmed. "Some photos. Uh, I think a wiring schematic of some kind." He swallowed hard. "Hair samples in a vial."

She stared hard. "Someone stole hair clippings from my home?"

Lucas said nothing.

"Why?"

Lucas said nothing again. He wasn't sure what he could say.

"And this is what you do?"

"No, no, no. Like I said, I'm not one of them. I'm trying to stop them."

But he felt the sour, medicinal taste of the lie in the back of his throat. He wasn't one of the Creep Club, not in any official capacity. But he was getting the feeling there was some thread that tied them all together. He did all the things they were doing, but he was a natural monster, not a trained one. That, in many ways, was worse.

"Okay," she said, not sounding convinced. "So what do we do?"

"Well, like I said, I was looking at the Blackboard, paying attention to all the faces on the photos—all the people pictured who were targeted for projects—and it occurred to me how many of those faces were brown, black, yellow. A few of them white, but only a few. And I started wondering why that is, and when I began looking at the names, I noticed most of the people had—what's the politically correct way to say it—*ethnic* names. Not Americanized names, you know."

Her eyes were hard flint. "Yes."

"And here were photos of these people and videos and things from their homes, and it just struck me, this isn't random. I mean, we're in Washington DC, and—"

"Homeland Security."

"What?"

"That's what you're dancing around. You think we're all being watched by Homeland Security, because we have foreign ties."

"I know it sounds crazy."

She smiled. "Ask any Japanese American who was herded into an internment camp during World War II if it sounds crazy."

He thought he saw a tear starting to form in the corner of her eye, but then her eyes shifted and became that hard steel again.

She looked at him. "So what are we gonna do about it?"

He smiled. "I was hoping you'd say that," he said, "but I need to ask you something first." He dropped to a knee on the floor.

"If you're going to propose, remember I'm already married," she said.

He smiled. A little humor. Good.

He rolled up his pant leg, exposing the manacle. "Unfortunately, I'm already attached too."

She crouched on the floor beside him, examining the manacle for a few seconds.

"Ever seen anything like it?" he asked.

She nodded. "You wouldn't believe the kinds of things I've seen," she said. "It's pretty basic."

"So can you get it off me?"

She looked at him. "Sometimes, basic isn't so good. No high-tech way of overriding it, or bypassing the code, or anything like that. You mess with it too much, you—"

"Blow off my leg."

She stood again. "Yeah." Pause. "What happened?"

He stood, retreated to the couch again. "You know that saying, no good deed goes unpunished?"

She came to the couch to sit by him. "Yeah."

He indicated the manacle on his ankle. "There's your proof. I tried to save a guy from people I thought were planning to kill him. Turns out, I shoulda tried to save them." He let out a bitter chuckle. "I think the guy's Russian Mafia, and he didn't take kindly to my heroics. Coincidentally, he's also on the Blackboard."

She stared at the manacle. "And so this is his way of making sure you do what he wants."

"Yes."

"And what is it he wants?"

"Wants me to lead some people to him, like lambs to slaughter. People he's convinced I'm working with. Only one problem with that."

"What's that?"

"Those people don't exist. Not that I'd lead them to Viktor anyway, but I think he's convinced I'm with a rival crime gang or something."

"There will be override codes," she said. "To shut it off, or to reset the timer."

He stared. Far away, in the kitchen, the refrigerator's compressor kicked on with a whoosh.

"Thanks," he said. "But I'm pretty sure he won't be sharing."

"Then we have to figure out another way to stop him."

"I've been working on it, believe me."

She flopped back against the couch, stared at the ceiling. "I think I need a drink. How about you?"

He nodded. "Make it a double."

A few minutes before nine o'clock that evening, Lucas stood across the alley from Saul's office building, waiting.

Waiting for what, he wasn't sure.

He looked at the building. Lights illuminated the lobby where two men sat at a guard station; outside, security cameras scanned the building's perimeter.

As Lucas watched, three quick bursts of light flashed from the hedge by the row houses. A signal. Quickly, Lucas unshouldered his backpack and retrieved his new flashlight, then returned three quick bursts.

He waited, but no other signal came. After a few minutes, he put his flashlight back and continued to wait.

Moments later, he felt someone in the dark alley with him, moving lightly in the deepest shadows. He smiled. "Nice to not see you again, Snake."

Moments later, Snake spoke from the darkness near him. "You ready to do this?"

Lucas kept his gaze on the building. "Does it matter?"

"No."

"Then I guess I'm ready."

Snake held a two-way radio to his face and spoke into it. "Give it to us in thirty seconds," he said. A squelch of static responded, followed by a woman's voice simply saying, "Okay."

Snake answered Lucas's question. "Can you wait for thirty seconds?"

"I suppose I can spare that."

They stood quietly, watching the building. The woman's voice spoke on the two-way radio again. "Ten seconds."

Then the block went dark. Everything in the building dropped to complete blackness, the lights extinguishing immediately.

"Now," Snake said, springing into action. "Run."

Three figures jetted across the street to the building, and Lucas followed. Silently they opened one of the side doors, then moved toward the stairs and sprinted up them to the second floor. There, they all filed into a small utility closet.

"Generators will kick on any time," Snake said.

As if on cue, they heard an odd roar that lasted for just a few seconds, followed by a hum. A weak sliver of light spilled in beneath the crack of the door they hid behind.

"Generators run the basics," said Snake. His flashlight came on, illuminating his face in the darkness of the utility closet. "None of the cams, but the alarms are live." He smiled. "Most of them, anyway."

"How'd you get us in the side door?" Lucas asked. "Typically, in a power outage, the whole place goes into lockdown."

Another smile from Snake. "Yeah," he said. "Typically. But then, this isn't your typical power outage. It's good to have contacts." Snake shined his light above them, showing the pipes and electrical conduit intersecting floors above. A makeshift rope ladder hung from above, and Snake grabbed it. "We have about ten minutes before the computers go through their systems checks and reboot completely, and we need to get to Saul's office on the fourth floor. Elevator's out with no power, and the stairs are definitely off-limits. So here we go."

Snake scrambled up the ladder, Clarice and Kennedy followed, and Lucas brought up the rear.

A few minutes later, they exited the utility closet on the fourth floor.

Snake spoke into his two-way radio. "We still clear?"

The woman answered. "You got about five more minutes."

Snake put the radio back in his pocket and led them down the hallway to an office door. At the door, Clarice and Kennedy clicked on lights strapped to their heads, opened the door, and slipped inside. Snake waved Lucas inside next, then followed him into the office and closed the door behind them.

They set to work, searching files and desk drawers, but finding nothing. Snake suggested they look in the acoustic tiles of the ceiling, but after Kennedy boosted Clarice up for a peek, she shook her head.

"Two minutes," said the woman's voice on the radio.

Snake held the flashlight on Lucas's face. "Any ideas, Humpty?" he said. "That's why you're here."

Lucas followed his flashlight's beam around the office until it settled on something that made him stop.

A cuckoo clock, mounted on the wall.

"The clock," he said.

Kennedy scrambled to the clock, pulled it from the wall. Behind it was a small space, just big enough to hold the two or three file folders that were hidden there.

"Okay," Snake said. "Grab it and go."

Kennedy pulled out the files and stuffed them in his pack, and they sprinted out into the hallway again.

"One minute," came the woman's voice on the two-way.

They scrambled into the utility closet and back down the ladder, then out onto the first floor. As they dashed into the hall, the main lights flickered.

"Power's on again," Snake yelled. "Let's go." He sprinted around the corner, and the others followed.

A high, ear-piercing alarm began to sound as iron gates quickly dropped into place at each end of the hallway.

They came to a stop, and Lucas looked at him. "What now?"

Snake looked around them. "Punt," he said. He ran into the nearest office, appearing moments later with a large chair. Snake went to the closest window and threw the chair at it. The glass cracked, but refused to break.

He picked up the chair and threw it again. More cracks.

Behind them, they heard one of the security guards. "Drop that chair or I'll shoot!"

Lucas looked back at the security guards, and just as he'd feared, he saw them standing at the nearest gate; both had their guns drawn and trained on them.

Lucas heard glass shattering, and he turned to see Clarice scrambling out the window.

Something whizzed by his ear, and a hole opened in the wall next to him, spraying him with chunks of concrete.

Kennedy was working his way out the window now, and Snake had drawn a gun. He aimed it at the security guards and pulled the trigger twice; both guards slumped to the ground at the gate.

Lucas turned to look at Snake again, and the gun had disappeared.

"Something tells me that's not the first time you've fired a gun," Lucas said.

Snake nodded grimly, then went out the window.

Lucas followed and dropped to the ground, following the other three to a nearby van. The driver, wearing a black ski mask, listened as Snake whispered something to him, then put the van into gear and wheeled away from the curb.

Two blocks later, headlights bounced into place behind them. The back window of the van spiderwebbed and shattered as a bullet hit it.

"Go!" screamed Snake as he moved to the back of the van, his pistol drawn. He sat beneath the shattered back window, his eyes boring into Lucas.

"What are you waiting for?" screamed Clarice. They raced around a corner, tires screeching as the top-heavy van tipped onto two tires. A few seconds later, the SUV caught up to them and tapped the back bumper.

"That's what I'm waiting for," said Snake. He stood and swiveled, pointing his gun and firing at the driver's side of the large SUV before it drifted away from their rear bumper again. It plowed into a row of parked cars, coming to a stop with a shuddering screech of steel.

"I really hope there's something good in those files, Humpty," he said as he looked at Lucas again. "I'd hate to go through all this only to find out your friend's been hiding downloaded photos of swim-suit models."

The van's driver made a couple more turns, throwing them around in the back of the van, and then they were on an interstate, picking up speed.

The air being sucked out of the broken window sounded like a jet turbine. Snake stood from his crouch a bit and surveyed the area behind them for several minutes before he was satisfied they weren't being followed.

They stayed quiet for a few minutes, all of them catching their breath and collecting their thoughts as the wind whistled through the giant hole at the back of the van.

Twenty minutes later, the van slowed, took an exit, and pulled into a parking lot. Lucas recognized the surroundings as a rest area, even though he couldn't say where, exactly, this one was.

The van parked, and Clarice pushed open the back doors.

Standing at the back of the van, gun drawn, was someone Lucas recognized immediately—even in the hazy orange glow of the rest area's security lighting.

Himself.

Snake started to raise his gun, but then hesitated as his face blanched. "Dad?" he said as he stared at the figure for a moment.

Snake's head snapped back as a shot hit him in the forehead, and before Lucas had a chance to move, he saw/felt/heard bullets hitting Clarice and Kennedy.

Now he stared at his own face behind the sights of the pistol. He felt the van rocking, and heard the driver screaming as he tried to get out the door.

His Bad Twin moved the barrel of the pistol a few inches and fired at the driver, then swung it back on him. Lucas stared back at the face of the shooter, hearing the struggled gurgling of the driver dying behind him.

Staring into a mirror reflection of himself, especially one who killed so easily, terrified him in a deep place inside. A deep place usually only occupied by the Dark Vibration.

"Go ahead," Lucas said, hearing his voice come out as a strained whisper.

With his gun, the shooter pointed to the bag that had fallen from Kennedy's dead grasp. "Don't forget your papers," his own voice said to him.

And then, the shooter replaced the gun in a hidden holster and casually strolled away.

Lucas stayed frozen for a moment, waiting. Surely something else was going to happen. Surely he would be taken or shot or captured or . . . something.

But nothing did.

After a few moments, he slowly crept to the open door at the back of the van and scrambled to the pavement, clumsily falling as he did so. His actions, normally so fluid and natural, felt stiff and awkward. It was the fear, he knew, coursing through his veins.

Lucas had rarely felt fear, true fear, in his life. And yet, in the last few days, it had been a steady part of his diet. Why did the sight of this pursuer, the one wearing his own face, terrify him so much?

He ran around the side of the van to the driver's door and opened it. The driver was breathing wheezily, and he looked at Lucas with panicked eyes. No doubt he'd seen the face of the man who shot him, and thought he'd returned to finish the job.

Lucas spun around his backpack, looking for his TracFone. Then he thought better of it and looked inside the van; sure enough, a cell phone sat on the console between the seats. He reached across the dying man to grab the phone, flipped it open, and dialed 911. He panicked again when he realized he didn't know exactly where they were, but the 911 dispatcher said he had pinpointed the location on GPS.

Good thing he'd decided to use someone else's cell phone. Did TracFones have the built-in GPS feature? He didn't think so.

He closed the driver's cell phone and put it on the dash, then looked into the man's face. "Help's on the way," he said. "You're gonna be just fine."

A lie, but he felt the situation called for it; no one should die without thinking he had a chance.

The driver closed his eyes for a few seconds, and Lucas thought he was going to lose him. But suddenly the driver grabbed his arm in a painful vise.

"The shooter," he said, his voice sounding like liquid. "Did you see him?"

Lucas nodded. "Yes," he said. "And I'm sorry. It wasn't me, even though—"

The man tightened his grip, shook his head. "'Course it wasn't you." He took a pause for a labored breath. "It was Charles Manson."

TWENTY-SEVEN

10:41:43 REMAINING

Later, after Lucas had made his way to the rest stop on the opposite side of the interstate and flagged a ride from a trucker, after he had spent a sleepless early morning wandering the streets, he was, once again, caught in that dead zone between night and day. The Metro wouldn't start running until five thirty, so he decided to walk.

He now had about eleven hours to go before his leg was blown off. And that was just the start of his problems.

As he walked, he glanced down one of the side streets and saw the bright sign of a convenience store still glowing; someone hadn't shut off the lights even though it was now past daybreak.

He needed something, anything, to eat. He could just slip into this store, grab something quickly, and be on his way again.

He approached the store and opened the front door, looking around for the ATM machine he knew had to be there. There was one in the back corner, but not one of ATM2GO's machines. At least he didn't think it was; he didn't see any signage to that effect. Unless ATM2GO had ways of tracking the cameras inside every ATM machine, in which case he was in serious trouble no matter where he went. Not that it mattered now; they didn't need to find him to kill him. The lovely anklet he wore was proof of that.

He nodded at the cashier, who sat behind the counter watching a small television. The cashier didn't even look up as he passed.

After pouring a cup of coffee and grabbing a sandwich from the cooler, he went to the counter and set down his purchases.

The cashier, annoyed, finally was able to tear his eyes away from the program. When he saw Lucas, he immediately did a double take. He tried to hide it, but he wasn't much of a poker player.

Lucas became dimly aware of the sound from the television, even though he couldn't see the screen.

It was one of the news channels. "Once again, we're following this breaking news story. Officials are searching for a suspect in the shooting deaths of four people found in a van at a rest stop on the Beltway. This image, taken from security cams at an office break-in earlier in the evening and enhanced, shows the suspect."

Lucas didn't need to see the screen to know who they were talking about. He stared at the cashier, who had obviously gone into stall mode, visions of his own television interviews dancing in his eyes. "You gonna ring me up?"

"Something's wrong. Register's locked. If you give me a few minutes, I'll see if I can get it working."

Obviously, the cashier wasn't much of a liar either.

"No worries," Lucas said, acting as if everything were perfectly fine. "I'll just use the bathroom."

"Oh, yeah. Okay."

Lucas turned and moved toward the back of the store, sure the cashier had already pressed a silent alarm. He walked beneath the sign marked RESTROOMS, but instead of turning down the small hallway to the bathroom, he kept going straight, through the area marked EMPLOYEES ONLY and out the back door.

Immediately he began to run, moving as fast as he could go and not stopping until he'd run several blocks. In the distance behind him, he heard a siren.

Sounded like the kid at the convenience store had fixed his cash register.

This day was getting better all the time. He'd been tied to the disappearances of Anita Abkin and Ted Hagen (who were now dead, he reminded himself), then to a break-in at a secret government agency, and now to the murders of four other people.

And to top it off, the person who had killed the last four people wore his face. He wasn't sure what the dying driver was talking about with that Charles Manson comment—perhaps his brain had been flashing random images as he died—but Lucas knew what he had seen: himself. Killing.

After resting and catching his breath, he began walking again. He turned toward the west, walked two blocks, than went down a back alley until he came to a manhole cover. Once there, he went to the Dumpster nearest the manhole, felt around the back, and retrieved the length of construction rebar he'd hidden there months ago.

With that in hand, he went to the cover, pried it out of its seat, and returned the rebar.

He crawled down the iron rungs, paused to replace the manhole cover, and disappeared into the depths of the DC sewer system.

Several tunnels and shortcuts later, he was hiding under the catwalk at the nearest Metro station, waiting for the trains to begin running. He had changed into the extra set of clothing he carried in his backpack and put on the Washington Nationals cap backward. That and the sunglasses were the best he could do now. There were cams in the Metro stations, he knew, but very few of them actually on the cars themselves; most of the security cams were at the gates, which he'd bypassed.

He stared at nothing, curled into a ball, until he heard the rumble of a train approaching the platform. He had no destination in mind yet; his plan was to simply ride the train for a while, collect his thoughts, make his plan. There was nowhere else he could go at the moment. He didn't want to take another cab, because . . . well, because the Metro was part of his home. He needed to get back to some familiar territory, and the Metro was it. Yes, it was dangerous, but at this point, everywhere was dangerous.

The train pulled up to the platform with a hiss, and he waited for the doors to open. He took off his backpack, chose a seat at the back of the last car, hunched down, turned his cap around again to pull it over his face, and tried to rest. As soon as his eyes closed, his mind began to wander.

(Humpty Dumpty had some great falls.)

The words hovered in his mind, but he let his thoughts go

deeper as he listened to the shudder of the train join the rising Dark Vibration deep inside his own soul.

Soon his mind took him back to the rooftop of the orphanage. As he crouched on the rooftop, the last vestiges of twilight disappeared into the dark purple of night, and the sounds of far-off activity—people laughing? people singing?—filtered to him on the breeze.

He looked at the city, admiring the lights wavering in the dissipating heat of the day, and he knew those lights were close—so close he could touch them. And so he put out his hand, his small, ten-year-old hand, to grasp the lights that were so near.

But then he felt the wetness on his hand. His hand wasn't reaching into the night sky, but into a deep pool. A deep pool formed by burbling springs. And he wasn't on a roof but on a stone walkway that ran beside the springs. Those lights, the lights that he wanted so desperately to touch, were deep inside the pool, and the water created optical illusions; each time he felt sure he was about to touch one of the warm, glowing orbs, it shifted direction, darting away from his grasp.

Frustrated, he looked on the pathway ahead of him, sure he would see the backs of the couple walking away. Maybe he could call out to them, stop them, convince them to come back and catch the lights for him.

But there was no couple on the walkway. Instead, it was an old man, sitting on a crate, battered guitar clutched in his hands. His fingers moved over the strings, and he rocked back and forth, his eyes closed in pain, as he sang.

Got those crumblin' down blues, baby

Got me some crumblin' down blues

Got those crumblin' down blues so bad

Feel 'em clear down in my shoes

Did me some dancin' with the devil

Said he'd have to take his dues

Now I'm digging with that shovel

Cuz I got them crumblin' down blues

As the man sang, Lucas saw it was true. He was crumbling, his hand cracking and turning to dust, and then his arm, and then his shoulder, and then every bit of him, disintegrating into dust and falling toward the deep lights in the bubbling spring.

He awoke with a start, immediately holding up his hand and looking at it, as if to make sure it was there before his mind totally left the dream. He looked around him; there were only three other passengers in his car. Outside, unfamiliar terrain rolled by.

At the next stop, he stepped off the train onto the platform and wasn't surprised to hear the nearby wail of a familiar guitar, the hushed growl of a man singing.

He followed the sound to the other side of a nearby bus shelter, and there he saw the Blues Man who had haunted his dream. His head rocked back and his right foot tapped out time as his hands slid across the frets, massaging sorrow out of every note.

When the song finished, Blues Man opened his eyes and stared straight at Lucas, almost as if he expected him to be there. He nodded as he picked a few more notes on his guitar, an interstitial piece between songs.

"Whatcha wanna hear, son?" the man asked.

Lucas shrugged. "I don't know."

The man smiled, closed his eyes as if concentrating on a pleasant thought. "That's part of the problem, ain't it?" he said. He tested a chord a few times, liked what he heard. "Howzabout I play you something you need to hear instead? Folks get too caught up on what they want, they don't ever hear what they need."

Without waiting for an answer, he launched into the next song.

> Spinnin', you got me spinnin' all around
> Spinnin' so much I ain't never been found
> And when you tell me you don't mean it
> I don't mind much, baby, cuz I seen it
> So maybe I don't like the way it sounds
> But the answer is I'm spinnin' all around

Lucas listened to the rest of the song, transfixed, the world around him forgotten. Finally, as the song finished and the man's eyes opened again, Lucas pulled a five-dollar bill out of his pocket and threw it into the guitar case. "Thanks," he said. "I think I'm spinning myself."

The Blues Man nodded but said nothing.

Lucas started to head back down the tunnel, but decided maybe he'd spring for a cab again. Only one person to recognize him in a cab, as opposed to hundreds of people on the Metro. Especially people riding back to the heart of DC on the morning commute. People who would be thrilled to recognize him and help authorities.

He smiled, thinking of Viktor's words. People ready to be heroes.

He hailed a cab, thankful when the driver barely paid any attention, then told him where he wanted to go. After that, he pulled out his TracFone.

A few moments later, Saul answered. "Well, if it ain't my good friend who can't seem to keep himself out of the news. Kind of early in the morning, isn't it?"

"We need to talk."

"I'd say we do."

"That Java the Hut you love so much—is it open early?"

"Open early, open late."

"Then I'll see you there in fifteen minutes."

"Okay," said Saul. "This time, though, you can buy."

09:27:13 REMAINING

Saul was already at the coffee shop when Lucas arrived. He was sitting at one of the tall tables, his heels hooked on the bar of his chair, carefully blowing the heat off his latte. The lid sat on the table in front of him.

"Thought I was gonna buy," Lucas said.

Saul shrugged, indicated the seat opposite him with a hand. "Let's just say I'm not a man known for my patience," he said.

Lucas sat, noticing Saul had bought him a cup of coffee and poured him a glass of water. "Decaf?" he asked.

Saul nodded.

"Thanks," he said, picking up the water and drinking. He gulped down half of it, feeling the ice cubes shift in the glass before he set it back down again.

"Killing people at rest stops is thirsty work," Saul said.

"I didn't kill anyone."

"I know that. Unfortunately, the TV stations don't seem to agree." He paused, looked at Lucas's head. "Nice hat."

"Thanks. Really goes with the glasses, don't you think?" He tugged at the large glasses.

Lucas looked around the coffee shop, paying attention to other customers. No one seemed overly interested in their conversation.

"So what are you here to tell me, Humpty?"

Lucas stared hard for a few moments. "I know."

"Know what?"

"About your back-door deals. Your work with Guoanbu."

Saul narrowed his eyebrows together the slightest bit, picked up his latte, and blew over the rim again. "What work would that be?" *Blink, blink, blink.*

The blink was this guy's tell; like the kid at the convenience store, he wasn't much of a liar. A wonder he'd ever made it as an agent. Lucas held up the bag he'd retrieved from Kennedy's dead hands.

"The work in these files," he said. "Interesting reading. Your contact at Guoanbu—your cute code name for him is Beast from the East, I think—drops money for you regularly. In return, you've been giving him names of agents—agents, oddly enough, who all seem to have died."

Saul took his time stirring his hot coffee, continuing to stare at its creamy surface as he spoke. "And where did you come up with these files?"

"Your offices, last night. Took them with us in the van, and then I took them with me after . . ." Lucas paused, swallowed. "After the shooter."

"I see. And what about the other files?"

"What other files?"

Saul smiled. "Don't you ever watch TV? The newsers have been very careful to say authorities have recovered some files from the van, which are—hmm, how did they say it? 'Important to the on-going investigation, although details can't be provided yet for national security reasons.' Something to that effect." Saul sipped his latte, grimaced.

Lucas looked hard at Saul. "No other files in the van. I got all of them."

"So you said. But let's get back to the fascinating subject at hand: this little matter of two sets of files. If you didn't leave behind any files, someone else must have planted them."

Lucas took another drink. "How'd you do it? How'd you set us up at the rest stop? How'd you even know we were going to stop there?"

"You're sniffing down the wrong trail."

"Who else would it be? You knew what files we had from your office."

"If you took files from my office, they must not have been that important. I'm not missing them."

"And your home."

Saul flinched, the slightest bit, which brought a smile to Lucas's face.

"You've got a thing for cuckoo clocks," he said.

Saul said nothing but placed the lid back on his cup and drank. This time he showed no reaction. Instead, he changed subjects. "I said I wanted information on your friend Snake and the others, not that I wanted them dead."

"I didn't want them dead either."

"But you had no choice."

"No, I didn't do it. There was someone there at the rest stop. He killed everyone in the van."

"Everyone except you. You might want to practice your story a bit before they drag you in."

"What, like you don't know all this? It had to be you, your Guoanbu contacts, at the rest stop."

Saul set his coffee down again. "You're trying to hardball me. I can roll with that. But let's not cry when the other kid on the playground punches you back."

Lucas switched gears and tactics. "Look. Here's what it comes down to. I have these files, and I know you want them."

"That's where you're wrong."

"Why do you say that?"

"Because you're being played. Sounds to me like a lot of different files floating around. What makes you think you haven't been getting spoon-fed?"

Lucas, stunned by this thought, sat in silence.

"Fact is, the only thing you have I'm still interested in is contact with other Creep Clubbers. Although, at the rate you're plowing through them, the Creep Club itself might not last," Saul said. "So like it or not, you're gonna have to trust me now; you're in this deep, and it's getting deeper all the time. Let's just clear the air; start by showing me what you have."

Lucas smiled. "So these files are planted and mean nothing to you. But you'd like to see them anyway."

Saul stared. "It's the only thing we've got."

Lucas thought for a moment, grabbed the bag, and pulled out the files, flopping them down on the table.

Saul began paging through the documents, his latte forgotten for the moment. Lucas waited patiently, studying the man's face. No reactions, as far as he could tell.

Finally, Saul pushed away the files, leaned back in his chair, and pulled out a pack of smokes. He pulled one from the pack with his lips, tilted the pack at Lucas.

Lucas smiled. "I think I told you before, smoking will kill you."

Saul lit his cigarette, put the lighter back in the folds of his jacket, and smiled. "I hope it's smoking that does kill me." He considered the floor while he spoke. "Where'd you get those files?"

"I told you: your office. Last night."

Saul tapped some ash onto the floor. "What I mean is, who sent you on this trail?"

Lucas stared silently.

"This stuff," Saul said, waving his hand, "is worthless to me. Means nothing to me. In fact, I can guarantee you the files found in the van are identical to these. And the person who sent you for those files, well, that's who I need to concentrate on."

Lucas watched Saul take another puff of his Camel, unsure how to play his next move. He hadn't expected a curve ball quite like this. What could he do to . . .

Well, he could put Saul and Viktor together, of course. Play them against each other, watch the fireworks. But that was a very bad idea—he could get his hand blown off by that kind of fireworks.

Not to mention his leg.

"What? Like a meeting, you mean?"

Saul looked at him, stared for several seconds without blinking. Amazing. He looked away again when he spoke.

"That'd be a start. But you're running out of time."

Lucas nodded, thinking about the bomb on his leg. If only Saul knew.

TWENTY-EIGHT

Lucas wandered aimlessly, unsure what his next step should be. Saul's words had unsettled him. Was he really being played? Were there really two sets of files? Why?

He shook his head. No, not possible. He, himself, had creeped Saul's house, unknown to him, and found the hidden information. Saul was the one trying to game him now. Part of the territory. Saul *had*, after all, been very interested in the files at the coffee shop. And he'd immediately requested a meeting with someone who didn't exist.

Just as Viktor had.

He thought, again, of putting the two of them together. For Viktor, Saul would be the mysterious heavy who was backing Lucas's efforts to infiltrate his mafia territory; for Saul, Viktor would play the part of the double agent feeding him files. The two could cancel each other out, the world would be rid of a thug and a traitor to the U.S. government, and all would be right again.

Of course, Lucas's leg would explode, and he'd die in the effort. But the greatest heroes were always the tragic ones, weren't they?

It was no good; no matter how many times he ran it through his head, he saw nothing coming of a meeting between Saul and Viktor—let alone the vast entourages they would surely bring.

These thoughts, along with snippets of his dreams, filtered through his mind when he found himself at his hiding spot near the Lincoln Memorial. The packages Saul had given him were still hidden there, behind the loose stones, but he knew his subconscious mind had brought him here for one thing in particular.

The cube.

He retrieved the cube from its hiding place and turned it in his hands, over and over, looking for some kind of irregularity, some kind of clue, on its surface. He found none.

He put the cube in his backpack, knowing already where he was going next.

Half an hour later, he stood in front of the giant brick church, the Blackboard waiting inside. The Dark Vibration was cycling up now, bringing him first to the cube, now here. And so he went inside the building, flipped on the lights that illuminated the giant wall of nails and strings, and stood in front of it. After a moment, he felt compelled to drop to his knees, and even though this was no longer a church, even though there was no longer a cross or an altar here at the front of the sanctuary, he closed his eyes.

It wasn't exactly a prayer, because Lucas knew, deep inside, he had no prayer. It was a quiet moment for a lost soul chasing a lost cause. But strangely, it was fine. He would fail, yes, but he would follow the trail to its bitter end.

When he opened his eyes, he felt a warm spot on his forehead. Above, somewhere in the deep recesses of the church ceiling, a tiny shaft of light had pierced the darkness through a hole in the ancient roof, and somewhere in the deep recesses of that room, the shaft of light had found his forehead.

Perhaps startled by the sudden light, a pigeon flew from its perch above, dropping low until Lucas could almost touch it, then circling him a few times with a frantic flapping of its wings, and finally flying toward the open door of the church and freedom.

As it flew, Lucas knew it was the most beautiful bird human eyes had ever seen.

He stood. And suddenly, he knew what he had to do.

08:01:19 REMAINING

Amazingly, the fourth-floor space above Dandy Don's Donuts looked untouched since he'd last been there. Lucas half expected everything to be gone, tossed into a Dumpster, but all of it was still there.

His totems lay scattered as he'd left them, waiting.

He leaned over and picked up the scarf. The faint perfume was still there, just barely, but it brought back memories of Tricia. Her effortless laugh as she shared jokes with her coworkers. Her tendency to bite her upper lip when she was concentrating on something. Her—

He shoved the scarf into his backpack, forcing himself to stop thinking of Tricia and his invented memories for her. It was time to put this right.

After the scarf, he bent and picked up the other mementos. The photos. The notes. The knickknacks. All of it. Last of all, he retrieved the photo of Noel and her kids, their faces caught in perpetual smiles on their camping trip. She had been the last one before . . . before all this had happened. So she was the freshest in his mind. He ran a finger over the frame of the photo before turning it over and putting it into his pack with everything else.

He pulled out the TracFone and checked the time. Almost seven thirty, which meant the day was just starting for the people who lived in the open, the people who laughed and talked and celebrated the day while they sat at desks topped by photos of their smiling families.

Not the best timing. He would rather do this after hours, but thanks to the manacle on his leg, he wouldn't live to see the end of this workday. He was now sure of that. So he'd have to do it now.

He found an old stocking cap, still stuffed into the hole in the wall near his old makeshift altar. He put it on, replacing the Washington Nationals cap, and adjusted the giant sunglasses once again. A stocking cap in DC during August wasn't exactly the best plan, but he didn't have time to cut or color his hair at the moment. He added a large bandage on his cheek, knowing it would attract more attention than the rest of his features. When asked to describe him, most people would say, "He had a big bandage on his face."

Properly dressed, he sat for a few moments, eerily calm for the first time in days, feeling he was on the verge of . . . being free. Maybe for the first time ever.

He decided to go down to Dandy Don's for a farewell doughnut.

Yes, Viktor would be able to find him there. Yes, someone might recognize him. Yes, he might be caught by police. But did he care? No,
he did not. None of it mattered now; he was beginning to feel more
fatalistic than ever. If he were caught, what of it? He'd only be in custody a few hours before blowing up.

After getting a pastry and a cup of coffee and sitting at a table in
the corner, he spun around the backpack, fished around inside, and
brought out the photo of Noel and her kids. The photo still spoke
to him, yes. All of the totems did. But he had an overwhelming need
to look at this one in particular.

The photo was a moment of pure joy, unfettered happiness, never
ending because it had been frozen on film.

He looked into the eyes of Noel and the kids, unable to control
his own smile as he imagined the joke, the private moment, they must
have been sharing.

As he looked, something shifted in the photo—something behind
the young boy, on the left side of the photo.

Lucas blinked, glanced around, as if scared someone else had
witnessed what he'd just seen. But he was alone with his pastry and
his cup of coffee.

He looked back at the photo and, yes, something was moving
behind the boy. Water. He'd not noticed before, but the family was
standing in front of a pool of water.

Actually, they were standing on a stone path beside a pool of
water.

And in the background, the movement he saw was a bubbling
spring, gurgling air to the surface and hiding bright, twinkling
lights deep in its depths.

The lights wavered inside the spring, and Lucas could hear it now: the gurgling spring, the call of birds in the distance, the soft sigh of a breeze in the leaves of the giant trees over them.

Why hadn't he seen this before? It was in the photo all along. He reached out a finger, drawn by the surface of the spring, but as soon as his finger broke the plane of the photo, the sensory details disappeared. Instead of the birds and breeze, he heard the clinking of coffee cups and the murmur of people ordering. Instead of a bubbling, wavering spring, he saw a flat image of three smiling faces.

And yet, when he brought his finger away from the photo, he noticed something odd indeed: at the tip of his finger, a single drop of water formed, then suspended itself, frozen in time for a moment, before slowly dropping to the floor.

Without thinking, he placed his finger in his mouth, and the last traces of water were still there. He could taste the fresh spring, and all those sensory images returned for a fraction of a second. He closed his eyes, trying to hold on to that image—

(*Humpty Dumpty had some great falls.*)

—then opened his eyes again, staring out at the small restaurant space.

Across from him, along the wall that hid the utility closet in front of the men's bathroom, he saw an eye peeking out. His own viewing platform, the one he'd hastily put together in this very space.

And now someone was using it to spy on him.

He jumped to his feet and moved across the space toward the men's restroom as fast as he could. The hole was still there, barely visible to anyone but him, but he knew the eye was gone before he'd even risen from the table.

And yet, he had to go to it. To see.

At the restroom, he threw open the door and rushed in, put his shoulder into the door of the utility closet when it wouldn't open.

The closet was dark and empty. As he knew it would be. But as he stood and carefully surveyed every available inch of the closet, he felt a soft, barely there draft of air kiss his face.

He looked above him and saw one of the ceiling tiles pushed to the side.

He stepped up onto the slop sink, then quickly put his foot against the nearest wall and sprung off of it, propelling himself up and catching the lip of the hole in his hands. The frame for the acoustic tiles sagged and sank a bit, not designed to hold his weight, but then he grabbed the solid framing above and boosted himself into the tight space, listening.

Nothing.

He felt the breeze pushing steadily on his face. Several feet away, toward the back exterior wall, he saw the giant ductwork for the kitchen's exhaust fan. He recognized it immediately; it was the very ductwork he'd used to access the utility closet a few days before, when he'd built his observation deck. Now someone else had used it. A panel in the ductwork was missing, creating a gaping maw. He made his way across the space, careful to avoid the wiring, and peeked into the duct.

Down the small tunnel of ducting, a hole opened onto the exterior of the building. He followed it. This was the source of the breeze. The vent he'd carefully removed and replaced a few days ago lay on the ground. Probably kicked away in a hurry.

Someone had followed him here. Someone had used his secret

route into Dandy Don's. Had hidden inside his observation deck in the utility closet. Had barely escaped by scrambling through the ceiling and kicking away the vent to the outside of the building.

And yet, none of this surprised him.

He pulled out his TracFone and checked it again. It was time for him to go to work.

He walked steadily down the alley, leaving behind Dandy Don's Donuts forever, and began making his way to the first office.

05:22:07 REMAINING

In just two hours, Lucas had been to a dozen different office spaces. Today the occupants of those offices, those cubicles, those reception desks, would find items they thought were 'long lost. A family photo, a card from a friend, even, in one case, a favorite scarf.

Now Lucas stood at the reception desk of the office where Noel worked. He pulled an envelope out of his backpack, smiled at the receptionist. "Dropping off a package for Noel," he said, hoping he looked the part of a bicycle messenger.

The receptionist, bored, looked at the envelope that held the camping photo of Noel and her kids, oblivious to the magical totem inside. "I'll make sure she gets it," she said.

He turned to leave the office. No need to hide in the ceilings and utility chases now. He could use the elevator. He could walk out as just another person who belonged here.

Yes, he could do this.

TWENTY-NINE

04:59:55 REMAINING

Exhausted from all his visits, Lucas returned to the only place he now felt safe. The church.

Inside his own skin, he felt cleansed. But outside was a whole different matter. He was down to just a few hours now, and he really had no choice: setting up a meeting between Viktor and Saul was the only thing he could do. And hope that somehow—and he wasn't quite sure how—he could get the bomb off his leg before it exploded and killed him.

He'd worn down his reserves yet again, and his body screamed for sleep. But he couldn't. Not now. Even though he felt somehow lighter, cleaner, the last few days had exacted their toll: his reserves were bottoming out, his whole body a raw, exposed nerve.

Without bothering to look at the Blackboard or anything else in the church, he found the door to the basement, flicking on a light switch that illuminated rickety wooden steps into the darkness below.

Lucas descended the steps, moving slowly until he reached the bottom. Here, the yellow bulb above the stairs did no good; it was darkness beyond, because the basement had no windows of any kind. He found his flashlight, thumbed it on, and swept the beam around the room.

Like the upstairs, it was a huge space, unencumbered by walls or partitions; he could tell where walls had once been, but they'd been ripped out at some point. Just a few supporting columns remained.

In essence, the basement was a giant space. The beam of his flashlight moved past stack after stack of boxes. Most of them were labeled with years and names, but nothing else. At first glance, Lucas estimated a couple thousand boxes, but as he kept finding more rows, he thought his estimate might be low.

He wandered down rows, and finally stopped to look inside one of the boxes labeled *1998—Sculley.* Inside, he found the box segregated into two separate compartments. The first compartment held files. Inside the files were several photos—people in restaurants, people in offices, people in homes, with many of the faces repeated. Surveillance photos. Various scribbled notes, dot matrix printouts, facsimiles, and other documents were stuffed here as well. But the printouts were scrambled—coded, as Snake had said.

The other compartment held objects. A couple of DVDs, each marked with the word *Archived,* followed by dates within the past few years. Video footage, he guessed. Here, also, was what looked like a toy gun, some tape, a length of rope, something that looked like an unlabeled prescription bottle, and a tube of lipstick. All of the items, with the exception of the DVDs, were sealed in plastic bags, as if they were valuable pieces of evidence that couldn't be contaminated. He smiled. Yes, he recognized that tendency; his own mementos, his totems, had always been precious to him, and he wanted to keep them safe. That's why he'd always arranged them in such a precise pattern, because . . . because they had to be. Because the Dark Vibration inside demanded it.

He opened another box nearby and found the same kind of two-compartment setup. Satisfied all of the boxes contained essentially the same thing, he felt oddly comforted.

He'd given up his own totems, locked the door on that part of himself this morning. But now he was surrounded by thousands of totems—more than he had ever seen before. Ironic, yes. But Lucas was too tired for irony.

He moved down the row to the far end of the basement and found a giant shelving unit built into the back wall. The shelves held several tools, including one that caught his eye right away.

A hacksaw.

After he converted his flashlight to an electric candle and set it on one of the shelves, he sank to the floor, the hacksaw in his hands.

A hacksaw was built to cut through metal, of course. The kind of metal that was wrapped around his leg right now. He pulled up his pant leg and looked at the manacle, a merry-go-round of red lights illuminating its surface. He could cut it off right now, and what would it really matter if the bomb exploded? This was a nice place to end it all, as nice a place as any, this church where he felt . . . comfortable.

He held the saw up in the dim light from his electric candle, ran his finger lightly along the teeth of the blade.

A hacksaw could also cut bone.

That was another option; just cut through the bone of his lower leg above his ankle. He'd need to get to a hospital eventually, yes, but he could stanch the bleeding with a makeshift tourniquet made from his belt. Then he could make a plan for using the hospital, put together an alias so he couldn't be tracked.

It wasn't a perfect plan, but he would live.

Resolved, he took a deep breath, rolled up his pant leg to his calf. He set the blade of the hacksaw just an inch above the blinking manacle, closed his eyes for a second, drew the blade across the skin just a bit. A thin trail of blood followed the fresh cut.

Do it, do it, do it.

Another deep breath.

Doitdoitdoit.

Uncharacteristically, he felt tears welling in his eyes, and within seconds, he was sobbing, the tears flowing for the first time in years. For the first time since he'd been a young boy in the orphanage. Somewhere in the distance, he heard the hollow *thunk* of the hacksaw falling to the dirt floor.

Lucas pulled his legs toward his body, wrapped his arms around them, and pulled himself into a tight ball.

The tears came harder than ever.

04:27:04 REMAINING

While in the fetal ball, he turned everything inward and blocked the outside world. It was like his deep relaxation state, in some respects, but done in reverse. His observational state, which he had perfected after years of practice, heightened his senses, made him supremely aware of the world around him.

In contrast, the long minutes in the basement deadened all his senses, putting him into a coma of sorts.

In spite of it all, the crying and the coma were somehow cathartic; in an odd way, he felt refreshed. Unafraid, even. More like his normal self, which hadn't experienced true emotions for so very long.

Maybe returning all his totems had been better for him than he'd realized.

He made his way back to the steps. Even his backpack felt lighter. How long had he been down there? Only twenty minutes or so by the clock, but it felt more like twenty hours.

At the top of the steps, he turned off the light switch and opened the door to the main floor of the church. Closing the door behind him, he paused in the morning haze and listened for several minutes. Even though the sun was shining outside, large swaths of the church, including the Blackboard on the front wall, remained shrouded in darkness. As if the building knew it had deep secrets to hide.

He was sure he was alone, but it was best to take a moment to listen anyway. While he was in his semi-catatonic state, he hadn't been aware of his surroundings; he'd been drawn completely inside himself.

Satisfied no one was in the building with him at the moment, he started to move toward the main doors, his mind already chewing on possible sites for the meeting.

But something stopped him. Just a few hours ago in this church, he'd stepped up to the Blackboard and prayed for some kind of deliverance. Well, perhaps not exactly prayed, but he had stopped for a moment of silence, had let his fear and frustration and fury come rolling out of him in one long moment. Had uncaged everything fearsome inside him, letting it all out into the light for the first time.

And then, when he'd opened his eyes, he had seen a shaft of light and a bird, breaking away from the confines of this space. Something had happened in that moment, something he didn't quite understand. And yet, he didn't need to understand it to be part of it.

Perhaps. Perhaps he should spend another moment in silence. Focus his thoughts.

If there was ever a day he needed focus, it was today.

Lucas moved to the front of the church, flicked on the lights to illuminate the giant Blackboard, and dropped to the floor, closing his eyes. He centered his thoughts, breathed deeply a few times, opened his eyes.

Immediately, he felt as if he'd been slammed in the stomach with a sledgehammer; if he hadn't been kneeling, the sight on the Blackboard would have brought him to his knees.

He gasped a few times, trying to get his breath, and felt himself starting to tremble. This was a new fear, something he'd not felt before, and it had been awakened in him in a fraction of a second.

The Blackboard had been changed sometime within the last several hours. The photos of the roughly two dozen Creeps were still on the board, attached to nails. And the strings that attached the Creeps to their current projects were still there. But now, all those strings had been rearranged, and all of them were attached to a single nail, holding a single photo.

A photo of Sarea, his one and only friend from the Blue Bell Café. The new project of every person in the Creep Club.

04:15:36 REMAINING

Lucas scrambled to find the TracFone in his backpack and paused to remember the number Sarea had given him; in a few seconds, he saw the numbers flashing in his mind, and he dialed them. No answer, her phone flipping to voice mail after just a few rings.

At the beep, he spoke. "Sarea, this is Lucas," he said. "I need you to call me as soon as you get this. It's an emergency. The phone number should be on your caller ID right now."

After hanging up, he retrieved the number for the Blue Bell Café from memory and dialed it. After five rings, a voice he didn't recognize answered. He asked if Sarea was working and was told it was her day off.

He hung up, unsure whether to feel relieved or concerned that Sarea wasn't working. That meant he would have to go to her apartment. He'd been there before, without Sarea's knowledge; the self-admission caused his cheeks to burn as he thought of it, but at least he knew where to go. He hadn't been inside, of course; that was back in the days so long ago when he had his strict code of ethics that said he didn't break into people's homes. Since then he'd been in at least three private homes. So much for ethics.

He sprinted out the front door of the church, momentarily blinded by the bright sun—already hot—in the morning sky. And here he was, still wearing a stocking cap.

Yes, today was going to be a hot day. Unbearably hot. He scratched at the bandage attached to his cheek, as if there really were a wound underneath, itching and healing.

He started walking toward the Metro stop, then broke into a run after just a few steps. He had to hurry, had to get to Sarea. This was—

what day? His brain was scrambled, misfiring, making his body feel foreign as he tried to run in it. Putting himself in danger, well, that was something he could handle. But to go after Sarea, the one and only person who had befriended him . . . that awakened a rage inside he was already having a hard time controlling.

At the station, he raced past a newspaper box displaying today's edition, and the large headline slowed him for a few seconds: FUGITIVE SOUGHT. Another story on him, no doubt. He wanted to buy a copy of the paper and read the story, but he didn't have time. All the same, he looked around suspiciously, scanning the people swirling around him for signs of recognition. No one seemed to be paying attention.

At least he had that going for him: everyone looked, but no one saw.

Lucas stripped off his jacket, going down to just a T-shirt, and put the jacket in his backpack.

He continued down the block, then into the construction zone blocking a portion of the street. He grabbed a hard hat off the folding table at the fence perimeter, put it on his head, and moved inside the fence as if he knew exactly where he was going.

And he did; he'd scouted this construction site previously, and it offered a good back door to the nearby Metro tunnels.

He made his way to the giant hole in the street and climbed down the rungs on one of the ladders; at the bottom, he nodded a greeting to a man hefting a jackhammer as he disappeared into the darkness at the back of the underground compartment.

Five minutes later, he was inside the security walkway for the tunnel, knowing overhead cams were picking up his images but betting his construction hard hat would hide his face and identify him as someone at work.

He made his way down the catwalk, opened the AUTHORIZED ENTRY ONLY door, and went directly to the restroom inside the station to lose the hard hat.

After that, he stood on the platform with about a dozen other people, waiting. He looked at the schedule; he'd have to take the Green Line down south several stops, and the next train was still about five minutes away.

He pulled out the TracFone again, dialed Sarea's number. He hung up once the message started to play, then waited patiently, keeping his head down and looking at the ground directly at his feet.

Yes, he'd been by Sarea's apartment. Never inside it, of course, but he'd dreamed of it, hadn't he? He'd imagined the interior of her place, pictured himself under her bed, just a few feet away from where she slept, listening to the sound of her breathing as if it were a metronome.

Even now, that thought excited him as much as it shamed him. He wasn't one of the Creep Club, not in name. But was he any different?

It's a drug, he heard Donavan's voice say. *Once it's in your veins, you need more.*

At last the train pulled to the platform, pushing away his dark thoughts in its wake. He waited for the doors to open and walked on with several other passengers after a few people exited.

The doors closed behind him; the train began to move away from the station. Ten stops to Anacostia, the stop nearest Sarea's apartment complex in southeast DC. How long would that take? Forty-five minutes? Maybe longer?

Too long. Far too long.

He needed to take a cab. He should have tried that first, but his brain still felt thick and gelatinous, in shock after seeing Sarea's photo on the Blackboard. The Metro was home to him, and the place his feet automatically carried him when he wasn't thinking.

At the next stop, he slid out the doors and sprinted for the stairs. At street level, he went directly to the curb and hailed a cab.

The driver looked at him without interest, but nodded when he gave an address.

"How fast can you get there?" Lucas asked.

"How fast you wanna get there?" the cabbie asked.

"Fast as Benjamin Franklin can go," he said, pulling out the last hundred-dollar bill he had on him. He'd probably die later today anyway, and he couldn't take the money with him.

The driver smiled and put the pedal to the metal.

In the backseat, Lucas tried to make himself relax, but it felt as if more than his mind was betraying him. His muscles were shaky and overworked, and his eyes felt as if they'd been dipped in alcohol. What was wrong?

He closed his eyes, concentrated, began forcing his body to go into its deep relaxation state. He needed to be as alert as possible now. Breathe in. Breathe out. Breathe in. Breathe out. Block out all outside stimuli, concentrate on nothing but the Dark Vibration inside.

After a few minutes, when his heart rate matched the thrumming of the Dark Vibration, he let the outside world begin to filter back in. But now, his senses were heightened. First, touch. He felt the seat beneath him, fabric flaking off, worn padding deep inside. He felt the cold plastic of the armrest on the door, the minute crack in the handle. Next, smells filtered into his consciousness: old leather, oil from the overworked cab engine, spicy food lingering in the car's interior.

He turned up the sound, listening as cars and traffic whirled around them, as the cab's radio squawked something about a stop by police officers, as the brakes of the cab squeaked, as the cabbie said, "This'll just be a minute."

Finally, Lucas opened his eyes, knowing even before he opened them that the cab had slowed and was pulling to the side of the road. Colors were richer now, details brighter. His body was completely relaxed, his heart rate only thirty beats per minute, as he casually turned his head and saw the police cruiser, siren flashing, just off their back bumper.

He knew, without having to think about it, what was happening. Someone had seen him. Perhaps on the train, perhaps getting into the cab. Perhaps the cabbie himself had made a call to authorities.

Who said publicity didn't work?

He watched the faces of the officers as the cab slowed to a stop, and in his heightened state, Lucas knew he must act immediately, before the cab and the police cruiser stopped. Once they were parked, the police would be out of the car, guns drawn, holding back nothing in their effort to apprehend a suspect wanted for the murders of several people. No matter which side of the cab he chose to make his escape at that point, he would be trapped.

He slid across the seat to his right, pulled the knob to disengage the door lock, and yanked the lever to open the door. As he did this, he folded his body into a ball, rolling as he hit the pavement.

Coming out of the roll, he rose and ran on the balls of his feet, moving quickly across the sidewalk as shocked faces stopped to look at the man who had just jumped from a cab and was now running full speed.

But that world was in slow motion, and Lucas, in his heightened state, was moving at double time. Even before he'd leaned out of the cab door, even before he'd tucked into his roll, he'd picked his first target: an alley half a block away. He moved quickly, changing direction as he bobbed through the crowd of pedestrians.

Behind him, he heard one of the police officers command him to stop, but he was ahead, so far ahead of them, darting down the alley.

He could slip into one of the Dumpsters here in the alley, yes, but that would be expected, wouldn't it? Instead, he found a back door to some kind of restaurant—an Italian restaurant working on today's lunch specials, his heightened sense of smell told him before he'd even reached the door—and he slipped through it.

The officers would have backup on the way now, perhaps even on the scene, and they would expect him to go through the restaurant, find his way to the street at the front.

And so he did.

He ran through the restaurant, screamed a hasty "Where's the front door?" at one of the surprised workers, kept going without waiting for an answer. He found his way to the front door, stopped, turned down the small hallway on his right, and ducked into the men's restroom.

Because it was still morning, and the restaurant was a few hours away from opening, he had the restroom to himself. He scanned the area, looking for the room's weaknesses. An exposed industrial ceiling, with a giant pipe for the air return running the whole length of the room. No tile to hide above.

He looked at the sink. A small vanity, but probably too small even for him. There were two stalls, of course, but those would be the first things inspected.

He looked at the giant overhead pipe again. Maybe it could work. He probably had two minutes or so before the cops figured out he hadn't slipped out the front of the building, and then another couple until they searched the bathroom.

Lucas went into one of the stalls, checked the distances. After a few moments of calculating, he stepped onto the toilet and launched himself at the wall behind it, at the same time bending to catch the top of the stall's iron divider. Now his body formed a crude triangle, with his feet wedged on the back wall and his hands grasping the divider. Slowly, he walked his feet up the wall until he'd reached the height of the divider, then he brought his bottom leg to the top of the divider while his top leg still held his weight. Quickly, he took his foot off the wall and transferred his weight; he tottered dangerously for a few seconds, but then he had the foot on the stall under him, and he was able to regain his balance and stand on the divider like a tightrope walker. He edged to the front of the stall.

He couldn't quite reach the pipe, but he was able to grasp one of its ceiling brackets with both hands. Stepping off the door of the bathroom stall, he swung his body up and onto the pipe like a high jumper going over a bar belly first. When he landed on the pipe, he felt the ceiling brackets shift a bit, but they held. Dust from the top of the air return filtered down to the floor, but after a few seconds, the air was clear again.

Lucas hugged the top of the pipe, waiting. Finally, he heard someone come in the front door of the restaurant, yelling something at the

workers. The voice moved closer until he was able to make out the
last few words: ". . . sure he went out that way?"

One of the officers, he knew, coming to check the bathroom. Lucas
turned himself to his side, putting his hand against the ceiling above
and wedging himself on top of the pipe. The pipe's width would hide
his form, unless the police officer moved far to either side of the pipe
and examined the ceiling. He hoped that wouldn't happen.

He heard the door squeak open. "Give it up now, son." Lucas
waited, remaining quiet. He heard the officer's shoes squeak on the
fake tile of the bathroom floor, but couldn't see what was happening: the pipe blocked his view of what happened below as much as
it blocked the floor-level view of his own body.

A couple more steps, and then the shoes squeaking more. Metal—
handcuffs, maybe—jangled on the officer as he turned.

A few seconds later, one of the stall doors below slammed open.
Then the next. More footsteps, going toward the sink, checking the
vanity cupboard.

Lucas heard a deep sigh, a muttered curse under the breath. Finally
the officer spoke. "This is Fisher. All clear in the men's restroom."

A crackling voice answered Fisher, indicating the women's restroom was clear. Another reported the kitchen search was in progress.

Lucas heard the door to the bathroom swing open again, then
begin to whisk shut.

Unfortunately, that's when the TracFone in his pocket started
to ring.

THIRTY

The bathroom door swung open again, and the officer's voice bellowed, "Show yourself."

The phone rang once more. He was sure it was Sarea—he had to move to silence it—which would give up his location. And doing nothing would let the phone continue ringing, which would also give up his location.

He said, lowly and clearly, "I'm going to answer the phone."

"No, you're not. You're going to show yourself."

Lucas slid his pack around, found the phone, and fished it out. At the same time, he grabbed one of the ceiling brackets with one hand and slid himself down to a hanging position before dropping to the floor.

The police officer, a large, beefy man who was breathing heavily behind red cheeks, looked at him with his mouth agape.

The caller ID showed Sarea's number calling back, so he pressed the Answer button. "Sarea, listen. This is Lucas."

On the other end of the line, a voice that wasn't Sarea's interrupted. "Lucas. What a wonderful name. Much better than Humpty." He recognized the terrifying voice immediately. Hondo. "Sarea can't come to the phone right now. She's a bit tied up."

Lucas glanced at the police officer, who was pointing something at him, something that wasn't a gun, and screaming for him to get facedown on the ground *now*.

In his ear, Hondo's voice came again. "Sarea needs you, Lucas," he said, emphasizing his name carefully. "You know where she lives, don't you?"

"Listen, if you—" But that was all Lucas got out, because he saw something coming from the thing the police officer was holding, something that looked like a tiny dart on a wire, and then the tiny dart-thing was on his chest, and then a huge wave of white static overwhelmed him and he was falling, falling, falling, and as he was falling he was smelling something like an electrical short, yes, an electrical short filled with white static.

And the white static turned into black pain.

03:22:03 REMAINING

When he awoke, he thought he was still dreaming, remixing his moments in the back of Snake's car. His hands were bound behind him, and he was traveling in the backseat of a car to . . . somewhere he didn't know.

So yes, he had to be dreaming, because all of this had happened

to him before, he knew. Soon Clarice would pull over and let him
out of the back of the car, and they would be at the giant church
with the Blackboard.

He opened his eyes, saw the wire cage separating him from the
officers sitting in the front seat of the police cruiser.

No dream. And he definitely wasn't going to a church.

He would be taken into police custody, thrown into a small room
for a couple hours, questioned for several more, then booked and
thrown into a jail cell until he could post bond.

Unfortunately, by that time, Sarea would be attacked by Hondo
and the remaining members of the Creep Club would want revenge
because they thought he had killed Snake, Clarice, and Kennedy.
After all, the papers had said as much.

Even his own eyes said so—he'd seen the shooter.

On top of that, he would be dead because his leg would explode
some time in the next few hours. Maybe while he sat in the inter-
rogation room.

His mouth tasted like he'd been chewing on ashes from a fire-
place, and his ears rang with a slow, steady roar.

"What . . ." he creaked, but his voice barely came in a whisper.
He cleared his throat, swallowed a few times, tried again as the
police officer riding shotgun—the beefy one who had shot him—
turned to look.

"What did you do to me?" he asked.

Beefy Cop smiled. "I tased ya."

Tased, tased, tased. Suddenly, an image came to his mind, a young
man being held by police officers and pleading, "Don't tase me, Bro."

A taser. Yes, Lucas was familiar with the contraption, something of a stun gun that pumped several thousand volts of electricity through the intended victim, incapacitating said victim for several minutes.

"Count yourself lucky," Beefy Cop said. "We had orders. Been up to me, I woulda shot you with the .38."

"Well," Lucas said, working his jaw a bit more. "Lucky me."

They drove in silence for a few more minutes, and as they did, Lucas's despair grew. His eyes scanned the cruiser's interior, and his mind turned over every possibility he could think of. Force the car to crash? No; the mesh cage and handcuffs prevented that from happening. Unlock the car door and slip out, the way he'd been able to do in the cab? No chance; he knew the doors of these police cruisers couldn't be unlocked from the back. A careful look at the windows of the cruiser showed the glass was reinforced, which ruled out spinning to his back and kicking the glass—something he doubted could easily be done even with regular auto glass.

With no viable options available, he would have to wait until they got to the station. Maybe, during the transfer from the car to the cell, he'd be able to break free and make his escape. His hands would still be bound, but he didn't have many choices.

Barring a miracle of some sort, it was his best option.

They drove on in silence for a few more blocks, the officers not seeming to be in any particular hurry. And with each passing second, the futility of it all weighed heavier on Lucas—so much so that he finally had to scream in rage and frustration.

Both Beefy Cop and the more athletic one in the driver's seat jumped, startled by the guttural cry that escaped from his lips. Beefy Cop turned to say something to him, and in doing so, missed Lucas's miracle, coming to meet them from the passenger side of the vehicle.

A giant black SUV, doing at least fifty, and hurtling at the police cruiser without slowing.

03:05:49 REMAINING

To Lucas, the impact sounded like an explosion: a giant *whump* that knocked the wind out of him as the mesh cage in front of him crumpled.

For a few seconds, he heard the painful sound of metal shuddering against metal, something like fingernails on a chalkboard amplified a million times, but then there was an odd moment of silence as he felt the cruiser tipping and rolling to its side.

He tumbled in the backseat as the car flipped a few times and finally came to a stop. Now the only sounds were a low, menacing hiss of escaping steam and the squawk of static from the car's shortwave radio.

He wasn't sure whether the car was resting on its roof or on its tires, but it didn't matter: he saw that the fortified glass window beside him had indeed webbed in a million tiny lines. He swung his legs around and kicked at the glass; it fell away like a heavy curtain.

He started to slide out of the window when he heard a croaking voice: "Stop."

He looked back over his shoulder, and Beefy Cop had his trusty .38 drawn, pointed at him through the mesh. Beefy Cop was still strapped in, and a large flap of flesh from his forehead was hanging down over his right eye, pouring blood down his face, but one clear eye stared straight at him behind the barrel of the pistol.

Beefy Cop smiled a crooked smile, his teeth painted pink by

the blood in his mouth. "Looks like I'll get to use my .38 after all," he said.

Lucas watched as the finger on the trigger started to tighten, and he couldn't help it; he had to close his eyes. He didn't want to see the gun go off in his face. He heard the giant wallop of the gun inside the cramped space, hammering once and then twice, and he squeezed his eyes even tighter, surprised at how painless, how almost effortless, it was to be shot at point-blank range.

THIRTY-ONE

Lucas opened his eyes once more. Yes, he could see. Maybe he'd been shot in the head, but both of his eyes were intact, and no blood was running into them.

A few seconds later, he felt someone tugging at his feet, pulling him out the car window.

When he was totally outside, his first thought was, *Ah, so the car landed on its roof.* Crazy. And his second thought was pure terror, because the person who had pulled him from the car was the one person he was most afraid of seeing.

It was the assassin who had been stalking him. The assassin who wore his face.

03:03:57 REMAINING

The man who wore Lucas's face slipped a semiautomatic weapon with a silencer into a hidden holster, flipped Lucas onto his side, and began fumbling with keys. Lucas looked back inside the car and saw two thin streams of blood drizzling from the unmoving bodies of the police officers.

Numbly he realized he hadn't been shot at all. The man currently unlocking his handcuffs had shot the officers.

His pursuer stood and offered a hand to Lucas; Lucas, overcome with revulsion at the thought of touching the other man's bare skin *(his own skin),* boosted himself to a sitting position and then stood.

The Other was larger than he—heavier, thicker across the chest, and taller—but the face was still unsettling. "Are you okay?" his face asked him with his voice.

Lucas opened his mouth, closed it again, decided it was best to speak. "Yeah. I think I'm okay, all things considered."

"What do you see when you look into my face?" the man asked.

"What?"

"The face. Whose face do you see?"

"I see . . . me."

The man pursed his lips *(his own lips)* for a moment. "That's a new one," was all he said as he held out something for Lucas.

Lucas looked at the man's offering and saw it was another pistol much like the one the man had just secreted away, right down to the silencer attached to the tip.

"What's this for?" he asked weakly. He felt as if he were on drugs of some kind, drugs that filtered everything he said through a thick layer of cotton.

"Oh, I think you've used one before," the man said. He handed two more clips to Lucas. "It's a Taurus 45-caliber. You've got a full clip in there, plus these two extra, which means thirty rounds. Think you can make thirty rounds last?"

Lucas nodded, and the man smiled; Lucas hoped he didn't look that unsettling when he smiled.

"You'd better get going. You're still twenty minutes from Sarea's," the man with his face said.

Lucas looked from the pistol back to his own face, but the mention of Sarea brought some life back. "Yeah," he said, finally putting his hand behind his back and tucking the gun into the back of his pants. He briefly considered putting it in his backpack, but he might need quicker access.

"Take my car," the man said.

Lucas followed where the man was pointing and saw the steaming hunk of the black SUV, pink coolant trickling from the mangled radiator. "Doesn't look like it will get me far," said Lucas.

The man smiled, hit the button on the key fob in his hand. "That wasn't mine," he said.

Behind the SUV, another black vehicle—this one a nice sedan—hiccuped and flashed its parking lights. "That one's mine." He tossed the keys to Lucas.

Almost as if on cue, the warble of approaching sirens floated through the air. Odd, now that Lucas thought about it: there were no other cars, no pedestrians, on this street. He looked at the next block and saw traffic flowing; same with the traffic a block behind them. But here, at this intersection, there were only the two twisted heaps of what had once been cars and the black sedan, waiting with its driver's-side door open.

Lucas turned to look at the man with his face once again, but the figure was gone.

After a few more seconds, Lucas was gone too.

02:48:12 REMAINING

The man with his face was wrong.

Lucas wasn't twenty minutes away from Sarea's apartment complex; he made it there in less than fifteen.

As he neared the complex, he let his foot off the accelerator. He had considered speeding into the parking lot, leaping from the car before it had fully stopped, and letting the automatic pistol mow down everything that moved.

But that wouldn't be smart. He had to be careful.

He parked the car down the street, left the keys in it, and made his way down the sidewalk to Sarea's building. No sense trying to hide; they knew he was coming. They wanted him to come.

Pausing to shift the load of his backpack, Lucas went up the walkway toward Sarea's apartment. He climbed the steps to the second floor, considered knocking, and decided to try the doorknob.

It moved easily.

Pushing the door open with his left hand, he reached behind his back and pulled out the pistol as he entered the apartment.

Music—familiar music—filled the entryway, which led directly to the living room. Something bluesy, with a slide guitar.

Abruptly, Sarea came around the corner, dressed in a bathrobe with a towel on her head. Her eyes caught Lucas standing in the doorway, pointing a gun toward her.

"Just for future reference," she said, "you could probably ring the doorbell next time."

He stepped into the apartment, closing the door behind him and locking it. "You always take showers with your door unlocked?"

She shrugged, readjusted the towel on her head. "What do I got to be afraid of? I grew up here."

If she only knew. Lucas began moving through the apartment, methodically searching. He went into the living room, scanning the walls and floors. He stood on the couch, pushed up one of the ceiling tiles.

"Hey!" Sarea called, moving across the floor toward him.

"Hang on, I know what I'm doing." He winced as he said it. He knew what he was doing a little too well. With the flashlight from his backpack, he scanned the area above the ceiling tiles; as he swept the beam, it picked up a flash of silver in the corner near the front door.

He replaced the tile, looked at Sarea. "Can I borrow a chair for a second?" he asked as he moved toward the small dining nook.

"I guess," she said, watching him pick it up and take it over to the front door.

He put the chair in place, stood on it, and pushed the ceiling tile above out of the way.

"Hey, I got some other furniture in the back, if you want to stand on that next," she said.

He ignored her again, pulling away the small camera attached to the top of the acoustic tile, its lens aimed at a small, precisely drilled hole.

He stepped down from the chair, held out the camera for her to see.

Sarea looked at it in wonder, unconsciously pulled her robe a bit tighter. "What's that?" she asked.

"It's a camera," he said as he continued to scout the apartment, opening cupboards and inspecting the walls. "You've got three others in the ceiling over the living room and the dining area here. Probably more in other parts of the apartment." He moved into her bedroom, the gun loosely held at his side.

She followed him, now more intent. "So are you looking for more cameras now?" she said.

He looked at her. "No. I'm looking for someone who might be hiding."

"Who?"

"Could be a number of people."

He stood on the bed, pushed aside the ceiling tile, looked around. "Your bedroom's clean," he said as he put the tile back into place and hopped off the bed. "Can you be ready to go in five minutes?" he asked.

She frowned. "Ready to go where?"

He moved past her into the hallway. "I'm still working on that."

He began checking the heat registers in the hallway.

"So," she said. "I'm just supposed to drop everything, pack up, and run away with you with five minutes' notice but no idea what's going on?"

He turned to her. "Yeah, that's pretty much it."

She smiled. "Okay, Lucas. As long as we're on the same page." She shut the door softly.

He finished checking the rest of the apartment, finding a few more cameras, but not what he had feared: someone from the Creep Club, hiding inside the apartment.

He went back to the living room, sank down in the couch, listened to the blues guitar on Sarea's CD player.

What did this mean? He had expected a war zone here at Sarea's; he was sure, when he got here, he would find her place surrounded by Creep Clubbers ready to take him down. Instead, they seemed to be alone.

Were they watching? He was sure of that; the cameras said as much. Maybe they were planning an ambush. Maybe they had snipers outside, ready to pick him off when he walked out of the apartment.

The song on the CD player ended, moved to the next selection. His whole body froze when he heard the song begin. He recognized it, even before the man's voice began to sing.

> Got those crumblin' down blues, baby
> Got me some crumblin' down blues
> Got those crumblin' down blues so bad
> Feel 'em clear down in my shoes

He stood, slowly, and walked to the CD player. He picked up the jewel case sitting beside the player, studying the image on the cover. It was one of those old-style black-and-white portraits of a man sitting stiffly, unnaturally, his guitar perched on his lap. The man's deep, expressive eyes looked off to the side—not at the camera—as if he were pleading with someone just out of sight. A porkpie hat sat on his head.

"You a fan?" Sarea spoke from behind him.

He whirled around quickly, almost guiltily. She'd done nothing to her hair, which was kinky and pulled against her head after the shower. Hadn't even put on makeup of any kind, and yet she looked to Lucas like the most beautiful sight he'd ever seen.

She nodded her head at the CD case. "Mad Billy Weevil. You a fan?"

He looked at the jewel case again, as if it were the first time he'd ever held such an object.

> *Did me some dancin' with the devil*
> *Said he'd have to take his dues*
> *Now I'm digging with that shovel*
> *Cuz I got them crumblin' down blues*

"I . . . don't know," he admitted.

"Classic," she said. "He, Robert Johnson, Leadbelly, Blind Lemon Jefferson, a few others. The Delta Blues."

Lucas said nothing, so she moved across the room and pulled the case from his hands.

"We'll bring it," she said, pulling the disc out of the player and putting it in the case before tucking it into her bag. "What about a disc player?"

Lucas stared, unable to say anything. Even though the room was silent now, the song still echoed in his head:

Those crumblin' down blues.

Sarea shrugged, pulled the compact player from the shelf. "It's got batteries," she said, unplugging it. "We'll bring it." She stuffed it in her bag and turned to him. "Okay. Ready to go."

He nodded, forced himself back to the moment. They needed to go . . . where, exactly? What he needed was a safe house. A place that was isolated, unexpected. A place where he could take Sarea for a few hours and trust that she would be safe until this all ended.

He frowned. He could only come up with one possibility, and he didn't want to go there. It was too much to ask.

"We gonna go or not?"

He looked at Sarea. "Yeah, we're gonna go."

He opened the door and stepped into the great unknown.

THIRTY-TWO

They drove in silence for several minutes.

"Nice car," Sarea finally said. "Where'd you get it?"

"It was a gift," he said.

"A gift? From who?"

He smiled bitterly, turning onto the next street. "You might say it was a gift from myself."

She nodded. "So you were just washing dishes for the fun of it."

"Something like that."

More silence, then Sarea rummaged through her bag. "I saw the news on TV. The paper too. The way they talk, I should be scared of you." She pulled out a copy of the day's newspaper, the one with his face printed large.

"You're not a hat person," she said. "But you're big stuff—main story on the front page."

He shrugged as he reached into his pocket to get the TracFone.

"Who you calling?"

"Her name's Leila."

He dialed the number from memory and heard Leila's voice answer after one ring. "Hello?"

"Hi, Leila. This is . . . uh . . ."

"The front page of all the newspapers?"

"Yeah. Lucky me."

"Big press conference on TV right now too."

"Press conference for what?"

"Well, at the scene of the shooting, they found some files."

"They already said that."

"Yeah, but now they're revealing what's inside them."

"Which is?"

"They say those files detail a security breach with some Chinese intelligence agency."

"Guoanbu?"

"Yes, that's it."

Lucas had brought those files with him, showed them to Saul. So there *were* other files left in the van, which meant there were duplicates. Saul had been right.

"Listen," he said. "I need to ask you a favor—a favor I have no right to ask, but you're the only person I can think of."

"What is it?"

"I need to protect someone. I need a safe house where I can drop her off for a few hours," he said.

"Protect this someone from whom?"

He smiled. "That's a good question. Mainly from the people who monitored your home."

"If I remember right, one of those people was you."

"Not until the end. There's a whole group of them."

"What did she do to put them on her trail? Commit the mortal sin of being born in another country, like me?"

"Close. She befriended me."

"If they've been here before, it's not like they'll have a hard time finding her."

"That's just it, though. I think they'll expect me to head somewhere else, not circle back around."

The other end of the line was silent for a few moments; then Leila spoke. "Bring her," she said. "Sounds like maybe I shouldn't put away my gun just yet."

"Maybe not."

Lucas hung up, put the phone into his pocket, glanced at Sarea. She had the CD from her house in her hands—the disc by Mad Billy Weevil. She held it up, and he nodded, so she slipped it into the disc player on the dash.

The music started, a song he didn't recognize. But he recognized the playing style; it was unforgettable.

"You got a lot to tell me, Lucas. A whole lot. I think I've been pretty cooperative, dropping everything to come with you like this."

"Why? I mean, you did it, no questions asked."

"Because you asked. Because I want to help you."

A dark sigh escaped his lips, and he shook his head. "That's why we left. People after me were trying to come after you."

"I figured that part out."

She said nothing else for several seconds, so Lucas prompted her. "And?"

She cocked her head toward him. "And nothing, Lucas. You expect me to be mad? You expect me to go all damsel-in-distress, break down in tears? You ain't seen where I grew up, ain't seen what I've seen. You're not getting a guilt trip from me. Seems like you're tripping over it enough on your own."

He smiled at that, made another turn. The first song on the disc ended, and the second began to play. He recognized this song instantly, listening to the opening bars before the man's voice began to sing.

Spinnin', you got me spinnin' all around
Spinnin' so much I ain't never been found
And when you tell me you don't mean it
I don't mind much, baby, cuz I seen it

"This is faster," he said, almost without thinking about it.

"Faster than what?"

"Faster than he played it at the station."

"Yeah," she said. "Lots of people play Mad Billy's old songs."

"No," he said. "It was him—the guy on the cover. I heard him play this."

Sarea went silent for several seconds, and he turned his head to see her staring at him.

"What?"

"Why do you say it was him?"

"The picture on the cover. It was him. He was even wearing that crazy hat."

Sarea stayed silent for a few more moments.

"What's the big deal?" he said. "So he's fallen on hard times. Lots of musicians playing the streets."

She sighed. "The big deal is, that picture on the cover was taken in 1931—one of only three confirmed photos in existence. And the last known photo before he died."

Lucas snapped his head to look at her again. "Died?"

"Stabbed in a bar down in Louisiana."

They drove a few more minutes, listening to the song, neither of them saying anything.

Finally Lucas broke the silence between them. "That picture. I thought it was one of those old-time studio shots, you know. Supposed to look old."

She smiled. "The Delta Blues—several men started playing down in Mississippi during the Great Depression, you understand. And they were like this loose group; they all listened to each other, borrowed from each other, traded on each other's stories and legends."

Lucas glanced in the rearview mirror, counting at least four cars in line behind him now.

"Robert Johnson—you've heard of him?" Sarea asked.

"I think so."

"He's maybe most famous. And maybe most famous because of the legend around him. The legend of the crossroads."

"The crossroads?"

"He always told the story of standing at these crossroads in Mississippi, meeting the devil, selling his soul for music."

"So what's that have to do with Mad Billy?"

"Well, like I said, they borrowed each other's stories, even borrowed each other's songs, built on them, you know? Took what the other had and added to it. So even though Robert Johnson is the one famous for selling his soul, he wasn't the first to stand at those crossroads. He followed Mad Billy, the legend goes."

"So Mad Billy sold his soul, then?"

She smiled. "No. No, he didn't. He refused the deal, which is why Robert Johnson had the chance. Funny thing is, though, they both died almost the same way."

"So turning down that offer for his soul didn't help him much, did it?"

Sarea shook her head, exhaled loudly. "I think you're looking at it wrong, Lucas. Looks to me like Robert Johnson didn't get much for his soul."

The song about spinning ended, and the "Crumblin' Down Blues" began. After the first verse and chorus, Sarea spoke again.

"Thing is," she said, "that ain't all about Mad Billy Weevil." She touched his arm. "Legend says, since then, Mad Billy appears to certain people."

"Like a ghost?"

"Something like that. A sign."

"A sign of what?"

"Appears to folks standing on the edge of losing their own souls. Showing them the way out, the story goes."

Lucas turned onto the street that led to Leila's home. "I got some news for you," he said. "I don't have a soul."

01:48:11 REMAINING

Leila opened the door to them as they walked onto her front porch, not bothering to wait for the doorbell or a knock. She shook Lucas's hand, then offered her hand to Sarea after he introduced them.

"Well," she said. "I guess we'd better get off this porch." She turned and went back into the house, and they followed. He saw Leila hadn't been kidding about putting away her gun; she had two pistols and a shotgun, along with several rounds of ammo, sitting on the floor of the living room.

Leila obviously noticed the two of them staring. "Either of you fired a gun before?"

Lucas was surprised when Sarea nodded her head, went across the room to pick up one of the pistols, and released the clip to check the cartridges.

Leila turned to him. "You?"

"I have my own," he said, retrieving the pistol his Bad Twin had given him after the accident.

Leila picked up the shotgun, loaded a few shells into the magazine, and pumped it once to chamber the first round. "You go do what you have to do," she said to Lucas. "We'll be just fine here."

"Okay," he said. He turned, started to go back out the door, then stopped and faced them again.

"I'm sorry," he said abruptly.

Both of the women stopped, looked at him. "For what?" Leila asked.

"For getting both of you involved in this," he said. "I'm putting you in danger, and you could die, just for knowing me."

Leila bent and picked up the other pistol. "Lucas," she said. "I was already dying. Just doing it slowly. This way, maybe I get to make up for not doing anything for so long. For believing I couldn't do anything." She held him in a strong gaze. "This isn't all about you. It's something I have to do too." That said, she walked into the next room.

He looked at Sarea. She smiled.

"We ain't dead yet, Lucas. Let's not act like it."

He nodded, closed the door, knowing it was the last time he would see either of them.

THIRTY-THREE

01:44:25 REMAINING

Back on the road, Lucas sped toward the District again, ready to head for the church.

But after a few miles, he pulled to the side of the road. It was time to die, he knew. He just wasn't sure how it was going to happen yet. Somehow he had to stop Saul, Viktor, and Hondo in the next few hours. All that before he could turn attention to the bomb on his leg.

He dialed Sarea's phone number. As he expected, Hondo answered.

"Is your girlfriend missing her phone yet?" Hondo said when he answered. "I hope I'm not using up all her minutes."

"Are you gonna tell me what this is all about? Why you stole Sarea's phone?"

"I want a new project. We all do. Do you know none of us—none of us in the Creep Club—has ever caught a murder on video? Not a real one. A shame, really. That's why we were all excited when Kennedy and Clarice were going to catch you on tape. But then . . . well, I guess you took care of them, didn't you? Along with Snake."

"That wasn't me."

Hondo laughed. "Hmmm. That's not what the news channels are saying. You telling me I maybe shouldn't trust big media?"

"For someone who's lost a few friends recently, you don't seem too broken up, Hondo."

"Oh, you got me. You really got me. Donavan, Snake. To tell you the truth, I'm glad to see them dead—all the better for me. Sorry to see Clarice and Kennedy go, though. They had possibilities."

Lucas closed his eyes. He listened to a few moments of silence before Hondo spoke again.

"Well, this is indeed a wonderful conversation, but I need to get going."

Lucas's eyes flicked open immediately.

"Where?"

"Where do you think? Gonna drop by and see your gal friends. Dilbert remembers the way there, of course, but we also have GPS coordinates."

"How?"

"You're kinda slow today—sure you got enough sleep last night? If I managed to get into her bag to take her cell phone . . ."

"You put a geopatch in her bag."

"Ah, now you're catching on."

Lucas swallowed hard, then put the car in gear and swung back the opposite direction on the street he was driving down, cutting off several cars in the process. "But if you wanted to kill me, why not just do your setup at Sarea's apartment—jump me there?"

Hondo laughed. "You ever hunt?"

"No." Lucas thought the longer he kept him on the phone, the more distracted he would be. And maybe, the longer it would take them to get to Leila's house.

"Well, you ask anyone who hunts about their favorite hunting story, you know what they tell you?"

"No."

"They tell you all about the day. All about the terrain, the weather, the tracking, the chase. No one ever talks about actually pulling the trigger. Pulling the trigger isn't the fun part; it's the end of the fun part, actually."

"So you did it all for fun."

"Oh, I'm expecting some great footage out of this—especially because we've already got cameras all over that house. Thanks to Dilbert." He paused. "Your first project is about to begin, Lucas. Unfortunately, it's also your last."

The connection went silent as Hondo ended the call.

Lucas immediately called Leila's number. When she answered, he said, "They're coming."

"I know," she said.

"How did you know?"

"Like I said before, Lucas. This is something I have to do. So I know."

"Have you seen anyone?"

"Not yet."

"You're about to."

"Why's that?"

"Because I'm heading back right now."

01:36:25 REMAINING

Sarea met him at the door again and led him to a small breakfast nook with a computer on the table. Leila was sitting there, staring at a screen that presented six different cam shots. "The crazy thing is," she said, "we've had security cams on the house the whole time. No alarm ever went off, though." She stared at Lucas for a second. "Not until you tripped it."

Lucas stared at the cam shots. "These people are good with technology," he said. "They figured out some way to override your alarm system."

"What was his name?" Leila asked.

"Who?"

"The guy—the one in my house."

He nodded. "I don't know his real name. Dilbert is what he goes by."

She nodded. "How many will there be?"

"I don't know. If it's all of them, something like twenty. Wait, make that sixteen—four of them are dead now."

She looked at him, her eyes narrowed a bit.

"Long story for a different day," he said.

"So what are they going to do?" asked Sarea. "I mean, how will they attack?"

Lucas looked at her. Attack. That was a good question. Right up there with: *How do you get rid of a bomb that's going to blow off your leg in less than two hours?*

But one question at a time.

He'd heard the excitement in Hondo's voice, the junkie rush of the drug pounding in the veins. And now he realized, this really *was* a project to them.

They would kill him, kill Leila and Sarea, yes. But they wanted to record it, to document it. To them, that was the most important thing. All of them were juiced up on the thought of seeing three people die on camera.

"Can we kill the power?" he said.

Leila turned and cocked an eyebrow at him. "Kill the power, shut off our security system and all our surveillance cameras. Yeah, that sounds like a good idea to me."

"Look, you already know they bypassed your security. And I'm betting they've tapped your cameras, because they—"

"—because they want to record what the cameras see," Leila finished.

"Exactly. That's what drives us. Them, I mean. We make it harder for them to record, none of your cameras, none of your lights, we distract them a bit."

Leila nodded. "Breaker panels for the upstairs are right behind you. More in the basement, but just for the water heater, the furnace, and the garage."

"Okay," he said. "How about flashlights? I have one, but do you have a couple extras?"

"Hang on," Leila said. She left the room for a few minutes, then returned with two flashlights, handing one to Sarea. Loaded with guns and lights, they were ready.

"Now," Lucas said, "we shut down the power, and then we go to the basement. Not as many access points, and—"

"Harder to record in the dark basement, unless they have infrared cameras," Sarea finished.

"They will have infrared cameras, you can bet on that," Lucas answered. "But, yeah, we'll make it more difficult."

Both women nodded.

"Let's go." He turned around, opened the breaker box, and began flipping all the switches.

A few minutes later, they walked out of the office and made their way to the basement door. Light spilled through the large windows on the main floor, but as soon as they began descending the basement steps, they needed to turn on their flashlights.

They worked their way down, all of them breathing heavily as they felt the darkness—and what would soon be in that darkness—pressing in around them.

"Back here," Leila whispered, swinging her flashlight. "There's a utility room. Only one way in—we can hold them when they try to come after us."

Lucas began to follow, but then the enormity of it all overwhelmed him. Here they were, three of them, trying to hold out against more than a dozen. And they were going to trap themselves inside a room in the basement. Impossible. What had he been thinking? He needed another way out of this.

"Careful, the ceiling's kind of low here from the furnace returns," Leila said.

Furnace. The word stuck in his mind.

"What kind of furnace?" Lucas asked.

"Natural gas, but this probably isn't the time to talk about home improvement."

"Don't go to the utility room," Lucas said.

Leila stopped, spun the flashlight around on him.

"You got a better idea?"

"I might, if you have a set of tools down here—crescent wrench or pliers."

"Toolbox in the utility room."

"I'm thinking we maybe do a bit of work on that furnace."

Leila smiled, obviously catching on. "I like the way you think."

"Really? You're okay with it?"

Sarea spoke up. "Would somebody tell me what's going on?"

Leila looked at him. "We unhook the gas supply from the furnace, let natural gas seep into the house."

Lucas took over. "The gas should actually rise, pool in the upstairs. Right now, all the power's off up there. But when they find the breaker box and flip the power on again . . ."

"Electricity and gas. Bad combination," Sarea said. "Let's do it."

"Hang tight," Leila said. "I'm gonna go do it right now."

"What?" Lucas said. "No way. This is on me. Bad enough we're going to blow up your house."

Leila's flashlight wavered in the dim light, and Lucas felt her hand on his arm. "You think I'm sorry to see this place blow up? I'm doing it. You guys go open the window and we'll slip out the back. You remember where the window is, I'm sure."

He considered for a moment, thought it best to pick his battles elsewhere. "Okay," he said. "Just remember to flip the breakers down here too."

She said nothing, but he felt her turn and leave.

Lucas led Sarea toward the window he'd entered just a few days before and opened it. He peeked outside, looking for activity but seeing none.

A few moments later, the rotten-egg scent of natural gas surrounded them; both he and Sarea moved closer to the open window to breathe the fresh air from outside.

Leila returned, a smile on her face. "Valve's wide open. Don't know how much gas we're pumping in here, but I bet it's a lot."

"I can smell it already," Sarea said.

"Okay," Lucas said. "Now we need to get out of here. But we can almost guarantee, if they're here and getting ready to come in, they're watching all the exits—maybe not so much back here by the basement window, but we have to assume someone's going to see us and warn them."

Sarea raised her gun, fully visible in the shaft of light coming through the window. "Then we'll shut them up before they can say anything."

He nodded. "I'll go first. I'm gonna head for the back of the garden shed, and I'll stop there to cover for each of you. When we're all at the shed, we'll head to those trees just off the back of the property, hopefully be able to circle back around."

"Then what?" Sarea asked. "We don't have a car or anything—the one we were using is still out front, and I doubt we'll get back to it. Even if it survives the explosion."

Lucas shrugged. "One problem at a time. I'll just be happy if we all get out of here without blowing ourselves up." He winced as he said it. Even if he avoided this explosion, another one was waiting for him soon.

Upstairs, they heard a scraping sound. The front door, opening. Time was running out.

"Okay," Lucas said, his voice dropping to a whisper. "Who's coming after me?"

"Sarea is," Leila said. "Captain's the last one off the ship."

Sarea turned and looked at Leila, but said nothing.

"Sounds good," Lucas said. "Here we go."

He didn't have time to think, only to act. He boosted himself through the window, stayed crouched in the shadows for a few moments, scanned the backyard. No one was immediately visible.

He sprinted to the rear part of the backyard patio, crouched behind one of the giant planters. Still no sign he'd been seen. Now it was a sprint of about twenty yards across open lawn to the shed. If people were watching, this was when they would likely shoot.

Lucas took a couple deep breaths, launched himself across the thick, lush grass. He sprinted halfway, then shifted ninety degrees for a few yards, hoping to throw off anyone who might be leading him.

Good thing. A report sounded, and he saw a small puff rise from the lawn right where he would have been if he hadn't made the unexpected shift.

He turned back toward the shed again and ran as fast as he could, sliding on the ground and crawling behind the shed on all fours.

His breath came in ragged gasps as he replayed the last few seconds in his photographic memory. Where was the shooter? He analyzed the bullet's impact on the lawn, realizing the shot must have come from his left as he ran to the shed.

That meant he could slip around the back of the shed, get a look at the other side. He had a few feet between the shed and the fence, fronted by a hedge that ran down the property line.

He went around the back of the shed, still on his hands and knees, and put his head to the ground so he could see beneath the heavy branches.

About ten yards away, he saw two feet standing behind the hedge. Without waiting, he aimed his gun at the calf of the near leg and squeezed the trigger, then raised the gun a few inches and pulled the trigger again. The silencer did its job, making only a soft *plunk* with each shot.

He saw the legs collapse, and he immediately scrambled beneath the hedge, rising to his feet and squeezing between the fence and the hedge to reach the body lying on the ground.

He had no idea what kind of shells his Bad Twin had loaded into the pistol, but the man's leg had been shattered. The other shot had opened a red hole in the man's side, and he was now crumpled against the chain-link fence, glassy eyes staring at nothing. His pistol was on the ground a few feet away, and his left hand still clutched a two-way radio.

"Kramden," a voice squawked over the radio. "Kramden, what did you say?" The radio stayed silent for a few seconds, then the message repeated. "Kramden, talk to me."

Lucas recognized the voice. Hondo.

He quickly snatched the radio, made his voice gruff in hopes of disguising it, and keyed the mike. "Never mind," he said. "False alarm."

"Copy."

Lucas took the two-way and squeezed back beneath the hedge to the rear of the garden shed. Sarea was already there, panting, and a few seconds later, Leila came around the corner.

"Where you been?" Sarea asked. He held up the two-way radio, now squawking with other communications among the Creep Clubbers.

"Let's go," Leila said, running for the trees. Lucas and Sarea followed, and they scrambled through the cover.

After a couple hundred yards, Lucas stopped and keyed the mike on the two-way again. "We need everyone in the house, now!" he screamed, hoping he sounded authoritative enough. He threw the two-way on the ground behind a small bush and kept running.

Come on, come on, Lucas said to himself. It has to be soon, or they'll figure out what's happening and—

As if on cue, a giant *whoom* sounded behind them. Even behind the tree cover at the distance they were, Lucas felt the heat of the blast, along with a strong shock wave, blow past them. Branches bent and swayed, and leaves began floating down around them as they turned to see the damage.

The house had exploded, he had probably sent twenty people to their deaths, and he didn't regret it in the least.

No, he didn't have a soul.

Several minutes later, they came out of the woods into a small clearing. They found their way to the end of a cul-de-sac with a few large homes surrounding it, bookended by a few open lots with FOR SALE signs pounded into the bare dirt. A new subdivision.

But it wasn't the subdivision that stopped Lucas. It was the car, a newer black sedan sitting at the end of the cul-de-sac and idling.

No one was inside it.

Leila peered at him. "Looks like the car you brought to the house," she said.

"Doesn't just look like it. It is," said Sarea.

"How do you know?" asked Lucas.

She shrugged. "I just know." She began walking toward it, and Leila followed.

When they reached the car, they checked to make sure it was empty, then climbed in.

"You sure you didn't plan this?" Leila asked from the backseat.

"I didn't," Lucas said. "But someone did."

He looked at the clock on the car's dash. By his calculations, he had an hour and change before the manacle on his leg exploded. He wanted to check it, but not in front of Sarea and Leila. They had enough on their plates for right now.

So did he, for that matter.

As they sat in the car, catching their breath, images jumbled in his mind.

(Humpty Dumpty had some great falls.)

"He only had one," Sarea said.

He turned. "What?"

"Humpty Dumpty only had one great fall," she said. "You just said, 'Humpty Dumpty had some great falls.' It's 'Humpty Dumpty had a great *fall*.' He only fell once."

"Oh. I . . . didn't know I said it out loud." But now the words *great falls* kept sticking in his mind, and they somehow fit something deep inside where his soul should have been.

Great falls.

"So," Leila said again. "What, pray tell, is our next step?"

Lucas started to speak, but Leila's comment stuck in his mind. Pray tell.

He smiled. "We're going to church."

THIRTY-FOUR

01:02:59 REMAINING

Back on the interstate, they drove in silence for several miles. Sarea dug in her bag, brought out a pack of cigarettes. She put one in her mouth, offered one to Leila—who accepted it—then tilted the pack toward him.

"I don't smoke," he said.

"I know," she answered.

He smiled, took one of the smokes, let Sarea put flame to it with her lighter.

"You wanna tell us what's happening?" Leila finally said from the backseat.

"I'm not quite sure," he answered.

Sarea looked at him. "Give it a try."

He smiled. "Okay."

For the next several minutes, he filled them in on Viktor and Saul, skipping the part about the explosive attached to his leg. No sense adding to their stress.

When he was done, Leila spoke. "What about your ankle? Is it okay?" she asked.

He looked at her in the rearview mirror. Oh yeah—he'd already told Leila about the bomb; he'd forgotten.

"You hurt your ankle?" Sarea asked, sounding concerned.

"Yeah," he said, glancing at Leila in the back again. "Old injury, but I think it'll hold out another hour."

Leila dropped the subject.

He wheeled into a convenience store, parked in the front.

"What are you doing?" Sarea asked.

"I just need a coffee or something. Thought you guys might want a quick break too."

"Good idea," Leila said.

He caught her gaze in the mirror again.

"Okay," Sarea said. "Let's make it quick, though." She opened the door.

"Only thing is," Lucas said, "no way I can show my face in there, you know? They're looking for me everywhere. So maybe . . . would you mind picking up the coffee for me?"

Sarea studied him for a few seconds, then relented. "Okay," she said slowly. "I'll get you a coffee. Anything else?"

"No, that should do it."

Sarea put her foot on the pavement and started to get out of the car.

Lucas grabbed her arm. "And thanks," he said. "For everything."

She smiled. "You're welcome. For everything."

He let go and watched her walk toward the store.

"What about you?" he said to Leila in the backseat.

After a few moments of silence, she spoke. "I understand, Lucas. I had to blow up my past, you have to blow up yours." She opened the door. "I'll make sure she stays safe," she said, and then she slid out of the car and walked toward the front door of the store.

He put the car in reverse, backed out of the parking spot, and wheeled out onto the street again.

Humpty Dumpty was heading for his great fall.

00:58:14 REMAINING

Lucas shut off his cell phone, knowing Sarea would try to call. He'd already had his share of trouble from a phone ringing at the wrong time today. He needed time to think, time to make his plan, and the church was the place to do it.

He drove down the interstate, took the exit, and made his way toward the church. After parking several blocks away, he checked the clock on the dash. How much time before the bomb detonated? Less than an hour, for sure. But enough time for a quick good-bye at the church, then maybe try to set up a meeting with Saul or Viktor. Maybe he could take one of them with him.

He walked toward the church, catching a glint of sun as it reflected off the nearby Quonset hut.

He stopped when Viktor stepped out of the front door. Two other men, thick and dark, followed him. One of them was Garlic Breath.

"Ain't like no church I ever saw," Viktor said when Lucas approached.

"What are you doing here?" Lucas asked.

Viktor paused, looked. "I got your message," he said.

Lucas stared. He'd left no message, but he had an idea who had. His Bad Twin. One of them.

"You look disappointed to see me," Viktor said. "You should be eager to have that clock reset—which I'll be happy to do after our little meeting."

"Meeting?"

Viktor looked at him, puzzled. "You said you set up a meeting with your backers. Now I'll find out who—" Viktor's gaze caught something over Lucas's shoulder, stopping him in midsentence.

Lucas turned and looked. He was unsurprised to see Saul walking toward them, a briefcase in his hand.

"Let me guess," Lucas said as Saul approached. "You got my message."

Saul knotted his brow, looked back at Lucas, staring above his head as usual. *Blink, blink.* "You said to meet you here." He glanced at Viktor and his men at the front door, just behind Lucas. "These must be the . . . ah . . . the people you were telling me about," he said.

"This is Viktor Abkin," Lucas said. "Viktor, meet Saul."

"Saul? A very Jewish name. You don't look Jewish," Viktor said.

"And you don't look like you're from Belarus. But that's what your accent tells me."

Viktor eyed him suspiciously. "Very good. Most just say Russian; you have an ear for regional differences."

Saul smiled, shrugged. "Comes with the territory. Once had a major interest in Belarus." He smiled again. "And Russia."

Saul started to put his hand in his coat, and the two burly men behind Viktor moved for their guns.

"Whoa, whoa, there, cowboys. Just going for my smokes."

The two relaxed a bit, watching carefully as Saul slipped his hand inside his jacket and retrieved his cigarettes. He shook one into his mouth, offered one to Viktor, who shook his head, and then offered one to Lucas.

"I told you before," Lucas said, "I don't smoke."

"Well, no better time to start."

Lucas smiled. "You know what? You're right." He took one of the cigarettes from the pack and put it between his lips, then waited as Saul lit it for him.

Saul glanced at Lucas, gave a small, almost imperceptible nod. He started to put his cigarettes back in his jacket pocket, paused, arched his eyebrows at the two men behind Viktor. The two men relaxed, and Saul let his hand disappear into his pocket.

Suddenly his hand reappeared, this time with a gun in it. He shot Viktor and his two henchmen quickly; three shots, three seconds, and it was over.

Immediately, Lucas felt Saul's arm around him, and they were falling through the door as the world around them erupted in gunfire.

Lucas immediately pushed away, rolling to the side and coming out of the roll in a crouch. Saul had shot the other three because they were the most immediate threat, but Lucas knew he had to be next.

He came out of the roll, retrieving his own gun and pointing it toward Saul. Saul pushed himself up on his hands slowly, putting his gun on the floor next to him, making no attempt to use it.

Outside, the gunfire continued; a few stray bullets hit the wall of the church, and one splintered the jamb of the doorway they'd just rolled through.

Saul struggled to a sitting position on the floor, just adjacent to the doorframe. He looked at Lucas, gritting his teeth. "You gonna trust me enough now to tell me where you really got those files?"

Lucas noticed a patch of red spreading beneath Saul's leg. He let his eyes lock with Saul's. "You mean the files that prove you're working with the Chinese Guoanbu?"

Saul smiled. "Shoulda expected. You're new to this game. You don't even know."

"Know what?"

"Know anything." Saul spied his recently lit cigarette smoldering on the floor a few feet away, leaned over to retrieve it. He put it between his lips, took a few puffs.

Outside, the gunfire had stopped, and now only echoes rang in Lucas's ears. "Who's out there?" Lucas asked.

Saul smiled. "Maybe no one left, judging from all that shooting. Guess we'll find out in a few seconds, won't we?"

Moments later, a figure appeared at the door, pointed the gun toward Saul, and fired point-blank. The figure wheeled and pointed his gun at Lucas, smiling.

"Did you miss me?" Donavan asked.

THIRTY-FIVE

Lucas stared in wonder. Donavan, who had been missing since . . . well, since the beginning.

"What . . ." Lucas stammered. But it was all he could get out.

"Quite the surprise, I know," Donavan said. "But count yourself lucky. You've been part of the perfect operation, Humpty. Or Lucas, I should say. I've known that all along, I should tell you."

Donavan moved across the floor, keeping the gun pointed at Lucas. "Worked pretty well, don't you think? Stories will be hitting the papers, tying your friend over there to Chinese intelligence sources, and we'll be able to wipe the whole slate clean."

"What slate?"

"Long story. There's just one loose end to wrap up right now."

Lucas dropped his gun, no longer caring. He'd reached the end of everything. His nerves were too frayed, his mind too tired to care.

"You're going to have to shoot me like this," Lucas whispered. "Unarmed."

Donavan smiled. "I'm sorry, did you think you were the loose end?" he asked. Abruptly, Donavan pointed the pistol at his own head and pulled the trigger.

00:43:18 REMAINING

Lucas closed his eyes for a few moments, and when he opened them again, his vision swam in tears. He was lost, hopelessly lost, in something far beyond his understanding.

"Hello, Lucas."

A new person at the door. Someone he didn't recognize. The man stepped through the doorway and walked across the floor toward him. Lucas thought his ears were buzzing from all the gunfire, but then he realized it was the man who was buzzing: yellow-and-black bees hovered around him in a giant cloud. As the man stopped to stand in front of him, more bees flew in through the doorway. No, they weren't bees, Lucas noticed on closer inspection, but wasps.

Lucas scrambled for his gun on the floor, trained it on the man, who seemed unconcerned. "Who are you?" Lucas asked, not sure he wanted to know.

"Who are any of us? That's a question we must all ask ourselves at some point—and a question I'm hoping to help you answer in a moment. Call me Swarm; it's the only name I've known."

Swarm walked toward the Blackboard at the front of the church, flicked on the switch that bathed it in light. He shook his head. "I knew, someday, it would end up like this. It had to."

"What had to?"

"This project."

Project—what everyone in Creep Club called their odd fixation.

"So you—" Lucas began. "You're a member of the Creep Club."

Swarm spun around and began walking toward Lucas. "Let's take a ride, Lucas. I have a car waiting outside, and as you can imagine, this place will be crawling with law enforcement soon. No way to cover up several hundred rounds fired in just a few minutes. Not even I can do that."

Swarm held out his hand, offering to help Lucas to his feet.

Lucas stared a few moments as sirens wailed in the distance.

"Hear that?" Swarm asked, still holding out his hand. "Time to go."

Lucas let the man help him to his feet and followed him to the door. Out on the street, as promised, a black sedan waited, its back door hanging open. Without waiting, Swarm approached the car and got in, sliding to the other side to make room for Lucas. After a few seconds of hesitation, Lucas slid in behind him.

Immediately the car began to move; two men sat in the front seat, but all Lucas could see was the backs of their heads. Even so, he felt his terror starting to rise a few notches.

"You feel it, don't you?" Swarm said without looking at him. "Fear."

Lucas swallowed, trying to calm his nerves. "Yes," he admitted, without really knowing why.

"Scientists scoffed at the existence of human pheromones until 1982," Swarm said. "Animal pheromones they had no problem with, but they couldn't buy into human pheromones. Well, most scientists, anyway; the ones I worked with were convinced."

Swarm turned to him and smiled. "That's what you're feeling—pheromones. We have, unfortunately, the two men in the front seat to thank for that. They're part of one of my newer projects—a little something I call Dark Fear. A bit of genetics, but mostly good, old-fashioned pheromones, pheromones engineered specifically to light up the part of your brain that controls the fight-or-flight reflex. Scent, believe it or not, is the most deeply imprinted sense in your brain; you can't retrain it."

He looked at Lucas again. "I think you've probably met these men before," he said, gesturing at the two in the front seat.

The two men swiveled their heads to look at Lucas, and he had a good view of their features. Not for the first time.

Both of them wore his face.

"These . . ." he stammered. "They've been—"

"Yes, they have," Swarm interrupted. "Believe it or not, with phero-mones, with the body's sense of smell—and to some extent, taste—you can fool the other senses. That's why all the agents in Project Dark Fear can appear to anyone as the person who scares them most."

"Who scares them most? But they—"

"You see yourself, I'm told. That's an unusual one, I must admit, but perhaps not unexpected, considering everything you've been through. Lots of times, we get movie influences: Jason, Freddy, Hannibal Lecter, that kind of thing. Adolf Hitler. Mothers and fathers a surprising amount of the time. I, myself, see the man who conditioned me. Raven."

Swarm went quiet for a few moments.

"The van driver said he saw Charles Manson," Lucas whispered.

"Manson's in the top ten."

They drove in silence for a few minutes as Lucas tried to process

all this information—especially as his heart trip-hammered, terrified of the two in the front seat. He prayed they wouldn't turn
around again.

Lucas looked back at Swarm, tried to ignore the cloud of wasps.
The insects seemed calm, almost drugged. Most of them hovered
within a foot of his head, until they tired and landed on his head or
shoulders. They crawled, unhurried, around his skin before flying
again. In many ways, it seemed as if the man were a human hive.

"I'm sorry for the wasps, on top of it all. When I was the project,
the experiment, if you will, they didn't understand nearly as much
about pheromones, genetics, anything. Mostly synthetic drugs back
then. They were trying to create a Super Soldier, a drone who sacrificed himself to save his homeland. The way drone wasps do."

Lucas closed his eyes, wishing for the first time he was in the
midst of a firefight between Viktor's mafia men and Saul's secret
agents. This was a bit too Twilight Zone for him.

"You deserve an explanation, Lucas, and that's what I'm here to
give you. Because I also created another project, one called Inside
Information. Or, as you know it, the Creep Club."

"You started the Creep Club?"

"Yes. Two dozen people, beginning with Snake. He knew more
than the others—I needed someone to be a contact, a liaison with
government agencies, since I don't officially work for any agency
myself. Officially, I don't exist. Like you."

Swarm dug in his pocket and produced something Lucas had forgotten all about: the small black cube from Saul's briefcase. Where
had he left it? How did Swarm find it? Swarm turned it in his hands,
over and over, as he spoke.

"Project Inside Information began about twenty-five years ago,"

Swarm continued. "It was my brainchild, a way around the age-old question of what you do with intelligence agents who get caught. In an ideal world, of course, they don't get caught alive. Like Donavan—perfect example. If they follow their training, as he did, they kill themselves first. But that doesn't always happen. Add in the temptation to be a double agent . . . well, you can see some of the difficulties."

"Like Saul—um, Saul Slater."

"You really think he was a double agent?"

"He . . . I found files."

"Just as you were supposed to. I was sorry it had to be Saul; he really was a good agent. But he was getting a little too close to the truth, so he had to be part of the cover-up."

Lucas felt like he was about to get sick. "That's what I am too," he said.

"You're catching on," Swarm said. "My idea for Inside Information was rather simple: we create agents who don't know they're agents, you see? Enlist very young people for our purposes. Very young people who seem to have a . . . let's call it a predisposition . . . for this work. The right build, the right mental capacities, as determined by their schoolwork, that sort of thing. Work with them for years, conditioning them. Some like to use the word *brainwashing*, but I find that somewhat distasteful. I like *conditioning* much better."

"These kids," Lucas said, afraid of the answer to the question he was about to ask. "Did they come from orphanages?"

Swarm smiled. "I know what you're asking, Lucas, and the short answer is: no, they didn't come from orphanages. But there's a longer answer you'll want to hear. Well, maybe *want* isn't the right word, but an answer you should hear." He tilted his head at the ceiling of the car, considered for a moment.

"Long story short, we began Project Inside Information during the Cold War era, used participants to keep tabs on ambassadors, foreign dignitaries, that sort of thing. Perfect cover, you see? If the person gets caught, he is nothing more than this creepy Peeping Tom. He doesn't even know he's collecting information or evidence."

"Evidence to bring back to that church."

"Yes. All the files, everything going back to the church. Not horribly secure, I grant you, but once again, something unexpected—hiding information in the open. Anyone who investigates, finds out anything about the church . . . well, they'd just find this group of creepy Peeping Toms once again, wouldn't they?"

"That's why you conditioned them to revere the place, treat it as holy. Didn't want them snooping through old case files."

"Exactly. And really, a church was the obvious choice, wasn't it?"

Lucas's legs felt weak. The whole Creep Club had been an intelligence operation of manufactured monsters. But what did that make him? A natural freak? He'd never been part of Creep Club, and now, the one group of people he'd felt remotely connected to was forever gone. By his hand, no less.

"I can sense what you're thinking, Lucas. Indeed a tragedy—one of many associated with this project. Anyway, when the Department of Homeland Security was formed, you can imagine some of the more legitimate intelligence agencies took a great interest in Project Inside Information. Creep Club."

"They started monitoring people with foreign ties," Lucas said.

"For a while it was successful. But then, as I said, as more and more legitimate agencies became aware of the project's existence, the information became unstable. Until eventually someone started gathering information on the project, threatening to be a whistle-blower."

"Saul."

"Yes. The existence of a project that spies on foreign-born U.S. citizens . . . well, very messy. A PR fiasco. And so, we began to make it someone else's project."

"Guoanbu. You set up Saul as a double agent, and now, when the story hits the media, this will look like the work of the Chinese."

"And the shootings here, the explosion at your friend's house, those will be linked to Guoanbu doing some sudden housecleaning. It's pretty messy now, but it will all wrap up rather cleanly. And to make it all happen, these Dark Fear agents." He gestured at the two in the front seat.

"They tried to kill me."

"Just the opposite, actually. You would have been dead at least three or four times without their stepping in. In the Dandy Don's building, they woke you up and got you out of there before a couple of Viktor's thugs found you. They took care of the police with that convenient car crash when you got yourself in trouble. And of course, they provided your ride at Leila's house."

"But they blew my cover at the Creep Club meeting, and they left messages with Viktor and Saul, telling them to meet me at the church."

"I needed you to get back in the middle of it. I tried to help Snake hold on to control, you know, but things were getting out of hand. He knew someone was about to blow open the Creep Club, he just didn't know who. So I had to feed Saul to him—but not too much of a force feed, you understand. Needed to come from a third party. I knew Snake would protect you, find out what you knew, because he was hungry to find out who the whistle-blower was."

"So your Dark Fear agents—the guys in the front seat. You say you sent them to protect me, to help me. Why? Am I just some random connection, a fall guy for you?"

Swarm smiled. "You are my greatest project, Lucas. My emergency escape. My End Game."

"Emergency escape?"

"Come on, now. You know you always plan your emergency escape before you start. So, for Project Inside Information, I chose one person who was very special. I did many, many hours of extra work with this young man, teaching him all the techniques of Creep Club, but keeping him separate, keeping him rogue. Just in case. I even invented a fake background for the young man—conditioned him to think he had been in an orphanage from a very young age, when, in fact, he was part of a family until age six. But he doesn't remember that, doesn't remember any of that, because he was conditioned not to. He was conditioned with memories that never existed—memories of an orphanage, memories of being a loner who just liked to escape and lie on the roof, staring at the lights of the city. But those were false memories; in reality, the young boy spent most of his time locked in a large steel room. So he doesn't remember any of his *real* memories, none at all. Except."

"Except what?" Lucas demanded, suddenly finding his gun in his hand and pressed against Swarm's cheek. Swarm made no move to stop him, and neither did the two men—or things—in the front seat.

"Except, I saw something of myself in this young man. I didn't want to totally cut his ties to his past, because . . . because I had all my ties to my past cut." His eyes swiveled, held Lucas's gaze.

Lucas felt the hand holding the gun trying to shake, but he calmed it. This was a lie, had to be a lie. Memories of the orphanage flashed back to him, so real. The far-off lights of the city, the bread baking in the kitchen . . .

"What researcher made the initial breakthrough in human pheromone research?" Swarm asked. His eyes were staring intently, thin black dots.

The answer came to Lucas immediately. "Dr. Winnifred Cutler," he whispered, and his mind bloomed with a full history of major pheromone researchers. How did he know that?

"You see? You remember, because I planted those memories, those lessons, in your mind. Try this: the four DNA nucleotides in genetic sequencing?"

"Adenine, cytosine, guanine, thymine." Lucas swallowed, felt his dry throat click.

"How did you learn to drive at the orphanage?" Swarm asked.

"I . . . I . . ." Lucas stammered. He filtered through his memory banks, looking for driving lessons but finding nothing.

"You didn't learn to drive at the orphanage, because it never existed. You learned to drive in my program—not just cars, but many different vehicles. You could even pilot an M-1 tank, if needed."

Lucas let the hand holding the gun drop to the seat, feeling his body go numb all over.

"In many ways," Swarm said, "you were nothing more than an organic computer. We cleared your hard drive and loaded it with all new information."

He went silent, and Lucas closed his eyes, hoping the silence would last.

It didn't.

"I don't know who I am, and it haunts me every day," Swarm said quietly, almost wistfully. "More than these wasps, more than the hundreds of people I've killed, more than Raven, who conditioned me from a very young age. More than all of it put together. I will never know who I am."

Lucas opened his eyes again and stared at Swarm.

"So as part of his conditioning," Swarm said softly, "I taught this boy a phrase that would keep some semblance of his former life alive. Something of himself."

Lucas stared. "Humpty Dumpty had some great falls," he whispered.

"That will be your starting point," Swarm said. "Your key to unlocking your past." He held up the cube. "Your past in here." Swarm turned his attention to the front seat. "This is far enough; pull over when you have a chance."

Lucas looked out the window; they were at a large landfill. Seagulls wheeled in the brilliant blue sky above.

Lucas turned his attention back to the cube. "But this," he said. "This is from Saul. He gave it to me."

"Did he?" Swarm asked. The wasps around his head seemed to be a bit more agitated now, perhaps stirred to more activity by the stench of the garbage surrounding them.

Lucas thought for a moment. "You planted the cube in his case," he said.

"Yes." Swarm opened the door on his side of the car, got out. He leaned back in the door, motioned for Lucas to follow him. Neither of the two in the front seat made any move to exit the car. Good.

Swarm shut the car door behind him and walked to the front of the car. He turned, waited. "I promise you, I'm not going to do a thing to you," Swarm said. "I don't think you've totally figured this out yet."

Lucas approached Swarm carefully, pointing the gun toward him. When he got close, Swarm abruptly took a few steps and grabbed the gun's barrel. He sank to his knees, put the barrel of the gun to his forehead.

"And now, you have to finish your job," he whispered. "You are my emergency exit. My End Game."

He looked up into Lucas's eyes, and Lucas noticed tears forming there.

"I conditioned you. I shaped you into something inhuman. I killed hundreds of people—hundreds. For that I deserve to die. But before that, I was also conditioned. My identity was erased. All memory of who I once was. And for that"—he lowered his gaze, staring at the muck on the ground at his knees—"I *want* to die."

Lucas paused, letting his eyes wander over the giant cloud of wasps that surrounded both of them now. The wasps settled on the gun, on Lucas's own hands, but they made no move to sting him.

Lucas thought a moment. "You're still playing me," he said. "My DNA is all over that church. My prints are on this gun. I shoot you, this whole thing—along with everything else these past few days—gets tied to me."

Swarm smiled. "The two Dark Fear agents in the car have been instructed to take you anywhere you want. Inside the box, the cube, is your new identity."

Swarm closed his eyes expectantly, waiting.

"One question first," Lucas said, his finger on the trigger. "How do I open the cube?"

"You will know when the time is right."

It would be easy—so easy—to blow off Swarm's head. He had tortured innocent kids to create the Creep Club, invaded the lives and homes of countless people, probably killed many of them. Surely he deserved it, and it would feel so good to send Swarm out as his own last act on Earth.

But he couldn't.

He lowered the gun. "I got news for you, Swarm." He bent to pick up his cube. "I'm gonna be dead in another few minutes, no matter what happens."

He threw the gun as far as he could, watching it land in the heap of crushed refuse; immediately, seagulls flocked to inspect it.

"And you're gonna have to live, knowing your grand experiment—your End Game—failed. You're looking for deliverance in the wrong place."

He turned and walked back to the car. As he walked away, he was sure he could hear sobbing.

Lucas was surprised to discover he had a soul after all. And it wasn't for sale.

00:05:21 REMAINING

Once he was back inside the car, the driver turned the vehicle around and drove them away; Lucas turned and watched the figure of Swarm, still hunched, still on his knees in the garbage, recede behind them.

A few minutes later, on a suburban street, the driver finally spoke, jolting a new wave of terror in him. "We're taking you to a new car. Nothing quite like this, but it should be good enough to get you out of town."

Lucas smiled. "Well, if the two of you want to live, I suggest you get rid of me. Like now."

The one sitting in the passenger seat turned, looked at him with Lucas's own eyes. "No need to fight us, Lucas. We're helping you."

"Oh, I'm done fighting," he said. "It's just, I have a bomb strapped to my leg, and it's going to go off any time."

00:00:32 REMAINING

The driver slammed on the brakes, bringing the car to a sudden halt along the curb; he climbed out his door and flung open Lucas's in mere seconds. "Let's see it," he said.

Casually, Lucas turned and held out his left leg. He closed his eyes, feeling like he was ready to explode. Ha ha. Ready to explode. Viktor had actually done him a favor, because he didn't want to live. Not like this. Not knowing what he now knew about his life. It had all been one big lie.

(Humpty Dumpty had some great falls.)

Bring it on, he thought. Time to let Humpty shatter into a million pieces.

00:00:00 REMAINING

He realized the driver was still looking at his leg and hadn't said anything for several seconds.

Lucas opened his eyes. "Well?" he asked. "What's the verdict, doc?"

"It's a bomb, all right," the driver said. "Only problem is, it hasn't been armed."

Lucas snapped his head off the seat, looked down at his leg. "What do you mean?" he started to say. "It's—"

But something *was* different. The regular display of lights, marching around the exterior of the manacle, was dark. No activity of any kind.

The passenger doppelgänger had come around the car now; meanwhile, the driver disappeared to the back, and Lucas heard the trunk pop open.

"I've seen these before," the passenger said. "He's right. When they're armed, they have lights that count down the time."

"I know," Lucas said. "The lights were on when Viktor's guy clamped it on me."

"So what did you do to deactivate it?" the passenger asked. "These things are kind of primitive, so if you mess with them too much . . ."

Lucas shook his head. "I didn't do anything," he said. "That's what I'm trying to tell you. Last time I checked, the thing was lit up like a Christmas tree."

The driver was back now, holding what looked like a large pair of bolt cutters. "Well then," he said, putting the cutters on the manacle, "looks like you got yourself a Christmas miracle a little bit early."

THIRTY-SIX

THEY DROPPED HIM OFF OUT NEAR FALLS CHURCH, HANDED HIM THE KEYS to an older four-door car, and suggested it was probably a good idea for him to keep heading west.

He agreed that was a good plan, but wasn't sure what to do. Where to go. They'd still be looking for him; eyes would be everywhere.

They started to roll up the window and drive away, but then Lucas stopped the driver. "Just a question," he said. "Out of curiosity. Your faces—you look like something terrifying to anyone who sees you."

"Yes," answered the passenger.

"So what do *you* see when you look into a mirror?"

The driver smiled. "I see a reflection," he said. He rolled up the window and wheeled away from the curb.

Lucas sat on the curb for a few seconds, massaging the area where the manacle had been bolted to his ankle for the last two days. What had happened? Why had it quit working? He didn't know.

He held the cube in front of him, looking at all its surfaces in the bright sunlight. Same as ever: he could see no hidden hinges, secret doors, seams of any kind. He hit it against the concrete curb as hard as he could a few times. A few flakes of concrete chipped away, but the box remained unscathed.

Maybe the gun, or some explosives. He stood, put the cube in his backpack. This wasn't the place for guns or explosives.

He sat again, stared at the sky for a few minutes, noticing the deep azure above him, the whispering wind in the trees, the far-off cries of children playing.

He was here, despite the odds.

After a few minutes, he pulled out his TracFone and turned it on, started to dial Sarea's number from memory.

Wait. That wouldn't work. Hondo had Sarea's phone, and it was probably gone now—along with everything else in Leila's home. He had to find them, but how?

He looked at the neighborhood around him. A library, with free Internet access, was several blocks away. He could maybe try to track Sarea's geopatch, but he thought showing his face was a very bad idea.

Abruptly, his cell phone rang, and he answered it.

"Lucas?" Sarea's voice. Mad.

He smiled. Lucas. Who was Lucas? Just an invention of Swarm. "Yeah," he said. "It's me."

"What kind of stunt are you trying to pull, ditching us like that? I've been trying to call you every ten minutes."

"Yeah, Sarea," he said. "It's nice to hear your voice too."

She paused on the other end of the line, and he could hear her breathing coming in short gasps. After a few seconds, she gave a deep sigh, and he could almost sense her coming down.

"Are you okay?" she asked.

"Yeah," he said. "Okay as I can get. Leila still with you?"

"Yes. Said she wasn't going anywhere until we heard from you."

"Where are you?" he asked.

"We're in that charming strip mall right next to the convenience store where you dumped us."

He smiled. "Let's see," he said. "I think you'd probably be about two blocks from a Metro stop," he said.

"I don't know," she said.

"I do. You know how you keep asking me when I'm gonna take you out for a cup of coffee?"

"Yeah. I remember something like that."

"Can you and Leila meet me at the GMU stop? Take the Orange Line—it's the last station. The farthest west. I'll buy you a cup of coffee there." He paused. "Actually, you'll have to buy it, because I can't really show my face anywhere. But I'll pay for it."

"Yeah, because that worked out so well for me last time," she said before she hung up.

He looked into the sky again. It was still blue.

"SO LET ME GET THIS STRAIGHT," SAREA SAID, PUTTING HER COFFEE IN the cup holder as they sat in a crowded parking lot. "You had a bomb attached to your leg that whole time, and you didn't say anything to me?"

He shrugged. "We had other things to worry about."

Leila shifted in the backseat. "You know," she said, "I've been thinking about that. Only thing I can come up with is, something shorted
it out. Fried the wiring. An electrical surge of some kind." She smiled.
"You didn't get struck by lightning, did you?"

He returned the smile. "About the only thing I haven't been hit
by in the last few days. I've—" He stopped, a memory coming back
to him suddenly.

"What is it?" Sarea asked.

"Well, I didn't get hit by lightning," he said. "But I got hit by several thousand volts of electricity."

"And you conveniently left this out of the story too?" said Sarea.

"It was . . . I dunno. This morning. Remember I said the cops
were taking me in after they caught me at that restaurant? Well, I
didn't think anything about it until just now, but they tased me."

Leila smiled. "A taser. That's 50,000 volts."

Lucas turned around. "How do you know?"

She smiled. "I helped design it."

They fell into silence for several moments until Lucas spoke to
Leila again. "So," he said. "What now for you?"

She shrugged. "Got a court date for the little kneecapping thing,"
she said. "But somehow, I don't think the charges will stick. My house
blowing up, well, that might be another matter. Maybe I need to head
back to Venezuela, lie low for a while. After that, who knows? Maybe I
need to go back to work on some weapons designs. Been thinking
about something that detects and blocks surveillance signals. Start
drawing up some plans."

"And what about you?" he said, turning to Sarea.

"What about me?"

"What do you have planned?"

"I don't plan, Lucas," she said. "Life's more interesting that way."

He smiled. "Well then," he said. "What if I tell you my plan?"

THREE DAYS LATER, HE AND SAREA WERE SOMEWHERE IN THE MIDWEST. He had raided a few of his cash stashes before they left, but he knew it was more important to get out of town fast. They'd started with about five hundred, but they were starting to run low, and they'd have to stop soon. They had thought about hiding at Sarea's for a few days, but it seemed too dangerous, maybe for both of them. There might be other rogue members still following up loose ends, investigators following up on a tip that Sarea and Lucas had been friendly at the Blue Bell, dropping by to ask her a few questions unannounced.

And so, when he'd suggested they leave DC in their rearview mirror, he was thrilled to hear her say yes. Not many people could do that, just pick up and leave. But not many people were like Sarea, were they?

No wonder the Connection was so strong with her.

Maybe they'd just drive until they ran out of cash, stop where they were, and find some work. He knew how to wash dishes, after all. She could wait tables. The world always needed dishwashers and waitresses.

She had agreed immediately when he asked her to do some traveling with him, to discover . . . whatever there was to discover.

The first two nights, he searched for a way to open the cube. Both nights he came up empty-handed.

On the morning of the third day, Sarea asked him to stop at a discount store so she could pick up a few things. He was happy to do so, and he lay out on the hood of the car, staring up at the sky above, so close it felt he could dip his finger in it. Out here, a few states away from DC, he felt safe to show his face; he wouldn't immediately be recognized.

He hoped.

"Hey." Sarea was back, clutching a small bag. "I got you a little surprise." She opened the passenger door and climbed inside.

He smiled, slid off the hood, and jumped into the car.

She held up a compact disc for him to see.

"Mad Billy Weevil," he said, recognizing the photo of the blues guitarist.

He started the car, and she slipped in the disc as he put the vehicle in gear and started to inch out of their space.

> Spinnin', you got me spinnin' all around
> Spinnin' so much I ain't never been found
> And when you tell me you don't mean it
> I don't mind much, baby, cuz I seen it

The words resonated in his mind, and his last vision of Mad Billy Weevil came flooding back. *I'll play you what you need to hear*, Billy said, and then launched into a song.

This song.

He put his foot on the brakes. Behind him, in the parking lot, a small red car honked in frustration. Lucas paid no attention, but made a sharp turn back into the parking lot.

"What is it?" Sarea asked.

"It's . . . something I need to hear," he said. He turned to the backseat, found the backpack he no longer felt the need to wear but couldn't quite part with yet, and unzipped it. Inside, he found the cube.

Cube in hand, he opened the door and stepped out.

"What are you doing?" Sarea asked.

He smiled. "I'm spinning," he said.

He set the cube on the ground, then tipped it up on one of the corners and tried to twirl it like a top. The cube flopped around a few seconds, coming to a quick rest.

He picked it up and tried again, giving his wrist a solid flick as he did so. The cube whirred on its corner, creating a blur as it moved. After several seconds, it slowed and then came to a stop on one of its sides.

But now, a small door in one of the cube faces had slipped open. Inside the door was a small button.

He looked at Sarea, who was smiling. Inside the car, Mad Billy had begun to play a long solo.

"Go ahead," she said. "Push it."

He put his finger on the button, and the whole face popped open. Inside were a photo and papers, all folded.

His heart beating fast now, he pulled them out. First was the photo: a mom, a dad, and a young boy—maybe four years old—standing beside a body of water.

A body of water that looked to him very much like a spring of some kind.

On the faces of the three people in the photo, he saw looks of pure joy. Pure love. Pure living. It reminded him in many ways of all the photos he'd ever taken from offices, but mostly of Noel and her kids.

He turned over the photo. On the back it said *Mom, Dad, and Shane. Heritage Springs State Park.*

He handed the photo to Sarea. Next was a small card with a handwritten name and address.

James and Helen Mercer
3227 Marigold Way
Great Falls, MT 59403

He felt his breath stop when he came to the city name.

Great Falls.

(Humpty Dumpty had some great falls.)

I planted that phrase in you, to help you remember who you are.

And then, as his breath returned, flashes of memories began to return with it. Some of them, most of them, filled with feelings of terror. Dark corners, tied to a chair, hearing a long tape repeat phrases in his head over and over. Slide shows, flipping through images and implanting them in his brain.

But beneath those memories, he also discovered something else. A red bicycle. A high, trilling laugh *(Mom's laugh, that was Mom's laugh)*. A bubbling spring, and a couple, hand in hand, walking ahead of him.

He called out to the couple, and they turned to him, smiles on their faces. When he ran to them, they took him into their arms and held him.

There were more items inside the cube: a birth certificate, driver's license, and passport for Shane Mercer, who lived in Great Falls, Montana; the license and passport had photos—recent photos—of him. How, he didn't know. And finally, a cashier's check for $100,000 made out to Shane Mercer.

He showed the items to Sarea.

She looked at them thoughtfully, then back to him. "Are these . . . is this . . . you?"

He nodded. "I think so." Then: "You ever been to Montana?"

"Never, but I hear it's a nice place, Lucas."

He smiled. "I guess we'll find out."

ACKNOWLEDGMENTS

THIS BOOK WILL FOREVER BE ETCHED IN MY MEMORY; DURING ITS CREATION I was first diagnosed with, and then treated for, follicular non-Hodgkins lymphoma. As I write this, I'm cancer free and doing well—and even able to see the many positive ways cancer has changed me, thanks in large part to the many people who have entered my life as a result of it. These include my network of family and friends who were there from the beginning, as well as Dr. W. Thomas Purcell and the entire Cancer Center staff at Billings Clinic; GlaxoSmithKline, makers of Bexxar; Dr. Michael Snyder, Dianne, Tina, Kim, Rex, and everyone at Community Medical Center for their care during my treatment; Karl Schwartz of Patients Against Lymphoma and Betsy De Parry for their support and information; everyone in my Monday evening group; countless friends on the lymphoma.com message boards and other online venues; and inspiration from more than 500,000 people currently living with lymphoma.

I am also indebted, as always, to my lovely wife and lovely daughter, who are my constant sources of joy. Thanks also to my agent, Lee Hough, editors Ed Stackler and LB Norton, as well as Allen Arnold, Amanda Bostic, and everyone at Thomas Nelson Fiction for their invaluable contributions. I owe you all Dr Peppers.

MUSIC CREDITS

Silversun Pickups, David Crowder Band, Peter Bjorn & John, Okkervil River, Fratellis, Future of Forestry, Mates of State, Rilo Kiley, Weezer, Derek Webb, Kingston Trio, Better Than Ezra, Fountains of Wayne, Wilco, Pixies

DISCUSSION QUESTIONS FOR
THE UNSEEN

1. Compare your feelings about Lucas at the beginning of the book with your feelings about him at the end of the book. Did your opinion of him change? Did you identify with him? Why or why not?

2. If you asked Lucas what he most wants at the beginning of the book, what would he say? Would he be truthful with you? Would he be truthful with himself?

3. The members of Creep Club live vicariously through the people they monitor and record. In light of recent trends such as YouTube and "reality" television, do you think our society mirrors this odd fascination? What are the implications—bad and good—of our more transparent world?

4. Lucas feels a Connection to his co-worker Sarea, and even though he's entertained thoughts of spying on her life, he never has. Why do you think this is?

5. At the end of the book, Sarea willingly goes with Lucas—first to escape her apartment, then to travel with him across the country. What does this willingness say about her as a character? About her relationship with Lucas?

6. Lucas has an odd habit of collecting photos and other souvenirs from the people he observes, calling them "totems." Why do you think he does this? What do the totems represent for him?

7. Throughout the book, Lucas tells us: "People look, but they don't see." Mad Billy Weevil, the blues musician, says: "People hear, but they don't feel." What do you think they mean by this? Do you agree most people go through life looking but not seeing, and hearing but not feeling?

8. At the end of the book, the character Swarm says he sees himself in Lucas. How is he like Lucas? How is he different?

9. Lucas repeats the mantra "Humpty Dumpty had some great falls" throughout the book, which leads to some obvious connections with his past. But do you think there's also some symbolic significance in this phrase? Can Lucas himself be seen as a "Humpty Dumpty" kind of character? For that matter, can we all be seen as "Humpty Dumpty" characters in our own lives?

10. At a key point in the story, we find out the person Lucas is most afraid of is . . . himself. Why would he be afraid of himself? Do you think other people may be afraid of themselves? Do you think Lucas is still afraid at the end of the story?

11. Toward the end of the book, Sarea recounts the famous tale of the crossroads and the musician Robert Johnson, then suggests Lucas is in the same position. What's the main "crossroads" moment Lucas faces? What is his decision? Do the effects of his choice begin to appear by the time the story has ended?

ABOUT THE AUTHOR

T.L. Hines writes "Noir Bizarre" stories, mixing mysteries with oddities in books such as *The Unseen, Waking Lazarus,* and *The Dead Whisper On. Waking Lazarus* received Library Journal's "25 Best Genre Fiction Books of the Year" award.